LOVE HARD

A HARD PLAY NOVEL

NALINI SINGH

Copyright © 2020 by Nalini Singh

eISBN: 978-1-942356-68-4

ISBN: 978-1-942356-69-1

Cover image by: Jenn LeBlanc/Illustrated Romance

Cover design by: Croco Designs

OTHER BOOKS BY NALINI SINGH

Shield of Winter

Shards of Hope

Allegiance of Honor

The Psy/Changeling Trinity series

Silver Silence

Ocean Light

Wolf Rain

The Guild Hunter series

Angels' Blood

Archangel's Kiss

Archangel's Consort

Archangel's Blade

Archangel's Storm

Archangel's Legion

Archangel's Shadows

Archangel's Enigma

Archangel's Heart

Archangel's Viper

Archangel's Prophecy

Archangel's War

Thrillers

A Madness of Sunshine

For detailed descriptions of these books, as well as additional titles, visit Nalini's website: www.nalinisingh.com.

PROLOGUE

"Yo, gearhead!"

"If I make like I can't hear you, will you go away?"

"Nope. So what'd you do to get in detention? I thought you were the Upstanding Student of the Year. Isn't that what the shiny trophy said?"

"What's the deal with detention? Do we just sit around?"

"Don't worry, I'll give you the lowdown—*after* you tell me what you did to land your golden-boy halo in here."

"I helped lift and carry Mr. Boucher's car to the other side of the school. He thought it'd been stolen."

"Hah! That's pretty funny. Especially since Mr. Bozo's the reason I'm in here."

"Yeah? What'd you do?"

"Told him to his face that he was a big bully with a small dick. He was hassling Callie about answering stuff aloud in our last class, like getting in her face and whacking his stupid ruler down on her desk. And you know Callie."

"Shit. She okay?"

"Got the guilts because I have detention, but hey, she

I

didn't make me point out Mr. Bozo's small dick. She wanted to go to the dean and explain and stuff, but I said, 'No way, Cals. I *earned* this detention, and I'm gonna do it proudly.'"

"You're all right, Jules."

"Ugh. We are not friends, *Jacob*. That's Juliet to you."

1

JACOB ESERA VS. AN AGGRAVATED GHOST IN STILETTOS

Jake's big brother was getting married.

Gabriel had taken his sweet time falling for a woman, but when he had, he'd fallen *hard*. Charlotte Baird owned Gabe's heart, and Gabe was not only fine with that, he reveled in it. Not surprising given how the Bishop-Esera men had grown up—in a home with parents who adored each other to this day.

Their mum kissed their dad each and every morning, rain or shine or occasional grumpiness. And while not an overly demonstrative man, their dad had never shied away from admitting that their mother was his lodestar.

As Charlotte was Gabriel's.

"Have you seen Charlie today?" Jake asked Gabe as the six of them finished getting ready.

Gabriel, Sailor, Jake, Danny, Fox, and Harry.

Four brothers; Fox, a rock star who'd been adopted as family because his wife was best friends with Gabe's Charlotte; and last but not least, Gabe's best friend from his pro-athlete days—tall and quiet Harry with the big body and massive shoulders of a rugby prop. He and Gabe had stayed close even after Gabe's injury took him out of the game. Jake had actually played alongside Harry for a year before the other man hung up his rugby boots in favor of a new career as a pilot.

"I wish," Gabe grumbled as he put on his suit jacket, his shoulders wide and his body as muscled as when he'd played professionally. "I tried to lure her out of the apartment last night while the women were having their party, and she messaged me emojis of champagne glasses, flames, and a fireman. I'm probably going to go home to find a stripper pole in the living room."

Jake glanced down to fix his tie. He and Charlotte had become good friends since Gabe introduced her to the family, so he was well aware that Charlotte had been teasing Gabe. Strippers weren't Charlie's style.

The champagne though, that was real. Jake had delivered the box himself after picking up the special order featuring not just the bubbly but bottles of blueberry and strawberry wine.

A bright blue and vivid pink respectively.

It being early morning, Charlie and her friends had been readying themselves for a champagne breakfast. Their plans for the day included manicures and pedicures and a trip to Auckland's Sky Tower for a harnessed bungy jump. Petite Charlie had been wearing a T-shirt that said: T-REX TAMER on the front. The back had borne a cartoon drawing of a bow-tie-sporting T. rex holding a bespectacled mouse in his arms.

The mouse had been wearing a wedding veil.

Cake and cocktails had featured heavily in the women's post-jump plans.

When Jake checked on their hangover status this morning, he was told that everyone was functional. Apparently Charlie and the others had jumped off the Southern Hemisphere's tallest building not once but *twice*. They'd been the last group of the day, and when—high on adrenaline—they'd asked the instructor if they could book another jump even though jumps were over for the day, he'd winked and taken them up for free.

None of which Jake was authorized to reveal.

While the women jumped off tall buildings, the men had gone black water rafting deep in the caves of Waitomo, finishing off the day with beers around a campfire. Included in the group had been a number of others. Those men were already in the church, acting as ushers, while the six of them stood in Sailor's large living area, only minutes from getting into cars for the drive to the ceremony.

It was the second time in his life that Jake was to be a groomsman.

The first had been eight years ago, at Sailor's wedding. He'd been a carefree sixteen-year-old kid then, with no awareness that his life was about to change forever in the two years to come. That kid might be long gone, to be replaced by a single dad with the sweetest little girl anyone could want, but one thing hadn't changed: he was as happy for Gabe as he'd been for Sailor.

"So you're leaving for your honeymoon right after the reception?" Fox said after Danny helped him knot his tie; Fox could belt out a rock anthem like nobody's business, but he was no expert at the whole suit-and-tie business.

"Yeah." Gabe stood in place while Harry pinned a "rose" to the lapel of his suit jacket. Fashioned from the pages of an old romance novel, the floral artwork looked ridiculously delicate against Gabriel's stone-gray suit, but the juxtaposition worked. Just like Charlotte and Gabriel did. The last part of the men's outfits would be the open leis of green foliage they'd wear around their necks, the ends falling on either side of their chests, a respectful nod to Gabriel's stepfather's culture.

"Flights to Samoa are all booked. Bags are packed and waiting in the car." A smile creased Gabriel's cheeks.

Jake's phone rang into the low murmur of male voices. Glancing down, he felt his stomach clench. "I better take this. It's Coach."

His brothers all looked over. "Good luck," they said in unison.

Breath tight in his lungs, Jake ducked out and into the rambling garden of Sailor and Ísa's sprawling single-level villa. He loved his brothers but couldn't take this call in front of them. He needed time to gather himself back together and prepare to lie through his teeth if it turned out to be bad news—no fucking way would he ruin Gabe's wedding day.

The grass was a lush green under the winter sunlight, the vines crawling up one side of the villa dotted with small blooms of bluish-white. Camellias in blush pink glowed against the fence in the distance, behind a garden planted with winter color—Jake recognized the vibrant pansies and yellow-orange polyanthus blooms because he'd helped plant them. A child's bike stood propped beside the garden, its frame a glossy red and the handlebars festooned with ribbons.

Jake saw it all, processed none of it.

"Coach," he said after putting the phone to his ear, "just give it to me straight." He'd been out with a broken arm for a good chunk of the previous season, but he'd played his heart out for his regional team—the Harriers—in the months leading up to selection for New Zealand's upcoming championship series against Argentina, Australia, and South Africa.

The Harriers had taken the regional championship, though their archrivals, the Southern Blizzard, had made them earn the trophy. The pundits were predicting a heavy Harrier and Blizzard presence in the national squad, along with several standouts from teams that hadn't shone as a group.

That squad was being announced on Wednesday.

Danny's selection was a certainty, his current form phenomenal. According to all three of his brothers, Jake was the best first five-eighth in the world right now, but the New Zealand selectors had a deep pool in which to fish—and the shadow of injury haunted him. Also, no one usually called the players ahead of the official announcement. Legend was, Coach only called when it was bad news... like if a player was being permanently dropped.

"I figured you'd say that," Coach Lincoln Graves said. "Short version: you've done a fine job getting back into fighting shape, and you're playing the best I've ever seen you play. Safe hands and magic feet. Well done, Jake—you'll be in the squad we announce next week."

Jake slumped against the white wall of the villa.

"I'm giving you an early heads-up because I wanted you and your brothers to feel free to celebrate the wedding without this hanging over your head," Coach continued, his voice barely penetrating the buzz in Jake's skull. "If anyone but Gabriel, Sailor, Danny, or your parents ask, you know nothing."

Jake managed to get out a few words. "I won't tell anyone else."

"Right. I'd better head out or Neeta and I'll be late to Gabriel's wedding. Talk more at the reception."

Jake just stood there in the sunshine after Coach hung up, gulping in huge lungfuls of the crisp winter air. He hadn't known how terrified he'd been until this moment. Rugby was the only thing at which he'd ever truly excelled —the one thing he could use to build the kind of future he wanted for Esme. He might've started off as a teen parent, but he was well on the road to making sure she'd never be disadvantaged because of that.

No one would ever make his daughter feel small or a mistake; the children of rugby professionals got treated with respect. That went double for the children of those who played in New Zealand's famous black jersey; Esme would be a little superstar on the playground.

"Flippin' flip!"

He frowned at the sound of that husky female voice, a strange sense of knowledge murmuring at the back of his mind. That hadn't sounded anything like Sailor's wife, Ísa, but he'd been a bit zoned out, so it wasn't as if he'd been paying full attention. What reason would any woman *but* his brother's wife have to be here right now? All the women in the family—his and Sailor's daughters included—were with the bridal party.

Stepping away from the wall and through an arbor of fragrant purplish-pink blooms, he said, "Ísa? Did you forget...?" His eyes landed on the woman currently balancing on one foot while she slid her black stiletto heel back on the other foot.

That heel had grass and dirt on it.

Not only was her footwear inappropriate for a garden, her dress was... Narrowing his eyes, Jake hauled his primitive male brain past the sensual impact of her lush body, the heavy weight of her breasts revealed by the vee of her midnight-blue dress—a dress that wasn't dealing well with her current precarious position. It was also of a soft, satiny material that made his palms itch to touch.

Itch or not, if a rugby groupie had managed to get past the property's locked gates, he'd throw her out on her shapely rear. He'd permit nothing to ruin Gabe and Charlotte's day.

Silky black hair streaked with bronze and red shifted over her shoulders as she lifted her head, her skin a creamy shade of brown. Dark eyes full of fire and annoyance smashed into his.

"Juliet?" His neurons misfired, his brain white noise. "What are you doing in my brother's backyard?"

A roll of those wildly vibrant eyes as she finally lowered her foot to the ground. Her dress fell over her curves to reveal a wrap design that was technically decent, but—on that spectacular body—was the definition of indecency.

Wrangling his mind into some sense of order, Jake scowled and squared his shoulders against the visceral sexual heat in his gut. For *Juliet*.

"Esme broke her glasses." Her body might no longer be all pointy elbows and gangly bones, but her voice was that same low contralto with an edge. "Ísa said you'd have a spare set in your car."

Jake still had no idea what the hell this ghost from his past was doing in Sailor's backyard, but his paternal instincts trumped any and all other questions. "Is she hurt?"

"No, she's fine." Red-lipsticked mouth glossy and full, a hand with manicured nails featuring tiny glittering stones. That hand held a set of keys. "She and Emmaline were playing and she tripped—right onto a bunch of cushions. Glasses just landed wrong."

Jake was already moving to where his gray SUV was parked in Sailor's drive. The electronic gate was open at the

9

other end, a hot-pink compact blocking the exit. The number plate read: S3XⅡ.

His lips tightened as he unlocked the SUV and reached into the glove box. Grabbing the glittery white glasses case his daughter had chosen with glee, he handed it over. He'd long ago become used to keeping a spare—having a little girl who wore glasses and who was despondent when the world became a blur was a quick learning curve.

"Thanks." With that, Juliet sashayed back down the drive, her skyscraper heels making any other form of movement impossible. Her hair was longer than he'd realized, reaching almost to her lower back. His eyes caught on her hips, on the curves of her butt, before he realized what he was doing and flushed.

"You're not wearing that to the wedding are you?" he asked in desperation.

A hitch in Juliet's stride, then a scalding glance over her shoulder. "Still got that stick up your butt, I see." Sliding into her car with a slammed door, she zoomed off down the street.

Jake slumped back against his car.

And his brain *finally* connected the dots.

"You'll get to meet my friend Jules at the wedding," Charlotte had said. "The one from pastry class. You two apparently went to the same high school."

As that high school's roll of students had been well over a thousand, Jake hadn't really thought anything of Charlie's statement. Neither had he seen Juliet when he dropped off the wine and champagne. She'd either not attended the festivities or had been in another part of the apartment.

And never, not once, had he connected Charlotte's pastry-making friend Jules with snarky and tough Juliet.

Why the hell would he? The Juliet he'd known had been all detentions and trouble and a messy braid.

Now she was *making pastry*? And he'd been *checking out her breasts*?

"Jesus Christ. *Juliet*." He shook his head, trying to shake out the crazy.

2

THE BAD INFLUENCE AND HER COLD,
DEAD HEART

J uliet strode into the den of chaos that was Charlotte
and Gabriel's home. "Ta-da!" She held up the spectacle case while keeping a tight lid on her
simmering temper.

Jacob Esera was lucky this was his brother's wedding or
she'd have had him eating grass. Juliet was no athlete, but
her throwing arm was hella-accurate. A whack on the head
with a well-aimed stiletto, and Mr. Judgy McJudgypants
would've face-planted. Because she wouldn't have aimed for
the head on his neck. Oh no, she'd have aimed much lower
down, right where it would've hurt the most.

The image mellowed her temper into grim satisfaction.

"You got it!" Grabbing the case, Esme opened it and slid
on her glasses—the frames were electric blue, the glass
crystal clear. "I knew Daddy would have it!" Then she
slammed her tiny body into Juliet's legs, hugging her tight
with skinny arms. "Thank you, Jules!"

Bending down while trying not to wobble—she hadn't
had a chance to kick off her heels—Juliet picked up Esme
and hitched her on her hip. Even at age six, Jake's little girl

was petite and light. Probably the smallest in her class. Just like Callie had been.

"A girl has got to have her accessories," she said past the sucker punch of memory, and got a giggle.

"Sweetie, Boo! Time to put on your dresses."

Esme wriggled down to race off toward her grandma. Joy whispering over the sadness that had hit her out of nowhere, Juliet slipped off her heels out of respect for Charlie's gorgeous wooden floors and wandered over to where the makeup artist was putting the last touches on Ísa.

Charlotte's future sister-in-law was a bridesmaid, alongside Juliet and fellow pastry-class graduate Aroha. Charlotte's detective friend Mei Lee was the final member of the bridesmaid quartet. Matron of honor duties had gone to Charlotte's best friend, Molly.

"You look spectacular," Juliet said to Ísa. "Straight out of a Renaissance painting." All wild red hair, flawless skin, and a sense of contentment that drew Juliet.

"Thanks for doing that for Esme." Ísa squeezed Juliet's hand.

"My pleasure," Juliet said as Charlotte floated down the hanging spiral staircase with Molly by her side.

"Why am I nervous?" the bride said with an enormous but shaky smile when she reached this floor, one hand pressed to her chest and a flush gracing the pale gold of her skin. "I'm *so* ready to marry Gabriel!"

Juliet couldn't help her surely goofy smile at Charlotte's giddy happiness. The other woman looked like an old-world princess in a wedding dress of ivory lace with a wide skirt and a gentle bateau neckline. The sleeves were long, the lace there and over the slope of her shoulders unlined.

Juliet's friend had decided to wear contacts for her wedding rather than her usual metal-rimmed glasses; her hazel eyes were gorgeously outlined by lashes that curled up at the ends, her eyelids dusted with the barest shimmer. A pop of color came from her lips. Plump and pink, they drew the eye in a way that was lovely rather than overtly sensual.

As for Charlotte's blond hair with its tendency to curl, the hairdresser had put it in a soft updo with enough tendrils around her face that the style made Juliet sigh it was so dreamy and romantic. Juliet could never pull off that look, but on Charlotte? Utter perfection.

Her friend's entire face glowed.

"It's happy nerves." Molly hugged Charlotte from behind, the lush orange-pink frangipani she wore behind one ear vibrant against the wavy black of her hair.

Charlotte had seen similar flowers in Auckland's Winter Gardens the day Gabriel proposed to her. Her bouquet was made up of paper roses formed from the pages of romance novels, intermingled with the fragrant tropical bloom and tied with a "rope" of the same green leaves as the leis the men would be wearing.

"Jules, your flower." Aroha tucked a frangipani behind Juliet's ear.

"Thanks, babe." Juliet took out her phone and snapped a few photos just as Mei appeared from the balcony, phone in hand and poker-straight black hair cut in a short, sharp bob against the light brown of her skin. The senior detective was currently at the tail end of a major investigation and had probably been checking in with her people.

"We got the bad guy," she'd said to Juliet yesterday, before their heart-thumping scream of a jump. "My team can wrap it up. No way would I miss Charlotte's wedding." Her uptilted eyes had met Charlotte's as she said that, something unspoken but powerful passing between two women who'd been born a decade apart and appeared wholly unlike one another despite their matching petite builds.

Mei was tough and confrontational, Charlotte stubborn and sweet.

Yet that they were tight was undeniable.

Juliet knew, however, that Charlotte's closest friendship was with Molly. The two women had met in nursery school, might as well be sisters. As Juliet and Callie had once been.

Now Molly reached for a flat, square box on a side table and carefully lifted out a necklace. Created of two strands of white gold that came together in a knotted waterfall, the simple piece was elegant and timeless.

Charlotte's hand fluttered to her chest again, her eyes wet as Molly draped the piece around her neck. "I can feel my mum hugging me." A shaky whisper. "She would've been so happy to be here today, to see me marry the man of my dreams."

Juliet's softer self might've turned to stone long ago—she'd been known to joke about her cold, dead heart—but even her eyes stung. She'd never had a loving mother figure, not one she remembered anyway, so she had no understanding of the kind of love that had Charlotte closing her hand gently about the falling strands of the necklace as she bowed her head—but she understood that love existed. She'd witnessed it multiple times in her life.

Jake with Callie back in high school.

Her boss Everett with his partner Rufus for so long now.

Charlotte with Gabriel.

"No tears." Aroha, all wild curls and kindness and generous curves under dark brown skin, walked over to Charlotte. "You'll ruin your makeup." Her voice was wobbly, the hug she gave Charlotte as big and warm as her heart.

Somehow, all six of them—Ísa included—were

suddenly hugging in a wash of laughter and emotion. Juliet didn't even care that she might catch some of this sweetness and joy and start to believe in happy-ever-after.

Clearly the wedding virus had already infected her system.

Then Esme and Emmaline ran out of the spare room, dressed in their flower girl outfits, and it turned into an even mushier group hug. The final person to join in was Alison, Charlotte's future mother-in-law, her maternal touch somehow managing to enfold them all.

They separated to find the hairdresser and makeup artist wiping away tears.

Her gaze misty, Charlotte bent down to kiss both Emmaline and Esme on the cheek. With eyes of devastating blue, Emmaline was nearly as pale as her mum, Ísa, while Esme had Jake's intense brown eyes but skin of a lighter brown than his.

A mark of Callie's genes.

Juliet's best friend in high school had often complained that she was so pale she burned if she even *looked* at the sun. Little Esme wouldn't have that problem, Juliet thought, her chest tight at the memory of the laughing young woman with hair of silky blond and studious eyes of blue hidden behind black-framed glasses.

Callie would've been effervescent with happiness to see her baby today, all dressed up and excited.

"You look like princesses," Charlotte said to her adorable flower girls.

"No, you do!" both girls cried before asking for photos with the bride.

The hairdresser and makeup artist took their leave at the same time—to profuse thanks from the entire bridal party.

As soon as Juliet had snapped their photos, Esme and

Emmaline ran over to the large standing mirror someone had propped near the balcony doors. The early-afternoon sunlight poured over them as they admired their dresses in the mirror.

"The necklace is the something old," Molly said into the quiet.

"And the dress is something new." Alison ran a hand down the lace of Charlotte's sleeve. "I'm certain this'll become an heirloom; it's so lovely."

Two little girls danced in the light as emotion filled the room anew, the sunshine caressing their dark hair. Emmaline's a pure black, Esme's silkier and less manageable and with hints of chocolate brown in the black. Another mingling of two very different people. Another sign of love.

As was this moment with Charlotte.

"As for your something blue..." Stepping forward, Mei raised Charlotte's hand, and Aroha slipped on a thin sapphire-and-diamond bracelet that all of them had pooled their money to buy.

It didn't matter that Molly and Alison could've each bought it on their own—what mattered was the symbol of friendship, a memory of this time together. As delicate as the bracelet was, it perfectly suited Charlotte's small bones. It also went very well with the platinum-and-emerald bracelet from Gabriel that pretty much never left her wrist.

"Oh." Charlotte's hand fluttered to her mouth, her nails polished to a shine and coated with a shimmer of pale color. "This is so beautiful. You didn't have to—"

"Of course we did." Carefully picking up the gauzy veil that had been draped over a sofa, Juliet handed it to Alison.

Molly, both hands pressed together and eyes shining, leaned against Juliet. "Your something borrowed, Charlie," she whispered.

Alison's throat moved as she secured the veil to Charlotte's hair, using a graceful and fine tiara that flawlessly matched Charlotte's sense of style. "I'm so glad my stubborn Gabriel convinced you to marry him," she whispered after fixing the veil in place. "You light him up, my beautiful girl, and I see the same light in you when you look at him. May you always be each other's starshine."

Juliet had to look away for a second, the lump in her throat in danger of smashing her cold, dead heart back to life. Everyone was bustling to get ready to head out to the church by the time she pulled herself together. Aroha asked Juliet to check the back of her dress to make sure everything was in place.

"You look amazing." Juliet fixed the shoulders of the midnight-blue A-line dress with a high waist, vee neck, and long sleeves that Aroha had chosen for herself.

A small, warm hand slipped into Juliet's in the aftermath.

Glancing down, she found herself looking straight into a pair of big brown eyes framed by glittering blue spectacle frames. Callie was there in that moment, in the shape of Esme's face, in the way her smile was a little lopsided—and in the solemn seriousness with which she examined Juliet.

Calypso "Callie" Simpson had always had a solemnity to her, but intermingled with that had been a deep generosity of heart. Gearhead and elite athlete Jake, on the other hand, had always had a hint of the stiff-lipped Puritan in him. Just enough to make him and Juliet firm nonfriends.

Looked like that hint had become a full-blown case of stuffed-shirt syndrome, she thought with an inward scowl just before Esme said, "You look pretty, Jules."

Clearly, Esme had learned her manners from relatives other than her father. "*We* look pretty," she said with a grin and a squeeze of that fragile hand. "Let's go knock 'em dead." Especially Jake.

It was a point of honor now. Because the boy she'd known had grown fully into those wide shoulders and long legs that had been a promise the last time she'd seen him. And in that instant when she'd first looked up from putting her heel back on, she'd wobbled internally... before her brain processed the fact that it was Jacob Esera she was ogling.

She could hear Callie's laughter now. Her best friend was probably rolling around the floor in heaven while tears of sheer hilarity streaked down her face. For such a nice person, Cals had sure had a wicked sense of humor.

Anyway, it had to be all the wine last night. The fumes had clearly still been in her system during that split second of disorientation when she'd looked up and seen a hot— and *built*—man who'd sent a distinct "zing" through her lady parts.

Jake "Golden Boy" Esera and Juliet "Bad Influence" Nelisi?

Nope. Nope. Triple extra nope.

3

FEATURING AN INDIGESTIBLE MOUSE
AND GOO-GOO EYES

J ake couldn't see Juliet in the audience that sat ready
for the bride to make her entrance.

Maybe she'd been held up by that run to pick
up Esme's glasses. Still, he scowled—she should've
made an effort to be on time. It'd be just like Juliet to swan
in late and cause a ruckus. He could still remember that
time she strode in half an hour late into a full-school assem-
bly. Most students would've scuttled into the cavernous hall
with its walls and floor of polished wood, trying not to be
noticed.

Juliet had walked in bold as you please, no concern on
her face.

"Why do you look constipated?" Danny muttered to him
in Samoan as the six of them got themselves sorted by the
altar.

Jake shot his brother a shut-up look, but Danny was the
youngest in a brood of four boys. He'd long ago learned to
ignore any such cues.

"Seriously, bro," he said, switching to English. "Do you
need a pill?"

Narrowing his eyes, Jake silently promised his baby brother that payback delayed was payback well thought out. "I just want everything to be perfect for Gabriel and Charlotte."

Grinning with the rash confidence of someone who hadn't felt Jake's wrath in a while, Danny slapped him on the shoulder. "You don't have to worry about that. As long as Charlie doesn't ditch him at the altar, our big bro couldn't give a shit what else goes wrong. She's what he cares about."

Jake knew Danny was right, but he couldn't still the nerves. Worrying about the people he loved, the people who were important to him, was part of his nature. He'd always been inclined that way, but it had gotten much, *much* worse after Calypso's death. It didn't matter that no amount of worrying would've stopped the spread of the bacterial meningitis infection and saved her life. Jake couldn't stop his compulsive need to protect and shield his own.

The only good thing about it all was that—thanks to the counseling sessions his parents had forced him to attend after Calypso died—he was fully aware of his overprotective tendencies and how much damage they could do to an innocent soul. So he fought against those urges every hour of every day. Esme would *not* grow up suffocated by his need to keep her safe.

His daughter would grow up free and a bit wild, just as he'd done.

Given that two weekends ago, she'd used the aftermath of a rainstorm as a chance for a gleeful mud bath, he thought he was doing okay. Especially since she'd enticed him into the mud bath with her delighted laughter. They'd lain there, two very cold and muddy people under the bright winter sunshine, and the world hadn't fallen down.

Esme hadn't caught the flu or some weird mud-borne

disease. No, she'd had the time of her life, and he'd taken another breath. Maybe he'd be fully able to relax by the time she reached adulthood. One could only hope. Because having to constantly battle his protectiveness was more exhausting than any game he'd ever played.

Beside Danny, Gabe's friend Harry said, "What are you two whispering about like little old ladies?" His voice was a deep rumble, his clean-shaven jaw as square and solid as his shoulders.

"My baby bro doesn't know when to shut up," Jake muttered while Danny refused to look the least bit cowed.

A rustling swayed through the audience before Harry could respond, a gentle wind of expectation. On its heels came the first sounds of a lilting melody, the composition done especially for Gabriel and Charlotte by Charlotte's friend Aroha—who now sat at the grand piano at the far end of the church.

Jake had a moment to notice that her dress was the same deep blue as Juliet's, but no time to process that knowledge before the doors at the back swung open. Two adorable little flower girls walked in side by side, both dressed in their "girl princess" dresses—as described to Jake by his daughter. Those dresses were white and calf-length with skirts fluffed out by netting and belt sashes of a blue identical to Aroha's dress.

His heart squeezed as it always did at seeing Esme's sweet face.

The two girls wore flower crowns woven with miniature frangipani flowers, bright green leaves, and tiny white blooms, and carried little baskets full of blush-pink petals. Their shoes were sparkly and buckled securely on two pairs of tiny feet, their smiles enormous. They did their assigned task with teeth-biting-down-on-lower-lip concentration, carefully scattering the petals as they walked.

Esme looked at him at one point and beamed, her smile gap-toothed as a result of the loss of her first baby tooth—a lower central incisor—just a week earlier.

He mouthed, *Good job, Boo.*

Her smile expanded to cover her whole face, and his heart, it threatened to explode out of his chest. He'd done so much wrong in his life, but somehow he was getting this right. His little girl knew that she was loved, that she was the most important thing in his life.

Movement at the doors, three adult women following the flower girls. One was family: Sailor's wife, Ísa; the second, Charlie's detective friend, Mei. However, it wasn't Ísa or Mei who held his attention. It was the tall, curvy, dangerously sexy woman behind Mei.

Jake's mind short-circuited.

"She wasn't at the rehearsal," he found himself muttering.

"Did you forget, old man?" Danny murmured sotto voce. "Charlotte said her other friend from pastry class couldn't come to the rehearsal but that you're supposed to partner her today."

What?!

"Anyway," Danny continued, "pretty sure she isn't in any danger of messing up the aisle-walk deal. In case you didn't notice, there's only a single lane."

Jake fought the lowering of his brows—the last thing they needed was for him to be caught glowering in his brother's wedding photos. His entire family already thought he needed to lighten up; his parents were gentle in their encouragement that he go out, let his hair down, but Danny straight up called him an "old man in a young man's skin suit."

His baby brother liked to live recklessly.

As for Gabe and Sailor, they'd matured young for different reasons, so were less on his case, but he saw the concerned looks when they thought he wasn't looking. He figured they'd ease up as he continued to be successful in his career and in raising Esme—happiness came in different forms, and his came from giving his daughter the best life he could.

So yeah, no glaring at Danny in the photos.

And no staring at this sharp-tongued ghost from his past.

Juliet had disappeared without warning halfway through their final year of high school; student gossip had it that her family had decided to transfer her to a stricter school after she nearly got suspended for the third time. Calypso had been so anxious, certain that Juliet wouldn't leave without telling her, but a sympathetic teacher had confirmed that Juliet had officially transferred out of their school.

Gone without a trace—at least until Calypso finally began to receive emails and texts from her friend a month later. At the time, Jake hadn't asked too many questions about what had caused Juliet's sudden departure. He'd had bigger issues to deal with. But seeing her now, it brought it all back—the excitement and innocence of their teenage years, the way Juliet and Calypso used to pass notes in class, the occasions he'd caught them giggling hysterically together.

He also remembered skinny and lanky Juliet spending half her life in the principal's office while small and plump Calypso had been an honors student destined for a top university. But when a befuddled Jake had asked Calypso why she hung around with the troublemaking Juliet, his girlfriend's defense had been staunch.

"You don't know her," she'd said in that quiet way she had of doing, until he had to lean close to hear her. "Jules and I've been friends since primary school. She's funny and kind and she's never once let me down. You should give her a chance."

Jake had been determined to try to get along with Juliet for Calypso's sake—and he had to admit that she'd made him laugh more than once with her acerbic comments and razor-sharp wit—but they'd never been anything but wary acquaintances at best. Calypso had been the bond between them.

Well, Calypso's skinny best friend with what used to be elbows of doom—she'd utilized those pointy weapons on him more than once—had become distinctly and sensually curvy, her hair sleek and straight rather than a fuzzy braid. But in her eyes lived the troublemaking spark that had always made him want to grind his teeth.

Behind Juliet came Molly, her smile gorgeous. Her hair was dark, her body draped in a midnight-blue dress that fell gracefully to the floor, and she held a small frangipani bouquet bursting with color, the same as Juliet and Mei and Ísa.

The bridal party came to stand across the aisle from the groomsmen. They were uneven in number because Aroha was at the piano, but Harry would stop by the piano on the way out, offer her his arm as her assigned escort.

Jake's mother, already seated in the front pew, waved Esme and Emmaline over, and the two girls took their seats between their grandparents. Jake could feel the pride and joy emanating from both his parents.

The music lilted into a wedding march rewritten for Charlotte and Gabriel, snapping him back to the here and now. And there came Charlotte, lovely and radiant. She was walking up the aisle on her own—she desperately loved her parents, wanted to honor them by walking with their memory at her side.

Jake had been hanging out in her kitchen with her when she'd shown him the heart-shaped medallions she planned to attach to the backs of her heels. One held the name of her father, the other the name of her mother.

"So they can walk me up the aisle," she'd said thickly, wiping away her tears with one finger.

Her eyes were luminous behind her veil today, full of an incandescent love, all her attention on Gabriel. His big, brawny brother looked awestruck. Gabe was always in charge, the CEO of his life and his world, but when it came to Charlie, he was a man slayed by emotion.

Jake's diminutive future sister-in-law was the only person he knew who could stand toe to toe with Gabe and get Gabe to back down. He knew they'd be happy, the same way he'd known Sailor and Ísa would be happy.

Both couples had between them the indefinable something shared by Jake's parents—a sense of bone-deep comfort that existed beyond the passion and the love. The knowledge that this person would accept them always, even as they changed and grew through the years to come.

Gabe stepped forward to take Charlotte's hand in his. A gentle laugh rippled through the entire church at his readiness to do this. He grinned, unashamed about his desire to make Charlotte his wife.

Their pastor, a smile on his seamed face, stepped forward. "Dearly beloved..."

. . .

JULIET'S STONE heart was taking a beating today. First, all
that ridiculously beautiful love among the women, sprin-
kled with sparkling little-girl joy, and now this. Gabriel
Bishop, one of the toughest men to ever grace the rugby
field—*the* freaking Bishop—had his petite bride's hand
clasped firmly in his, his heart in his eyes and his eagerness
to be her husband unhidden. And Charlotte, just glowing,
her happiness a physical pulse that took them all down like
sniffling bowling pins.

Juliet couldn't believe she was about to *cry*. She swallowed in desperate self-defense against the stupid wedding
virus. She'd girded her loins for this, told herself that she
was proof against wedding bells and goofy lovestruck eyes.
Her armor of cynicism, tough as a crocodile's skin, would
protect her.

After all, the one genre of book she refused to read was
romance. She wasn't a snob about them, had devoured
hundreds as a teen. But she couldn't make herself believe in
happy-ever-after anymore, not after everything that had
happened. Except there it was: a great big fat happy-ever-
after right in front of her.

The Charlotte whom Juliet had first met had been a shy
mouse with fear shadowing her world. It had been
surprising and utterly delightful to see her bloom under the
attentions of the Bishop, of all people. Big, tough, relentless
Gabriel who ate mice for breakfast.

Turned out Charlie was indigestible.

Now here the two were, their devotion so deep and true
that Juliet expected to see little cartoon love hearts popping
up over their heads.

And oh my God, Ísa was making goo-goo eyes at Sailor,
and had she just seen Joseph Esera, senior member of the

Samoan community and stiffly formal in his mien, send his wife an "I love you" look?

Ugh. This family was going to test her decision to stay cold and cynical.

Jake was still scowling at her. The sight perked her up; at least some things never changed. A scowl was Jake's default expression when it came to Juliet. He'd never been able to grasp why his good-girl girlfriend was so loyal to her bad-girl best friend.

Poor Callie, Juliet had always thought, stuck with such a stuffy stick of a boyfriend. But, having seen how he'd smiled and encouraged his daughter just before, Juliet was forced to grudgingly accept that maybe Jacob Esera had his good points.

That Esme was a child confident in her right to be loved was obvious, and though Juliet wanted to credit the elder Eseras for that, the fact that Jake kept a spare pair of child-sized eyeglasses in his car smashed her favorite theory to splinters.

Gabriel's voice—*very* firm—as he said, "I do. Definitely. Forever. No out clause."

Juliet grinned through her incipient sniffles.

Charlotte's response to the pastor's question was softer but just as vehement. "I do. Forever and ever."

Seriously, they had to stop being so adorable—how was she to keep up the curmudgeon act? She was smiling so hard that her cheeks ached, fluffy happy rainbows dancing in front of her eyes.

"You may kiss the—"

Gabriel lifted Charlotte up by the waist before the pastor finished, and she threw her arms around his neck. The kiss they shared was hot and loving and went *just* a bit too long for the staid old church—and probably for all the tut-tutting aunties who lived to lecture everyone on acceptable behavior.

But even the pastor was grinning at Charlotte and Gabriel's enthusiasm, his brown face marked by life and lit with love. Lips kiss-wet, the bride and groom turned to face the guests, and the whole crowd rose up to cheer and shower them with flower petals as they walked back down the aisle.

4

IT INVOLVES JAKE'S THIGHS

Juliet had missed the wedding rehearsal because the plumbing in her kitchen had chosen that day to pack it in, flooding the entire area. She'd felt terrible for canceling, but Charlotte had assured her it was fine. She'd then sent through a quick list of instructions, so Juliet was prepared to slide her arm through Jake's as the bridal party followed the newlyweds.

Molly and Fox. Ísa and Sailor. Mei and Danny. Aroha and Harry. Juliet and Jake.

She'd actually found the idea of seeing Jake again in this context kind of funny. Who would've thought the two of them would end up arm in arm in a church wedding? Had a fortune-teller forecast that back when they'd been teens, they would've both gagged and asked for their money back while Callie groaned.

Anyway, it was just a short walk. No biggie.

Except for the frisson of... something that had hit with a vengeance the first moment they laid eyes on each other in his brother's backyard. She wanted to brush it off as irritation or annoyance, both things she was very used to feeling around Jake, but she knew full well the weird fluttering in the pit of her stomach was nothing of the kind.

The last time she'd felt anything near that flutter, she'd been on her couch eating strawberry-swirl ice cream while wolf whistling at the fit actor who played her favorite doctor on *Shortland Street*. But that had been a mere whisper in comparison to this massive reverberation that had zapped her entire system to speechlessness.

Guilt bit into her.

She shook it off, almost able to see Callie rolling her eyes at her. Her best friend knew Juliet'd had zero salacious thoughts about Jake when he'd belonged to Callie. Her thoughts had leaned more toward culpable homicide. She had no reason to feel guilty just because her adult body was insane enough to be attracted to Jacob Esera—who smelled far too good next to her.

Like freaking mountains and manly man and all that other stuff they talked about in aftershave commercials. She'd always made fun of those commercials, but now she was like the token brainless woman in the most recent ad, the one who wanted to snuggle up to her man and just *smell* him.

Well, too bad.

Her urges weren't getting no satisfaction. She'd rather stick a fork in her eye.

"He's amazing, Jules. Just give him a shot."

"With a tranquilizer dart you mean?"

Even as the memory of Callie's laughing shove against her shoulder made her lips twitch, Jake's muscles clenched under her palm. He was probably also clenching his jaw. At least if she wanted to confirm, she could just glance across —they were the same height, but only because she was wearing heels. At five eight in bare feet, she was tall for a woman, but all the men in this family were over six feet in height.

It irritated her that Jake had the physical ability to look down his snooty nose at her.

Deciding to focus on something else, she glanced around, taking in the smiling faces and teary-but-happy eyes. Everyone in their best clothes, their coats abandoned in the cloakroom to reveal bright, happy color. Structured and beautiful puletasi—full-length dresses, or skirts and tops, featuring traditional prints—on the women with Samoan heritage. Flowy lines and block colors on others.

As for the men, some had broken out a crisp lavalava—a traditional Polynesian skirt—to go with their shirts and ties, while others stuck with suits, but everyone was in formal gear. That, she knew, hadn't been a demand by the bridal couple. She had a feeling it was simply expected in this church.

Juliet's grandparents' congregation had been similar.

When two mischievous flower girls ran sneakily past to follow directly behind the bride—on best behavior once they'd reached their destination—her lips kicked up. Other children had wiggled out to stand at the aisle end of the rows of seats, all the better to see the bridal party. A small Indian boy wearing the cutest Indian-style gray suit, complete with silver embroidery, shot a sunny smile Juliet's way, his cheeks round and his eyes dancing.

Juliet recognized him as belonging to Ísa's funny and intelligent friend, Nayna. Having gotten to know and become friends with Charlotte, too, over the time since Charlotte had fallen for Gabe, Nayna had joined them for the prewedding festivities. Her handsome husband had been part of the male cohort, and had acted as an usher today.

Their gorgeous little boy was going to be trouble as a teen, Juliet thought with a sense of kinship. She looked forward to seeing him dance at the reception. Because no Samoan family wedding was ever without dancing—and from all she'd seen, Gabriel Bishop deeply respected his stepfather's heritage, so there'd be dancing, of that she had no doubt.

Juliet intended to dance until her feet hurt. One of her best friends had just married the love of her life; it was a night to celebrate and to *not* consider the opinions of a certain male member of Charlotte's chosen new family.

Jake probably considered dancing indecorous.

The doors were open, the afternoon sunshine pouring in as Gabriel and Charlotte stepped out to be met by another hail of petals from the guests who'd managed to get out before the wedding party headed down the aisle.

Laughing, the couple ran to the gleaming white stretch limo that'd eventually take them to the reception. First, the entire bridal party—Alison and Joseph included—would stop for photos. Ísa's siblings, Harlow and Catie, had also been ordered to come along to the photo session as the newlyweds wanted shots with the entire family.

According to Charlotte, Harlow and Catie had spent so much of their teenage years with the Bishop-Eseras that Alison and Joseph treated them the same as their boys. And though both had been abroad during Gabriel's courtship of Charlotte, Juliet's friend had come to know and fall in love with the two in the time since.

Charlotte had included Catie in all the prewedding celebrations.

Honestly, Charlotte's heart was the biggest thing about her. Juliet had wondered if, once Charlie came to know her, she'd run fast in the opposite direction—because Juliet's heart was as heavily shielded as Charlie's was open and generous.

But Charlotte insisted on believing that Juliet had "a heart so generous" she had to protect it against hurt. Juliet had decided not to disabuse her friend of that notion or to share the fact she still threw random objects at the screen when her pinhead ex showed his lying face.

Since she couldn't afford to keep replacing her TV, she threw soft objects while pretending they were rocks hitting Reid's swollen heads. Yes, both of them. The one above his shoulders and the one he went around swinging in the face of any woman vaguely blessed with breasts and an ass.

But Reid had no place here, she thought with a breath that had her lungs filling with Jake's manly-man scent. *Damn it.* Exhaling as quickly as she could, she kept her mind on what was to happen next. While the bridal party did the photos, the guests would make their way from the church to the reception venue to be plied with food and drink and entertained by acts put together by the children and teenagers in the extended-kin group.

With how both Gabriel and Charlie valued family— including friends who had become family—Juliet had a bet going with Aroha that the two would begin birthing their own private rugby team within the next nine months.

A year at the latest.

She and Jake didn't say a word to each other as they walked to the second stretch limo. It was big enough to fit the entire bridal party and yet somehow—*thanks, universe*— Juliet found herself trapped in a corner with the heat of Jake's body pressed to hers. He'd gotten a whole lot bigger since the last time she'd been this close to him: big shoulders, muscled thighs, ripped biceps, all were kind of a given with rugby men. He *was* sleeker than heavily built Gabriel, but in rugby, muscle was a matter of degrees.

A sleek, elite rugby player was still pure hard muscle and bursts of incredible speed on the field, their fitness and toughness legendary. Jake's thighs were probably like rock.

For all that's holy, Juliet, stop thinking about Jake's thighs!

Her mind immediately wandered to what it'd be like to bite down on one of those thighs and whether his warm brown skin was dusted with black hair all over or— *Stop, Juliet! Stop this insanity at once!*

"Cut it out, you two." Sailor's words had her cheeks going blazing hot... until she realized he was talking to Catie and Danny—who'd been sniping at one another from opposite sides of the limo. "Put down the swords for one day."

"They wouldn't know what to do with themselves then." Ísa laughed. "The last time the two of them were on good behavior, they ended up so traumatized that Catie had to leave the country."

"Ha ha," Catie said, the skirt of her flowy, breezy dress arranged neatly over the knees of her prosthetic legs.

Honestly, Juliet wouldn't have known they were prosthetics if Catie hadn't whipped one off during yesterday's celebrations to show off a new way to attach it to her stump. The younger woman had also shown Juliet a picture of a skin that gave one prosthetic the look of a cybernetic leg.

"My faves are my racing blades though," the champion runner had said. "I'm the wind on those."

At twenty-two, Catie was at home in her body in a way that Juliet had never been at her age. She'd been physically awkward even at her best, all skinny arms and legs and bones that felt uncoordinated and too big for the world; she'd also been reeling from the collapse of her marriage six months earlier.

But man what a difference breaking free from Reid had made.

The women's magazines might taunt her for "eating away her grief over the end of her marriage," but Juliet much preferred the way she was now. She felt ownership of her body, enjoyed the way it moved, how it looked. As if she'd grown into those bones, finally hit her stride. The women's mags could go suck on their fake sympathy. She was going to flaunt her curves and love her life.

Anyone who tried to judge her could go sit on a cactus.

Jacob Esera especially.

"Here." Jake handed her a flute of champagne.

Sailor was at the front end of the seating area in the limo, pouring sparkling golden liquid into clear flutes held out by his wife. Who he winked at just then, a wicked smile creasing his cheeks.

"Thank you." Juliet made sure her fingers didn't brush Jake's as she took the flute. But it didn't do much good when the rest of his body was pressing up against the side of hers. The man was a furnace.

"Why the death glare?" Jake raised an eyebrow.

"That's my resting bitch face."

The faintest warming of his eyes—and yeah, that was potent—before Molly tapped him on the shoulder to pass him a flute. Taking it, he didn't seize the opportunity to talk to someone, anyone, else. Instead, he shifted his attention back to Juliet after thanking Molly. "To clarify, is that your only resting face, or am I the recipient of a special one?"

Juliet almost laughed, would've probably snorted champagne bubbles up her nose if she'd given in. "I have a repertoire." She smiled her fakest smile, just to see what he'd do. "But don't worry, you only have to remember this one—it's the only one you'll ever see."

Wide eyes. "I think you need to consult a doctor, Jules—your face seems to be cracking in the most bizarre way."

She absolutely would've snort-laughed this time if Sailor's voice hadn't cut through the limo. "To Gabe and Charlie!" The second-eldest of Jake's brothers held up the flute in his hand after everyone had a drink—with Esme and Emmaline given soda in lieu of alcohol. But that soda had been poured into "grown-up" glass flutes that each girl held with utmost care.

Heart threatening to go scarily mushy again, Juliet raised her flute along with the others. Jake clinked his flute to hers and they drank. Their eyes locked in silent combat, part of a battle that had been going on since the day Callie tugged Juliet aside at lunchtime and whispered that "Jake invited me to come watch his game!"

Callie had been like a tiny star that day, she'd been so buzzy and bright. Juliet hadn't understood what her scholarly best friend saw in the gearhead jock who swaggered around the school thinking he was all that and tomato sauce, and seriously, what kind of a date was it to invite Callie to watch a bunch of sweaty boys slamming into one another?

But in the end, she'd had to admit that Jake treated Callie like a goddess.

Like his just-married brother, Jake didn't hide it when he was into a girl. He used to wait outside Callie's classes to walk her to the next one. Callie, in turn, had turned up to every one of his rugby matches, Jake's personal cheer squad. She'd dragged Juliet along despite all of Juliet's attempts to wriggle out—Juliet liked sports, but standing on a muddy and freezing winter sideline while a bunch of equally muddy jocks chased a slippery oval ball hadn't been her idea of a good time.

But she'd gone, because Callie had always been her truest friend. It would've been easy for the other girl to drop her as they grew and Juliet's grades began to slip, her suspensions and warnings rising at an inverse rate. Callie's parents had certainly not liked Juliet and often told Callie she could do better.

But Callie, nonconfrontational but stubborn, had ignored them.

Juliet's breath stuck in her chest, because in the end, she'd let down her friend. It hadn't been her fault that she couldn't attend Callie's funeral, but it still felt that way. She hadn't even been able to send flowers, she'd had so little money. Barely enough to pay for a small amount of data on the aged phone a sympathetic teacher had gifted her.

The only thing she'd managed was to send an email to Jake. Not to Callie's parents; they would've deleted it at once. Jake being Jake had replied to tell her that he'd received the email and that he'd read out her words of friendship at the funeral.

Before today, that was the last time they'd spoken.

"Oh damn." A drop of champagne slid wet and cool down her cleavage. Not thinking about it, she lowered her finger and wiped up, then licked the champagne off the wet tip.

Her eyes collided with Jake's while her finger was in her mouth. Heat burned her cheekbones. He was looking at her like she'd walked out of a cave wearing nothing but a bearskin and dirt.

Making a face at him, she sucked more deliberately before popping her finger out of her lips, just *daring* him to say something.

5

JULIET AND HER BLOWTORCH

Jake's entire body clenched against the raw sexual heat that smashed through him in a tornado that sought to level everything in its path. Setting his jaw, he forced himself to look away from Juliet's challenging gaze.

What the hell was wrong with him?

This was *Juliet*.

Constantly in detention, lippy with the teachers, barely scraping by on her grades, burr in his side, Juliet.

Beside him, she laughed in response to something Mei had just said, the hard-nosed detective more smiley than Jake had ever seen her. Juliet's laugh was big and husky and warm. Before, when she'd been all gangly limbs, it had seemed too big a laugh for her, but now it was just another weapon in her sensual arsenal.

That laugh wrapped around him, as soft and sexy as her thighs.

Because bad-girl Juliet Nelisi had grown into her bones, no more hard edges to her. Ah hell, who was he trying to fool? The woman was a hammer-to-the-head, bottle-ofwhiskey knockout, full of dangerous curves that made him want to explore her inch by inch... then do it all over again.

He curled his fingers into his palm, squeezing tight. He was no monk, but he wasn't exactly a man about town either; Jake took his time, chose his sexual partners with care. He didn't do one-night stands or give in to lust. Even if he hadn't been an intensely private man who wanted his daughter to grow up proud of her dad, he had endorsement deals based on his squeaky-clean image.

He couldn't afford to end up all over the tabloids.

The last woman with whom he'd had a physical affair was a reporter who did long-form hard news pieces. Rachel had been of the same mindset—she had a rising career that was as far from the tabloids as you could get.

Those tabloids as well as the gossipy women's magazines liked to run the occasional story about how he had a tragic past with "a lost love," but that was about it. Hard to wring salacious and scandalous from his determinedly uninterest-ing-to-the-media existence. There were only so many times they could reprint that old photo of him and Callie they'd managed to source from an old classmate.

Jake was the most boring-to-the-tabloids rugby player in the world, and that was *exactly* how he liked it.

Juliet, on the other hand, was a staple in those same magazines and tabloids. He hadn't followed her life, but it had been hard to miss the headlines back when she'd been married to Reid Mescall. He'd spot her face or name on a front page while in the line at the supermarket, notice it because of their shared history.

He'd never, however, bought the magazines or tabloids.

Jake frowned.

Now that he was thinking on the subject, he didn't remember seeing her on any new covers lately. But since her ex was a media hound, Juliet was of interest to the public by default. And this limo ride was taking an eternity, the erotic softness of Juliet's body sinking deeper into him with every kilometer they traveled.

He swore he could smell her scent—lush and addictive —even though, logically, that had to be impossible. There were too many of them in this limo. But each breath he took was going straight to a part of his anatomy that had no business being excited on this day. Having a hard-on in his brother's wedding photos was *not* on Jake's to-do list.

He was never so glad as when the limo finally came to a stop inside Auckland Domain. The sprawling green space in the heart of the city was special to Gabriel and Charlotte, and they'd decided to have their wedding photos here and also back at their apartment.

The view from their penthouse was an unbeatable one.

Because of the way everyone had been seated, he and Juliet were the last to get out. Once out himself, he turned automatically and held out a hand. His father had drilled it into him, into all of them, that they were to treat women with respect, like the knights of old in the fairy tales his mother had read them.

Of course, Joseph Esera had never had to deal with the fiery virago that was Juliet. Crunching on heroic knights was probably her favorite post-dinnertime snack. Afterward, she no doubt used their bones as toothpicks.

Today she shot him a dark look but put her hand in his and let him help her out from the low-slung vehicle. The shock of the contact ran through him, his body suddenly that of an irrational teenager who hadn't taken on board any of his rational objections to this inexplicable attraction.

Her hand was soft and warm with a slight unexpected roughness. She did something physical with her hands; he wondered if she'd kept up the metalwork she'd been so good at back in high school. She'd been one of the only girls in that particular class. Jake knew because he'd been in an adjacent class that dealt with car repair and engineering.

A snapshot came to mind of Juliet with her face half-hidden by safety glasses, expertly handling a welding torch. While his own teacher's back was turned, he'd managed to snap a picture of her as sparks flew around her face. He'd sent it to her at lunch—and been shocked when she replied with: *This is awesome. Thanks.*

That had been their politest interaction. Ever.

As far as hands went, his own were all kinds of roughed up. The kind of work he did in the gym to stay on form didn't allow for softness, and rugby wasn't exactly a gentle-man's sport.

"Thanks." Juliet released his hand the instant she was out on her feet.

"Gee, don't hold on too long," he muttered, though he should've been thanking her.

Another smile that came straight out of central casting for insincere. "Aw, little Jakey needs me to hold his hand. Come on now, baby." She held out a hand.

Tugging his suit jacket closed, he did up the button. "Did you forget to take your vitamins this morning? You're acting extra feral." He couldn't believe the words had come out of his mouth; only Juliet could make him regress to the point where he sounded like a seventeen-year-old dipshit.

Then Juliet laughed, that big husky sound washing over him like a caress. "You've gotten faster with the comebacks," she said, her eyes dancing. "Back in school, you mostly just tried a macho-stud glare."

That was because she'd been like an alien species with which he'd had no familiarity.

"Juliet! Jake!" His mother's voice, her hand waving them over.

The two of them began to move.

The limo driver had parked in a spot between the rotunda and the Winter Gardens—two huge greenhouses from the 1900s that housed blooms of every variety as well as tropical plants. Jake sometimes brought Esme here on rainy weekend days when the two of them were getting restless being cooped up inside.

They usually went by his brother's and picked up Emmaline too. His daughter's favorite thing in the gardens was the cacao tree when it fruited, while her cousin was fascinated by the hanging pitcher plants. The three of them would wander leisurely through the Winter Gardens, then —if the girls had been good—he'd take them for afternoon tea at the nearby café.

Weirdly, the two were always impeccably behaved on those days.

Jake bit back a smile at the thought, his eyes on their two little forms as they walked hand in hand between Ísa and Alison. Molly and Mei were ahead of them, holding Charlotte's train up off the asphalt of the parking area. The photographer and his assistant, meanwhile, had come ahead in their own vehicle; the photographer now waved Charlotte and Gabriel toward the rotunda while taking candid shots along the way.

His assistant lugged the gear for the more formal shots.

Unsurprisingly, the wedding party attracted attention from people out enjoying the sunny Saturday; smiles broke out over countless faces. A couple of kids were playing in the rotunda when they arrived but got quickly out of the way at first sight of Charlotte. A minute later, they sighted Gabe, then Jake and Danny, and their eyes rounded.

Rugby fans right there.

Since the kids had been so good about vacating their play area, Jake would make sure they got an autograph or a picture with him and Danny. He didn't think they'd be taking off before the wedding shoot was over—even now, one had turned to call over a couple on a picnic blanket who had to be their parents.

The photographer didn't bother giving Gabriel and Charlotte any instructions after the first few minutes—the two were so madly in love that everything they did was beautiful, their faces glowing. At one point, Gabriel scooped Charlotte up into his arms without warning, her veil trailing to the floor in a delicate waterfall. His tough-as-nails brother's face was a picture of delight, Charlotte's full of laughter.

Meanwhile, he and Juliet stood silent as sphinxes next to each other. It wasn't comfortable. It was very *uncomfortable*. Prickly. As Juliet had always been. Full of sharp edges that kept the world at bay. Only Calypso had been invited in.

"So you transferred to another school," he finally said, trying to make some kind of a connection, some kind of conversation in honor of the girl who'd touched both their lives. "Was it because you got expelled?" He hadn't asked too many questions of Calypso back then, had just been glad that she was no longer stressing about her friend's disappearance.

She'd been three months along by then.

"Was that the rumor?" Juliet made a face. "Tell me that at least I was suspected of having done something wildly scandalous."

He leaned in close, the scent of her intoxicating. "Affair with the principal."

"Ew!" A sudden poke at his upper arm. "You made that up."

"Did I?"

A look that told him the virago would wait for her revenge—then scorch him dead. "I got sent to Samoa," she said at last. "Phone confiscated, the whole strict discipline, straight-home-after-school thing. I only managed to message Callie after a teacher took pity on this lost transplant from New Zealand and gave me her old prepaid phone. I used to do homework for a couple of other kids to earn money to load it with data."

Because Juliet had never been stupid. No, she was extremely smart. He'd once seen her scribbling in her math book during a lesson and peeked over her shoulder, expecting to see a rude doodle. Instead, she'd solved the complex math equation the teacher was still patiently explaining. That she'd had such trouble with her grades probably had to do with the fact she'd worked most nights as well as on the weekends.

He'd had part-time jobs too, but nothing so onerous. "What about the money from your job here?" he asked, recalling the times he'd gone in late with one of his older brothers to pick up groceries and seen Juliet at the checkout. She'd been the picture of politeness to his brothers.

It had been weird.

So much so that one day, he'd gone back to fetch a chocolate bar he'd deliberately forgotten to bag and asked her if she'd been possessed by a nice demon.

Her response had reassured him that Juliet was still Juliet.

Today she shrugged, and it threatened to draw his eyes straight to the vee between her generous breasts. "I was a minor, so my aunt had access to my bank account. She used what I'd saved to pay for my ticket to Samoa."

Jake looked at the line of her profile, searching for all the things he could feel but that she didn't say. Her words had been offhand, without anger, but that was impossible after such a major forced shift in her life—especially one paid for with money she'd worked hard to earn. The Juliet he'd known had always been angry.

"Who did you stay with in Samoa? Grandparents?"

"Yup. My dad's parents."

"How was it going to school there?"

A pause before she said, "I had to repeat a grade." Words that held more unspoken things. "Let's just say things were a bit messed up."

Jake shrugged. "I repeated a grade too."

Dark eyes met his, a softness to them that cut him off at the knees it was so unexpected from this woman made of prickles and armored to the teeth.

"You're a really good dad, Jake," she said. "I think Callie would be beyond happy to see how you've raised your daughter. She had such dreams for her baby."

This wasn't a topic on which Jake spoke often, not even to his brothers. And he hadn't had a non-family best friend for a long time. Most of the guys his age who played rugby were still unfettered by family obligations and lived a life that he couldn't—and didn't want to—emulate. No late-night drinking sessions for Jake, no taking off on weekends away without planning well ahead of time.

He got along better with the older guys on the team, the ones with families of their own, but their mutual responsibilities meant they didn't hang as much. Because they got it, got that Jake's daughter was his responsibility and he loved her. He wanted to be there for her. Esme didn't have a mum, just him.

While his entire family was always around, ready to help, he was the one who kissed her good night and got her up in the morning. He was the one who went with her to get her school supplies, and he'd learned how to braid hair so he could braid hers.

All these things, and more, he usually never spoke aloud.

Today, however, maybe because Juliet had known Calypso, he found himself saying, "Yeah, I hope so. She would've been a hell of a good mum." Calypso had been the one with the plans, the one who'd made lists of what their baby would need.

"She chose Esme's name, didn't she?"

Of course Calypso would've shared that with her best friend. "And she made all these videos, talking to Esme while she was pregnant." Cradling her belly while speaking to her "sweet baby." "Esme likes to listen to and watch them sometimes."

Danny had helped Jake load all the videos into the cloud and set a backup so Esme would never lose access to them. "We do that on Mother's Day." His daughter had grown up knowing that she'd had a mother who'd loved her very much. "I just wish that Calypso could see who Esme's growing up to be—she would've been so proud."

Blinking rapidly, Juliet glanced away. They watched Gabriel and Charlotte kiss on the curly-haired photographer's redundant cue. Gabriel couldn't keep his hands off his new bride, and Charlie was his partner in crime.

"I heard it was fast." Juliet's voice was rough. "That the meningitis took her quickly."

"She didn't suffer." That would matter to the girl who'd been by Calypso's side since childhood. "She wasn't feeling well one night, and since it was so soon after the birth, my mum and dad drove us to the ER so the doctors could confirm it wasn't anything major. We thought the flu. They admitted her instead. She slipped away only hours later, despite all their efforts."

It still seemed surreal when he thought about it, that the vibrant young woman he'd loved with all his teenage heart had been brought down by a disease that didn't understand that she was a new mother with a baby she adored—and a scared boyfriend who was doing everything in his power to man up and give her the support she needed.

"Daddy!" A tiny sprite jumped up and down in front of him.

His entire soul smiled, the sadness of memory fading away into the past where it belonged. Because his future was right here in front of him, and she needed a man with a whole heart, a man who understood joy.

Going down on his haunches, he said, "I'm sorry, do I know you?"

"It's me, Esme!"

"I don't think so." He rubbed his jaw. "My daughter's a little girl, and you're a beautiful young lady."

She giggled. "I love you!" She leaned in to kiss him on the cheek before running away to join Emmaline and the kids who'd been attracted by the bridal party.

Yeah, he did okay. Even if he was scared all the time about fucking up.

Gut tight, he took a breath... and the scent of a lushly sensual woman bloomed on his tongue, in his blood. A woman whose bare legs were inches from him. Legs covered by smooth brown skin he wanted to stroke until he heard her purr. Thighs he could imagine pressed around his head as he did things with his tongue that might—finally—blunt the sharp edge of hers.

6

THE LADY PARTS, THEY'RE MISBEHAVIN'

Seeing Esme kiss her dad with such joy had Juliet smiling past the grief of the past. And seeing Jake crouched down that way, his daughter's tiny hands on his face as she held him in place for her kiss, had her heart doing ridiculous somersaults. All wide shoulders and dark hair with a tendency to curl, his voice playful as he teased his baby girl, he was lethal to Juliet's lady parts.

They wanted to tingle.

Gritting her teeth, she told said lady parts to calm the heck down. There was to be no tingling whatsoever where Jacob Esera was concerned. Then Jake rose to his feet as the photographer took several photos of Alison and Joseph with the newlyweds and she caught a hint of that manly forest-and-rain-and-sex aftershave of his, and her breasts joined in on the act, seeming to swell inside the cups of her bra.

"All right." The photographer clapped his hands. "Wedding party!"

Thank God.

Juliet focused all her attention on the lanky male, who

was very good-looking but incited no tingling whatsoever. A tingle-free zone, that's what she wanted and would achieve.

"Ladies, you're up!" the photographer said. "Then we'll do all of you together, then some other single and group shots. Groomsmen, you'll be the closers."

It was chaotic and wonderful, and Juliet's cheeks ached by the end. Maybe she'd lift her romance-novel moratorium, because this was a happy-ever-after in every way. Her own situation couldn't compare.

Reid the Pinhead had never looked at her the way Gabriel looked at Charlotte.

When the photographer banished Gabriel to stand with the men, Charlotte's husband clutched his chest and pretended to be heartbroken as he walked sideways down the steps of the rotunda. Charlotte laughed and blew him a kiss, and the photographer's camera shutter clicked.

Juliet sighed.

Aroha nudged her with an elbow. "Hah! Told you you'd fall victim to the luuuuurv bug."

"It's the wedding virus. Passes once the wedding is over."

"You sure? Saw you cozying up to Jake there." A waggle of her eyebrows. "Hubba-hubba."

"I once beat him up at school." In truth, she'd thrown a tomato at his head for reasons she couldn't quite remember, he'd dodged it, and they'd gone about their business.

Aroha's mouth fell open. "Seriously? You went to school with Jacob Esera?"

"Ugh, stop fangirling." Aroha was a rugby fanatic. "But talking of hubba-hubba, Harry's pretty hot." Though at this point, he could've been a three-headed weevil and she'd have said that to get Aroha off the subject of Jake.

Her friend looked down, an uncharacteristically shy smile on her face, and Juliet took a second and far more speculative look at Harry. Big, muscled—a bit too much for her, to be honest—and square. Square jaw, square face, square shoulders, a sense to him that said he liked things solid and in their place.

Aroha, by comparison, was wild, dazzling color and a wide-open heart.

But who knew what might happen when so many love pheromones were in the air? Just so long as they didn't infect Juliet. She planned to live a long and gloriously single life, complete with the adoption of at least five cats once she no longer had to travel for work.

"I hope you bang Harry like a drum—man looks like he needs to be unleashed," she said to Aroha, startling her friend into laughter that was caught by the photographer.

The groomsmen, when it was their turn, decided to have their pictures in among the ancient trees that grew all through the Domain. A group of big, gorgeous men with identical smiles on their faces. Blood relations or not, it didn't matter, they were so much birds of a feather. The effect didn't change even after Harlow and Joseph joined them for a shot.

Jackets came off, ties were loosened and then discarded, and arms went around each other. When Emmaline and Esme ran into the shots partway through, the men grabbed the girls and put them on their shoulders. And the photographer clicked on.

Before they moved to the greenhouses for the next set of photographs, the men grumbled but put their jackets and ties back on. Several of them, groom included, then paused to sign autographs for and take pictures with the little boys who'd been in the rotunda when they first arrived.

Juliet tried not to look at Jake while all of that was going on. He was also avoiding her. Good. Because they'd had their moment of togetherness—it'd all go downhill if they tried for any more.

At one point she bent down to fix the ribbon sash at Esme's waist when a shutter clicked, and she realized the moment had been captured.

Another time, Jake wrapped his arm around his younger brother's neck and hauled him down to ruffle his hair while Gabriel laughed, and the photographer captured that too.

"I'm starving," Charlotte said toward the end. "Seriously, does anyone have snacks?"

Laughing, the photographer promised he was almost done. And Gabriel leaned down to whisper something in Charlotte's ear that had her cheeks going pink before she turned to lay the side of her face against his chest.

Juliet pressed a hand to her heart. "They keep this up and I'm going to give them a citation for ridiculous amounts of adorableness," she said to Molly.

Charlotte's best friend wiped away a tear, utterly no help in assisting Juliet maintain her own composure. "I'm so happy for her. She's the kindest human being I've ever known."

That, of course, had Juliet sniffling as well—and damn it, she wasn't a crier. "Charlie tamed the T-Rex," she rasped to Molly, "so she must have *some* evil superpowers we don't know about."

Molly laughed at Juliet's reference to the nickname Charlotte had given Gabriel when he'd first taken over management of the company where Charlotte had then worked. He'd apparently fired people left and right, rampaging through the place. But he hadn't fired Charlotte. No, he'd seen her for exactly what she was: a highly intelligent and capable woman who was being woefully misused.

Thus had begun the battle of the mouse and the T-Rex.

Up ahead, Gabriel said something that made Jake grin, and damn if her breath didn't stick in her chest. Cheeks creased, hands in his pockets, and head slightly lowered so the sun glinted off the black strands of his hair, Jacob Esera was the definition of sexy.

It was a good thing he never smiled at Juliet that way. Because if he did, she might forget that they were sworn nonfriends. And that was her number one rule for dating now: friendship. Which was probably why she'd been celibate since recovering from marriage to the pinhead. Turned out that these days most men looked at her and didn't want friendship—they wanted hot, sweaty, no-strings-attached sex.

What a hoot that was for the girl one teenaged charmer had called a "walking stick" who'd probably give him bruises with her "pointy" bones. At least the salivating male reaction had quickly disabused her of the notion that Reid had tried to plant in her head: that her weight gain made her less desirable. Tell that to the guys whose tongues hung out of their mouths the rare times she went out for a drink with her girlfriends.

Unfortunately, her incredibly unearned reputation as a sex-hungry, gold-digging debaucher of innocent males came along with her. Those drooling men would sleep with her if she were foolish enough to accept an invitation, but they wouldn't be taking her home to meet the family. Juliet had too much respect for herself to accept that state of affairs. So it was a good thing she was an old hand at being alone.

Debauchery was overrated anyway. All those nights she'd gone out with Reid because "we have to be seen, babe," she'd ended up dog-tired and just wanting a good nap the next day.

"Time for the final photo!" the photographer called out. "Everyone, I need you back here!"

That final image was of the entire group against a backdrop of ancient trees. And because fate was laughing at Juliet today, she ended up sandwiched between Jake and Aroha. Then the photographer, surely in league with the devil, asked Jake to move in tighter and put his arm around Juliet's waist.

Heat.

That's all she felt. She didn't breathe until the photo was done. At which point she inhaled Jake's sexiness, and the tingles went from low buzz to a full-on vibrating concerto. "Did you bathe in deodorant?" she said to Jake when he caught her trying to sniff him.

Really, Juliet?!

"I find it gives me good all-over coverage," he said with a straight face.

Juliet's lower lip quivered, and she had to turn away to maintain her composure. There it was, that sneaky sense of humor that had always taken her by surprise, she was so used to thinking of him as Callie's straitlaced choirboy of a boyfriend. But every so often, out he'd come with a zinger.

"Look to the left," he murmured in her ear, his warm breath kissing her skin and that delicious scent in her lungs all over again.

Juliet did so instinctively and had to grin. The photographer wasn't done after all—Gabriel and Charlotte were currently posing with Esme and Emmaline, with Gabe holding Esme as if she were a rugby ball he was ready to throw, while Charlotte and Emmaline took positions as if to catch her, their bodies mid-lunge.

"He should do some shots of the entire bridal party as if

we're playing a game of rugby," Juliet found herself saying. "Bridesmaids against groomsmen maybe?"

"Sometimes, Jules, you're all right."

Even as Jake grabbed her hand to tug her to the rest of the bridal party, Juliet muttered, "That's Juliet to you, Jacob." But she didn't pull her hand away—and she really, really should have. Because Jacob Esera was never going to be anything but a mistake for a woman like Juliet.

Everyone loved the idea of joining the girls and the wedded couple in their game of frozen rugby. Teams were chosen, a ball borrowed from the same kids who'd been playing in the rotunda, and the "game" was on.

They took shots with pretend running and the "opposition" getting ready to tackle, others where Gabriel was boosting Charlotte up so she could grab the ball in a line-out, still others with the flower girls "arguing" with the referee—their grandfather, who'd borrowed the limo driver's red license holder and was holding it up as if sending one of the girls off the field.

Needless to say, the public in and around the shoot were taking some images of their own.

"Is it okay?" Juliet asked Jake at one point, aware the family was justifiably protective of the two young girls in their midst. "The photos by the public, I mean."

"Things like this, with ordinary folks taking a few shots, it's not a problem," he said as the photographer—having a grand old time with this new element of the shoot, told them to organize themselves with their arms over each other's shoulders—or around waists—depending on position, and bend as if forming into a scrum.

"Women on one side, men on the other," he ordered. "Girls, you're playing first five-eighth. Emmaline, you're on the men's team. First five-eighth is Jake's usual position on the—"

"We know!" both Esme and Emmaline cried, the two girls probably far better versed in rugby than the photographer.

"We just don't want the media stalking them," Jake added as the girls scrambled to take position. "Luckily the Kiwi public isn't keen on kids being hounded for photos, especially when we've made our position clear, so the mags and tabloids leave them alone."

"Or we'd burn them dead," Danny said, tone merciless as he got into formation next to Jake. "No interviews with any of us into eternity."

Yes, that would be a serious deterrent when their family had such enormous pulling power. Add in the fellow athletes who'd back them in solidarity and it would be a bad business call for any media outlet to breach that unwritten law of privacy.

"One, two, three!" The photographer took the shot.

And Juliet found herself looking straight into a pair of dark brown eyes that were far too intense and far too serious for a woman who was a bad influence. Yet the eye contact robbed her of breath, as if she'd truly played a hard hour of the most unforgiving ball game on the planet.

AFTERWARD, the wedding party—sans the bride and groom—went ahead to the reception venue, a stately old theater with a rich history. Antique chandeliers sparkled overhead as they walked into the space, dripping light across the ornate cornices that ringed the ceiling and falling across the deep blue velvet that lined the walls.

Charlotte had asked her bridesmaids if the color would

be too much, given the shade of their dresses, but the hue of the velvet was much darker than their midnight blue. Also, the theater was just stunning in its unashamed baroque glory—every single one of them had sighed at the romance of it when Charlotte brought them in for a sneak peek when she and Gabriel had been looking at booking the venue.

The tables were clothed in white, the centerpieces glass bowls holding flowers and tea lights floating in water. That was Charlotte's touch all the way. Simple but lovely. Gabriel's more pushy and bold nature came in on the masses of fragrant flowers piled in every corner. Literally *piled*, as if a flower truck had lost its load.

Come the end of the night and the kids were going to have a lot of fun with those floral mountains. Juliet, Molly, and the other bridesmaids were already planning a group shot with their bodies flung back against the blooms, and they intended to talk Charlie into joining them.

The newlyweds hadn't yet arrived, having detoured to their apartment for more photos and so Charlotte could change out of her wedding dress into a dress more suited for the reception and the planned dancing. When Danny— poker face in place—had suggested the bridesmaids should go with the newlyweds so they could help Charlotte with her dress change, his big brother had threatened murder.

From the look in Gabriel's steel-gray eyes, he'd had plans to do more than just help Charlotte out of her dress. Which was why Juliet wasn't the teensy bit shocked when the bride and groom arrived at the reception a little later than expected. Charlotte was radiant, a guilty flush on her cheeks but her hair still perfectly in place.

Gabriel just looked gorgeously smug.

He also looked smitten, which Juliet figured excused the smug.

Aroha sent Juliet a speaking look from down the table, her gaze sparkling. Had she been sitting beside Juliet, she'd no doubt have elbowed her into breaking out into a grin. As it was, Juliet had been seated between Jake and Fox. It was tempting to focus on Molly's tattooed rock-star husband and busy herself with random questions about the rock-star life, but she could hardly ignore Jake when he was sitting right next to her.

Especially when he was sending out that scent of his that wasn't just deodorant or aftershave, but Jake. She'd figured she'd build up a tolerance after so much exposure, but no, the tingling was still proceeding without hesitation. Pushed to the edge, Juliet decided to talk to him specifically so she could incite their mutual aggravation with each other.

She was going to whack this ludicrous attraction stone-dead.

7

JULIET NELISI IS NOT A CHICKEN

"So," she said to him without warning, "you going to date that tennis player with all the red hair?" A serious stunner as well as gifted in her sport, the visiting athlete had, a week earlier, been asked in a radio interview which man she wouldn't kick out of bed if she had all the choice in the world.

Juliet would've bristled at the question if the two interviewers weren't renowned for such questions; it was their shtick. Anyone who came on their show knew their reputation well in advance, so it was never an ambush—and they were equal opportunity. Gender and sexual orientation didn't matter; they'd find a way to work sex into the interview.

The tennis player's answer to that latest volley?

Jacob Esera is a hottie. So serious and focused. I mean, imagine all that intensity in bed!

At the time, Juliet had been driving to a work meeting and had burst out laughing at the idea of anyone finding her old nemesis hot. Probably why fate had decided to slap her with the tingles that *would not stop*.

"If I wanted the world to know my business, I'd have a TV show," said nemesis muttered tersely. "I mean, who goes out and says that kind of stuff about someone they don't know?"

Lots of people, all the time. But not Jake. She'd never once caught even a snippet of his private life on TV or in the magazines—not that she'd been looking, but beloved as they were by the media, it was hard to avoid catching glimpses of the Bishop-Esera family in print and online.

"Don't die of shock, but I agree with you." She waited for Jake to laugh at her—after all, she'd done a ton of media with and for Reid. Her ex had told her it'd be good for his future career in television; he'd had plans to end up with his own late-night sports show or as an anchor on a long-running commentary show.

Young and in awe of Reid's career as a top professional athlete, Juliet had tried to be a supportive wife despite her discomfort at the intrusions into their private life. He'd even talked her into allowing reporters to follow them around to do a "day in the life of" piece. It had made her skin crawl to know people were watching her every move, and she'd nixed any further such stalking.

It had been the first time she'd defied Reid in their short marriage, and it had signaled the beginning of the end. The pinhead had wanted a brainless talking doll, not a living, breathing woman with her own thoughts and opinions.

"I figured Reid was behind the publicity you got," Jake said as the MC—one of Jake's uncles—called everyone to order. "You never were big on public stuff. Must've made you nuts to have it all out there."

Startled at the unexpected understanding, she was glad of the MC's announcement that the formal part of the reception had begun. First came the cake cutting, interspersed with joyful laughter, then a toast made by Sailor on behalf of the entire Bishop-Esera clan and responded to by Molly on behalf of Charlotte.

Charlotte's parents might've passed away, Juliet thought with an ache in her already overworked heart, but she very definitely had a family.

Joseph then got up to welcome Charlotte into the family, his speech so full of warmth and love for this "new daughter" that tears ran down Charlotte's face. Gabriel kissed them away before rising to his feet with a murmur to his bride. Meanwhile, a couple of cute little second cousins dressed in lavalavas printed with hibiscus flowers, their feet and upper bodies bare and their round faces awash in grins, began to do a dance that was more enthusiasm than skill.

The two couldn't have been more than five or six years of age.

The adorable factor was off the charts.

Juliet didn't think anything of Gabriel's departure from the wedding party table... until she felt Jake's warmth leave her side a minute later, followed by Fox on the other. Sailor and Danny had already disappeared.

No freakin' way...

But then the music altered into a fast dance rhythm, and the cute second cousins scarpered off with giggles—or as if they'd been coached. And onto the dance floor stepped Gabriel Bishop... with five gorgeous groomsmen. No ties or leis now, but they'd kept on everything else.

Blowing Charlotte a kiss—a Charlotte who had her hands clasped over her mouth—Gabriel took a step to the right... and the entire group of six stepped into a routine that was a gift from a groom to his bride.

It was also a testament to the athletic skill of the men involved. Because they could *move*. Gabriel and Harry might both be heavily built, but right now they were pure masculine grace. As for Jake... Juliet had caught the odd news replay of him on the rugby field, but those glimpses had done zero justice to the beauty of the man in motion. Add in the heartbreaker smile he'd brought out as well as the grins he shared with the others, and she was in danger of a fatal heart event.

The tennis player was more right than she knew: Jake was a serious hottie.

Glad she'd thought to get her phone from Alison, who'd been babysitting all their phones in her handbag, she hit Record, then propped the phone up against a water glass so she was free to just watch. The choreography was amazing, all the men perfectly in sync—and all so obviously having a good time that their joy was infectious. Grinning, Juliet glanced at Charlotte to see that her friend had all but melted, her delight effervescent.

The men brought down the house.

And Gabriel got a passionate kiss from his delighted bride while the others laughed and grabbed glasses of cold drinks to cool down from the dance.

She glanced at Jake as he slipped into his seat beside her. "Jacob Esera, I didn't know you had that in you."

A fading hint of the grin he'd sported on the dance floor. "It's my big bro's wedding, Jules. We did it at Sailor's reception too, you know—different routine though." He shoved a hand through his hair, then took a long drink from his glass.

Juliet found herself hypnotized by the movement of his throat, the tendons strong and defined. A hint of perspiration dotted his skin. She wanted to lean in and lick it up, her thighs clenching under the table.

Cheeks hot and a shocking slickness between her legs, she forced herself to look away and saw that the criminally cute cousins had returned to finish their number. Or to act as decoys to distract from another planned surprise. Because it took her a few minutes to realize that Fox hadn't returned to the table.

Her eyes narrowed just as the music altered and the impish kids ran off a second time.

The now jacketless rock star, the sleeves of his shirt folded up to reveal a stunning dragon tattoo that twined around his left arm, was at the microphone in front of the live four-piece band. His lip ring caught the light as he turned to grin at the quartet.

Gabriel, love brilliant in his eyes, rose from his seat beside Charlotte at the same moment and held out his hand to his bride. She slid her hand into his without hesitation, and the two of them walked out onto the dance floor.

Charlotte's reception dress was sleeveless, ankle-length, and hugged her body with delicate elegance. Made up of cream-colored fabric with a high neck, and a lower—but not scandalously low—back with a soft cowl design, it was graceful and sexy without being too much. It perfectly suited Charlotte's personality and comfort zone.

Fox's gritty voice flowed into a smoky ballad that made Juliet shiver, the words were so beautiful. The chorus was formed around the words: *Be mine. I'm yours.*

Sometimes the simplest things hit the hardest.

She also appreciated that the lead singer of one of the world's most successful bands was careful to keep his voice in the background so that the spotlight stayed on Gabriel and Charlotte. Though Gabriel was much taller than Charlie, they didn't look mismatched on the floor—their bodies were too naturally in sync for that, with Gabriel's tenderness and devotion for Charlotte as evident as her love and adoration of him.

When Gabriel spun Charlotte out in a swirl, Juliet's friend's laughter filled the old theater.

"It's time for the wedding party to join the bride and groom," the MC said as Fox ended the song to hand things back to the band, and dear God, she wasn't ready for this.

Because her assigned partner for this dance was Jake.

"Try not to stab me with those heels." Jake held out his hand.

"Sorry, I make no promises." Heart thudding at the idea of being pressed up against him, she almost told him to partner Aroha, except that Juliet Nelisi was no damn chicken. Also, Harry had already stepped up to Aroha— with a quiet determination on his face that had been legendary during his time on the field.

Today it said he wasn't open to trading partners.

Wrapping a wide-eyed Aroha in his thickly muscled arms, the former rugby loosehead prop swept her away.

Internally gritting her teeth, Juliet gave in to the inevitable and let Jake lead her to the dance floor. The feel of his arm sliding around her waist, all hard muscle and heat, threatened to steal her breath. Unlike Harry, he wasn't overtly big, but he was so tautly muscled, with such wide shoulders that she felt intensely feminine and *small* in a way that was a shock to her system.

Juliet was used to being tall and shapely and owning it.

Maybe she needed to relax her friends-only rule. Because if this lunacy was what resulted from celibacy, she wasn't impressed. Meanwhile, her nipples tightened to nubby points that made her grateful she was wearing a padded bra. The last thing she needed was for Jake to feel rigid boob-buttons poking his impressive chest.

As it was, despite the way he held her—with absolute respect—her breasts continuously brushed his chest. She'd never been exactly small up top, and he was *built*. Some friction was unavoidable.

Great. Now she was thinking about friction. About skin sliding against skin.

Taking a deep breath, she tried to do the yoga breathing she'd learned in a class her boss had organized for the entire E. E. Designs team. Except her inhale brought with it the scent of Jacob Esera. The same scent that made her want to snuggle her nose into the strong column of his neck and breathe deep.

Her hand clenched on his shoulder.

He glanced down, his jaw tight and no hint on his face of the devastating grin he'd sported during the dance. "What?" It came out kind of a terse growl. "You trying to dig your talons in and draw blood?"

Juliet smiled, oh so sweetly. "Oh, looks like you decided to return that stick to a certain part of your anatomy," she said before she could stop herself. Seriously, it was supremely irritating that while she was all stupid tingles for him, he obviously couldn't wait to get rid of her. If fate was going to laugh at her, couldn't it laugh at him too?

A flush kissed his cheekbones. "Mature, Jules. Real mature."

Even as her breath caught at the sign of human emotion, Juliet smiled with the poise of a nineteenth-century debutante. "If maturity means acting like an eighty-year-old geriatric with permanent grump syndrome, I'll pass." Actually, he hadn't been too bad today—but he was a whole lot more... solemn and *old* than he'd been back in school.

Not the kind of age that showed in the face, but something deeper, more profound. Some of that could be explained by life and loss. He was a dad now—a good one—and he was a professional athlete at the top of his game. Yet those things didn't explain the deep sense of "tightness" she felt in him, as if he was containing himself until his real self could only find freedom in tiny bursts.

In contrast, while his teenaged preoccupation with mag wheels and shiny rims had made her roll her eyes, it had been very human. "You still do the car thing?" she asked when he took the higher road and didn't respond to her provocation. "That old junker you were obsessed with fixing has to be as good as new by now." She'd gone for more than one ride in that car, sharing the back seat with another friend while Calypso and Jake sat up front.

"Some of us have responsibilities." A pointed look at the hand she had on his shoulder.

A hand bedazzled with nails boasting diamantes and sparkles. She'd made plans to get the fun but deliberately over-the-top nails removed for the wedding in favor of a simple nude, but Charlotte had caught on and would have none of it.

"I want you to be *you*, Jules." Fierce voice, hazel eyes intent. "Complete with dramatic nails and skyscraper heels. Just like I want Mei to look like she can kick everyone's ass without breaking a sweat and Aroha to be all big hair and big heart."

All Charlie had asked was that her bridesmaids and matron of honor wear midnight blue. It was the five of them who'd coordinated the dresses so that the styles meshed when they were together. Each suited the woman who wore it, and Juliet knew all of them were planning to wear the dresses again.

As for the nails... "Oh, these?" She gave Jake another dagger-sweet smile and deliberately dug them in. "They make great stealth weapons against disapproving old men."

Thank heavens the song came to an end at that moment.

Even her wall of snark and sarcasm was beginning to crumble under the weight of her battle against this aggravating one-sided sexual tug. While Charlotte and Gabriel and the others—Aroha and her hulking partner included—continued to dance on, she and Jake separated with alacrity.

The MC muted the lights at the same time until the dance floor held the spotlight.

Others from the crowd began to meander onto it, including a stunning blonde who made a beeline for Jake. Juliet couldn't help glancing back to see his response. Smiling with every appearance of relieved happiness, he held out his hand.

Gee, she thought bad-temperedly, *as if I needed any more evidence that the tingles are an unrequited joke at my expense.*

Jake clearly had a type. Calypso might've been sweetly plump, but she'd been as blond as Jake's current partner, with the same serene grace—a grace that Juliet would never possess. It was something you were born with; Juliet had always been too loud, too dramatic, too much the street fighter used to grappling for survival.

"Dance?"

She looked up to find herself facing another big man—this wedding was bursting at the seams with rugby players, current and former. "Sure," she said and walked into his arms with the fervent hope that her hormones would fixate on someone—*anyone*—other than Jacob Esera.

Fate, however, wasn't yet done cackling at Juliet.

8

JAKE STARTS A FIGHT (AND TEXTS A CAT)

Even though he held an accomplished and beautiful woman in his arms, Jake was very aware of Juliet disappearing into the crowd of people milling around the dance floor. Her height made her easy to spot until she became lost in the shadows created by the muted lighting outside the dance area.

"I'm going to get a complex if you keep scoping out that seriously foxy bridesmaid."

Jerking his attention back to Rachel, Jake flushed. He'd invited his former girlfriend as his wedding date because his parents liked her, and he knew her presence would make them happy and hopeful for him. They deserved that on this day. Rachel held no torch whatsoever for Jake and was well aware of his motives.

The two of them had broken up when they realized their relationship was just endless trying on both their parts; there was no passionate joy, no desire to simply hang out with the other person, nothing but two people who liked each other and didn't want to cause hurt. It had been a relief to both of them when Jake turned to her and said, "Rach, you gonna be heartbroken if we break up?"

"Thank God you said it," she'd replied and gone to grab a bottle of champagne from her fridge. "Let's drink to a long and happy friendship."

Attending the wedding as his date was a kindness on her part, and here he was, ignoring her in favor of a woman who'd sashayed away without a backward look.

"Sorry. Juliet's always been able to get under my skin." How many times had she made a dig at him that caused him to retaliate in just as juvenile a manner? Anytime the two of them got within five feet of each other, the missiles began to fly.

Rachel cocked an eyebrow. "Is that right? Funny, when one of the problems with us was that I couldn't rile you up. Ever."

"That's because you're a sane, sensible woman who doesn't try to pick fights." Though their harmony didn't extend to dancing—moving with her around the dance floor took a little work because she was shorter by half a foot. And seriously, that was no excuse when Gabe and Charlotte were pulling off pure grace despite their height difference.

Juliet had probably hexed him into being a klutz. Because irritatingly, it had been effortless to dance with her —she fit his body perfectly. He'd been viscerally aware of the plump fullness of her breasts pushing against his chest, the generous swell of her hip just inches away from his palm, the way her back dipped so beautifully.

It made a man think about kissing the curve of her spine.

As for her cleavage... Jesus! Lord save him. He'd had to keep his eyes rigidly over her head or he'd have been staring at her breasts like a lech. Maybe his brothers were right. He needed to get laid.

Except his body only wanted one woman.

The one who was a burr under his skin, an aggravation that wouldn't stop.

Rachel laughed again, all sweetness and no sarcasm. It was nice. He should react to nice. Instead, he reacted to dagger words and patently insincere smiles designed to provoke.

"I dunno, Jake." Rachel's gaze was acute, that of an investigative reporter at the top of her game. "Maybe you need a woman who unsettles you. Life would never be boring."

He shook his head. Firmly. Very. "Trust me, Juliet doesn't 'unsettle.' She overturns, disrupts, capsizes." A tornado had nothing on Juliet. "The only time Calypso got into trouble at school, it was because she was smoking in the bathroom with Juliet."

Scowling, he tried to locate the object of his thoughts in the crowd, finally spotted her dancing with one of Gabe's single rugby friends. "She should come with a Bad Influence warning above her head. In red neon." And why was she smiling at that hatchet-faced bruiser with genuine sweetness when all Jake got was snark and fury?

Rachel chuckled. "Oh my God, you sound so shocked and staid. I'm going to start calling you Grandpa Jake if you keep that up."

Great, now Rachel was comparing him to an octogenarian too. Clearly Juliet's influence was catching, even from a distance.

"Funny thing is," Rachel said with a small frown, "the face of your sexy nemesis is so familiar. I could swear I've seen her before."

Jake didn't jog Rachel's memory. Some things were off-limits even when he and Juliet were annoying each other. But he should've known that Rachel's brain was too much of a steel trap for the information to elude her for long.

"Oh my God." A dangerous brilliance on her face. "She was married to Reid Mescall."

"Rach, you won't—"

"Gossip isn't my beat," she said at once. "Also, I'd never use a private family affair to pass on a tip to another reporter."

Well aware of her airtight ethical boundaries, Jake exhaled quietly—and tried not to look in Juliet's direction. Did she have any idea how many wives her dance partner had left in his dust? Four at last count was what Jake had heard. The man obviously had serious moves, because even a mother couldn't love that face, which had taken more than one beating.

Maybe Juliet went for rough rather than clean-cut.

Rachel's voice brought his attention back to the woman in his arms. "I knew Reid was an idiot the first time I interviewed him, back when I covered sports, but having seen his ex in the flesh *and* having seen the friends she keeps—says a lot about a person, that—I can now state categorically that Reid Mescall is a *major* idiot. Imagine not doing everything you could to hold on to a knockout like her."

Jake had zero disagreement with Rachel's conclusion. Juliet's ex-husband *was* a prize idiot. But not for the reasons Rachel had listed. No, Reid was an idiot for a whole other reason—the same reason Jake had never tried to get between Calypso and Juliet—Juliet's capacity for fierce loyalty.

That time when Calypso got caught smoking with Juliet, Juliet had tried to take all the blame. In the end, she'd taken enough of it that the school hadn't put anything on Calyp-so's record.

Calypso had fought Juliet over that in front of Jake, but Juliet had been adamant. "You're going places, Cals. Another demerit won't much change my record, but it'll mess up yours. I'm doing this—you back me up."

"Jules—"

"You back me up, Callie. And when you're a rich fancy-pants lawyer, come bail me out when I get in trouble."

Any man who not only gave up that kind of loyalty but rewarded it with a smear campaign? Well beyond an idiot and straight into asshole territory, Jake thought as the song came to an end and another single male asked Rachel for a dance. As an amenable Rachel moved off in the guy's arms, Jake checked on Esme—who was having a grand old time running wild with the other children—then went hunting Jules.

He was starting to think she'd ditched the reception when he finally saw her seated in a hidden alcove with a giant slice of wedding cake on a saucer. She cut into it with a fork as he watched, slipped the tines into her mouth. Her lashes drifted shut, her lips pursed; he could almost hear her moan of pleasure.

His cock twitched.

No, no, no. He couldn't twitch for Juliet.

Yet he haphazardly grabbed a slice of cake for himself before going over to join her in the alcove.

She glared at him. "This is my spot. Go. Away."

"I don't see your name on it," he said and took a seat. The alcove wasn't that big, and his shoulder brushed hers, his hip pressing into a lush feminine curve. He was crowding her on purpose. Because the thing was... he wanted to fight with Juliet.

Dangerous as it was, he hadn't felt this alive in a long, long time.

Her eyes flashed. Then she elbowed him under the guise of getting comfortable.

"Oof." He rubbed his ribs.

"Oh, did that hurt?" She pointed her fork in his direction. "So, *so* sorry."

Jake was grinning when his father appeared nearby. "Son," he said. "Sorry to interrupt, but Uncle Tama wants to get home and his car isn't starting."

"I'll have a look." Jake took the keys his father held out... before he turned to Juliet and said, "It's dark out. Mind coming and holding the torch for me?"

Joseph Esera broke in. "Oh, I can do that."

"No, Mr. Esera." Juliet's smile was warm and generous. "It's your son's wedding. Stay, enjoy. I'm sure it won't take Jake long to fix things." She kept up that smile as Joseph patted her on the shoulder and told her she was a good girl before he walked away to tug Alison into a dance.

At which point Jake got the death glare magnified.

Driven to antagonize her by a madness he couldn't shake, he took a bite of cake before rising to put his plate down on the alcove seat. "Cake's gonna have to wait, Jules."

"Where's the damn torch?" She put down her own cake and stood.

"In my car," Jake said automatically before realizing they'd come here in a limo. "On second thought—we'll have to use our phones."

Juliet took his phone when he handed it to her, then swung by the head table to pick up hers too. They'd just stepped outside when his phone flashed with light, a message popping onto the front screen.

Shuddering, Juliet handed it over. "I think it's one of

your groupies. Take it before I gag."

The text was from a Trixi Kitten. "For your information," he muttered after quickly scanning it, "that's the name of my great-aunt's cat."

Juliet stared at him. "Do I look like I was born yesterday?"

"Read the message." He held it out.

Folding her arms, she tilted her head to the side, just daring him to continue.

He held it up right in front of her face so she couldn't miss the message: *Jake, dear, are you checking your uncle's car? Can you come look at Great-auntie's in the next week? It's making a strange noise and it scares me. Meow – Trixi Pussy*

A kind of strangled sound erupting in her throat, Juliet nudged aside his phone. "Does she always..."

"Write messages as if it's her cat?" He nodded. "She's a perfectly sane human otherwise. Last week she beat everyone in her local pub quiz so she could win a nodding-cat thing."

"The whole... er... pussy thing?"

"She's eighty-nine. As far as she's concerned, it means cat." Jake rubbed his face. "She stood next to me while I was inputting her number and kept asking me why I didn't list her as Trixi Pussy."

Juliet's laughter sounded like it was torn out of her. And the cock twitching got worse. That didn't make sense. Why was her laughter turning him on? Or maybe it was the way she looked when she laughed, so open and warm and... as if she'd make him that way. Not this staid, solid stranger he sometimes felt he'd become.

Shaking off the thought because his solid and staid nature was what made him a good dad, he pointed to a pale blue VW Bug. "That's it."

The two of them walked across the parking lot, which was empty of all other signs of life. Just rows of cars—some bedecked with flowers and streamers in honor of the wedding—and a few standing lamps that cast just enough light so people could find their vehicles. Useless, however, for looking at an engine.

The land sloped down on the other side of the car, the old theater surrounded by manicured grounds that often hosted outdoor plays. Maybe he'd bring Esme to one of those, he thought absently as he unlocked his uncle's car, then tried to start it to see what sounds it made, if any.

Juliet stood outside, tapping her toe on the tarmac and looking like a fantasy straight out of the midnight hours, times when Jake's brain went its own merry way. Sex dreams weren't exactly a surprise for a single male who had a sex drive he hadn't been feeding, but the dreams had always been amorphous and erotic. No faces, nothing but sensations that led to frustrated arousal.

He had a feeling that was about to change.

When the hell had Juliet grown those curves?

Wishing he hadn't left his jacket in the event space, he popped the hood before getting out of the driver's seat; hopefully the dim lighting would conceal the interest in his pants.

"Here." He handed her his phone. "I think I know the problem," he said, propping the hood open.

The scent of Juliet washed over him as she stepped close enough to shine the torchlight from both phones into the engine.

"Tell me where you want it," she said, and his brain decided to put those words in a totally different—and dirty —context.

Gritting his teeth, Jake said, "Where you have it is good."

Not responding to Jake's comment because she'd become fascinated by the way his muscles moved under the fine white fabric of his formal shirt as he bent over the engine, Juliet told herself to breathe. She also reminded herself that she'd already had this conversation with herself and decided the physical attraction was pure nonsense.

But jeez, did the universe have to make him so gorgeous? There, fine, she'd admitted it. The gearhead jock had grown up into a panty-melting adult who adored his daughter, loved his family, and was kind to his elders. Even a great-aunt who liked to text using her cat alter ego.

He might have a stick up his butt, but Juliet would still like to *see* that butt.

Juliet Nelisi, you stop checking out Jake's butt. STOP.

But the man was muscled everywhere. It was hard not to eat up the eye candy when it was right in front of her. Also, since a visual was all it would ever be, she might as well enjoy... except, this wasn't just a random hot guy.

This was Jake.

"My arms are starting to hurt," she muttered, because keeping him annoyed with her was an excellent and time-proven way to foster distance.

"Sorry," he said, his focus obviously on the engine. "I almost have it. It's just a loose... There." Rising to his full height, he went to put his hands on his hips.

Juliet, her own hands full of phones, whacked his upper arm with one to stop him. Of course it was all taut biceps and heat. "Grease."

He looked down at his hands. "Shit."

"Go wash off in the bathroom. I'll wait here." She knew he had to start the car, check everything was okay.

He hesitated, a frown on his face as he took in the empty parking lot. "Sit in the car," he said at last.

"Gee, Jake, I don't know how I survived life without your advice."

Juliet's deadpan words had clouds moving across his face. "You know, you're right. You'll probably just stab anyone who attacks you. Probably with one of those weapons on your feet. No wait, I forgot your elbows."

"Keep going and you'll get a demonstration of just what I can do."

He glared at her one more time before shifting on his heel to walk back to the venue. Except he only went three steps before turning to her. "Seriously, Jules, just sit in the car, okay? Or I can't go inside and you can't have cake."

Juliet went to snap a comeback but decided to hurry this up. The faster he got cleaned up, the faster they could get this done with and she could get away from Jake and his potent aphrodisiac of a scent. "Fine, grandpa." Ignoring the growl-like sound that came from his direction, she slipped into the driver's seat and shut the door, then pointedly pressed the lock.

As she watched him walk off at last, she exhaled a shuddering breath. It was easy to be annoyed with him for acting all protective and overbearing, but a small part of her was shaken by how his care had made her feel.

No one had ever been protective of Juliet's safety, not that way.

Her aunt didn't care when she came home so long as she didn't embarrass the family. Her grandparents in Samoa had set her a strict curfew, but it'd had nothing to do with protectiveness. It had to do with control.

As for Reid, the only thing he'd ever cared about protecting was his own ass.

As she sat there, she allowed herself to wonder what it'd be like to have Jake's brand of protectiveness all the time.

"It'll probably drive you crazy," she told the nutty part of her that was enamored of the idea. "He's probably the kind of man who, if you go out after dark, will ask you to text him to verify you've reached your destination."

Still... what he'd asked today, it hadn't been an assault on her independence. It also wasn't a major deal to reassure another person that you were safe. Might even be nice knowing someone would care if you didn't check in. Her friends were wonderful, but they weren't hers in the way Gabriel was Charlotte's; Juliet wasn't their priority, and that was normal.

Being Jake's priority...

"Enough, Jules. That way lies madness." It had been a nice wedding-virus-induced fantasy, but the fact of the matter was, she and Jake were dynamite and a flame. Even if he wasn't so totally not interested in her, they'd drive each other to homicide.

He reappeared in the distance, a tall and broad-shouldered silhouette she'd never mistake. Unlocking the car, she stepped out, attitude wrapped around her like armor.

"That took long enough," she said when he got closer. "Were you moisturizing in there?"

That was when she noticed he had something in his hand. A saucer holding a big hunk of cake and a fork.

"Here." He thrust it at her while taking his phone so she had a hand free. "Caterers cleared away our half-eaten pieces, so I got you a new one."

Damn it. Now he was giving her cake?

Juliet was not going to cave and jump his bones. He'd be horrified—it'd almost be worth it to see the look on his face. But she'd never live down the embarrassment of being rejected by Jake of all people.

Putting her own phone on the hood he'd just closed, she

forked a piece of the decadent concoction into her mouth to shut herself up from saying anything stupid.

"You're welcome," Jake said as he stepped past her to open the car door.

"I only lost my cake because you made me hike out here," Juliet pointed out.

His response was to start the engine. It purred.

Hallelujah!

Switching it off, he stepped out and locked the door behind him before putting the keys in his pocket. "I spoke to my uncle on the way out—he's decided to stay a bit longer." He looked at her cake. "That's a big piece."

"Yep. And it's all mine." Belying her self-satisfied words, Juliet used her fork to cut off a piece and nudged it in his direction on the saucer.

A small smile as he picked it up and popped it into his mouth.

Juliet didn't know why they stood there in the parking lot, sharing cake, but they did. Afterward, the plate empty of anything but crumbs, Jake picked up her phone to hand it to her, and they walked back into the theater in a quiet that was weirdly comfortable.

No barbs. No sniping. Jake's hand a light touch on her lower back as he walked inside a step behind her.

Protective.

Dangerously attractive.

"Jake, there you are," said the woman with whom she'd seen him dancing.

A woman nothing at all like Juliet.

Fantasy nicely crushed.

Good. Now maybe the tingles would get with the program.

9

HOW TO MURDER YOUR BROTHER

Two days after the wedding and Jake was in a foul mood.

Standing in front of the mirror after his shower, he glared at the idiot who'd thought this deal was a good idea. Past Jake needed his head examined. And Present Jake needed to stop waking up hard as a rock after erotic dreams featuring a certain sharp-tongued bridesmaid.

Back in school, his English teacher had marked down his writing efforts for "lack of creativity." It turned out his brain had been saving all its creativity to drive him insane with increasingly down-and-dirty fantasies. Crazed, he'd even jerked off prior to falling asleep in the hope it'd keep the dreams at bay.

Nope. Even in his dreams, Juliet played by her own rules.

She teased and she laughed and she made him wake sweat-drenched and frustrated.

His phone rang.

Towel hitched around his hips, he walked into the bedroom and—after seeing that it was Gabe—picked up.

"Why the hell aren't you concentrating on your honeymoon?"

His big brother's response was quick and brutal. "Wanted to make sure you didn't chicken out of today."

"I couldn't even if I wanted to," Jake muttered, tugging off the towel to pull on a pair of white boxer briefs. "The damn contract is airtight."

"Excellent." Total lack of sympathy. "We need to set you up for what happens after you retire from the game. The body doesn't last forever, Jake."

Because Jake knew Gabe was speaking from painful experience, he made himself take a breath, released it slowly. "I know, I know," he said. "But seriously, Gabe, an *underwear* commercial?" He was going hot under the skin just thinking about it.

"Face it, little bro." Gabe chuckled. "You're a heartthrob. Getting caught snuggling Esme after that championship win did great things for your marketability."

Jake rubbed his temples. He'd hugged his daughter because he'd wanted to hug his daughter. Her tiny face had been so excited in the stands that he hadn't been able to stop himself from running straight from the field to her. She'd laughed and told him he was "stinky," but she'd hugged him back with boundless love.

Gabriel knew all that. The cool-eyed talk was to remind Jake that this was about ensuring Esme's future as well as his own. Because the fact of the matter was, the underwear-commercial contract would net him a ridiculous amount of money—money he could sock away for a rainy day. Money that would provide a cushion if he got injured and could no longer play.

Unlike Gabriel—and despite their parents' efforts—Jake didn't have the best education. Between raising Esme and keeping up his rugby career, his younger self had maxed out. He'd never been one of the brainiacs in the family anyway. He could play rugby and he was good with his hands, with mechanical things.

In high school, the latter had been purely about cars.

Though he'd almost forgotten the old junker Juliet had mentioned, the one his parents had allowed him to keep in one half of their double garage on the condition that he mow the lawn every two weeks while the car was in there. He'd mowed a lot of lawn. He'd also spent all his discretionary money on bringing the junker to a "mean" standard, one that would inspire envy in his friends.

In the end, he'd made it nice enough to sell for a few thousand bucks—money he'd contributed toward baby stuff for Esme. The loss of the car had been worth it for the look on Calypso's face when he told her they could get the nice brand of baby buggy instead of the supercheap one.

His parents and older brothers would've given them whatever money they needed, but he and Calypso, they'd wanted to buy the baby gear on their own. God, they'd been so young. So unprepared for the adult world in which they'd found themselves. But that one moment, it had been happy. Innocent.

"I won't chicken out," he promised his brother. "It's not like I went into this blind." Gabe had told him to take the offer, but only after Jake had considered it himself and laid out the pros and cons.

In the end, it had been Jake's call.

"By the way," he said. "I got the newest investment statement yesterday—thanks again for doing that for me." Jake put any extra money he had into Gabriel's hands because Gabriel was a genius when it came to money. Already, Jake had enough put away that Esme could study whatever she wanted in the future. He also owned his own place and had the funds to ride it out if a run of bad form kept him off the field for a period.

He was determined that his baby girl would have the same kind of solid foundation his parents had given him.

"No thanks needed. I'm fucking proud of you, Jake." Blunt words from a brother Jake had idolized as a boy—and, honestly, still did. "A lot of people would've given up at the first hurdle, but you just put down your head and kept going. Now go look sexy."

"I'm going to kill you."

Laughing, Gabriel hung up.

Afterward, Jake pulled on jeans and a long-sleeved T-shirt, then ran his fingers through his hair to put it into some sort of order—not that it mattered. According to the run sheet he'd been emailed yesterday, he'd be in "hair and makeup" as part of the torture session he was contracted to attend today.

The run sheet had been signed JULIET.

Just his luck that the woman overseeing the shoot had the name of the one who was haunting him. Juliet would probably cackle with delight at the odd coincidence. Jake wasn't laughing.

Thankfully, this Juliet was likely to be a no-fuss marketing manager who looked nothing at all like his Juliet.

His Juliet.

Two words he'd never predicted he'd string together. But not only was she haunting his dreams, he kept thinking of her at odd times throughout the day. Especially of how she'd shared her cake with him, of how it had felt to walk back to the party with her in a silence that was easy, and of how she'd caused him to come alive inside in a way that made him feel hungry and guilty at the same time.

Scowling, he wandered into Esme's bedroom. The sight of his daughter fast asleep, arms and legs flung out like a tiny octopus, made short work of the scowl. He grinned, still not sure how such a small human managed to take up so much room. She still snuck over to sleep in his bed now and then. On those nights, he could guarantee he'd wake to find himself clinging to the edge of the mattress while she sprawled all over.

Crouching down beside her bed, he brushed strands of silky black hair off her face and kissed her on the soft warmth of her cheek. "Time to wake up, Boo," he said, as he'd been doing for years.

Mumbling a grumble, she turned in to him, arms rising to wrap limply around his neck.

Gathering her up, he held her against him and stroked her hair as he carried her into the bathroom. First he set her down on the counter, then he wet a cloth with warm water and wiped her face. She screwed up her nose, stubbornly keeping her eyes closed. Well used to this, he put the face-cloth down on the counter and gave her ribs a gentle tickle.

A giggle, her lashes rising.

Without her glasses, her brown eyes looked so big and vulnerable.

Yawning, she watched in silence as he put toothpaste on her sparkly blue toothbrush branded with the face of a fairy princess. As she grimaced so that he could see her teeth, he began to brush her pearly whites.

She woke up properly halfway through and took over the task.

He knew it wouldn't be much longer before she wouldn't want to be carried into the bathroom this way, before she wouldn't want her daddy to wipe her face to wake her up. Jake would miss this morning routine but knew they'd find a new one. He was proud of the strong and independent little girl she was becoming.

After lifting her down from the counter to her feet, he left her to finish up her "morning business"—a phrase she'd picked up from Emmaline, who'd picked it up from Sailor. A younger Emmaline had always woken early and, fuzzy blue blankie tucked firmly under her arm, had toddled after Sailor around the house, asking him what he was doing.

"Morning business," had been a sleepy Sailor's stock answer.

Smile returning, he went into Esme's bedroom to tidy up. He made sure to put Mr. Mouse in his customary position against the princess-branded pillow, where he'd be waiting for Esme when she got home from school. It still kind of stunned him that the baby girl who'd fit into his hands was going to school, but she was six years old now and an old hand at the student deal.

Room tidy, he told her he was going into the kitchen to make breakfast, and she said, "I'm gonna wear blue today!"

There'd been a time when Jake chose her clothes, but she'd begun to want to dress herself six months ago, so now he just kept an eye on things to ensure she hadn't left a button undone or put on a shirt inside out.

Once in the kitchen, he prepared a warm glass of milk, then made toast. With Esme, it was either toast or cereal for a week or two at a stretch. At the moment, it was toast. With her grandmother's homemade marmalade and not a hint of anything else.

Woe to him if he contaminated it with his own natural peanut butter.

That done, he got to work making her lunch. It didn't take long, and he was soon closing the lid of her princess lunchbox, which he then put in her princess backpack. He had no idea when this blue-princess phase was going to be over, but it showed no signs of losing steam.

At least it made birthday gifts a cinch.

"I'm here!" she announced, bouncing into the room.

She'd chosen to wear her favorite black leggings with blue sparkles, paired with a long-sleeved T-shirt with—of course—the blue princess's face emblazoned on it. Over the top, she'd put on a denim jacket that Ísa had given her for her birthday.

In her hand was a hairbrush and a sparkly blue hair tie.

While she scrambled up into a chair at the kitchen table to eat her breakfast, he took the hairbrush and began to smooth her hair back into a ponytail. Man, but he loved her current choice of style. For a while it had been the blue princess's freaking French braid, and he'd had to watch online videos to figure it out, then hit up his sister-in-law for further instructions.

Her hair done, he joined Esme at the table to eat his own breakfast: heavy on the protein at the moment because he needed to bulk up a touch more for peak form. "I have a meeting later today," he said as they ate.

"Will Grandpa pick me up from school?"

"No. Uncle Sailor. He's going to take you and Emmaline with him to an out-of-town nursery."

Beaming, she bounced up and down in her seat. Not only was Emmaline one of her "most favoritest" people, getting to ride along with Sailor was an adventure. He always found a strange plant to show the girls, or a new fruit for them to try. Last time it had been an experimental kiwifruit variant that had a burst of red at its heart.

"I'll pick you up after dinner." He tweaked her nose. "You can tell me all about your adventures."

After breakfast, she helped him clean up.

"Time to head out," he said afterward and grabbed his keys and phone for the walk to the local primary school. Once there, Esme gave him a kiss on the cheek before running off to join friends, who were playing on the swings before class.

Jake, meanwhile, turned around to go torture himself by participating in an underwear commercial. Seriously, he was going to murder his own past self for thinking this was a grand idea. "It'll be easy, Jake," he muttered once he was back home and in his SUV. "You'll be in and out, Jake. Oh, no biggie, Jake, but they might want to oil your abs. Argh!"

The drive to the large warehouse where the filming and associated photo shoot was to happen took him forty-five minutes in the heavy morning traffic, but at least there was plenty of parking at the site. After slipping his SUV into the spot next to a teammate's insanely beautiful yellow Porsche 911 with its air-cooled flat engine, he got out at the same time as the other man.

"Ready to get your kit off?" Leo asked with a grin, his green eyes dancing and his mop of dark brown curls wind-tumbled against skin of a deep caramel shade that came from what he called his "melting pot" genetics. "Hope you've been doing those crunches."

"According to the radio, I'm not the one who got caught stumbling out of a club at midnight," Jake said before exchanging a fist bump with the other man. "I thought your girlfriend was a redhead." The tabloids had apparently caught him with a black-haired supermodel from Bulgaria.

"So last week, man." Leo wolf whistled at another teammate who'd just gotten out of his own vehicle, a top-of-the-line black Ferrari F8 Tributo with incredible engine dynamics. "Can't wait to see you seminaked, hot stuff!"

That got him the finger from the tall and quiet Fijian-

Kiwi winger with skin two or three shades darker than Jake's.

"My mother is going to disown me," Viliame muttered.

"After she shows off the pictures to all the church ladies," Leo predicted as the three of them waited for the final victim to emerge from the other side of Vili's vehicle, with whom he'd caught a ride.

With amber-blond hair he tied up in a bun when on-field and a small beard, Christian played Gabriel's former position, had the same build, and seriously looked like a Viking, hence his on-field nickname. The women went crazy over it—but the Viking was of the same mindset as Jake and Vili. No partying, his focus on the game.

They walked into the warehouse together.

A shapely behind encased in a black pencil skirt was bent over a table not far from them, the woman's long bronze and red-streaked black hair pulled back into a neat braid.

Leo nudged Jake with his elbow. "Forget the Bulgarian beauty. My tastes have undergone a curvy shift."

Jake was barely paying attention. Surely, *surely*, fate couldn't be that cruel. But oh, it was. Because when the woman rose and turned toward them with a smile, a clipboard held in her arms and a Bluetooth headset tucked over her ear, it proved to be the same woman whose mouth and body and breasts taunted him nightly.

His Juliet.

10

JAKE TAKES OFF HIS CLOTHES (NO OTHER ENTICEMENT NECESSARY)

J uliet had known he was coming. His name was right there in her run sheet for today. The fact her temporary assistant had messed up the original sheet and accidentally left off his name so she'd only found out yesterday shouldn't have made a difference. She had this job because she could handle unexpected events.

Everett relied on her to be the calm, practical center of E. E. Designs.

Yet heat stung her cheeks while an odd sensation twined through her abdomen—and not just because she'd had the most erotic dream of her life the previous night, with Jake front and center.

No, it was because, though dressed-up Jake was good-looking in a preppy kind of way, dressed-down Jake was the type of man she could imagine having a pizza with while laughing over a comedy show on television... before they got sweaty, dirty, and very, very naked.

Shakiness or not, she was smiling and words were coming out of her mouth. "Gentlemen, it's lovely to see you.

Would any of you like coffee, tea, a shot of liquid courage before we get you into hair and makeup?"

Three of the guys laughed. Of course the one who didn't was Jake. As was often the case, he was looking at her with a slightly disapproving expression on his face. Well, that was the last time she shared cake with him. She fought the urge to narrow her eyes; she had to be professional and adult in this environment.

"No caffeine until after the mostly naked shots are taken," Leo said, a flirtatious grin carving deep grooves in his cheeks.

Juliet ignored the signals—in a diplomatic way. She knew his record, and it involved a new woman every night of the week. Leopold "Leo" Naughton also seemed to be the subject of back-to-back tell-all stories in the gossip mags. Most featuring kittenish, pouting creatures who told anecdotes of his "breathtaking prowess" in bed, followed by his "coldhearted rejection."

When confronted about the stories, Leo would smile a cheeky smile, shrug, and point out that he was young and single and so were his lovers. He'd then turn up at the hottest clubs with a new woman—or two—on his arm.

Men loved his swagger.

Women had been known to throw their panties at him.

So yeah, even if Juliet had been looking for another athlete lover, which she would never ever, *ever* do, even on pain of having her teeth removed without anesthesia, it wouldn't be Leo.

"How about the rest of you?" she said with a smile.

Viliame, Christian, and Jake all just pointed to the bottles of water her assistant had stacked on the table for them. Unsurprised at their desire to keep things clean before the shoot, she turned to lead them into hair and makeup. *Someone* was definitely checking out her ass; she could feel the appreciative male gaze.

Probably Leo.

It annoyed her that part of her was hoping it was a certain stuffed-shirt Esera.

"Today's photographic and recording team is a compact but highly experienced one," she said as she walked, because keeping her mind on business kept it off Jake—who was going to be all but naked in the very near future.

Her knees threatened to lock.

Clenching her gut, she continued on. "All have impeccable professional records. You can be assured they won't leak any images ahead of the launch—though, of course, if you want to take any for your own social media, please feel free." Her boss would be ecstatic at the free publicity.

"Leo is always near-naked on his accounts." Christian's distinctive baritone. "This'll be business as usual."

"Yeah, man," Vili said. "I had to rinse my brain with mental bleach after I scrolled down and nearly got traumatized by your pubes. Blankets are supposed to *cover* you."

"Jealous, boys?" Leo flexed one ripped arm. "I have the bod and the moves, so why not show it off?"

One of the men snorted. It wasn't Jake. Jake had been silent since the moment he walked in, but she could feel him staring at the back of her neck, the laser beams of his eyes drilling into her skin.

"So," she said, having reached the hair-and-makeup station. "We'll be doing individual as well as group shots before we record the commercial. Who wants to go first?"

Predictably, it was Leo who volunteered; Christian went with him.

"Viliame, Jake, if you'd follow me to our locker room set," she said with commendable calm. "Our photographer and camera crew will talk you through the planned shoot so you can get straight into it after Christian and Leo are done."

"Call me Vili." The winger smiled at her while Jake remained stone-faced.

Deciding to take that personally since she'd seen him smiling at other people—hell, he'd even smiled at *her* during the wedding—she lost the battle to remain friendly and professional. "You're doing a wonderful job with the tall, dark, and silent look, Jake," she said with what others would see as a playful smile, but Jake would know for a pinpoint strike.

Vili gave a big laugh and slapped him on the shoulder while Jake's eyes flashed.

"Good," he said without cracking even a miniscule grin. "It means I can get this over and done with quickly."

Jeez, why didn't he just take out a sign: I can't wait to see the back of Juliet.

Her blood heated, the fire of battle licking through her. Well, Jacob Esera wasn't the only one who wanted to salt the earth and chant incantations to ensure their paths never again crossed. Too bad that was impossible with the contract between him and E. E. Designs.

Keeping a sweet smile on her face through sheer effort of will, she led them to the media team that'd be shooting both the print and television ads. Everett was also there. Many business owners would've left a campaign like this to an ad agency, but Everett had a distinct vision of how he wanted his designs showcased, which was why Juliet— instead of an outside ad exec—was overseeing the entire thing.

It wasn't the first time Everett had taken this approach; he not only wanted full control of his brand, he had the kind of mind that came up with great ad concepts. As a result, Juliet had handled more than one shoot for him—though this one was, without doubt, the biggest.

Today, her silver fox of a boss, slender and tall, shook the men's hands. "I'm so glad you decided to be a part of this campaign. I think it's going to be phenomenal."

Though Everett was doing a great job of sounding cheerful but composed, Juliet had seen him dance the Macarena in his office when first Leo, then the others, had signed on. This would take his design business to the next level—these four men were *extremely* expensive, but their impact was massive in a country where rugby was all but a religion.

Add in the other major rugby-playing nations where they had a following and Jake, Leo, Vili, and Christian were worth every penny. So regardless of her irritation with Jake for inciting this insane unrequited attraction inside her, she was happy for Everett. Her boss came across as urbane and sophisticated and more upmarket than down to earth, but scrape away the posh veneer and he was one of the good guys. It was nice to see him succeed.

While the technical crew and Everett spoke to Vili and Jake about today's process and reviewed the creative vision on which all four men had already signed off, she fought the urge to go over and shake Jake. If he didn't lose the stiff face and stop doing an amazingly lifelike impression of a robot, he was going to drive the crew crazy and draw out the shoot to a frustrating length.

Her phone buzzed in the midst of her attempt to send him "loosen up" signals with her mind. Glancing down, she saw it was Wesley, the billboard guy, aka CEO of the company that owned half the billboards in the city. She answered at once—her temp assistant had messed up a second time and lost a critical billboard.

Needless to say, Juliet couldn't wait for her actual assistant to return from maternity leave. "Tell me you can do something for us," she said to Wesley, her fingers metaphorically crossed.

"Juliet, my love, do you practice witchcraft?" he said in his raspy chain-smoker's voice. "Because that's the only way I can explain this."

Juliet began to grin. "It's not nice to tease a girl, Wes. Gimme."

"Someone just pulled a booking. You've got the central Queen Street billboard, the big daddy."

Juliet did a fist pump in the air... just as Everett, Jake, and the others turned around. Hanging up after confirming she'd personally arrange for prompt payment, she said, "We have the new Queen Street mega-billboard."

If anything, Jake went even stiffer. Everett, on the other hand, was clearly fighting the urge to break out into song and dance again.

Vili's teeth flashed white in that enormous smile that made him such a favorite with fans. "Me in my undies on Queen Street, huh? Not bad for a kid who couldn't get a date for the school ball. Worth my mother's wrath."

Christian and Leo emerged right then from hair and makeup. Neither had been too smoothed or polished— Everett wouldn't have booked rugby players if he'd wanted pretty. This ad campaign was all about playing off the men's rough masculinity. Though, according to her body, Jake was plenty pretty.

The damn tingles wouldn't stop.

Promising said body an ice-cold bath tonight if it didn't

behave, she forced a smile. "Vili, Jake, if you'd please head into hair and makeup."

Face like granite, Jake went to turn that way when his phone chimed. Glancing down at the screen, he said, "Give me one minute. It's my daughter's school." While Viliame continued on, Jake stepped away to have a quick conversation.

"Is everything all right with Esme?" Juliet asked afterward.

"She forgot her flute at home—but music class isn't until later this afternoon, so I can drop it off after we finish here." Curt words before he strode off to join Vili.

Juliet was tempted to ball up a piece of paper and throw it at his head.

Professional, Jules. Be professional.

Since Everett was here to oversee the shoot, she made her way out into the winter sunshine of the parking lot to make a number of calls, including one to their accounts department to expedite payment for the billboard. Suppliers, distributors, manufacturers, she dealt with all of them on a daily basis. She knew more about this end of the business than her immediate superior, Iris—which was why Everett paid her such a competitive salary.

"I would cry like a baby if you ever quit," he'd said to her more than once.

Her expertise was also the reason why, as of twelve months ago, she was no longer listed as Executive Assistant: Operations and Supply on the company website.

Juliet's new title was Vice President: Operations and Supply.

Creative Everett and his pragmatic right hand, Iris, had made it plain that Juliet was being groomed to take over Iris's position when Iris retired in three years' time. The slow transition of power was why Juliet was here at the shoot—Iris had overseen the contracts while Everett dealt with the ad creative, but Juliet had been handed the duty of ensuring it all went according to plan.

Iris was a call away if Juliet needed her, but this was her baby.

It made her laugh sometimes, that huge title and attendant responsibilities for a girl whose highest qualification was a diploma from a six-month course that taught office management. But she was good at her job, that much she knew—even Reid had never managed to convince her otherwise. Not that he hadn't tried. But that was par for the course with the pinhead.

A tap on her shoulder had her turning around. "Everett. What is it?"

"I've got to join my mom at the hospital. Kalia and her team have a good grasp of what I want, but can you direct the rest of the shoot?"

"Of course. Is everything going okay with your mom?" She knew the other woman had been in for a number of surgeries.

"Hopefully she'll get a clean bill of health—doctor just had an unexpected opening and asked her if she wanted to move up her final checkup. She called and I said, 'Go for it.'" His face was soft with love; an intensely private man, Everett was only this open with a rare few people. Juliet counted herself lucky that both Iris and Everett thought of her as a friend; she respected both of them enormously.

"Good luck," she said with a hug before the two of them parted ways.

She returned in time to see Leo direct his megawatt grin at rangy Kalia Nguyen while Christian laughed in the background. The camera clicked, and she already knew it'd be a good image. Leo's cheeky flirtatiousness would shine, causing women across the country to swoon and guys to want to be like him.

Juliet enjoyed the view while ticking off a mental checklist of necessary images.

Then out walked Jake.

Her blood buzzed in her ears, her skin prickled, and all at once, it was difficult to breathe. Because clean-cut Jacob Esera wasn't quite as clean-cut as she'd thought. She'd have known that already if she actually *watched* rugby on television, but unlike the rest of the nation, she wasn't obsessed with the sport. She'd watch if it was on at a friend's place, but she tended to treat it as background noise, her focus elsewhere.

Which was why she'd missed the fact that Jake not only had a delicious dusting of chest hair, he had a Samoan-influenced tattoo that covered his left pectoral muscle and curved over his shoulder, then down to wrap around his biceps. The work was intricate and expert, the design following the musculature of his body. Within that were precise geometric shapes born of a traditional and respected art.

"Leo, Christian, you can take a break while we warm up Jake and Vili for the filming."

Kalia's clear and confident voice startled Juliet out of her stunned stare. At least she hadn't gone slack-jawed or started drooling. And the men didn't seem to have noticed—they were too busy hassling one another about being oiled up and sexy. Jake was the only one not smiling; the man looked like a wooden board that just happened to be in the shape of a human male.

Juliet's temper ignited.

About to haul him aside to remind him of his contractual obligations, she caught the faint flush on his cheekbones... and suddenly remembered: Jake was *shy*. Not in a way that had stopped him from making friends or having a girlfriend, but enough that he'd never been one of the boys on their school's rugby squad who'd whip his jersey off over his head when he got sweaty or muddy.

The only time she'd seen him shirtless before now was when she, Callie, Jake, and a bunch of their friends had piled into a couple of cars and gone to the beach. He'd been fine then, probably because hanging out at the beach in board shorts was something he'd done often enough to be used to it.

His stiffness today had nothing to do with her.

Why, though, was the man doing an underwear commercial of all things if he was so uncomfortable with it? Especially when he had no reason to *be* uncomfortable. Muscled in a sleek way, Jake's body spoke of strength and hard work. Every cell in Juliet's body vibrated with the urge to kiss, to touch. Ah hell, she wanted to jump on him and cling like a lemur while she licked and sucked.

Right at that moment, however, she was more worried about his comfort than her misbehaving hormones.

Must be the ghost of her loyalty to Callie.

"Vili, Jake, let's start off casual," Kalia said. "Walk around as if you're in the locker room after a game. Ignore the cameras. We're not here."

Vili grinned and mimed grabbing a towel.

Kalia kept up the patter, inserting a few bad rugby jokes into the mix that had the winger laughing.

Jake continued with his flawless impression of a mannequin.

11

TROUBLE

"We need to get the tattoo." Juliet came to stand right beside the photographer. "No way the Goody Two-shoes I knew in high school would get ink."

All three of his teammates hooted.

"You knew him in high school?" Leo said. "Our Jakester was a saint back then too? You know the fans have started calling him the Saint, right?"

Actually, Juliet hadn't known that. "Figures," she said as Jake mock-punched Leo. "He managed to get the prize for Sportsman of the Year *and* the principal's Innovation Award for an idea to do with a part for car engines. Don't ask me what. But the school called his parents in for a special meeting and suggested he might want to aim for a degree in mechanical engineering."

"No fucking way." Leo elbowed him. "You've been holding out on us, Jake. Next we'll be finding out about your secret PhD."

Shoulders loosening at last, Jake looked down for a second before glancing back up. "That's Dr. Jacob Esera to you," he said with a slight half smile that was a punch to the solar plexus, it was such a gorgeous mix of shyness and pride and embarrassment and amusement all at once.

Kalia began to click away, though the other woman's camera was no longer making any sounds. *Clever.*

Jake relaxed even further as his teammates continued to razz him, and Juliet gave the recording crew the signal to catch it. They had a script for the commercial, but this kind of casual, funny banter would play even better if the players would agree to release it once they'd viewed the footage.

Jake's lighthearted expression only darkened when his gaze landed on Juliet.

She smirked at him. "So, Mr. Innovation Award, tell us about the tattoos," she said, realizing a beat too late that maybe he'd gotten them after the worst event of his life.

Her stomach dropped.

"Sure, Queen of Detention."

Jake's annoyed answer melted the ice that had begun to form in her blood. The last thing she ever wanted to do was bring up his final days with Callie. Because one thing was true: Jake had loved her best friend with all his teenage heart. Juliet hadn't needed to witness it to know he'd been devastated by her death.

Vili was the one who egged Jake on this time. "Queen of Detention?" He looked Juliet up and down in a way that was so good-natured she couldn't take offense. "Nah, you look like you got straight As and were teacher's pet."

Juliet took a theatrical bow. "Proud holder of the school record for most detentions in a row. Even saw Jake there... *one* time."

That set the others off again, and it was only when the hassling had calmed down that Jake said, "Tattoos are tradition in our family. Gabe, Sailor, Danny, and I each got to choose a design and received pieces of it on major birthdays starting from when we turned eighteen."

"You cry?" Christian said to Jake, then angled one foot to show the small tattoo on his anklebone. "I wept like a baby, man."

Viliame whistled. "Right on the bone? Better you than me."

Leo, meanwhile, had his hands on his hips and was shaking his head. "I prefer to keep this sexy canvas pristine," he said, pious as a monk. "No one with a frickin' needle and ink is getting anywhere near it."

Catching the rugby ball Juliet threw into the mix, Christian aimed it at Leo. "Pussy."

Leo caught it, spun it to Jake. "By which you must mean a man with high levels of intelligence."

Grinning, Jake, who'd been voted the "safest pair of hands" in rugby two years past, spun the oval ball into Viliame's big hands. "How about the lion emoji the fans use for you online? Full size on the chest."

"Nah," Christian said in that deep voice of his. "You know he wants an elephant—with a certain part of his anatomy as the trunk."

"Hey, not my fault you're jealous of my trunk," Leo retorted without pause.

"Oh, ouch." Christian clutched at his chest. "That might hurt if you weren't a shrimp."

"Yeah, well, better a sexy shrimp than a floppy flounder."

Christian, known for his intense and unsmiling expression on-field, doubled over. "Floppy flounder? Jesus."

All four of the men were laughing now, and Juliet knew her team had plenty of footage that could be cut for an excellent commercial. The words spoken didn't matter as there'd be a voice-over for most of it. What Everett had needed was relaxed interaction between the men, the impression of them hanging out in a locker room—while wearing designer underwear.

Shoving a hand through his hair, his eyes bright with humor, Jake looked straight at the still camera. Juliet didn't think he'd done it on purpose—Kalia was moving around too fast. But from what she could glimpse on the computer to their right, to which Kalia's camera was automatically feeding the photos, the shot was impossibly perfect. Jake's abs were defined in beautiful relief, the light caressing his tattoos, his hair tumbled enough that he looked like he'd just rolled out of bed.

The boxer briefs he had on were black with a partial design on the right-hand side that was subtly spotlighted as a result of his position.

It couldn't have been a better shot had they choreographed it.

"I messed up my hair," he said with a grimace. "Do I have to go back and get it fixed?"

"No, we're good," Kalia reassured him. "Another few shots of you alone, then Vili, and we're done."

Jake didn't stiffen up again, but he exited the faux locker room the instant Kalia announced she had everything she needed from him. "I have to drop my daughter's flute off at her school," he said to the other guys.

Juliet's phone buzzed as Jake disappeared into the changing area, but she spoke to Kalia before answering. "With Vili, we want playful along with a bit of swagger. I'll be back after I handle this call."

"No sweat," Kalia said, her eyes already on her model. "I couldn't take a bad picture of Viliame if I tried."

Leaving Kalia to it, Juliet stepped outside. She was

finishing up her call when Jake walked out. He paused, as if about to say something, then strode on toward his SUV.

"Bye, Jake," she said after hanging up the call, relief cool and heavy twining with another, thornier emotion. "Thank God that's over." She wouldn't see him again for six months, at the next contracted shoot.

Plenty of time for this alien attraction to fizzle out.

That night she dreamed of tracing the coils and shapes of his tattoo with her tongue, fantasized about licking sweat from his skin after a hard game of rugby, and woke at midnight to the impression of his strong body pinning her to the bed while he smiled down at her.

"Oh hell."

Juliet was in trouble.

JAKE LAY in bed at one in the morning, staring up at the ceiling. He was usually an early-to-bed, early-to-rise man, but today his mind wouldn't stop running around in circles.

The shoot had gone far better than he'd expected.

A little because of the guys and how not seriously they'd taken it, but mostly because of Juliet. Though it hadn't been until bedtime that he'd realized she'd picked up on his nerves and deliberately distracted him.

It was a whole lot terrifying that Juliet, of all people, knew him well enough to discern that. He could still remember the first time he'd seen her. Her hair had been messily braided, her uniform skirt torn slightly along the hem, and her uniform shirt haphazardly tucked in. Yet there'd been a kind of pride to her that dared him to make a comment.

Not that Jake would have regardless. He'd been raised better than that. His mother would've clipped him upside the head, then sent him out to spread fresh manure over her entire vegetable garden if she'd heard that he was critiquing girls' clothing.

Too bad he'd forgotten his mother's lesson on the day of the wedding.

Back in school, it hadn't been Juliet's clothes that roused his interest anyway. It had been her air of not giving a single fuck. Pretty much the only time she hadn't given that impression was with Calypso. Every so often, he'd find them together and they'd be laughing, their heads together. But Juliet's softness had only been for her best friend.

Jake never got anything but hackles and snark.

Now that same defiant girl was tensing up his insides. His urge to poke and play with her had only gotten worse since the shoot, after he'd seen her in action in her chosen field of work. That her boss had left her in charge of such a major and expensive endeavor said a hell of a lot about the trust the man had in her.

God, she'd looked hot being all competent and professional.

He'd wanted to stroke his hand over the curve of her butt the entire time. His palm still tingled. But most of all, he'd wanted to cross words with her, just to have her focused on him, even if it was only to aggravate.

He knew she thought him a stuffy ass, but he didn't care.

He didn't feel stuffy when he was with her. He felt young and a little wild and had sex on the brain in a way he hadn't since he was a teenager who'd just discovered girls.

His body began to harden even as his brain flashed bright red warning signals.

Jake had never been attracted to the type of woman who bragged about being a WAG—a wife or girlfriend of a sports star. That was exactly what the tabloids had branded

Juliet during her relationship with Reid Mescall, and even though the attention hadn't been her doing—the label slapped on her rather than claimed—her past notoriety would mean a media onslaught the instant Jake was seen with her.

It was the very thing he'd spent his entire professional career avoiding.

He fisted his hand against the sheet.

Why was he even thinking about this? It wasn't as if he planned to ask her out. Ask *Juliet* out? Was he nuts? She'd laugh herself into a coma, then shred him to pieces for having had the nerve to think she'd give him a second look. Though... he felt weirdly hollow at the idea of not seeing her again for months.

Maybe he could nudge Charlie into inviting Jules over for dinner, then invite himself. Or he could find out her favorite coffee shop and... "And what, Jake?" he muttered to the ceiling. "Start creeping on her there so you can pick fights with her?" His blood heated at the idea of engaging with her, even if it was to fight.

"Cut it the hell out," he ordered himself, "and go to sleep."

His subconscious had other ideas. He woke with an erection so rigid it was painful, the scent of Juliet in his head and her laughing voice in his ear. Most of all, he remembered how her eyes had danced as she'd teased him at the shoot by calling him a Goody Two-shoes.

Groaning, he glanced at the side table to check the time, then grabbed a wad of tissues and quickly took care of the problem. He'd just gotten rid of the evidence and washed up, his sweatpants back on, when his daughter ran into the room. This was the one thing they never told you in the parenting books—that for a single father, finding a few minutes alone for the most basic physical relief was a bit of a magic act.

"Daddy!" Scrambling up onto the bed, Esme made a spot for herself under the duvet.

He slipped back in, then leaned up on his elbow to look down at her. "Why are you awake?"

"I just am." She played with Mr. Mouse's bedraggled ear, all nonchalance. "I dreamed about a cute doggie. He was so nice and he had a waggy tail and he licked my face and made me happy."

Yeah, Jake hadn't been born yesterday. Instead of asking about her "dream," he said, "Since we're both up, shall we make pancakes?"

Her face lit up, the cute doggie forgotten. "Even though it's a school day and you gotta eat proteins?"

It was amazing what she picked up; one conversation on the phone with a team nutritionist while she was in the room and she not only had the word protein in her vocabulary, she'd figured out pancakes weren't on the menu.

"Special treat for both of us," he said. "Let's go."

As he boosted her up onto the kitchen counter so she could stir the batter after he put it together, he thought, *It's all worth it.* He'd allow nothing to jeopardize her smile, the light in her eyes. He definitely wasn't going to hook up with a woman who had bad girl stamped all over her. A woman whose mere existence in their world would lead to a media circus.

A woman who'd shared her cake with him.

A woman who'd seen his discomfort at the shoot and found a way to ease it.

A damn smart, accomplished woman who kicked ass in the business world.

Jake clenched his gut, because the woman Juliet had

become drew him like nobody's business. Tempting as it was to fight the attraction by focusing on her past, people weren't their pasts.

If they were, he'd still be the scared, irresponsible kid who'd gotten his teenage girlfriend pregnant. Instead, he was an elite athlete who represented his country on the world stage, and he had a daughter who was growing up into a spunky girl who might one day take over the world.

That future conqueror helped him polish off a second helping of pancakes, and they were both dressed and ready to head off on their day when his phone rang.

Seeing it was his mother, he answered. "Mum," he said. "What's up?"

"First, let me say hello to my sweet girl."

He handed over the phone to an excited Esme.

"Hi, Grandma," she said before launching into an exhaustive description of all they'd done this morning, complete with special pancakes because they'd woken early and had time to make them and they were really delicious and she had *four* toppings and Daddy even had *strawberries* in the fridge. All said in a single breath, after which came even more. It was time to walk to school when she handed the phone back up to him.

"We're on our way out the door, Mum."

"I won't hold you up," Alison replied. "I just wanted to let you know that we're having a barbecue Saturday afternoon for the wedding party and close family and friends. Molly and Fox are leaving on Sunday to travel through the South Island, and I wanted to have a get-together before that."

A casual weekend barbecue with family and friends was nothing new for the Bishop-Esera clan. But today Jake's heart thudded, his skin hot. "Are you inviting everyone?"

Alison laughed. "Why, baby?" she said, because—according to her—he and his brothers would always be her babies. "Is there someone you want to leave off the guest list?"

"No," he said, and it was the honest truth; he *wanted* to see Juliet.

Couldn't wait to see Juliet.

Couldn't wait to aggravate her.

Couldn't wait to draw in the lush heat of her with every breath.

"What do you want me to bring?" he asked, his voice a touch rough.

Alison hung up after telling him, and Esme's chatter as they walked kept his mind off Juliet for a few minutes. Afterward, he drove himself to a conditioning session at the gym, joining Danny, Vili, and three other players. Pummeling out his frustrations on the punching bag proved satisfying, the burn in his muscles even more so.

He was exhausted when he fell into bed that night, but still he dreamed of a woman with dark brown eyes and long black hair streaked with bronze and red, who made him feel as he hadn't for an eon: young, alive, excited. She wasn't naked in this dream, and neither was he. No, they were dressed as they'd been at the wedding, and they were laughing together.

Jake woke to a smile on his face, an ache in his heart, and the knowledge that he was in big fucking trouble.

12

**THE (UNWANTED) (HIGHLY) RETURN OF
REID THE PINHEAD**

Juliet got out of the ride-share car, handbag slung over one shoulder and a white pastry box carefully balanced in her hands. The box was large and flat, a bit unwieldy. She decided to use her hip to shut the door rather than risk taking one hand from the box. As Aroha said, why have hips this bodacious and not put them to use?

"Thanks!" she called out to the driver as she did so. At least she was wearing sneakers today rather than high heels. The former wasn't her natural state, not anymore. She'd learned to wear heels after she began working with fashionista Iris—at sixty-two, with hair dyed in shades of candy pink and magenta, her boss slayed hearts all over town.

At first the heels had made Juliet feel less awkward and more like she belonged in the firm's—at the time—small reception area, but then she'd fallen in love with them. A few people thought she should play down her height and her curves, but Juliet had had more than enough of trying to please others. She loved heels, and she didn't care about the opinions of people who really should be *minding their own damn business.*

That said, even she wasn't about to turn up in heels to a casual backyard barbecue. A girl had to protect her shoes—and not look like a prat as she struggled to stay on her feet on soil that was apt to be a touch soft at the moment what with the rain they'd had last week. All of them had crossed their fingers and toes the bad weather would clear in time for the wedding, and oh what a glorious day it had been.

No need for the emergency shawls they'd bought to throw over their dresses.

Today, with the sun heating up the early winter chill, she'd gone for dark blue jeans that hugged her legs, simple canvas sneakers in a sandy shade, and a white shirt worn loose over her jeans. A couple of funky, colorful bracelets and simple hoop earrings finished off the look. She'd also gone for minimal makeup—a touch of gloss on her lips, a sweep of mascara on her lashes—and put her hair in a gently bouncy tail.

Looking down instinctively when she felt one shoe land on what felt like a pebble, she saw that someone—probably a child—had forgotten a couple of marbles on the footpath. She was nudging them gently onto the grass verge where they wouldn't be a hazard when she became aware of a pair of sneakered feet in her vision. Looking up with a smile, she was about to apologize for blocking the path when she felt her face freeze.

"I thought that was you," Reid said with his trademark smile, all blue-eyed, mahogany-haired charm and delight.

Dear God. The universe hated her. HATED HER.

Churning nausea in her gut, Juliet somehow managed to say, "I didn't realize you'd be at this barbecue." If she had, *she* certainly wouldn't be standing here. She should've figured that elite athletes from one sport would know and be friendly with players from another. That Reid was a cricket rather than rugby pro didn't mean the men wouldn't have run into each other over the years.

Though seriously, she would've expected Jake's family to have better taste.

"What?" He frowned, then glanced over his shoulder in the direction of the Esera home. It was protected by a dark green camellia hedge that had begun to bloom with pink-ish-white blossoms, but Juliet could just make out the sounds of people chatting as they enjoyed the afternoon. A child's laughter rose into the air right then, followed by the musical ripple of what might've been a guitar.

"Oh right," Reid said with a shrug, "that's where the Eseras live."

Juliet didn't reply. All she could think was that the ride-share car couldn't have gotten far. She could probably recall it in a matter of minutes. And if she threw the pastry box at Reid, she could run pretty fast in these shoes. But then the pinhead would see her run from him, and no way was Juliet giving him that satisfaction. Not again.

Reid pointed across the road. "I'm not doing any barbeque. We just moved into that rental. Me and Lisa."

Juliet's shoulders unbunched. "How lovely for you." She felt nothing but pity for the woman who'd hooked up with this waste of space. No, that wasn't right. Part of her was grateful to Lisa Swan for giving her the push she'd needed to leave Reid. She'd been seriously considering it for months beforehand, but it was his cheating with Lisa that had torn the final veil from her eyes.

"Nice as it is to chat"—*not*—"I have to get going. I'm already late." Her car, just back from the mechanic, complete with a hefty bill, had broken down as she was about to drive over. Not only was she going to ask the garage for her money back, she was considering putting some of her squirreled-away funds into a more reliable vehicle.

One of the major reasons why she had such trouble letting go of her hard-earned money smirked at her. Money flowed through Reid's hands like water—the man was thirty-one and had been paid the salary of a top athlete since he was twenty-two. He could've owned a showpiece of a home by now. Instead, he was still renting. And she didn't think he'd socked his money away in non-property investments either.

"Busy, busy," he said, smile undimmed. "I hear you're quite the businesswoman now. Congrats. Still single though, right? No time for play?"

Passive-aggressive weenie.

Wondering if he was draining Lisa's bank account as he'd done hers before she wised up or if the other woman had been smart enough to keep her money separate, Juliet stepped to one side and began to walk past him. When he put a hand on her arm, she gritted her teeth against the urge to rip him to metaphorical shreds.

Reid had always used and manipulated her frustration and anger to make her feel small and useless. She could fight forever with Jake and come out feeling buzzy and happy even if he'd scored a few points. But with Reid, she'd just felt like trash. Awful, stupid trash.

Never again.

It was a vow she'd made as she walked out of their marriage and one she intended to keep. She was no longer the needy and lonely nineteen-and-a half-year-old who'd fallen for Reid's shallow charm; the pompous prick no longer had any power over her.

"I think I hear your girlfriend calling for you," she said.

"Better go before she starts thinking you're hitting on your *ex*-wife."

He stepped closer instead of backing off.

"Juliet," another male voice said just as she'd decided to hell with decorum and was about to slam a knee right where it'd hurt Reid the most. "Problem?"

She looked up to meet Jake's eyes, saw his granite jaw. Heat scalded her cheeks. Of course he wouldn't want a scene outside his parents' home. "No, your new neighbor felt the need to say hello." This time when she pulled at her arm, Reid let go.

Jake waited for her to step over to him, then, to her surprise, put his hand on her lower back as he turned to lead her into the barbecue. Before they passed through the open gate, however, he turned around to say, "You should probably go help Lisa. She's lifting those big boxes by herself."

Reid's face tightened. "Just wanted to catch up with Juliet. She and I have a lot of history."

Then she and Jake were through the gate, and Jake stopped to close it behind them.

"You didn't invite him to the barbecue?" she asked as Reid crossed the road to his nicely maintained villa. She needed to be sure she didn't have to worry about running into her ex in the backyard; the Eseras seemed like the kind of people who'd be friendly to their neighbors.

"Guy's an asshole." Jake's gaze was flint. "He's everything that's wrong with professional sports, and my folks would be horrified if any of us considered him a friend. You should know that."

Juliet took her first proper breath since the initial contact with Reid; the rush of oxygen was energizing. "Glad to see that being an underwear supermodel hasn't affected your brains."

He raised an eyebrow. "Stop insulting yourself."

It took a second. Making a face, she used one hand to slap herself on the forehead while shoving the box at him to hold. She had total faith in his reflexes, and he didn't let her down.

"You're right," she admitted, because really, he had her on that point. "I must've been in a delusional state to ever think I was in love with that jerk." It was easier to make light of those years, easier to think of them as a foolish young mistake than to look back and see how badly she'd allowed herself to be treated.

Reid was an asshole, it was true. But she'd been an affection-starved doormat.

Jake was looking at her with an unreadable but intense expression on his face when she glanced at him.

"What?" She took her box back. "You never made a bad relationship decision?"

His answer made everything in her go still. "I have a daughter."

His words could be taken one of two ways: either that he was far more careful because he had a daughter to protect or that he'd made his mistake a long time ago. But Juliet wasn't confused about which one he meant. It had never been his relationship that had been the mistake, it had just been two teenagers not getting birth control right.

Callie and Jake, they'd fit.

It was why Juliet had been so hard on him—a part of her had worried he'd steal away her friend. But when he hadn't tried to get between them, had even invited her along to things like the rides in his souped-up junker, she'd started to think he might be all right. Given more time, they might've ended up friends... But then everything had changed for both of them.

"I have to be careful who I bring into Esme's life," he clarified, as if suddenly realizing how his words could be misunderstood. "Calypso was no mistake. Neither is Esme."

"I got what you meant," Juliet said, her neck a little stiff from having to look up at Jake in this position. "After I left Reid, I used to have nightmares where I had a baby with him. Can you imagine that narcissistic pinhead as a father?"

"It's enough to terrify anyone," Jake agreed.

"I finally made a voodoo doll from this old T-shirt of his that I found in my stuff, put a picture of his face on it, and stabbed it with tiny pushpins and the nightmares stopped."

Jake stared at her, his lips twitching. "You're making that up to mess with me."

"Am I?" She smiled enigmatically, painfully delighted to have teased a near-smile out of him. "These pastries are still warm. Let's set them out."

Jake, his expression yet amused, led her to the front door rather than around the side to the back. The villa was full of light, the wooden floors a warm honey that had been lovingly polished. Like so many of the old homes in the area, it had a straight front-to-back flow but had been renovated to be far more open plan than was traditional.

The kitchen, she saw when they reached the end of the hallway, had definitely been redone. Afternoon sunlight spilled into the huge space that was built for use, not for show. There was plenty of counter space, and the appliances looked well loved. Huge stacking glass doors that folded back at either end meant the entire back wall could be opened up to provide a seamless flow onto a pretty little patio surrounded by pots of blooming winter flowers, and from there, onto the verdant green lawn.

"Gimme a sec." Jake bent down to look in a cupboard, rose with a large wooden chopping board in hand. "You want to put your pastries on this?"

"Yup."

Dumping her purse with the others that had been placed on the kitchen table, she opened the box and began to take out the small savory pastries. Tiny croissants with ham and cheese, small cheese-and-spinach tarts, even miniature butter-chicken bites wrapped in delicious puff pastry.

When a big male hand snuck into the box to grab a flaky croissant, she found herself biting back a grin. Good to know that even Jacob Esera had a weak spot.

"Congratulations on your selection—and Danny's," she said. "I caught the announcement." It was hard to miss when the naming of the national rugby squad was a prime-time headline. Could also be she'd paid more attention than usual, her stomach tense with the alphabetical roll call until Daniel Esera's name was followed by Jacob Esera's.

"Thanks. Be good to play in the black jersey again." Having made short work of the pastry, he went and got something from the fridge before rejoining her. She watched as he arranged chili peppers and parsley around her baked goodies. The simple chopping board was suddenly a piece of art, her work showcased as if in a restaurant.

Agog, she locked eyes with him. "You like to cook or just make things pretty?"

"I cook. It's easier to stay healthy and on form if I know what's going into my body." He inhaled a butter-chicken puff. "Where did you buy these? They're amazing."

She put her hands on her hips and pursed her lips even as warmth jolted her blood; turned out she liked being complimented by Jake. Ugh. "I *handmade* these, so stop scoffing them in a single bite and appreciate my artistry. Charlotte and I met in a pastry class, remember?"

Jake literally shook his head a couple of times as if blowing away cobwebs. "I didn't think you took it seriously. I mean, you mostly brought junk food for your school lunch."

"I was a teenager." No one had ever taught her how she was supposed to eat or cooked for her; the few good habits she'd had, she'd picked up from Calypso.

"I'm glad you're eating better now." Approving words, Jake's face so serious that she wanted to bop him on the nose just to see what he'd do. "Food is fuel, and putting junk food into your body is like putting sugar into a petrol tank."

Juliet bit back a smile. So the gearhead *did* still live inside resolutely serious adult Jake.

"Talking of cars," he added, "where'd you park yours? There's a no-parking area down the street where the city occasionally tickets people even on weekends."

"It wouldn't start." She scowled. "Second time this month—and the garage promised me the problem was fixed."

Jake picked up the chopping board. "I can have a look at it if you want."

Juliet wasn't sure which one of them was more surprised by his absentminded offer. Because he went dead-straight right after, as if he'd remembered too late that it was Juliet to whom he was speaking.

Too bad for him, because she was going to accept. Jake had always been a genius with cars. "If you can fix Dixie, I'll bake you an entire tray of pastries."

A sudden unexpected tug of his lips that stole her breath. "Deal."

That was when Juliet realized she might've outfoxed

herself. Because now Jake was going to be inside her internal garage and thus effectively inside her home. He'd fill it up with that drugging masculine scent she was trying to ignore but that she wanted to sniff straight from his neck like a strung-out junkie.

Oh hell. What if she lost all her self-control and lemur-jumped him?

13

BRING IT ON, CUPCAKE

After a short freak-out, Juliet decided liberal use of air freshener when he came to look at her car would keep her hormones at bay. She'd just let Jake think she was a neat freak who enjoyed refreshing her home every five seconds.

Freak-out aside, the barbecue ended up being far more fun than she'd expected. Aroha was present, as was the rest of the bridal party, along with Nayna, her husband, Raj, and their cheeky little boy, Gabriel's rugby mates, and of course the Bishop-Esera family. She'd been wary about how the family felt about her beyond the natural joy created by a wedding. Given their close association with national-level sports, they had to be aware of the way the tabloids followed her around.

It made her want to pull out her hair, especially as she hadn't done *anything* the least bit tabloid-worthy since leaving Reid. Every so often, however, a reporter would snap a photo of her walking out of a coffee shop or leaving Everett's manufacturing plant and spin a story about how her "broken heart" had "never healed" or how she was "bravely rebuilding" her life after her "doomed romance" with Reid.

Juliet would give those reporters a real taste of doom if she ever caught them.

The only thing she regretted about ending her marriage was that she hadn't done it twenty-one months earlier—because one month post-wedding was all it had taken for Reid's dickish nature to come out. The man must've given himself a coronary pretending to be a good guy for the three months they'd dated prior to marriage.

The good news was that things had finally begun to calm down. New Zealand's two-year separation rule prior to the dissolution of a marriage meant her divorce from Reid had only become legal fact six months earlier. So now the magazines and tabloids couldn't even spin stories of their reconciliation.

Especially since she'd had zero contact with him in those two years.

"Juliet." Alison walked over to embrace her with a maternal warmth that caused Juliet's eyes to sting. "It's so nice to see you again." Lowering her voice to a conspiratorial whisper, she said, "Thank you again for organizing that bra for me—I just about cried when I saw the one I especially bought had shrunk even with handwashing, and nothing else would work under my dress."

"Oh, it was my pleasure." The small prewedding emergency had been easy to defuse for the vice president in charge of operations and supply for a lingerie company. "If you ever want anything like that, just let me know." No, she wasn't above sucking up to Charlotte's mother-in-law, not when Alison gave out hugs that potent.

The older woman's smile lit up the gray of her eyes. "I

might just take you up on that, sweetheart. You know how hard it is to find a good bra."

"The holy grail."

Tucking her hand into the crook of Juliet's elbow, Alison drew her toward a small group on one side of the lawn. "Come, let's go see what Harlow and Catie are plotting."

"Hey, princess!" Danny called out just as Juliet and Alison reached the step-siblings. "You painting your nails or you going to help me with games for the kids?"

Catie's eyes acquired a dangerous glint before she stomped off toward Danny. Juliet had yet to see the two of them have a civilized conversation.

"One day," Alison said with a sigh, "those two will decide to behave themselves."

Harlow, quietly sophisticated with his black-framed glasses and tailored clothing, slid his hands into the pockets of his pants. "Honestly, I'd start to worry about demonic possession if they did."

Molly and Fox came over to join them even as Alison laughed, and the conversation meandered down various paths, including details of the locations Molly and Fox intended to hit on their travels. But regardless of anything else, Juliet never forgot Jake. It was as if her body was an antenna tuned directly to his presence.

Desperation had her reaching for another glass of cold lemonade.

"Game time!" Sailor's voice boomed over the small crowd even as her hand touched the handle of the pitcher. "Gather the troops!"

Jolting, Juliet turned to see a buzz of activity as tables were moved out of the way and chairs repositioned. The Eseras had a large backyard for this part of the city, a green haven that morphed into a miniature rugby field in a matter of minutes. Unsurprisingly, the family had the transformation down to a fine art.

Given the available land area, they played in two teams of three. Jake was on the opposing team to his daughter for the first game, but he hollered and clapped along with everyone else when Esme zoomed over the try line with the ball tucked under her arm.

Juliet's cheeks hurt from smiling, her throat hoarse from cheering.

The Bishop-Esera men got their father to play as well, then dragged in their mother for a turn. Juliet got a clue when they pulled Molly onto the field, and began to back away very slowly. But it was too late.

"Hey!" Molly put her hands on her hips. "If I have to play, so do you."

Juliet groaned. "I am *so* not sporty." Jogging was the only physical exercise she'd ever adopted.

"It's fun!" Emmaline tugged at her hand. "Come on, Jules."

Since she couldn't exactly argue with the cute kid, she walked onto the field. She was replacing Danny, who walked to the sideline with Catie beside him. The two were muttering at each other, the words too low to hear.

Juliet's team consisted of her, Fox, and Emmaline.

Their opposition was formed of Molly, Esme, and Jake.

Juliet's heart kicked, but she kept her eyes on the prize. From what she'd seen, this family took rugby seriously, even when it was touch rugby in the backyard. American Fox had clearly already been taught the rules, because he knew exactly what to do when things kicked off. He slipped the ball smoothly back to Emmaline.

Who ran, then threw the ball back at Juliet. Just barely

catching it, Juliet sidestepped Molly to go for the try line. She was almost there when Jake made a lunge toward her.

She dropped the ball.

Everybody on her team groaned.

Little Emmaline threw up her hands. "Come *on*!" she cried, and it was so adorable that Juliet couldn't help but grin.

Jake meanwhile, was bending down to grab the ball. "You better up your game, Jules," he said, a glint in his eye that she'd never before seen. "I mean, you're getting schooled by a seven-year-old."

Oh, now it was on. "That's Juliet to you, Jacob."

"Restart!" Aroha, a rugby fanatic and the current referee, blew the whistle.

Juliet had never had so much fun in her life. Molly was in hysterics at one point, and Fox argued passionately with Aroha about a foul while Emmaline nodded sagely alongside him. Esme, meanwhile, scored a second time—and did a victory booty dance, pigtails bouncing and hands fisted. As for Jake, Juliet actually saw him laugh.

The sound rippled over her like a rough caress.

Annoyed at how badly he affected her, she redoubled her efforts to bring him down and finally succeeded in managing a touch that meant he had to turn over the ball. Taking it, she buffed her bright purple nails on her shirt and blew off nonexistent dust. "Oh, what's this? Superstar Jacob Esera schooled by a newbie. Tut-tut."

"You want to bring it, Jules?" The light of battle in his eyes, he made a come-on gesture with both hands. "I'm right here."

Smirking even as her insides went all hot and tight, she tapped the ball at Aroha's whistle, then passed it immediately to Fox, who passed to Emmaline. Then she and Fox put themselves to blocking Jake and Molly, which left Esme the only line of defense. And she was on the wrong side of the field.

"Try!" Aroha's whistle pierced the air as Emmaline put down the ball on the other side of the opposition's try line.

Juliet blew Jake a kiss. "Better luck next time, cupcake."

Hands on his hips, he smiled with slow deliberation... and a shiver raced up her body. She still wasn't ready for his counterattack. She couldn't seem to go anywhere on the field without running into a hard male chest or feeling a pair of hands at her hips—a legal touch that meant a ball turnover.

Her skin was electric by the time Aroha blew the full-time whistle and the teams swapped out, but far more scary was how much she'd enjoyed playing with Jake—and how much she was coming to *like* him.

JULIET DID a good job of avoiding Jake for the rest of the barbeque, eventually ending up on the kitchen tidy-up crew while he helped with the external cleanup.

"Just put it all in here." Alison passed over a large plastic container that could be sealed and put into the refrigerator. "Someone will hoover it up."

With everyone pitching in—including Esme and Emmaline and Nayna's little boy, the kids assigned to find any straws or bottle caps that had fallen onto the grass—it only took a short time to set the house and yard to rights.

Afterward, Juliet picked up her handbag, dug into it for her phone. She'd just opened up the ride-share app when Alison came by to put something on the table. "Oh, you don't need to do that," she said, catching a glimpse of the app. "One of us will drive you home."

"It's no bother," Juliet began, long used to looking after herself.

But Alison would have none of it. "It's dark, and you shouldn't be getting into a car with a stranger."

It was such a motherly thing to say that Juliet's throat swelled up. Her aunt had never been like Alison. No one in her life had been like Alison.

By the time she found her voice again, Alison was already calling out to one of her sons. "Jake, sweetheart, please drop Juliet home."

14

ONE NIGHT OF NAKEDNESS AND ONE NIGHT ONLY (WHAT COULD POSSIBLY GO WRONG?)

Juliet parted her lips, eyes flaring—she *really* did not need to be stuck in a car with Jacob Esera—but all she could come up with was "The girls can come along for a ride." Emmaline and Esme would make great chaperones—for Juliet. Because, as she'd already realized, this was an excruciatingly one-sided attraction.

Jake no more wanted her than he wanted Reid.

And lemur-lunge thoughts aside, Juliet wasn't into rejection. Part of the reason she'd fallen for Reid was how he'd made her feel wanted, accepted. For a girl who'd been rejected by every single living member of her family, that had been one hell of a drug. Reid had known it too—he'd found her at a vulnerable moment, and she'd spilled her guts.

Her ex had used the knowledge to hook her.

"The munchkins are exhausted." Alison smiled. "Ísa's already got both of them in the bath. Then it's into pajamas and bed with them. They're spending the night here—Joseph and I are taking them fishing with us tomorrow."

Across the kitchen, Jake grabbed his keys. "Ready?" His expression was impossible to read.

Juliet nodded—there really wasn't anything she could do without insulting Alison's kindness. "Thank you again for the lovely time."

Alison gave her a big hug. "We'll see you next time."

Holding the possibility of another invite close, Juliet followed Jake outside to a large gray SUV with a child seat in the back. The two of them didn't speak as he pulled out of the drive and—after getting her address—turned in the direction of her place. She found her gaze going to the house on the other side of the street. The lights were on inside, and there were people hanging out on the porch in front, beers in hand.

From the raucous sound of things, the drinking had been going on for a while.

"He's going to lose his place in the squad if he keeps that up," Jake said coolly as he drove out of the otherwise quiet suburban street. "His reflexes are already slower—you can see it when he plays. And cricket season is far from over."

New Zealand, Juliet knew, had a major test match coming up against archrivals Australia. "He could bounce back from the party lifestyle when he was younger." She remembered how Reid would roll out of bed bright-eyed and energetic no matter what he'd imbibed or inhaled the night prior. "I don't think he's accepted that his body can't keep on doing that indefinitely."

"I would've expected better of you, Jules. You were always smart."

"Thanks, Mr. No One Asked for Your Opinion."

Hands bone white around the steering wheel, Jake said, "Yeah, it's not my business." It wasn't an apology, not even close. Especially since he followed it up with "But the guy is a total flake. What the hell did you see in him?"

Security, love, a sense of home.

She hadn't known it was an illusion when she and Reid first got together, had taken his words and promises at face value. As for what he'd seen in her, looking back, it had to have been a combination of her need to give love and the fact she had no one else; Reid loved exploiting vulnerability.

"Callie told me your family banded around you two when you found out about the pregnancy," she said to Jake —because if he was going to ask personal questions, he had to be ready for the answers. "Each and every one ready to catch you so you wouldn't fall."

A wrinkling of his brow. "Sure."

"Other than Callie, I've never had anyone who would catch me if I fell," she said, in no mood to hold her punches. "Reid convinced me that he was going to be that person. So yeah, I was naive for falling for it, but I had my reasons. You don't get to judge me while living in the heart of a family that will *always* have your back."

He shot her a quick glance before returning his attention to the road. "You lived with your aunt. I remember Calypso saying that."

"Let's just say she was never meant to be a mother figure. *Annnnnd* that's enough of a heart-to-heart." Juliet turned her head to look out the window, the conversation just another reminder of the vast divide between them.

She might have fantasies about Jake, but the reality was — "What is that abomination?" Clapping her hands over her ears, she stared at the radio he'd turned on.

"Metal." He nodded his head along with the screeching on the radio. "You don't like it?"

She was almost certain he was messing with her now,

and the idea of it melted the coldness. "Sure," she said slyly. "Let's listen to it the whole way home."

Turned out Jake had ears of steel. She cracked first and changed the station. Jake's laugh filled the car. Reaching over, she shoved his upper arm without thinking about it. Electricity zapped up her arm. Her inner lemur sat up.

Shit.

Juliet took to staring out the window again.

Until at long-freaking-last, Jake headed down the lengthy drive that led to her two-bedroom unit. Set within a grouping of similar homes, it made her feel a part of something bigger than herself. Another illusion, but a harmless one she'd created for the lonely young woman who remained a part of her.

Unclipping her seat belt as Jake brought the vehicle to a halt in front of her place, she said, "Thanks. I appreciate the ride."

But Jake was unclipping his own belt. "It's not that late. I could have a quick look at your car while I'm here, then I'll know what tools to bring to fix it."

Juliet tensed, but she couldn't exactly tell him to leave without giving away the intensity of her reaction. "Sure. Let me open the garage."

"That's not your car" were the first words out of Jake's mouth as the garage door rolled back to reveal her dark blue compact. "Where's the pink thing?"

Oh. "Part of the company's fleet," she said. "I borrowed it while mine was in the garage." She made a face at him as she unlocked the vehicle, then popped the hood. "You really thought I always drove around with a car that has S3X11 on the number plate?" She was trying to avoid the media hounds, not flash her existence.

"Jules, predicting you has never been my strong suit."

As Jake disappeared behind the hood of her car on those words, she found herself tucking her hands into the back pockets of her jeans and rocking back and forth. She'd never had a man in this house who wasn't a tradesman. Jake took up a whole lot more space than her plumber or electrician.

"Anything obvious?" She fought the urge to pad closer.

"No, but I see a couple of likely suspects. I'll have to take a section of the engine apart to see for sure."

"I'll contact the garage."

"No, I can fix it." He looked around the side of the hood, a curl tumbling over his forehead and his eyes bright. "I haven't had a chance to work on an engine like this for a while."

Juliet could eat him up, stuffed-shirt ways and all.

Dear Lord, whatever I've done, I ask for mercy. Please end this torture.

God didn't listen to her fervent prayer. Probably because, prior to the wedding, she hadn't entered a church for five years.

It was an endless ten minutes later that Jake unhooked the hood and put it back down. "I'll bring the correct tools the next time."

Next time.

Juliet decided her car would stage a miraculous return to perfect function in the next few days. "Thanks."

Holding up his grease-stained hands, he said, "Mind if I use your laundry sink to wash up?"

As with most houses of this vintage and design, her laundry was an alcove cut into the garage. There was only one problem: "Laundry tap's not working at the moment. Plumber's coming back tomorrow with the right part to fix it." She waved him into the house with a sense of inevitability.

Air freshener or not, his scent would torment her all night.

After Jake ducked inside the bathroom and water flowed in the sink, she went to open the sliding doors that led from her lounge to her deck. The crisp night air was a welcome slap against her cheeks, the skies dark and dotted with stars. She had no view as such, but the land fell gently away on the other side of her low wooden fence to reveal a small stream. Lush ferns and other native plants grew in abundance around it.

"This is nice."

Juliet didn't jump though he'd entered behind her—her Jacob Esera antenna was working just fine. "Got the grease off okay?" she asked, and when he nodded, said, "I'll show you to the front door. You must be wanting to get home."

He met her gaze full-on, and the impact of those brown eyes was a punch that made her throat tighten, her stomach flutter. "Kicking me out, Jules?"

"That's Juliet to you," she responded automatically, wondering why he was still hanging around, why he was looking at her *that* way. As if she was the only woman in the entire world.

Her mouth dried up, her pulse thunder in her ears.

"You're right, you know," he said. "I've always had people around me who'd catch me if I fell."

Oh. That's what he'd stayed behind to clear up. "I shouldn't have made it sound like an accusation." Flushing, she broke the eye contact. "It's a good thing you have. I envy you."

"I know my family is my greatest advantage in life."

She found herself looking at him again, caught by how solemnly he said that.

Their eyes collided again, and this time the jolt was so visceral that a shiver rippled over her. Wetting her lips, she went to say she'd walk him to his car when Jake lifted his hand and cupped her cheek. Hot, a little rough, the gentle hold locked her in place, her chest rising and falling in a sharp rhythm.

"Jake, you have to go home." It came out a rasp.

"Yes." The slightest tremor in the hand that continued to cradle her face. "We're not right for each other."

"Nope," she agreed, the word hard to get out through the tension in her throat. "We'll drive each other to homicide."

"Double, you think?"

"Hundred percent certainty."

Neither one of them moved.

"I don't do one-night stands."

"Neither do I." She sucked in a desperate gulp of air. "It's just some weird chemistry thing." At least now she knew it wasn't embarrassingly one-sided... though that made the attraction far more perilous.

It also touched an old grief stored deep inside her heart. "Is this wrong?" she blurted out. "Because of Callie?"

"I never looked at you this way before." No confusion in Jake's face, nothing but blunt openness based on a bedrock of confidence. "You were just Calypso's annoying friend."

"And you were her irritating boyfriend." She and Jake, they'd never betrayed Callie, not even in thought.

An exhale inside her, a worry she hadn't realized she'd been carrying around, poofing out of existence. "You're still irritating."

"But I'm hot too." Jake's words were so deadpan that it took her a moment to realize he was teasing her.

"A little, maybe." Not her best effort since she was all but hyperventilating, but a woman had to try.

"I need a good night's sleep." Jake ran the pad of his thumb over her cheekbone, the heat in his eyes threatening to burn. "I have training on Monday."

Juliet's toes curled at the implied admission that she'd been keeping him up nights. Good. It was only fair. She, too, would be a wreck by Monday if they didn't deal with this. Deal with it out of existence. "We're not friends, so we can't be friends with benefits."

"Just once." Hand tightening on her cheek, Jake stepped closer, the furnace of his muscular body pure erotic temptation. "Get it out of our systems, move on."

A small voice piped up in the back of Juliet's head, reminding her of how much fun she'd had with him this afternoon. Fun that had nothing to do with sexual heat. *Don't risk it, Jules. What if one night of sex only addicts you deeper?*

Intense brown eyes locked with her own. "Yes?"

"Yes," she said, shushing that worried voice on a wave of naked want.

Then Jake's lips were warm and firm on hers, his hand sliding to grip the back of her neck, his chest crushing her breasts as he slid his free arm around her waist. Everything about him was hot and hard, including the erection pushing against her abdomen. Juliet felt shockingly soft, delicately female—and wanted in a way that made her head spin, the last threads of caution slipping from her grasp.

Wrapping her arms around his neck and anchoring the fingers of one hand in the thick black of his hair, she parted her lips. Jake kissed like he did everything else: with purpose and concentration. First he learned her mouth, learned exactly how she liked things, then he used that knowledge to make her weak at the knees.

Juliet was a confident woman, had made herself that

way through sheer strength of will, but the majority of her sexual experience had been with Reid. That didn't exactly leave her in any kind of shape to deal with a man who took his time making love to her mouth until her lips tingled and her toes curled.

Painfully tight nipples pushing against the white lace of her bra, she pressed into his body, her nails digging into his neck. He bit lightly at her lower lip before taking another kiss. In revenge, she deliberately pricked him with her nails again—and got a deep, wet kiss that was all tongue and sex for her trouble.

Juliet melted.

She'd never been kissed this long and with such open satisfaction, never had her panties go damp before a man so much as touched her breasts.

Lifting his head at last, both of them panting, Jake glanced toward the stream, then to the right and left. She had higher fences on either side, and the way the houses were positioned meant none of her neighbors could look in on them, but when he tugged her inside, she went without hesitation. The last thing she wanted was to give a lurking photographer with a telephoto lens a big payday.

It wouldn't be Juliet who'd command the high price. No, it would be straitlaced Jacob Esera caught making out with "Notorious WAG" Juliet.

Locking the sliding door behind them, Jake took another kiss, this one harder, his breath choppy. "Bedroom?"

15

CLEVER HANDS AND ORGASMS TO RUIN A WOMAN (*FANS FACE*)

Juliet moved toward her bedroom, crossed the threshold, and all at once wasn't sure what to do. It wasn't as if she made a habit out of inviting men into this room; in point of fact, Jake was the first man she'd invited in. But he'd walked into the bedroom behind her and he swept aside her hair to kiss her nape before she could stumble.

Juliet moaned.

He'd found that sensitive spot where her neck met her shoulder. Reaching back to grip his thighs, she angled her head a fraction more. She felt his lips curve against her even as he slid one hand around her waist and pressed it flat against her stomach. The idea of Jake smiling as he kissed her, of Jake enjoying doing things to her that pleasured her, it melted her in ways that were far deeper than sex.

She shoved aside that thought, because sex was all this would ever be. Even if they didn't aggravate each other nine seconds out of ten, she wasn't the kind of woman a man like Jake took home to his parents. There was a difference between being welcomed as a friend of the family and entering as a possible future daughter-in-law. No parent wanted a scandal-ridden partner for a beloved son.

Why was her brain even *thinking* these things?

Jake slid one big, warm hand up over her body to close it over her breast, shattering her into a kaleidoscope.

Desperate to feel his touch directly on her skin, she lifted her hands to the buttons of her shirt and quickly undid them one by one. Jake moved back the instant she was finished and drew the shirt off over her arms.

After dropping it to the floor, he returned to his previous position, chest pressed to her back and hand splayed against her stomach. It quivered, his heat and scent her own personal aphrodisiac. As he kissed his way down her neck and along her shoulder, she tried to put together enough brain cells to figure what she could do for him.

That was how this worked.

"I can't really touch you," she managed to get out, raising her hands to hook them around the back of his neck.

"You can touch me later." A deep-voiced response. "I don't want this over with quick, and it will be if you put your hands on me."

No man had ever said anything sexier to her. Bones liquid, she dropped her head back against his shoulder and let him do what he wanted. The rumbling sound he made in his chest transformed her blood into honey. He returned his hand to her lace-covered breast not long afterward, molding and shaping with unhidden interest before he used his thumb and forefinger to clasp her nipple, roll it.

She had large nipples, and they were ridiculously sensitive. Gritting her teeth against the sounds that wanted to come out—she was pretty sure they'd be whimpers—she found herself rubbing against him.

As she'd already discovered, Jake was a very smart

man, one who listened and learned. He released her nipple but only so he could explore her neglected breast, tease the other nipple. The rasp of the lace against her skin, it made those whimpers escape her control. Jake bit her lightly on her shoulder in response before stepping back.

Bereft, she tried to find her balance, but he was back in a matter of seconds. It was his bare chest that he pressed against her. There was a slight, delicious roughness to his skin, and she remembered the fine chest hair she'd noticed at the shoot.

Her fingers prickled, wanting to touch, to explore.

Nudging her head to the other side so he could kiss the curve of her neck, he reached around to the front at the same time and tugged the cups of her bra down beneath her breasts. Juliet looked down... and heat erupted underneath the brown of her skin. This seemed naughtier than if he'd taken off her bra, as if she was serving herself up in a frame of white lace.

She watched with her heart in her mouth and her throat parched as he put two blunt-tipped fingers around the rich brown of her nipple and squeezed.

Her thighs clenched, her eyes fluttering shut. She ground back against him, unable to stop the rawly sensual movements.

Jake slid his free hand up to close gently around the front of her throat even as he continued to pluck and roll her nipple with his other hand. Each touch shot an erotic bolt through her, the pleasure on the edge of pain.

"Can you come like this?" Rough, focused, a question that demanded an answer.

Juliet struggled to form words. "I don't know." No one had ever spent this much time on foreplay and never on her breasts. Jake, however, obviously liked things slow and maddening.

"Let's find out." Then the man with fingers clever enough to fix engines and hands strong enough to keep a rugby ball safe on the field set himself to Juliet's pleasure.

At some point she found herself falling back onto the bed, Jake standing between her legs, which half hung over the side. His eyes were hot, his hair tumbled as he leaned forward to brace himself with his palms on either side of her shoulders. A single instant of searing eye contact before he lowered his head and sucked her nipple into his mouth.

The cry that left her lips this time was more of a scream, her body arching up toward his. Continuing to hold himself up with one hand, he used the other to squeeze the breast he wasn't sucking, his thumb rubbing *hard* over the nipple.

She came.

Her entire body went stiff, her internal muscles clenched, and pleasure kicked through her in a languorous rush. Somehow her hand was in Jake's hair, clutching in a vain effort to find solid ground. The feel of his teeth as he playfully scraped her nipple before releasing it turned everything white for a second.

When she emerged from the haze, it was to spots in front of her eyes and to Jake looking down at her with a distinctly satisfied expression on his face.

"Now we know."

She wondered if she should be irritated by his smugness, but in all honesty, what would be the point? The man had earned the smug. She wanted to kiss him—he'd earned it so without question. Right now smug looked cute on him.

Also, she might be drunk on orgasm hormones.

That was *fine* with her.

Tugging down his head, she kissed him, all languid and

wet, while stroking the fingers of her free hand over the dark lines of his tattoo. His body was sleek and cut under her touch, his chest hair a delicious abrasion. All out of inhibitions, she licked her tongue against his.

He groaned before pushing off the bed into a standing position.

As she watched, he dropped his hands to the top button of her jeans and flicked it open.

"Up," he rumbled.

In no mood to deny him anything, she lifted her bottom off the bed. Her muscles felt like jelly, but she wasn't close to done. No, she wanted to know what else Jacob Esera could do with those clever fingers and that smart mind.

A tiny, rational part of her worried that he might ruin her for other men—because she didn't have to be a sex diva to know that he was good at this, *really* good. The kind of good that came from having an intense ability to concentrate on his lover. This wasn't paint-by-the-numbers or a predetermined set of moves. Jake was reacting to her reactions, as quick on the uptake in bed as he was rumored to be with strategy on the field.

So yes, ruination was a possibility.

But Juliet wasn't about to allow fear to stop her from living what promised to be the most sensual experience of her life.

It didn't take him long to pull off her jeans and drop them to the floor. He stopped, gazing down at her splayed-out body. At her light blue panties with white lace edging, a tiny white bow in the center. The white lace bra she'd matched with it continued to obscenely cup her breasts.

Blue socks patterned with pink flamingos wearing feather boas covered her feet. Aroha had given them to her as a birthday gift, and Juliet thought they were a hoot. But sexy? A big nope.

Jake's gaze, however, was on the rest of her. "Nice," he said, and her entire body clenched as if he'd mouthed the dirtiest thing on the planet.

It was the look in his eye. He liked what he saw, and he was making no bones about displaying it. A woman could get used to a man this blunt, this open—though that was the last thing she'd ever thought she'd say about Jacob Esera. The man was the definition of closed up more securely than a bank vault. Except, it appeared, in bed.

Bending to cup the back of her knee, he stroked all the way down to one foot. But instead of tugging off her sock without looking, he glanced down. His lips kicked up. "Cute."

Her stomach dropped. Jake was dangerous when he smiled.

"Let's leave those on."

She thought he was joking until he dropped her foot and went to undo the top button of his jeans. All at once, she didn't care about her flamingo socks. She watched, dry-mouthed and restless, as he finished undoing the button and began to lower his zipper.

"Do you have protection?" A solemn question, Jake's hand halting with the zipper barely undone.

"Yes, in the bathroom cabinet." She'd bought the box a couple of months ago in a fit of determination to get out there and strut her stuff. But when push came to shove, she'd balked at the idea of picking up a man in a club.

Juliet had nothing against people enjoying casual encounters, wished she could. A woman had needs that sexy television doctors alone couldn't fulfill. But the gawky, unwanted girl she'd once been continued to exist in her sexual self—she needed to feel comfortable with a lover before she could get naked. For her, sex required friendship at the very least.

Yet here she was, with a man who wasn't a friend.

Disquieted by the sudden return to rational thought, she was in the process of sitting up by the time Jake returned from the bathroom. He just put one hand on her chest and nudged her back down.

No real pressure; it asked her to make the choice.

Shivering and consigning rational thought to the morning after, she went back down, though she felt a bit ridiculous with her legs half hanging off the edge of the bed. But Jake seemed to like the view, his eyes on her as he tore open the sealed box and threw it on the bedside table after removing one flat packet.

Her panties grew even more damp.

Dropping the packet beside her thigh, he finished undressing.

Juliet stopped breathing. She'd seen him all but naked on the shoot, but it was different here, in the privacy of her bedroom. With the smell of him all around her and his eyes saying she was his favorite candy and he wanted to steal the entire box so he could eat her up.

Her besocked toes dug into the carpet, her hands fisting on the sheets.

Taking his thick length in a fist, he stroked once.

Juliet moaned.

He smiled, slow and devastating, as he ripped open the condom packet. As she watched, her breathing shallow and fast, he sheathed himself with slow deliberation. Her panties were so damp by now that she was self-conscious when he slid them off her legs, but Jake's attention was on other matters.

Gripping her under her rounded thighs, he hauled her forward until her hips were at the edge of the bed, then he spread those thighs wide and looked down.

Unable to take the intensity of the connection, she glanced away and to the side.

"Jules. Look at me."

Teeth sinking into her lower lip, she nonetheless obeyed his command. Though why the hell was it so hot that he'd demanded her participation? He didn't move until their eyes had reconnected, his chest rising and falling in a rhythm as rapid as her own.

"Are you wet enough?" He bent to kiss the inner curve of her knee.

Juliet nodded; any wetter and she'd be dripping.

But Jake lifted his head and broke out that dangerous, sinful smile. "Let me check."

He'd dropped to his knees and put his mouth between her legs before she could respond. Juliet's brain exploded, her eyes rolling back in her head. Giving in, she just rode the waves—rode his talented, *talented* tongue—and was wrecked by the time he rose back up and lifted her legs to spread her wide open all over again.

Eyes locked with hers once more, he stepped forward until the head of his cock nudged a part of her body that felt as if it had melted. Her thighs quivered as he began to push into her, the friction a delicious ache.

Juliet couldn't keep her eyes open any longer.

Jake stopped moving.

Chest heaving, she forced her eyes open. "You're annoying and aggravating in bed too."

This time his smile creased his cheeks and stabbed her in a place he had no business intruding. "You like me this way." He taunted her playfully, pushing in an inch deeper. "Stay with me. I want to watch you come on my cock."

Desperate for him, Juliet maintained the intimate link as he worked his rather large erection into her body. She was tight after her unintended celibacy, but he didn't hurt her. He'd made very certain she was slick enough to take him. And take him she did; he filled her up until she was shuddering from the sense of completion.

But of course he wasn't done.

Leaning down to brace himself with one hand on the sheet, her legs wrapped around his waist, he closed his free hand over her breast and tugged once again at her nipple as he began to move. Three long, easy strokes before his rhythm altered.

If everything else had been slow and maddening, this was hard and deep and raw. His hand clenched on her breast and his eyes locked with hers as he began to move faster and rougher, his breathing uncontrolled and harsh.

"Fuck, Jules!" he groaned, his neck muscles taut as his back stiffened.

His primal pleasure ignited hers. There was no more thought, just the scent of Jake in her lungs, the feel of his big, strong body powering into hers one last time before he collapsed on her, the musk of sex in the air.

She came so hard she nearly blacked out.

16

IT'S THE QUIET ONES WHO HAVE
ALLLLL THE MOVES

Juliet wasn't sure what she'd expected afterward. Maybe a bit of awkward fumbling to get dressed, followed by an even more awkward goodbye, but after withdrawing from her, Jake lifted her in his arms and shifted her so she was lying fully on the bed. Juliet was still stuck on the fact that he'd *lifted her in his arms* when he returned from the bathroom to lie down naked next to her.

Both their chests heaved, their breathing short and harsh.

She wore only her newly raunchy bra and her flamingo socks. Cheeks hot, she pulled the cups back over her breasts. That made her feel better even though she was naked, naked, *naked*, in every other location except for her feet. Those silly socks had her wanting to grin—it was ridiculous that they'd had brain-liquefying sex while she wore them, but it made her feel as if it had been far more than a physical act.

Jake raised one knee, his foot flat on the bed. The defined muscle of his thigh under a dusting of dark hair made her want to lick her lips, as if she hadn't just come so hard that her lights had blown. He was just so pretty. The kind of pretty that made a sex slave out of a usually sensible woman.

So was it any surprise that when he turned to her with a lazy glint in his eye and put one hand on the side of her cheek, she let him turn her head toward his and kiss her? The kiss was slow and deep and unhurried, flicks and licks and tasting.

Juliet turned fully into him and he seemed more than okay with that, pushing one tautly muscled thigh between hers while fisting his free hand in her hair. She'd thought it would end with a kiss, but oh, it didn't. It was slower this time, his rough-skinned hand stroking over her softness with open appreciation and his mouth a lush caress on hers.

She didn't even care that, the best foreplay of her life or not, she was tender from the first time—*it had been a while, okay*. She wanted him, wanted this. He let her explore him as she wished, as generous with his body as he was every other way in bed.

But when he nudged his hand between her thighs and rubbed all the right things with just the right pressure—after saying insanely hot things like "Slow or fast?" and "Move my hand how you like it"—she gave up and held on for the ride.

He felt even bigger inside her the second time around.

She was a jellyfish by the end, a soft squishiness of postorgasmic bliss. Jake took his time getting up to take care of the condom, as if he'd had the wind knocked out of him too. She watched him come back into the room, all bronzed skin and muscle and that stunning ink, and couldn't quite believe he'd had his hands all over her—and that she'd had hers all over him.

She lifted her foot. "It's hot."

He tugged off one sock, then the other... and dropped a kiss on the top of her foot.

Butterflies took flight inside her as he walked around the bed to lie down next to her again.

"That's just made the problem worse, hasn't it?" he said.

She nodded, strands of her hair stuck across her face and her skin damp with perspiration. They might've scratched the itch, but in doing so had turned it into a chronic ailment—because now they knew how good it could be between them.

No, not good. SPECTACULAR.

"I didn't know sex could be like that." The unsophisticated words slipped out past all her sex-addled filters.

Instead of laughing at her, Jake said, "That was not normal."

Phew. At least he was discombobulated too.

Silence.

Until she started to feel uncomfortable for the first time since this began. Shifting a little, she managed to tug a soft fleece blanket over her body. "What happens now?" Her heart clenched even though she knew not to expect any kind of ugliness from Jake—he'd never been that way, and she didn't think he'd changed, not with what she'd seen of him.

He was no Reid.

"I have to go home," he said very deliberately. "We need to think about this."

She wanted to quip that there was nothing to think about, but the fact that she was lying naked in bed with Jacob Esera and wanted to jump his bones again told her she'd be a big fat lying liar. The scorching chemistry between them...

"Okay," she said. "That's sensible." She couldn't believe she'd said that. *Sensible.* Like an old grandma. But she felt tentative, not knowing where to go or what to say. Sleeping with Jake hadn't been in her five-year post-Reid plan. It hadn't been in *any* plan.

Jake's dark gaze held hers, but he didn't say anything further before getting up to dress. Her eyes lingered on the sculptured lines of his body for a moment before she made herself get up and grab her robe from where she'd thrown it over a chair the previous day. Printed with red hibiscus blooms and green foliage against a black background, it was a silky mid-thigh-length thing from Everett's autumn collection four seasons ago.

He'd gifted it to her after she worked seven days in a row to secure a critical supplier.

And she couldn't keep fiddling with the belt forever.

Turning on her heel, she left Jake to finish dressing and walked out. She was making a cup of tea when he exited the bedroom, his hair messy from her hands and a few small marks on his neck from either her mouth or her nails. Heat kissed her skin, but she kept it calm, channeling her professional self. "Drive safe."

A curt nod before he picked up his keys. "I'll call you."

Because this was Jake, she thought he probably meant that, but he'd come to his senses soon enough. Because while she'd been in the kitchen, she'd glanced at her phone and seen an alert that said she'd been mentioned in a recent media article. It had been nothing bad, simply a reference to Everett's upcoming campaign with Jake and his teammates —but the reporter had noted that the campaign was being coordinated by "former cricket WAG Juliet Nelisi."

It was a potent reminder that the tabloids would never let her live down her past. And Jake had both a kid and a squeaky-clean reputation to protect. Some of his sponsorship deals would likely fall over if he was linked to a scandal, but even worse, it'd hurt his daughter—children heard things from parents and repeated them in the schoolyard.

Juliet respected Jake for his fierce protectiveness toward Esme. She knew what it was like to grow up without a defender, understood how much hurt could be done to a small heart by a few thoughtless words.

Never would she hold his desire to protect his daughter against him.

"It's all right, Jake," she said gently after she'd opened the front door for him and he'd stepped out. "You don't have to call." She tucked her hair behind her ears. "Someone will catch us if we do this again, and that wouldn't be good for either you or me."

Any contact with a sports star, much less a sports star of Jake's caliber, would bring the tabloids knocking on her door. They'd throw up old accusations of her being a "gold digger," would reprint those pictures of her falling out of nightclubs at Reid's side. She had a different life now, and if she kept her nose clean for a couple more years, maybe the tabloids and women's magazines would forget her.

Jake frowned, grooves in his forehead. "Jules—"

Shaking her head at him, she smiled softly before closing the door. The sense of loss that came with the action shook her. It'd pass, she told herself as the quiet of her home settled around her again. She'd loved the quiet after leaving Reid, loved the peace, loved knowing no one would hurt her with thoughtless words or actions in this sanctuary.

Today, for the first time, the quiet felt empty.

JAKE STOOD outside Juliet's door for long seconds before he

could force himself to move. Everything in him rebelled against just leaving after she'd shared her body so generously and sweetly with him. Jacob Esera didn't *do* that.

He didn't generally stay overnight with women, but that was because he wasn't about to leave Esme with his parents all the time. It was different on nights like today, when Esme was with her cousin and his parents had plans to do grandparent-grandkid things the next day.

Then he'd stay with his lover, wake up the next morning, make her breakfast. Because he didn't do one-night stands. The small number of relationships he'd had since Calypso had *been* relationships. He'd never gone into a single one thinking it'd just be sex—a conscious decision on his part.

His life, who he was, meant sex was available anytime he wanted. To a lot of women, the simple fact he played professional rugby was aphrodisiac enough; they didn't care if he had two heads or sacrificed baby goats in his spare time. But as evidenced by Leo's constant presence in the gossip media, that sex came with all kinds of consequences, and Jake wasn't into that. He preferred to take his time, choose lovers who treasured their own privacy and would respect his.

He could smell Juliet on him as he drove away. Lush and aroused and sweet. The latter had surprised him—that sweetness inside her. She'd never been sweet that he knew, but she'd been Calypso's friend, not his.

He squeezed the steering wheel against the memories of two teenage girls laughing together in the sunshine, both in school uniforms. One with silky, straight blond hair, the other wearing a messy black braid, their smiles equally bright. Calypso, soft and plump and gentle; Juliet, all sharp angles and striking bones, a hardness to her.

Calypso would never change from that gentle young girl; she lived in the same past as the teenage boy he'd been.

Because despite the way some of the magazines tried to play up his "devotion" to his "first love," Jake wasn't stuck in the past. He'd grieved Calypso and he'd done it hard, but he didn't cling to her. The brokenhearted boy had grown into a strong, confident man, and that man lived in the present. The same present that held Juliet.

Someone will catch us if we do this again, and that wouldn't be good for either you or me.

She was right. She was thinking. He had to do the same.

Because this wasn't just about his need for privacy. He'd caught glimpses of how the media hounded her after the Reid saga; was it any wonder she wanted to stay away from another athlete who'd inevitably draw the same intrusive attention?

Better he let her go so they could both live their lives in peace. Even if the time they'd spent together felt as if it had altered something fundamental inside him.

17

BREAKING NEWS! MAJOR SCANDAL!

J ake didn't sleep well that night, but he turned up to the team's morning training run ready to go. This was a deliberately public training session to celebrate the naming of the new squad; the public wanted to see them together as a group. Their actual training camp wouldn't happen for another three weeks, and most of the squad would return to their home bases in the interim.

New Zealand's top coaches had realized at some point that superfit athletes couldn't get any fitter beyond a certain point. Overtraining could actually lead to injury. The camp would be as much about mental strength and how to use that strength to win the game as anything else.

Today, however, the squad jogged up one of Auckland's volcanic cones in the lingering fog, and while everyone bitched and cursed, they all made it up without problem. The view from the top was breathtaking, the sun's rays breaking through the clouds to bathe the city and its various waterways in pale golden light.

Hands on his hips as the team took a moment to appreciate the view before they dropped for a punishing set of push-ups, Jake found himself thinking of another kind of beauty altogether: Juliet.

Pastry maker. Businesswoman. Allergic to sports. And wearer of flamingo socks.

He only had pieces of her, and now he'd never learn any more. His gut grew hot and tight, the taste of wrongness in his mouth.

"Drop!"

Jake snapped into focus, dropping to the ground to begin his first push-up. But even as he made sure his form was flawless, his reps perfectly in time, a part of his brain remained dedicated to its quiet cataloging of Juliet, the woman who could jerk his chain faster than anyone else on the planet. The woman with whom he'd had the most phenomenal sex of his life. And the woman with whom he forgot to be staid, serious Jacob Esera and became a younger man with far less weight on his shoulders.

The way down the mountain was easier, and he ended up beside Danny. His brother might be the youngest member of the squad, but he was as disciplined and determined as any of his older teammates. Yeah, Danny could party, but unlike Reid Mescall, the youngest Esera brother limited his big nights out to the off-season.

During the season, the entire squad ate clean, slept solid hours, and maintained strong bodies capable of brutal bursts of speed. Even Leo followed the team rules—he went out with a different woman every evening, but you wouldn't find any photos of him in the clubs after a certain time of night; underneath his womanizing surface, the man fans called the Lion was one of the best second five-eighths in the world.

"You see Boo and Sweetiepie this morning?" Jake asked his brother.

Danny had first put on the squad's iconic black jersey at age nineteen. He'd signed a major sponsorship deal six months later. As a result, he had far more money than most twenty-two-year-olds. Despite that, he hadn't gotten his own place, preferring to stay with Alison and Joseph when in the country.

Not to say that he was in his old room; no, Danny had his own apartment above the villa's detached double garage. He had privacy to come and go as he pleased, and their parents weren't the kind to monitor his movements anyway. It worked.

Jake himself hadn't moved out until Esme began to go to school. He could've never continued with rugby without his parents' support, much less made the national squad at age twenty-one. Ísa and Sailor, parents of an eleven-month-old at the time of Esme's birth, had also helped by passing on their own experiences and talking with him and Calypso in the late-night hours when they got up to settle a restless Emmaline.

After Calypso's death, Ísa had pumped milk for Esme for a long time.

His mother had talked him into counseling, then driven him to every single appointment to make sure he went. At the beginning, she'd gone with him and done most of the talking while he sat numb and broken, mechanically rocking the bassinet in which he'd carried Esme around, unable to let her out of his sight.

All three of his brothers as well as his father had run plays with him in the backyard to prepare him for selection to a local team after he fell away from the sport for nearly a year.

Sailor, the brother who'd never wanted to play professional sports, had watched and rewatched Jake's training videos— shot by academically inclined Harlow—to figure out minute variations that had continuously improved his performance.

Gabe had become his personal taxi service, private coach, and occasional emergency babysitter, rocking Esme in his arms while he walked the sidelines and conferred with the team coach. Not many people in rugby turned down the Bishop's advice when he offered it.

Catie'd come along when she was in the city, the faces she'd pulled making baby Esme giggle. Ísa had hugged him so many times, sensing his fear of fucking up and getting it all wrong. Danny, called up to the national squad two months before Jake, had made Jake eat, drink, and train to the squad's schedule.

So many hands, all there to catch him when he fell.

"Yeah." Danny's voice and grin cut through the echo of Juliet's voice. "The two were sneaking around at six this morning, getting out the cereal and milk. I spotted them in the kitchen from my place and came down to make them waffles. Just so you know—*I'm* the favorite today."

Jake felt his cheeks crease. "Did you use the teddy bear waffle maker?"

"You think I'm an amateur?" Danny snorted. "Of course I used the teddy bear one." The aged trees of the park that surrounded the volcanic cone passed on either side of them, the branches heavy with dark green foliage.

Another one of their teammates ran forward to join them. "I heard your bro got married." Ambrose's pale skin was brushed with a slight pink flush from the cold and the exercise, a tight knit cap snug on his shaved-bald head. "Congrats. Damn Bishop."

Jake was used to that worshipful tone when it came to

Gabriel. He probably sounded the same when he talked about his big brother's exploits on the field. "Yeah, it was a great day."

"Only you two left now." The heavily built flanker waggled his eyebrows. "Who will the wedding bells ring for next?"

"Since Jake is a monk," Danny quipped, "it'll probably be me. A child groom."

As the two laughed, Jake put down his head and ran on. He hadn't felt like a monk last night. Not even close. He'd felt good, that's what. So, *so* good. Until he'd wanted to curl up around Juliet and sleep through the night, wake with her in his arms.

"Yo, Jake!" Christian was running backward so he could look at Jake.

"Yeah?"

"Piri wants you to show him that move you did in your final game against us." A proud member of the Southern Blizzard, Christian scowled at the memory of the game that had put the regional trophy back in Harrier hands. "The one where you fucking defied gravity and set up a try in the last fifteen goddamn seconds."

"Could do with the help, man." Piri turned to look over his shoulder. "I don't want to be on the bench forever."

Jake considered it. "It won't work for you." The reserve lock's build was too different, his biggest strength his brute power and relentless work ethic, whereas Jake relied more on speed, acute accuracy in passing, and rapid sidesteps. "But I have an idea. Talk when we get back."

As Christian and Piri turned back around, Jake had a thought—he fixed things on the field all the time. His brain was expert at coming up with strategic plays on the run. In that championship final against the Southern Blizzard, the

Harriers' planned play had actually collapsed in a mess of fumbles and bad passes.

Not only that, but they'd lost a key player to a red card.

So Jake had rearranged the pieces on the rapidly moving chessboard and sent Vili over the try line. The stadium had exploded at the last-ditch win for the Harriers and the attendant loss for the Blizzard as Jake's teammates swarmed him and Viliame in a jubilant mass.

Given all that, why the hell was he just accepting that he had to walk away from Juliet? Did he want to look back when he was an old man and wonder what could've been? Did he want to go back to how he'd felt before Juliet woke him up with her snark and her wit and her laughter? Did he want to stew in regret and cowardice?

Fuck that.

Jacob Esera didn't walk away from anything. He figured out how to make the pieces fit, how to fix the problem, how to reshape the chessboard.

His priorities shifted, with Juliet going to the top of his private list. Because this, what was going on between them, it wasn't just scorching sexual attraction. It was far too complicated for that, even if Juliet would probably gnaw off her own foot before admitting it.

Jake set his jaw.

Sharing cake, picking up spectacles for a little girl, sniffling at the wedding when she thought no one could see, Juliet Nelisi was a complex, infuriating, beautiful package, and Jake wanted to know her inside and out.

AMPED NOW that he had a plan, he picked up his phone from the squad room when they got back. His family and Esme's school knew to direct emergency calls to Coach's cell, and everyone else could wait. Focus was key when you played at this level.

It wasn't until after he'd showered and packed up his gear that he glanced at his phone again. He grinned at the message from Esme. She'd sent him a selfie using her grandmother's phone, bright yellow life jacket on, and a child-sized fishing rod in hand. He could count her teeth, her smile was so joyously wide.

He sent her a return selfie of him with what she called his "serious face."

The team was now scheduled to visit a local school team where they'd watch the end of a weekend game, then throw the ball around with the kids—no doubt while being watched by an audience of parents and other students as well as random members of the public.

It sounded like a cynical PR exercise, but it wasn't. A lot of men in this locker room had come from grassroots rugby backgrounds and strongly supported junior rugby—Jake included. It was tradition in his family that they didn't play for the clubs during high school, just their school teams. And okay, maybe there was a bit of superstition involved too.

Gabe had been scouted while playing for his high school's First XV. Jake and Danny, in love with the game since the first time they'd watched Gabe and Sailor play, had religiously followed their big brother's path. Whether they'd had it easier or harder was a debatable question—yes, the scouts had turned up to their games to see if the Bishop's brothers had his magic, but that had meant a level of expectation-based stress Gabe had never experienced.

He'd counseled them to shut it all out. "Play for the love of the game. Play because when you slam the ball down past that try line or kick that goal, it's a rush you can't describe.

The minute you start playing for the selectors or the crowd, you lose your edge."

It was advice Jake held close even now.

While he waited for the others to get ready to leave, he decided to scan a couple of news sites. The usual bad news, weather, sports roundups.

Juliet Nelisi...

He snapped his eyes back to the place where he'd spotted her name. The piece featured an old photo of Reid and Juliet coming out of a club. The cricket player was holding a bottle of champagne in one hand, Juliet's hand in the other. Her hair flew back from her face, her glittery gold dress so short it barely reached the tops of her thighs.

She was painfully thin.

He frowned as he skimmed the article. To call it that was an insult. It was nothing but a "scoop" from a "source close to Juliet" stating that Reid and Juliet had "reconnected" and spent a "steamy night together." Since that had apparently been last night, either Juliet was far more energetic than anyone knew, or this was full of shit.

He'd bet his Harriers contract that Reid was the one who'd fed the gossip columnist.

The man was clinging to the last vestiges of his dubious fame even as he pissed away his athletic career—and he was using Juliet to get a couple of column inches. Asshole. About to text Juliet, Jake realized he didn't have her number.

A second's thought and he messaged his sister-in-law: *Issie, you got a number for Juliet? She left something in my car when I dropped her home after the barbeque.* No lie. Her scent was in the fibers of his entire vehicle and it was driving him nuts.

Ísa replied soon after with the number attached.

After thanking her, he tapped out a message to Juliet:

You need to sell a subscription to whatever tea you were drinking last night. I was wiped, but you decided to take on Reid too? Legend. – Jake

Her response lit up his phone half a minute later: *You're hilarious, Jacob.* She'd added a grumpy panda sticker.

Grinning, he tucked away his phone just as Leo reached him.

"Jeez, what the hell is that on your face?" the other man quipped. "Could it be that the Saint is having a moment of hilarity?"

Jake groaned; he hated that nickname, born of his serious on-field nature and ability to "miracle" difficult passes, but it showed signs of sticking like superglue. The Bishop and the Saint. People thought they were geniuses. "You forget I'm your ride home, Simba? I think you want to walk."

Throwing back his head, Leo roared. "King of the jungle!"

Multiple rolled-up towels hit his head.

18

NO ONE MESSES WITH JAKE'S PEOPLE

Esme was waiting for him on the porch of his parents' house when a frustrated Jake drove up late afternoon that day. Reid had screwed up all his plans regarding Juliet. One shot of him anywhere near her and the small media squall would blow up to nightmarish proportions.

So he'd gritted his teeth and stayed put... and kept checking his phone like a besotted teenage boy. But Juliet hadn't messaged him again. So he'd messaged her. No pain, no gain. *I found a picture of Reid and printed it out for your new voodoo doll.*

I'm trying to work here, had been the response.

On a Sunday?

I'm a vice president. Attached had been the meme of a serious-looking cat at a desk, spectacles firmly on. *I have admin stuff to clear at the office since I had to babysit a bunch of rugby players who think they're models.*

So, he'd written, *no to the voodoo doll?*

Find a piece of his clothing, minion. Then I shall do my spells. Now, this VP is going back to work.

Realizing she was serious, he'd stopped with the messages but had gone online and ordered a bunch of flowers to be delivered to her office. Roses in darkest red. Lush and bold and sexy. Like Juliet.

He'd paid the exorbitant Sunday rate to ensure delivery within the hour.

Knowing the attached note might be seen by nosy parkers, he'd written: *These reminded me of you. (Except for the lack of thorns.) – J.*

Another woman would've seen that as an insult. Juliet, however, had replied with: *My thorns are extra stabby today. Keep your distance.*

That had been four hours ago, and while Jake had let her get on with her work, he wasn't planning to heed the warning. For the first time in his adult life, he felt like taking risks. It was scary as all hell, but so had been holding Esme for the first time. So had been trying out for a team after his grief-and-shock-fueled hiatus.

With risk came incalculable rewards.

"Daddy!" Esme flew down the stairs to him.

Grabbing her in his arms, he spun her around. "Did you catch any fish for dinner?"

"No! My fishies was small, so I threw them back!" She wrapped one arm around his shoulders as he climbed the stairs.

He bumped fists with Sailor when he walked into the kitchen, unsurprised by his brother's presence. He'd seen Sailor and Ísa's vehicle parked outside. After putting his daughter down so she could run outside to play with Emmaline and her grandfather, he hugged his sister-in-law.

When he bent to peck his mother on the cheek, he got hauled down for a proper hug. "We're having fish and chips for dinner," she told him. "You've just volunteered to grill the fish. Ísa, you set yourself down and take a load off."

Jake caught his sister-in-law's faint blush, saw the glance exchanged between her and Sailor, and narrowed his eyes. "You two are keeping secrets."

Ísa burst out laughing, gray-green eyes sparkling. "I *told* you." She pressed one hand to Sailor's chest. "I said your brothers would figure it out the instant they laid eyes on us."

Hooking one arm around her neck, blue-eyed Sailor kissed his wife's temple. His expression and grin were that of a man living his happiness. "You're going to be an uncle again, bro."

A huge smile cracked Jake's face. "An oops, huh?"

Sailor threatened to deck him while Ísa laughed and said, "No, a planned joint project."

A backslapping hug between brothers, a gentler hug for Ísa.

"You better tell the others," he said afterward. "Gabe will beat you dead if he's the last to know, and Danny will sulk."

Sailor glanced at his watch. "Where is Danny anyway?"

"On an orchard out Kumeu way," Alison answered. "Birthday dinner for a friend from his sports psychology course."

While Sailor called Gabe, then Danny, Jake got more details out of Ísa, including that the couple had found out the week before the wedding but hadn't wanted to steal Gabriel and Charlotte's moment—but that had meant amusing stealth shenanigans where Ísa avoided alcohol without tipping anyone off.

"I have to apologize to the plants in Charlie's home," she said with a giggle at one point. "Poor things are probably drunk from all the wine I poured into the pots!"

The happy, celebratory mood continued through dinner

—and Jake kept thinking of how much Juliet would enjoy this casual get-together. If Reid hadn't stirred up the media, Jake would've had his mother invite her. Jules might tell Jake to take a hike, but she'd say "Yes, ma'am" if it was Alison who made the call.

Alison Esera hadn't raised no idiot.

It was post-dinner that the trouble hit.

Helping with the cleanup, he emptied the kitchen garbage bin, then walked out into the early-evening dark and over to the hidden spot behind the garage where his parents stored their external garbage bins. Once he'd dumped the slick black trash bag inside, he pulled the wheeled green bin out to the curb, having remembered it was trash pickup day on this street tomorrow.

It was as he was about to return to the house that he spotted the media van parked down the road. He frowned, but the reporter getting out of the passenger-side door wasn't looking in the direction of his parents' home. She was motioning for her cameraman to follow her to Reid's place.

Glad it was dark enough that the reporter hadn't spotted him, he melted away into a pool of shadows cast by the large jacaranda tree his mother had planted when she and his father first bought this place. It had grown as Alison's sons had grown, and come spring, it'd carpet the entire front area of their home in a shower of purple-blue blooms.

Jake had seen the photos of what had been a run-down and neglected villa back then, its paint flaking and its plumbing shaky at best. Gabriel and Sailor had helped their mother and new stepfather strip the paint, clean the gutters, replace old boards, and in the doing, they'd laid the foundations for the unbreakable family unit into which Jake, then Danny, had been born.

Across the road, the reporter and cameraman pushed

open a little wooden gate and strode up to Reid's front door. Instinct telling him to stay put, he watched as the reporter knocked. Reid's model girlfriend opened the door, all masses of mahogany-brown hair and stacked body.

Jake had actually met Lisa Swan once or twice. She was one of those women who hung around pro athletes. He wasn't into groupies, but she'd cornered him at a teammate's anniversary party. He'd come away from the conversation having revised his opinion of her—she was good at giving the impression of being an airhead, but she was highly intelligent once you chipped away that surface.

Now he saw her gesticulating. Though he was too far away to catch her words, it was clear that she wasn't telling the reporter to get lost. No, she seemed to be speaking *into* the camera.

A cold and angry feeling began to coalesce in the pit of his stomach.

Shifting so that he was behind the hedge, out of sight of the street, he pulled out his phone and looked up the news sites. The gossip sections had exploded. What had begun as a small and titillating piece about Reid and Juliet's imaginary renewed romance had turned into a huge cheating scandal.

He knew without a single doubt that Reid's girlfriend was doing the wronged-girlfriend bit right now.

Which cast Juliet as the evil mistress.

Muscles bunched and blood in his eye, Jake called Juliet. He knew both her closest friends were currently away from her. Charlotte was out of the country and yesterday, at the barbeque, Aroha had mentioned she'd be leaving the city today for a week in the Bay of Islands.

Juliet had been handling this on her own all day.

The phone rang and rang on the other end, and he was

beginning to think she wasn't going to pick up when she answered.

"What?" Her voice was curt, tight, sharp echoes of the angry girl he'd known in school.

Jake wanted to crush her to him, just hold her close so she'd know he had her back, that she didn't have to do this alone. "I wanted to check in, see how you're doing. I just caught up with the bullshit online."

A long pause before she said, "Why are you so sure it's bullshit?"

Because if there was one thing he knew in the deepest part of himself, it was that Juliet didn't lie or cheat; her up-front honesty was a core part of her nature. "I'm a master-mind. Want to see my Mensa membership card?"

"Great, you think you're a comedian these days," she muttered, but he heard the faintest thawing in her voice. "One of my neighbors called to warn me that the reporters were camped out in front of my place. I'm still at the office. I figured I'd book myself into a hotel tonight."

Now that pathetic excuse for a man was driving her away from her own home. "It's about to get worse," he warned. "Reid's girlfriend is currently giving an on-camera interview. Full drama."

The swear word that Juliet spit out was as blue as a summer sky. "I don't want to be part of any of this! Why is Reid forcing me into it?"

"Because he's a fame-hungry has-been about to get dropped from his team." Jake glanced over to see that the reporter and cameraman were striding back down to the van. Another media van, however, was just pulling in. *Jesus, it was going to end up a circus.*

"I'll survive." Juliet sounded like she was gritting her teeth. "I did the last time. Back then I was the vicious gold digger who broke Reid's heart—even though the only thing he has in the cavity where his heart should be is an alcohol-pickled prune." She snorted. "Reid conveniently forgot to mention that I'd signed an ironclad prenup, he'd pissed away his money, and oh, that he was sleeping with Lisa well before we separated."

Jake wanted—*needed*—to help her, offer refuge, while at the same time kicking in Reid's face. But this localized scandal would become a massive international one the instant his name was thrown into the mix. Reid would use Jake's far bigger profile to push his own in the media. Caught in the middle would be Juliet, who wanted to live her life free of media stalking, and Esme, innocent and sweet and sheltered from the kind of spotlight courted by those who sought to be celebrities.

But no fucking way was he just leaving Juliet to the sharks. They were far more to each other now than just old antagonists—and Jake looked after his people. "You don't need to get a hotel room," he said, thinking quickly. "My family keeps an apartment on the waterfront. It's empty right now."

It had been a gift to Alison and Joseph from their four boys.

Mostly his parents used it as their getaway place in the city. They'd go to a show, eat at one of the fancy restaurants, walk hand in hand down the waterfront. But Alison and Joseph had been adamant they'd only accept the gift if their sons promised to use it as well.

Gabe's home was in the city anyway, but Sailor and Ísa had used it for date nights, and Danny and his friends crashed there the times they went clubbing. Once in a while, Jake took the girls there for a treat. He'd order their favorite takeout, take them up to see the sparkling view from the Sky Tower, or out to get ice cream in Mission Bay. The two would sit with their cones alongside the fountain by the beach, feeling very grown-up at being out at night.

"That's very nice of you." Juliet's voice was stiff. "But I can take care of myself."

"I know." He was beginning to realize exactly how long she'd been doing that. "But let's try being friends, Jules. After last night, we owe it to each other. And friends step in when the shit hits the fan." It bugged him that she hadn't messaged him when things began to blow up, *really* bugged him, even though rationally he knew they didn't have that kind of relationship.

Not yet anyway.

A long silence before she said, "I appreciate the offer, but you'd have to come out of your way to give me the keys—"

"It's all electronic locks with numeric codes," he said. "I'll text you the address and the codes." He'd also tell his family the apartment was in use so no one would disturb her. "The place has excellent security. No reporter's going to ambush you in the hallways, and you can drive directly into the secure underground garage."

An aggravated sound on the other end. "When did you get so bossy, *Jacob*?"

He didn't know why he always wanted to smile when she said *Jacob* in that tone. "Survival instinct," he shot back. "You try having Gabe for a big brother. Steamroller has nothing on the Bishop."

A startled kind of laugh. "You're selling me on this apartment deal—especially with the drive-in garage."

Jake's shoulders began to unbunch. "So you'll go?"

"Yes," she said. "Just for tonight. Hopefully the circus will have calmed down by tomorrow."

Jake hoped so for her sake, but he wasn't positive, not

with Reid and Lisa fanning the flames. After hanging up, he quickly sent Juliet the details of the apartment and received a reply saying she'd message him once she was successfully inside.

Gut still tense, he fought off the urge to go across to Reid's and instead walked into the house. Everyone was back in the kitchen once again. Esme and Emmaline were whispering to each other in one corner, no doubt complaining about soon being woefully separated by their unfeeling parents, while the adults were gathered around, divvying up leftovers.

Food did not go to waste in Alison Esera's house. She'd experienced extreme poverty after her first husband drained their bank accounts and abandoned his family. Of her two boys then, Gabe had been the worst affected, but Sailor hadn't been far behind. It wasn't until he was a young teen that Jake had truly understood how lucky he'd been to be born into the stable, supportive unit formed by Alison, Joseph, Gabe, and Sailor.

Now he needed his family to extend their support to Juliet.

"I've lent the city apartment to Juliet," he said during a lull in the conversation before explaining why—including what he'd just seen outside.

His mother slammed down the knife she'd been using to cut the leftover homemade cheesecake. "That Reid Mescall shouldn't have anything to do with a good woman. I've seen his interviews, seen how he talks about her. It's disgraceful."

Ísa's expression was no less furious when she said, "Juliet was telling me before the wedding about how proud she is of this new launch she's coordinating—the one you modeled for, Jake—and it almost seems like Reid's trying to ruin that."

Jake didn't think Reid had planned that far ahead, but it didn't matter if the effect was the same. "Hopefully none of the really big media organizations will pick it up."

Sailor made a face. "You know it's all about clicks these days."

"At least they can't manufacture more scandal out of the fact she's staying at the apartment." Ísa was tapping out a message on her phone as she spoke. "I mean, everyone already knows she was a bridesmaid at Charlotte's wedding." Sending the message, she looked up, "I told her to call if she needs anything."

Jake hadn't even considered that the media knew the apartment belonged to his family. But his sister-in-law was right: Danny had, with Gabriel and Charlotte's permission, shared photos from their wedding day on his social media. The shots taken by the public had also gone viral when they were posted, especially the one someone had snapped of Charlotte laughing with her bridesmaids.

No one could use Jake's family to hurt Juliet.

19

ICE CREAM

Juliet was still second-guessing herself when she punched in the door code of the exclusive waterfront apartment. She'd had dinner delivered to her office, sharing the meal with Kalia after the photographer swung by to show her images from a catalog shoot she'd done on Saturday. The other woman had offered to get compromising photos of Reid so Juliet could blackmail him into silence.

"Because you know that fuckwit compromises himself all the time," Kalia had muttered over her chicken satay. "It'll be a cinch."

Juliet was seriously considering the offer. What use was it being a good person if a man like Reid could wreck your life on a whim? She'd said as much to Kalia, who'd nodded in agreement, her face the picture of sweetness while her dark brown eyes held pure vengeance.

Of mixed Vietnamese and Indian descent, Kalia might be tiny and soft-looking, but she knew how to hold a grudge —especially on behalf of her friends. Also, she competed in mixed martial arts as a hobby and could probably break Reid in half.

Click.

The red light on the panel went green to indicate the door was now unlocked.

Stepping inside, she locked the door behind herself, then put down the overnight bag she always had in the boot of her car. Every so often, Iris needed her to put out a fire and Juliet had to get on a plane on short notice. It was easier to keep a set of necessities and a couple of changes of clothes ready to go rather than rushing around to pack on the day.

The light switch beside the door was slightly illuminated to stand out in the dark, and she soon had the living area bathed in light. The entire back wall was glass. Water gleamed dark and silken beyond, what looked like a party boat festooned with lights floating some distance out. The islands of the Hauraki Gulf were visible as dark silhouettes against the night sky.

Her phone rang in her hand.

Glancing down, she frowned at the unknown number. This was her fiercely guarded private line. The call ended, but she got the ping for a voice mail not long afterward. When she checked, she felt her eyes widen.

Frantically exiting voice mail, she returned the call. "Alison," she said. "I'm so sorry I didn't pick up. I thought you might be a reporter."

"I understand, honey. I saw the dark side of the media when Gabriel had his injury—they were like parasites wanting to suck my boy dry when he was already hurting."

Juliet had never heard Alison sound so harsh. "Thank you for calling," she said, not quite sure what to do with the attention. Ísa's message had been surprise enough.

"I wanted to make sure you were doing okay." A warm tone that wrapped around Juliet like a blanket. "You're going to our apartment, yes?"

"I just stepped inside. It's beautiful."

"I'm not sure if there's any fresh milk in the fridge," Alison said, "but I always keep a packet of long-life milk in the pantry as an emergency backup."

Juliet had to sit down, her body felt so strangely weak under the wave of maternal attention. "Okay," she said. "I'll have a look."

"You should find plenty else to eat in the kitchen— frozen meals included. Danny and his friends know to stock things back up after they've gone through it like a horde of locusts. If you need anything at all, you make sure to call. It's an easy drive for us."

Staring out at the party boat on the water, Juliet blinked back tears and bit down hard on her quivering lower lip. "Thank you," she whispered. "That means a lot."

She was still sitting there, the phone in her hand and her throat hurting with suppressed emotion, when the screen lit up again. This time with a message: *Are you in the apartment? I have to put my little grumpy guts to bed. I'll call after.*

Juliet squeezed the phone. Suddenly afraid, she replied: *I'm here and going to bed. Talk tomorrow.*

That done, she sat there and stared out at the darkness lit only by the boat on the water. All those people partying and dancing and pretending to be happy. Maybe they actually were happy. Or maybe, like her, they had a loneliness inside them. A loneliness that wondered what it would be like to have Alison's attention anytime she needed, to be part of a big loyal family who'd back her against the world.

And to have Jacob Esera put his stubborn, serious mind to keeping her safe.

Terrifying thoughts for a girl who'd been alone her entire life except for friendships that were a bulwark against the dark. But Calypso was gone, Iris and Everett had families of their own, Charlotte was transitioning to the next stage of her life, and Aroha was falling fast for an equally smitten Harry. Even Kalia was heading off on one of her travel-photo projects soon.

Juliet felt like an island alone in the ocean.

"Don't be dramatic, Jules." Annoyed with herself, she pushed up to her feet. "Charlie and Aroha and the others aren't disappearing into outer space. It's just this mess with Reid that's screwing with your head. Put your phone on Do Not Disturb mode, sleep, get up with a fresh mind. It'll have blown over by morning."

Her phone buzzed. Of course it was Jake. The man did not give up.

Wondering why she actually kinda liked that stubbornness in him, she answered, "Can't you read?" It came out snarly.

"Did you bring home my roses?"

Juliet's eyes went to her work satchel, from the corner of which poked the head of a single dark red rose. She'd left the others on her desk at the office, their perfume lush in the air.

Kalia had taken one look at them and raised an eyebrow. "Wow, some dude knows what he's doing. No pansy-ass daisies like that guy who hit on you last time."

"Daisies are nice," Juliet had protested while fighting not to fondle the rose petals as she'd been doing since they were delivered.

"Yeah, for another woman." Kalia had pointed a satay

skewer at her. "You're not daisies, you're sexy red roses that smell like heaven." A long breath. "Tell me he's good in bed. I need it for my fantasies."

When Juliet almost choked on her own bite of satay chicken, Kalia's grin had grown to gigantic proportions.

"Oh my gawd. He's *that* good?" A shiver. "I hope he screws the bad day right out of you tonight, then lets you parade him through the streets tomorrow to stick it to Reid."

That last had put a damper on Juliet's giddy excitement. Roses were easy, private. Anything more public— *Juliet, you're a grade-A idiot.*

"Jules, you asleep?"

"No." She'd just been hit over the head with the fact she was sitting in Jake's family's apartment. How much more public could their support get? "Jake, this isn't going to blow back on—"

"You were Charlotte's bridesmaid."

"Oh right." Slumping back in the sofa on a wave of relief, she said, "Why are you bothering me? I want to get into my pajamas and eat a tub of ice cream."

"Go check if there's any in the freezer."

"Do I look like your slave?" she muttered nonsensically because sparring with Jake was instinct, but she went to check since she really wanted that ice cream. At first she thought she'd struck pay dirt, but when she opened the two-liter tub, she almost cried. "Someone left like a bite of strawberry in here."

"Danny," Jake said darkly. "What flavor's your favorite?"

"Rocky road," she groused while deciding she might as well eat the measly bite that was left since that was all she was going to get. "Why was Esme grumpy?"

"Poor mistreated thing was cruelly separated from her best buddy." Dry as dust, Jake's tone had her grinning. "I pointed out that she'd see Emmaline at school tomorrow and was told that I didn't understand because I had no best friend."

"Ouch." She licked the spoon.

"I tell you, Jules, kids are brutal." His amused tone didn't match his words. "Go get into your pj's. Night concierge will ring up in a bit." A sound in the background. "Gotta go. Esme just got out of bed for the fifth time to stomp to the bathroom. Time for me to be mean dad again."

He was gone before she could ask him why the concierge was going to be calling her. Hanging up feeling a whole lot better than she had before his call, she left the empty ice cream container and spoon in the sink for now. She'd wash up and find the internal recycle bin for the container after she'd changed and wiped off her makeup.

It was as she'd just finished braiding her hair into a loose tail, her body clad in a simple gray tank and pink boxer shorts, that the intercom buzzed. Not sure she should answer, she remembered what Jake had said and chanced a wary "Hello?"

"Hello, ma'am," said a crisp male voice. "We've just accepted a food delivery for your apartment. We'll bring it up now unless you have other instructions?"

Her toes curled into the carpet, a warmth deep inside her gut. "Please leave it outside the door after a knock. I'll grab it myself when I finish something I'm doing." She wasn't about to show off her braless tits to some random man—because said tits were large and the tank didn't exactly cover them enough for public view.

She was all but bouncing on her toes by the time the knock came. But she forced herself to wait another full minute before she cracked open the door and pulled the insulated carrier inside. Putting it on the counter, she zipped it open to find two tubs of rocky road ice cream.

Yes, some dude *definitely* knew what he was doing.

JULIET WENT to sleep full of ice cream and smiles, but when she woke at around six a.m., it was to find her phone's home screen littered with so many messages and missed-call notifications that it was pure gibberish. *Great.* One of her contacts had either decided to go into the gossip business or had inadvertently sold her out to a sneaky reporter pretending to be a business contact.

Quickly clearing away the notifications from unknown numbers, she smiled as she came to one from Charlotte. Her friend had called just after ten thirty the previous night, then followed up with a text message: *I'll help you kill him. Gabriel says he'll dig the hole to bury the body—and he'll plan the entire thing so no one ever suspects us.* Emojis followed—of shovels and pickaxes, then hugs and hearts.

Startled into a much-needed smile, Juliet shot back a reply: *I might just take you up on that.*

Kalia's message was a photoshopped image of Reid in which he had a paunch, a bad comb-over, and a unibrow. Below it, she'd written: *The future you escaped for the hottie sex god who sends you roses.*

Laughing, Juliet sent back a laugh-crying emoji in response.

Everett and Iris had both called yesterday to ensure she was all right. Aroha had also called then—and she'd joined Juliet in verbally eviscerating Reid, his character, *and* his fading athletic career. It had made Juliet feel so much better. Now she saw her friend had sent another message close to eleven the previous night: *Kia kaha, my heart. You're far tougher than Reid the Pinhead. All my love.*

Juliet's eyes burned. And she'd been feeling so lonely and alone before Jake called her last night. Here was her tribe. Here was her family.

The next message in her queue was from a surprising source: Molly. While she and the other woman had gotten along great, they hadn't known each other long enough to become friends. Then she remembered that Molly had been through a horrific media onslaught herself. She was probably messaging to commiserate.

But when she read the text, it said: *Jake let us know what was happening. You'll be getting a call from this number.* What followed was an American number and the words: *Pick up.*

She checked, saw that she didn't have a missed call from that number, but even as she was about to message Molly to ask what she'd meant, her phone lit up with the American number.

"Hello," she said, unsure what was going on.

"Juliet," said a confident female voice. "This is Thea Arsana. Molly's sister."

"Um, hi?"

"I'm a publicist. And sweetheart, you need a publicist."

Juliet's eyes widened as she finally clued in to the woman's name. Thea repped Fox's megamillion-dollar rock band. "I can't afford—"

"As if I'd charge you," Thea said in a tone that brooked no argument. "You're one of Molly's friends. Also, your ex is a dickhead. I have a hard-on for exes who are dickheads."

Head spinning, Juliet rubbed her forehead. "I don't need a publicist. It'll blow over."

A small pause before Thea said, "Have you seen the video his girlfriend gifted the media last night?"

When Juliet said no, Thea said, "I'm going to send you a link. Watch, then call me back."

Juliet did exactly as directed—she had a feeling not many people told Thea no. What she saw on the screen had her stomach roiling and anger knotting her gut. Lisa Swan, the woman who'd slept with *Juliet's then-husband*, had called Juliet a home-wrecker and a gold digger who wouldn't "remove her claws" from Reid.

But Lisa hadn't stopped with shredding Juliet's character, she'd intimated that Juliet had only gotten the job with Everett because of sexual favors. Worst of all, she'd sniped about how Juliet had managed to "worm" her way into the "wealthy and connected" Bishop-Esera family through her friendship with Charlotte.

"She's probably planning to hook one of the men." Lisa had curled her lip. "Since she's not too particular about if they're married or not, the Bishop-Esera wives better watch their men."

20

DO NOT MESS WITH JULIET NELISI

Calling Thea back on a wave of pure, blinding rage, Juliet fought to keep her voice even. "She is a lying disgrace to women everywhere!"

"I know that, sweetie. Did you notice how careful Ms. I'm So Overwrought was not to use any words the station would have to bleep out?"

"I didn't even notice that, I was so focused on not smashing my phone screen," Juliet admitted. "Reid slept with Lisa while we were still married. I never made it public." Though she'd been glad to be out of that toxic marriage, she'd felt humiliated nonetheless. Hard to feel any other way when she'd walked in on the two in her and Reid's marital bed.

Dickish move number two zillion.

Thea whistled. "Talk about pot and kettle—but we're not going to go down the road of exposing her. It'll just add fuel to the fire, and you know she'll lie her face off."

Juliet nodded, though Thea couldn't see her. "I've got no desire to rake up that muck either. It's in the past—where I wish Reid and Lisa would stay."

"I've put out some feelers," Thea said. "There's a reason they've orchestrated this media storm, and we're going to find out why."

Juliet squeezed, then flexed her free hand. "I've been trying to stay out of the spotlight. I want to have a normal life."

"Here's the thing," Thea responded in her crisp LA accent. "Right now they're writing the script. You can't win unless you take control. I can tell you how to douse the flames, but it'll mean a public appearance and statement."

Shoving off her blanket, Juliet strode to the windows that overlooked the water. "There's no other option?"

"There are always other options—but the easiest way to stop this is to be blunt and up-front and brutal in a way they won't expect. Don't play their games and don't hide—it'll make you look guilty when you have nothing to be guilty about." A short pause. "Right, I just looked up your boss. He's a dish. He also has a very muted online presence for someone with his level of success. Are you sleeping with him or have you ever slept with him?"

Juliet blinked, the insult burning her cheeks... until she realized this had nothing to do with insults. Thea just wanted to know what she was working with. "He's gay," she said. "He's also in a long-term relationship." Her stomach twisted again. "God, I hope his partner doesn't take Lisa's allegations seriously."

"Is he out?"

"Yes."

Everett was a private man, but he was open about his sexuality if the question came up—which it mostly did when women who didn't know hit on him. As Thea had pointed out, he was a dish. Kalia had been one of those enamored women, but the photographer had taken his gentle rebuff with cheerful grace and was now friends with both Everett and Rufus.

Clearly, the lazy-ass gossip columnist who'd done the initial upload had simply assumed Lisa's sexual allegation was a viable possibility.

"Why do you ask?" she said to Thea.

"Not our place to out someone who isn't." Thea sounded like she was tapping a pen on her desk. "What are the chances he'd let you use his name in a statement or make a statement of his own?"

Confused and overwhelmed, Juliet said, "Can I have a few minutes to brush my teeth and grab a cup of coffee?"

"Take the time you need, but remember, the faster we handle this, the faster it ends."

"I won't be long," Juliet said before hanging up and heading into the bathroom.

It wasn't until she had the coffee going that she called Jake. "Why did you sic Thea on me?" It had to have been Jake who'd contacted Molly and set things in motion.

"Because you need a barracuda, and Thea's a friendly barracuda." His voice was a little sleep-rough.

"How do you know?" she said, exasperated. "You just met Fox and Molly before the wedding."

"I'm a fan of the band."

"Oh." That wasn't so much of a surprise—he'd messed with her about the heavy metal, but he'd always blasted hard rock in his car.

"I've seen her on camera dealing with things over the years. I could tell no one messes with her."

Juliet bad-temperedly poured a mug of coffee. "So you took it upon yourself to organize my life?"

"I saw that recording late last night and I knew you'd be

drowning by morning," he said, unrepentant. "I threw you a life raft. Whether you take it or not is up to you."

It was annoying because he was right. He'd found her the help she needed, but he wasn't forcing her to do anything about it. "I suppose you expect thanks."

"What I expect are a few moments of peace before my daughter wakes up. Go away and let me drink my goddamn coffee."

He sounded so grumpy that she grinned. Looked like Jake wasn't a morning person. She grinned even harder when he hung up on her. Only he called back almost at once.

Answering, she said, "Yes, sunshine?"

"I forgot to tell you," he grumbled, "but I did a bit of ringing around last night. A few media contacts I trust. Not the gossip people, but serious journalists like Rachel—she was my wedding date and she's a good friend."

"What did you find out?"

"Reid and Lisa have been pitching a reality show to the networks. No one was interested because he's not even a D-list celebrity at this point. He's a drunk who's one failed selection away from total obscurity. Not much drama in that."

Rage was a scorching wind through Juliet. "I'm going to crush that little pinhead," she said with open fury. "After that, I'm going to come over and kiss you."

A grumpy "Don't come in the morning" before he hung up again.

Juliet immediately called Thea and passed on what Jake had dug up.

"Let me confirm that," Thea said. "Since one of the Bishop-Eseras is calling you, we don't have to put out a fire there, right?"

Charlotte's message had come late last night, after the recording had hit the gossip sites, and Jake had just told her he'd seen it. His response had been to connect her with Thea.

"Yes," she said, her throat rough. "They're backing me." A strange, beautiful thing.

"Good," said Thea. "While I check on the reality-show situation, your job is to talk to Everett, find out if he's okay with you using his name and referring to his sexuality. If not, we'll figure out another way."

Not only was her boss more than fine with her using his name and mentioning his long-term relationship, he was in a real temper. "Good thing Rufus knows I've never been attracted to women—and that I'm devoted to him. He rolled his eyes when we saw the video, kissed me, and told me not to waste my anger on that woman."

Everett clearly hadn't taken the advice, because he continued with, "But what if I were bi? Or our relationship newer? That bit of orchestrated drama could've hurt him." His voice was colder than she'd ever heard it. "If you need us to release a statement, we'd be happy to do so."

"I'll take care of Lisa and Reid," Juliet said, even more furious now—Everett was a kind and private man, and Lisa had hauled him into this with no regard to the damage she might do. "In fact, I will *more* than take care of them."

"I wouldn't bet against you, Jules. Go crush them. Oh, and Rufus says you should use his name too—I'm proud he's mine and he's equally proud that I'm his. I don't want anyone else pulling this shit."

Hanging up, she got herself dressed for the day, though she wasn't looking forward to driving into the knot of reporters who were no doubt clustered outside Everett's design studio and linked offices.

It was a stroke of luck that she always laundered, then put her favorite sleeveless dark green dress back in the overnight bag after wearing it. Tailored to shape around her body, it was made up of triangular panels. The first panel came over her breasts with the point on her hip. The second panel went in the opposite direction to end just above the knee. The third panel filled in the remaining space.

It sounded so simple, but thanks to design magic melded with a gorgeous fabric that didn't wrinkle, it made her look spectacular in a way that said she took no prisoners. Especially after she paired the dress with a pair of black stilettos boasting four-inch heels. Her hair she brushed into a sleek fall. She kept her makeup simple except for a pop of deep red on her lips.

She was a fucking vice president.

She was not the love-hungry young girl Reid had charmed into marriage.

She was also a woman who had a hell of a lot of friends. Real, would-back-her-against-all comers and bury-bodies-for-her friends. Friends who now considered Reid an enemy because he was her enemy.

As for Jake…

Her heart squeezed so hard that she had to drop that line of thought. It was too powerful, too scary. Because a man who'd fight for and beside her? It was the embodiment of every dream she'd ever had.

SHE WAS on the road and stuck in early-morning traffic by the time Thea called back. Putting the other woman through to her hands-free system, she said, "Thea, I'm here."

"I confirmed your information." A very barracuda-like

glee in Thea's coolly dangerous voice. "Now, here's what you're going to do."

Juliet listened and smiled. Maybe she didn't want the spotlight, but if Reid and Lisa were determined to push her into it, she was going to use it to burn the two of them to a crisp.

Thea signed off as Juliet pulled into the parking lot outside the E. E. Designs building. As she'd expected, the media hounds were waiting, no doubt slavering at the prospect of a bloodbath. She'd give them blood all right— but it wasn't going to be hers.

Getting out after she'd parked, her sleek work satchel in hand, she smiled at the hovering horde. The questions came thick and fast.

"Is it true that you and your boss have an intimate relationship?" was the loudest one. "That he promoted you because of it?"

Juliet allowed her smile to deepen. "Firstly, my job performance review and promotions come under the purview of Chief Operations Officer, Iris Truett. Secondly, the news that we have an intimate relationship has come as somewhat of a surprise to Everett and his partner, Rufus. Ms. Swan might believe I'm hot enough to circumvent sexual orientation, but alas, my wiles have failed miserably."

A reporter's mouth actually fell open in front of her.

"So," another one pushed on, "No basis in fact?"

"Everett and Rufus hosted both their families for a big dinner this weekend. It's not like they need me for a beard."

More than one reporter laughed. A couple, however, including the one who'd taped the interview with Lisa, were determined to take her down. "The allegations of cheating are more serious," she said sanctimoniously. "Especially as Lisa is pregnant."

Yeah, right. "It's come to my attention that Mr. Mescall and Ms. Swan have been pushing for a reality show titled *Superstar Love.*" It was Thea who'd unearthed that choice nugget; Juliet would've thrown up at hearing it if she hadn't been laughing so hard. "Unfortunately for them, no one has been biting."

A sudden quiet. She took the opportunity to forge on. "I have no need or desire to be on camera. I am the vice president of operations and supply of a company that is now trading in the high multimillions." A fact that terrified her on a regular basis but that Iris was teaching her to manage step by step.

The firm had older team members, but no one as integrated into the nitty-gritty of the business as Juliet. For the first time in her life, she'd found something at which she excelled, and she was lucky enough to have bosses who saw her skill and not her age or lack of a tertiary degree.

"Furthermore," she continued, "my tastes have improved vastly in the time since I divorced Mr. Mescall. These days I go for men, not spoiled little boys who throw tantrums to the media when they don't get their way."

She glanced at her watch. "Now, if you'll excuse me, I have a conference call with a large department store in New York that is itching to carry Everett's new collection." Everett deserved the plug after dealing with this bullshit.

More questions, this time about the deal.

"Patience," she said with a laughing smile. "All will be revealed in due time. But let's just say I've already booked a billboard in Times Square for our newest models."

21

INTERNATIONAL MOSTLY NAKED JAKE

Hair damp and a towel wrapped around his hips after the morning maintenance session at the gym with his Harriers teammates, Jake was about to reach for his phone when banter broke out among the team. This was a private location, the locker room empty of outsiders—which left the boys free to talk, no holds barred.

Soon everyone was shooting the shit and hassling one another.

A butt-ass-naked Ambrose yelled at Leo about the "pussy" weights he'd been lifting.

Leo's response was a raised middle finger and: "Yeah? Your girlfriend doesn't think I have pussy arms."

Everyone laughed. The joke was only funny because Ambrose's girlfriend was eight months pregnant with their first baby and so wildly in love with the flanker that they were a favorite with the entire country. No doubt the couple would be inundated with handmade gifts—apparently, the tiny black socks and tiny black hats and tiny black team T-shirts had already begun arriving.

Ambrose, good-natured and content in his relationship, grinned. "You only wish, Lion-Man."

"Yeah, yeah, you smug shit." Leo threw a towel in Ambrose's direction. "Cover up. We don't need to see your baby-making stick."

That had everyone cracking up again. Jake was still grinning when he dug out his phone to check how things were going with Juliet. He'd be very surprised if she hadn't taken total control of the situation by now.

He had a text from her as well as a missed call from his agent, Darren. He read the text first. It was ominous: *I promise I tried to talk them out of it. But it's you they want.* The words were followed by a smiley with its teeth stretched in a wide "oops" smile.

Eyes narrowing, he called Darren.

His agent didn't beat around the bush. "Everett Echert is calling in that bit in your contract that obliges you to give him ten days of your time for publicity and promotion. They want to use up five of those ten."

Jake leaned back against the wall, his muscles easing; trust Jules to mess with him by making it seem some big thing. At least now he could relax—she was obviously doing a whole lot better. "We'll have to clear it with team management."

"I already sorted that. You'll be back in time for the training camp—with a couple of days breathing room to get over any jet lag." Darren talked like the trial lawyer he'd once been, fast and confident. "I also asked if you could bring Esme with you. I know you like to take her on trips when you can."

That was because he had to leave her in his family's care so much during the season. "What? They want me to go around the country doing photo ops?"

"No," Darren said, then dropped the bombshell. "Everett just inked a massive deal with a major US-based retailer. That retailer wants to shoot a couple of promo pieces with you in New York, the big one for a billboard in Times Square. Sorry, my man, but you'll have to get in the underwear again."

Groaning, Jake shoved his fingers through his hair. "What about Vili, Leo, and Christian?" he asked beneath the buzz of conversation in the locker room. It wasn't only about visibility—he didn't want his teammates pushed aside just because a random buyer had decided Jake would make the better visual.

"They're fine," Darren said. "Everett's also inked several other deals. He and his team have been busy over the past few months. I have to let their agents give the guys the news first, but one's headed to Tokyo, another to Berlin, third to London."

Jake's eyes widened. "Everett's going global?"

"You better believe it. Buy Gabe a beer when you talk to him—I know he convinced you to take this gig, and because of that, you're about to make a shit-ton of money." Darren sounded like he was rubbing his hands in smug exaltation. "And don't forget to thank me, too, for negotiating you a contract that means you'll be paid extra for just breathing outside the country."

Jake's head spun as Darren continued on. "I'm sending the dates to your phone. Reply today and let me know if your cute kid is hitching a ride. I'll get the other side to arrange a babysitter for when you're on a shoot."

Jake stared at his phone after Darren hung up. He knew Esme would love to go with him—they'd done small daddy-daughter trips around New Zealand and she was always excited to travel. But the idea of her being watched by a stranger while he was on a shoot didn't sit right.

"Fucking Tokyo!" Phone to his ear, Viliame punched his fist in the air. "I'm gonna chow down on some butter ramen." He scanned the room. "None of you assholes better tattle to the nutritionist."

Leo was asking Vili what was going on when his own phone rang. Christian had already flown home to the South Island—they'd see him, Piri, and a number of others again when the national squad re-formed for the first proper training camp.

Not long afterward, Leo said, "This boy is going to strut his stuff in Berlin." Towel wrapped around his hips, he did a prancing walk down the center of the locker room.

Chaos erupted.

"Jesus Christ, Leo, have some respect for the sanctity of the locker room!"

"The greats would turn over in their rugby boots if they could see you!"

"Your smizing needs work anyway."

"Did you see how he wobbled on the turn? Three out of ten at best."

Leo, undaunted, took a bow. "At least I'm not so whipped I watch those modeling shows with my girlfriend."

"That's because you'd have to hang with a woman for longer than a night to actually have a girlfriend," Ambrose pointed out reasonably in his deep tone, the back of his shoulder bearing a tattoo of a love heart with the word BRIA inside it.

"What the hell is smizing?" Vili scratched his head.

Leaving the others to their banter, Jake got dressed, then grabbed his bag and headed out. They had a team meeting later today to talk over their season, but he was free for a couple of hours. The first thing he did after getting to the privacy of his car was call Juliet.

"New York?" he growled when she answered. *"Times Square?"*

"What?" she retorted. "You never had dreams of bright lights and fame?"

"Only when those lights illuminate a rugby field."

"Don't worry, Jacob. I'll be there to hold your hand."

Jake suddenly didn't give a shit about the giant billboard that would soon be sporting his underwear-covered family jewels. "You're coming to New York?" Heart thundering, he did an exultant fist pump.

"A senior member of the E. E. Designs team is going with each of you. It's Everett's brand. We have to manage it," she added, so prim and proper that he might've even fallen for it—if he was a sucker.

"Yeah?" he said slowly. "You gonna manage me, Jules?"

A hitch in her breath. "We will not be discussing that topic. And no more roses. My office smells like a funeral parlor."

He made a mental note to send her more roses every week—because that tone of hers? He'd heard it before. It was the one she used when she got flustered or scared and was trying to bluff her way out. "Don't worry, you'll have a tiny chaperone to protect your honor." Except when said tiny chaperone was sleeping—then all bets were off. "I'm thinking of taking Esme."

"Oh, you should!" Juliet's smile was in her voice, and he knew it was real. Juliet's snark was real and so was her delight. She wasn't much good at playing games or hiding how she felt.

"She'll adore it," Juliet continued. "I can keep an eye on her while you're doing the shoots and meetings."

That quickly, the decision was easy. He trusted Juliet, knew she'd care for Esme's heart. Not just because Esme was Calypso's baby girl but because that was who Juliet was as a person—twice when she'd ended up in detention, it had been because she'd decided to beat up bullies who'd been picking on weaker kids.

One bully had been a boy, the other a girl.

Neither had come out on top of Juliet. The woman was a ferocious warrior in defense of those she considered weaker and more vulnerable. Jake had been away on a rugby trip during the first fight, had found out what was going on after the second fight was nearly over.

It was a desperate text from Calypso that had sent him racing to the school's back playing field. He'd had to drag an enraged Juliet off her male opponent—a boy twice her size. She'd tried to kick the guy even as Jake literally lifted her away, knowing she'd be in even worse trouble if she landed a punch or kick that did more than bruise. As it was, she'd ended up in detention for a month.

Meanwhile, though the bully might've escaped adult punishment, he'd never lived down the fact he'd been beaten by a skinny girl half his size. And Jake had learned something—to keep his eyes open in a way he never before had. Busy with his love of cars and with rugby and with Calypso, he hadn't spotted the bullying.

"Did I ever tell you I had a talk with Paul Sweeney?" he found himself saying.

"Paul— You mean that preppy A-student bastard who lived to make weaker kids' lives hell?" A pause. "Though he did have a sudden change of heart partway through the year. Must've been some talk."

"No one wanted to mess with me or Danny. Not when we had the Bishop and Sailor for backup." Four brothers who stood as a single unit, one of them a rugby legend, another heavily muscled from his physical work, were enough to scare any bully.

"I was planning to kick him in the nuts before he had his awakening," Juliet muttered. "Then it was like he began to avoid me— *Wait a minute.* Jacob Esera, did you warn Paul against coming near me?" A deadly tone to her voice.

"I warned him it'd probably be better for his health and macho reputation. I mean, everyone knew what you did to Jiro."

Something that sounded like a snorted laugh. "Yeah, he wasn't such a big man then, was he?" She still sounded exactly as satisfied as she had a month after the altercation, when she finally got out of detention.

She hadn't been sorry for an instant.

Smile curving his lips, he said, "How's the whole Reid situation going? I've been in the gym for a couple of hours." A good, hard workout that had given him an outlet for his anger at what that ass was trying to do to her.

"I have crushed that worm under my stiletto," Juliet said, her tone razor sharp. "Unfortunately, the media is now in love with me. Idiots won't stop calling with offers to do a lifestyle piece on my 'rise from a woman scorned to a powerful player in the business world.'" Gagging sounds.

But Jake didn't laugh. "Were you?"

"What?"

"The woman scorned?" He'd just assumed she'd done the walking away, but if it had been Reid...

"I'd kick *you* in the nuts if you were standing in front of me right now." He could hear her glare. "No, I'm not pining for Reid the Pinhead. For your information, I was the one who kicked *him* to the curb." A hesitation in those words.

"Actually, I'm not proud of it. I didn't do any kicking. I just packed my stuff and walked."

Jake's hand clenched on his phone. "Were you afraid of him?"

"No, nothing like that." Another hesitation. "Shit. I found him in our bed with Lisa."

Jake wasn't a violent man, but Jesus fuck, Reid deserved a punch in the face. He said as much to Juliet.

"No, he deserves obscurity. Don't do anything that'll give him a chance at fame." An exhale. "Honestly? I was relieved to have such an open-and-shut reason to walk. I wanted to get out but kept hesitating. I don't know why."

"Because you're loyal." Once Juliet picked a person as hers, she stuck. "Reid's a fool to have given that up."

The pause that fell between them was taut with things unspoken.

Noises in the background from Juliet's end. "I have to go. Meeting."

After they'd hung up, Jake stared out his windscreen at nothing in particular, his mind on a tough girl who'd grown into a strong, intelligent woman. A woman who was about to go to New York with him. Americans didn't follow rugby much—which was why the whole Times Square underwear thing had knocked him for six. Maybe the US company had some secret marketing plan.

He didn't honestly care.

What he was interested in was that, until those billboards went up, no one in the vicinity was likely to recognize his face or care that he was part of the best rugby team in the world. He didn't have to worry about Reid using Jake's connection with Juliet to further drag her into the media.

Jake smiled... then called up the florist website to order another bunch of dark red roses. These he sent with the message: *Roses are red. Violets are blue. Stilettos crush worms. And so do you. ~ From the G to the VP.*

He wondered if she'd get it.

Four hours later he received a message that said, *Gearhead, you have too much time on your hands. ~ That's Ms. Vice President to you.*

The tightness in his chest that he hadn't been aware of carrying around eased in a rush of endorphins. Yeah, he had it bad for Juliet. And it still terrified him.

Leaning back in his office chair where he'd been paying the invoice for Esme's dance lessons, he turned to look at the photo of Calypso with Esme in her arms that he'd put on the shelf above the desk a while back.

"Hey, Calypso," he said, talking to a girl he'd once loved with all his teenage soul. "What if I get this wrong? What if I screw everything up?" His life. Esme's. Juliet's.

Calypso smiled back at him, sweet and content and forever a teenage girl.

Giving up on the admin for today, he pushed back his chair and glanced at his watch. It was almost time to pick up Esme. Deciding to start out early, he was halfway along the walk when his phone buzzed.

"Sailor," he said after glancing at the caller ID. "What's up?"

"Can you pick up Emmaline too? Small emergency at one of the nurseries. I'm hoping to beat the school traffic and head out."

"No worries. Want me to keep her overnight?" Emmaline had stuff at his place, as Esme did at Sailor and Ísa's.

"No. Ísa's teaching an evening class today, but it finishes at seven thirty—she should be able to pick Em up around eight. Thanks, bro."

After hanging up, Jake took deep breaths of the crisp air

and tried to figure out what the hell was going on inside him. He was deeply, passionately attracted to Juliet. He wanted to play with her. Fight with her. So why all the knots in his gut? It wasn't as if she didn't reciprocate—at least on the physical front. He could work with that.

Yet the fear continued to gnaw at him.

22

DANNY BECOMES A MAN OF THE CLOTH

A familiar figure up ahead by the school gate caught Jake's attention. "Danny? What're you doing here?"

"Inviting myself to your place for dinner," his younger brother said with a grin. "Dad's taking Mum to a fancy restaurant, and I didn't want to eat alone." He held out a fist for Jake to bump.

"I hope you're looking forward to chicken nuggets and mashed potatoes." Jake handmade and froze the nuggets in large batches to ensure they'd be healthy, and oven-cooked them instead of frying, but the girls considered it a treat nonetheless. "I'll throw in coleslaw if you chop it."

"Sold!"

Jake grinned; they both knew they'd be eating following the squad's personalized nutrition guidelines for each of them. However, that wasn't as difficult or as complicated as it sounded—he'd put in a chicken to roast, they'd do a ton of steamed or roasted vegetables, and that'd suit them.

Breakfast would've been a different story. Jake liked his peanut-butter-infused fruit smoothies, along with oatmeal, while Danny was more into egg-white omelets and avocado, maybe a couple of pieces of fresh fruit. The squad's nutritionist worked with each member of the team separately to give them advice while keeping in mind their likes and dislikes—because life would suck if they were on a weird-ass strict diet where they had to eat things they didn't enjoy.

The control was in their hands, but, in turn, they took the advice seriously.

Danny hooked a thumb over his shoulder. "I know you and short stuff usually walk home, but I have my Jeep—I was thinking if you were free, we could do a post-school drive to the bay. I bought a huge bag of those tiny carrots that she likes for a snack."

"Yeah, sounds good." Jake could do with the fresh air. "Emmaline's coming with us too."

The bell rang at that instant, and the school disgorged children big and small. Yet Jake picked out his daughter among the crowd without a problem, her spectacles catching the light and her pigtails messy.

Spotting him, she ran. "Daddy!"

He grabbed her, squeezed her tight. He needed the hug today, needed her warmth and innocence. When she wriggled, he let her go so she could bump fists with Danny.

"Where's your partner in crime?" Danny asked even as Jake scanned the drive for Emmaline's dark-haired head.

"There she is." Jake waved when he saw Emmaline's searching gaze.

Smile wide, she skipped over to him and he enfolded her in the same kind of hug he'd given Esme. As the girls were well used to being picked up by each other's parents, their uncles, or grandparents, Emmaline had no hesitation in falling in with them—especially when Danny mentioned the beach and chicken nuggets.

A short fifteen minutes later, the girls giggled as they ran around the neighborhood bay that had a patch of sand, some open grassy land, and a playground. Around it all was native bush. Come summer, Esme and Emmaline could swim in the bay, the water was so calm and clear.

Jake and Danny played with them for a while, then sat on the stone wall facing the sand, from where they could keep an eye on the girls.

"So, you ask Juliet out yet?"

Jake didn't groan; he'd long ago gotten used to having a little brother whose eyes were a touch too sharp. "How'd you figure it out?"

"Saw you two walk back into the wedding reception together—way you were looking at her, bro..." A whistle. "Let's say I never saw you look at Rachel that way. Also, you were totally scoping out her ass."

"Don't talk about Jules's ass," Jake snapped back without thought.

Danny's laugh was loud and delighted. Hearing it, the girls looked over and waved before returning to their examination of the shells lying on the sand.

"Like that, is it?" Danny leaned forward, the afternoon sunlight making the black strands of his hair gleam like jet. He had a bit of curl in it, as did Jake. But where Jake kept his cropped short and neat, Danny let his grow a little wilder. Just enough to touch the nape of his neck.

"I know who she is, by the way." Danny glanced back. "I was only two years behind you in school. It took me a while, but it finally clicked." Dark eyes on Jake before Danny turned back to watch the girls. "Is that the problem? That she was Calypso's friend?"

"No." Jake leaned forward to mirror Danny's position... and then he talked. Because while Danny could be a wiseass, he was also Jake's brother. And the Bishop-Esera brothers always had one another's backs. "I sent her roses."

"That's my man." Grin back, Danny clapped him on the shoulder.

Shoving a hand through his hair, Jake said, "I'm fucking scared, Danny."

"Scared?"

"Knots in my gut, and half the time I feel as if I'm having a heart attack." His chest would go all taut, his breathing shallow.

Danny's response was quiet. "You really like Juliet, don't you? It's not an easy, light thing like with Rachel?"

Jake's shoulders shook despite his tension. "Juliet is many things, but the words *easy* and *light* do not apply."

"I love her already." Danny nudged him with his shoulder. "I want for you what Sailor has, what Gabe has—that deep-down forever kind of love. I mean, don't you want your woman's face to light up when you walk into a room? Our big bros have that."

The idea of Juliet's face lighting up when she saw him, it punched all the air out of his lungs, he *wanted* it so much. "I'm not about to back off," he told his brother. "I just wish I could figure out this fear."

Danny gave him a strange look. "Jake, you haven't had a proper, serious relationship since your first girlfriend died almost overnight after being brought down by a sickness no one saw coming." He waved off Jake's attempt to interrupt. "Yeah, you went out with women, but you never took a risk again, never opened yourself up. Sounds to me like your Jules won't stand for that kind of bullshit and you know it."

Jake stared at his kid brother. "Jesus, Danny, are you a reincarnated priest or something? Where do you come up with this stuff?"

"I'm right though." Getting up, Danny brushed off the seat of his jeans. "I'm gonna take the girls to play on the swings. Sit here and ponder the knowledge that Monsignor Daniel Esera has bestowed upon you, my son."

Stunned by his brother's casual and devastatingly accurate analysis, Jake didn't move as Danny led the girls to the playground. Instead, he looked at the fear inside him... and he saw Calypso looking back. The first girl he'd ever loved, his heart all puppyish and excited and adoring. Her coffin had been so light against his shoulder as he led the pallbearers to her burial plot.

Her death had nearly broken him.

And now he was starting to fall in love again.

JULIET STARED at the two bunches of roses on either side of her desk. The second had arrived in a crystal vase. Just as well, because she only had the one retro milk-bottle style vase that she kept in a drawer for the days when she felt like picking up a bunch of cheerful blooms from the local shop.

Iris had pushed her cat's-eye spectacles down her nose when she saw the roses. "Since you haven't thrown them in the trash," she'd asked, tone arch, "I assume they're not from Reid?"

"No," she'd muttered. "They're from my personal pain in the rear."

"I do like his style."

As Juliet stood staring at the roses, she realized so did she—and it was freaking her out. Jake was flirting with her, but to what end? No way could this ever work between them.

Yet... he'd stood by her through Reid's machinations.

Not only that, he'd made her smile when all she'd

wanted to do was rage at the world. Each time she caught the scent of the roses, her lips curved. As for his cards, she had them tucked into a zippered pocket of her bag.

Serious Jacob Esera didn't seem the type to write silly poetry. But he had.

Teeth biting down on her lower lip, she took out her phone: *Sorry to interrupt the honeymoon,* she typed to Charlie, *but I have a question.*

Her phone pinged ten minutes later while she was finishing up the last emails for the day. *Piña coladas and sunshine—it's a hard, hard life.*

You forgot the sex, Juliet messaged back with a grin.

I'm currently watching my gorgeous husband walk around our beachfront cabin in nothing but a pair of old rugby shorts. Trust me, I have a certain physical activity permanently on the brain.

Chuckling because Charlie was probably blushing as she typed that, Juliet went to respond when Charlie said, *What's the question?*

Juliet made herself push through her hesitation. *Hypothetically speaking, if Jake sent a woman roses two days in a row, one with a poem attached, would that mean anything?*

Our Jake?!!!

Yes, your Jake.

Can I consult Gabriel? You'll be anonymous, promise.

Juliet decided she might as well get the info straight from the top. *Yes, okay.*

The next few minutes inched by.

Gabe says that either his brother has been possessed by aliens, or this woman must be special. Jake doesn't do courtship or flirting.

Juliet stared at the roses, thought about the messages he'd sent her, the silly poem, and her breath, it stuck in her chest. To have a man like Jake, devoted and steady and passionate, in her corner? It would be a dream.

Of course, even if she ignored the whole media drama, the dream could quickly turn into a nightmare. She and Jake weren't friends, and after her childhood, after Reid, Juliet *needed* to be friends with her lover, needed to be able to lower her shields with him. Needed to be able to cry and break and curl into him.

Right now all Jake had seen was her prickly outer shell.

What if the softness inside repelled him?

She was still thinking about that the next morning when there was a knock on the door. It sounded like the impatient knock of a courier, but she looked through the peephole to make certain. Seeing the familiar cranky face of her local courier driver, she opened up to sign and receive the package.

Carrying it to her kitchen counter afterward, she saw it had been overnighted from a local address. She opened it up with a frown to glimpse the jacket for the hardcover book *Humans of New York* by the photographer Brandon Stanton. Hands trembling, she opened the book. It took her a second to see that there was a pink sticky note poking out of a particular page.

Turning to that page, she saw it was a photograph of a couple in Times Square. They were re-creating that famous image of the sailor kissing a woman bent over his arm. On the sticky note were the words: *I'll bring the sailor suit if you bring the dress and the heels. – Jake*

Juliet dropped the book on the counter, only to pick it up an instant later to stare at Jake's scrawly writing. It was as terrible as it had been back in school. Her fingers traced the jagged lines. That was when she noticed the edges of the book bore a few small marks, and when she turned the pages, she saw the imprint of two tiny fingers on a photograph featuring a group of children—possibly in ink, maybe in juice.

This was Jake's copy of the book.

Jake, who didn't flirt, who didn't do courtship.

Heart thunder, Juliet decided to pack a dress and heels.

23
_____

A DEADLINE (ALSO, PHENOMENAL,
CIRCUIT-BLOWING SEX MAY COME UP)

Two days after Danny's weirdly wise bit of insight, Jake thanked his brother for dropping him and Esme off at the airport.

"I want a souvenir key chain in return," Danny said, squeezing Esme into a hug. "Boo," he said when he released her, "make sure he gets me the kind with a big fluffy apple. I don't want no tiny-ass doll apple. I want the serious shebang." He held out a hand, palm out.

Esme slapped it. "I gonna make sure, Uncle Danny."

After exchanging a complicated leftover-from-teenage-hood handclasp with Danny, Jake took his daughter's hand to walk to the departure area. Esme was excited both because they were going away and because she'd been given special permission to be off school, though she had to finish a bunch of homework during the trip.

"Daddy, are we going in a big plane?"

"One of the biggest."

Having had a message from Juliet this morning—a very prim and professional message that made no mention of the

205

book he'd sent her—he looked for her after they cleared security and reached the executive lounge. It was his daughter who spotted her. Tugging at his hand, she pointed excitedly toward the coffee bar.

Juliet was ordering a drink using the tablet mounted beside the barista's workbench, and though she was dressed in a relaxed pair of black pants that looked soft to the touch and a simple gray sweatshirt, his body stirred as if she were wearing her sexy bridesmaid's dress—or nothing at all.

Yeah, he liked her best in nothing at all, but he could grow to like those pants.

His hand itched. He knew what the swell of her hip felt like under his palm, knew the smell at the curve of her neck, knew how tight and soft her body was when he thrust into her and how sweetly she gave of herself in bed. Going down on her had been ridiculously fun for him; she'd gasped with such shocked surprise when he'd licked her into an orgasm.

I mean, things like that gave a man ideas. Mostly of doing it again. Even better.

"Jules!" His daughter bounced up and down next to Juliet. "Surprise!" She threw out her hands like a circus magician.

Beaming, Juliet knelt down to enfold her in a hug. "Hello, Boo." She pressed a kiss to his daughter's cheek. "Do you want a hot chocolate?"

Esme glanced over her shoulder at Jake, her eyes in full charm mode.

He grinned. "Since we're going on semi-vacation, knock yourself out." A little indulgence wouldn't hurt her.

Juliet winced as she rose to her feet. "Sorry," she murmured under her breath. "I should've asked you first."

"It's not a problem, Jules." He wasn't going to get bent out of shape because she'd been nice to his daughter; he *liked* that Jules was so naturally kind to his baby girl. "Can you order me a long black?" he added while fighting the urge to stroke his hand over her extremely fine ass—though if Danny ever mentioned said ass again, he'd deck his brother.

In all likelihood, Danny had done it on purpose. Pressing buttons was Jake's younger brother's specialty, especially when the button push led to revelations. It wouldn't surprise him in the least if Danny switched from sports psychology to law. Though he supposed psychologists were nosy as hell when it came down to it, and that suited his brother to the ground too.

What he didn't fight was his urge to ruffle Juliet. It probably wasn't good for his health, but Jake had decided on this risk—and once he decided, he didn't hold back. It was how he'd gone from not playing for a year to making a representative team in eight months. Fear be damned.

"You smell nice, Jules." He took a long breath after speaking those words under his breath. "I can almost taste you on my tongue."

A flush on her cheekbones, she focused on inputting their orders. "Oh, do you know how to use that tongue?" she asked, sweet as pie. "I thought I felt a vague brush down there the other night."

He grinned. "Guess I need to try harder. Lick and suck harder."

As she inhaled quickly, he grabbed a couple of bottles of water and located his offspring. It was ridiculously fun messing with Jules, but he had to tone it down or his cock was going to give the entire lounge a show. Esme proved to be peering interestedly at the jar of marshmallows on the counter, far above her reach.

"Later," he told her. "Let's go find seats."

"I have some already," Juliet said, then led them to a grouping of four with a small coffee table in the center.

Esme rolled her child-sized blue-princess carry-on to stand next to Juliet's sleek black one. "See, Jules?" she said proudly. "I got one too."

Juliet nodded and, with every appearance of interest asked Esme about the princess whose face was emblazoned on the front, a face that was now haunting Jake in his dreams, cackling with glee at all the money he'd thrown her way. After giving Juliet the history of the princess, his daughter took the opportunity to regale her with stories of all the places she'd taken her carry-on.

Juliet's airline app pinged midway to tell her their drinks were ready. Motioning at her to stay seated, Jake went to the counter to pick them up. He returned to find two dark-haired heads drawn together in deep discussion.

A deep, *important* thing twisted in his heart.

Something that had nothing to do with his tongue or his cock and everything to do with the reason for the fear that continued to dog him: Juliet mattered.

Putting down the drinks, he volunteered to hold the fort while the two of them went off to look at the available food. He needed the breathing space, needed to find his feet again.

Of course, Juliet swept them out from under him again the instant she returned from the catering area. "We got a plate for you too," she said. "Heavy on the nuts and cheeses. Esme said those were your favorites."

Juliet's phone buzzed even as she spoke the last word, and she excused herself to go answer it.

"I like Jules," his daughter announced following her departure. "She's nice. Real nice, not pretend nice."

Sometimes Jake thought his daughter was sixty years old rather than six. "What do you know about pretend nice?" he asked with a raised eyebrow.

She shrugged. "I just know." Then she stuffed half a slider in her mouth, as if he hadn't fed her for days before bringing her to the airport.

Shoulders shaking, he ate a couple of nuts and drank his coffee while keeping an eye on his baby girl to make sure she didn't choke on her spoils. And he waited for Juliet. He felt like a damn kid eager to catch a glimpse of the girl on whom he had a crush, his heart thudding at the idea of spending five days with her.

In a massive city where no one would care if a man named Jacob kissed a woman named Juliet.

"THAT WAS the US side's head of marketing," Juliet said upon returning to her seat. "He heard about the munchkin, saw a photo of you holding her after that championship game with her wearing your medal."

Jake stiffened. "Jules—"

She rolled her eyes. "Jeez, let me finish."

"Yeah, Daddy. You say it's rude to inter-wupt."

Properly schooled, Jake rubbed his forehead. "It is. Sorry, Jules." He could see Juliet's eyes dancing as he apologized through gritted teeth. It took all his self-control not to lunge across the space between them and kiss her amusement right into his own blood. "Carry on."

"I set them straight. No pictures of Esme without permission. I assured them you'd sue them into the ground if they breached that rule."

"I know Sue!" his daughter announced, caramel sticking

to the sides of her mouth because she was now halfway through a chocolate caramel slice.

Picking up a paper towel, he wet it with some water, then wiped it over her mouth. She sat patiently through it before returning to her treat. He looked up to find Juliet's eyes had gone soft, a little sad.

"Remember how much Calypso could eat?" Quiet words that wouldn't reach Esme. "I never could figure out where it went."

"How about that time she ate a whole pizza? At the game."

"Oh my God, I'd almost forgotten."

"I thought she was joking when she took a whole pizza and refused to share." Jake's cheeks creased. "By the time she got to the final piece, I think we were all watching her more than the game."

"The way she held up that box like a trophy at the end. Crying, 'I'm the champion!'"

They both grinned.

"Daddy," Esme said, "can I go sit in that?" She was pointing at a giant swing chair at one end of the lounge.

Jake nodded because the chair was both solidly installed and in his line of sight.

"You're good at letting her be independent while keeping her safe," Juliet said after Esme had run off.

"I'd be an overprotective monster if it weren't for Mum and Dad getting me help," he admitted, the words flowing in a way they hadn't for a long time—not even with his family. "After Calypso died, I wouldn't let Esme out of my sight for a second, even when she was being cared for by my own mother.

"It wasn't just Esme either—I'd check on Danny during the night to make sure he was breathing, call Sailor and

Gabe multiple times a day, make my parents check in if they went out." He shook his head. "Poor Ísa would actually put the phone down next to Emmaline so I could hear her baby chatter and be reassured she was healthy and happy."

"I can't say I blame you." Juliet looked down at her drink. "When you're a teenager, you don't expect death to hit like that, out of nowhere."

"Yeah." His entire world had crumbled in the space of twenty-four-hours as the meningitis ravaged Calypso; she'd been playfully tickling a smiling Esme as she changed her diaper one day, fighting for her life the next.

"Do you miss her?" Dark eyes that held a weight of memory... and a question that was a gray barrier between them. "Callie?"

He took his time thinking about that, his mind filled with a thousand faded snapshots. "I miss that our daughter will never know her. I try to keep her memory alive, but to Esme, Calypso's an image in a photograph, a face and voice on a screen."

He smiled at his daughter as she waved at him after managing to clamber into the seat of her swing, a tiny and pleased empress on a huge throne. "I miss the way she'd make quirky jokes it always took me a while to get. I miss knowing who she would've become as she grew. But I had to get past her death to be a good dad, a good man."

Nudging his head in Esme's direction, he said, "She needed me to get my shit together, be there for her, and that was the start, but we were also so young, Jules. In puppy love that's frozen in time." Sweet and soft and gentle. "I'll never forget her, and I'll keep her in my heart always because she —and who we were together—deserve that, but she's gone and the boy she loved has grown into a man she never knew."

He held Juliet's eyes. "I'm not carrying a torch for her."

Juliet was the one who broke the eye contact, but because this was Jules, she remade the contact a second later. "I had to ask. I won't settle for being second best, not even to my best friend. Neither will I settle for a surface fling."

He hadn't expected such bluntness, but he smiled slowly at the implication. "So we're doing this?"

"Five days," she said, her tone stern and no returning smile on her face. "Five days to see if we can be friends as well as lovers, if we can spend time together like civilized human beings instead of a lion and a wolf circling each other."

He wanted to kiss her, promised himself a hundred kisses once they were away from prying eyes. "Which one of us is the lion?"

"Jacob."

"Deal," he murmured. "Five days."

"Or we walk away." A huskiness to her voice now. "There's too much risk if it's not about more than the"—a quick glance around to ensure they wouldn't be overheard before she said—"phenomenal, circuit-blowing sex. I can't be linked to you if it's only for a short time. The media will savage me afterward."

Protective anger rolled through Jake in a tidal wave. "Five days," he said, even as determination settled into his bones. He *hated* the idea of Juliet having to face the cameras and the questions on her own, hated the idea of her out in the world without the shield of his name and the support of his presence.

Hated it.

Jacob Esera looked after his own. And Juliet was his.

Part of him had known it from the moment she first

made him come alive with her prickles and her generosity and her sensuality. It had just taken the rest of him time to catch up. But now that he had... Well, Jake was known on the rugby field for being a cool head under pressure.

Juliet was about to find out exactly how strategically Jacob Esera could think and plan.

24

JACOB ESERA'S STEPS TO A STEALTH COURTSHIP

A s always, New York was beautiful chaos. This wasn't Jake's first time in the city, but he'd only been twice before, both times while in transit to somewhere else. At least their time at the airport had gone smoothly—though not one but *two* camera crews associated with New Zealand stations had been waiting for their arrival.

It turned out Everett's marketing department had released a sneak peek of the ad by way of a "making of" video, and it had gone viral while they were in the air. Given the subject matter, however, the media questions had been softballs, and since he'd spotted the cameras early, he'd been able to ask Juliet to spirit Esme out of shot.

He'd worried the viral nature of the clip would nix his anonymity here, but then Juliet had pulled up the stats for the video and he'd realized New York had far more people than were represented in the figures. It was also highly unlikely anyone would recognize him from a short clip—especially since he now had all his clothes on.

"So many people, Daddy!" Esme declared when he took her for a walk in Times Square after checking into the hotel.

With it being early afternoon here, there was no way she'd wanted to stay inside the hotel. Neither did he, not after being cooped up in the plane for so many hours. But he'd given her a bath since she'd admitted to feeling "goopy" after the long flight, then had a shower himself.

During his shower, Esme had happily amused herself watching the wild world outside their hotel window—all while wrapped up in a giant hotel bathrobe. When he'd asked her if she wanted to try it, she'd jumped up and down and grinned. So he'd put her in it, rolled up the sleeves, and she'd trailed the robe behind her like a queen as she walked.

Now, in the summer sunshine on this side of the world, Esme wore a colorful little faux jumpsuit her grandmother had made for her. It was faux because while it looked like the "big girl" jumpsuits Esme had coveted, the pants could be pulled down if she needed to use the bathroom. A bright yellow with white daisies all over it, the fabric suited his sunny, happy daughter.

Her shoes were her favorite light-up princess sneakers, and he'd put two sparkly white barrettes in her damp hair to keep it out of her way.

Jake was far less colorful in his faded blue jeans and white T-shirt paired with his old black Doc Martens.

His daughter stared agog at the color and music all around them.

"Where's Jules?" she asked at one point.

"She had to work." Jake wasn't sure if that was true or if Juliet was using it as a convenient excuse—she'd turned wary after that honest exchange in the lounge. Or maybe she'd caught the hunting glint in his eye and realized he was playing for keeps.

"Ask her if she finished her work," Esme insisted even as he was plotting how to lure Juliet out into the open. "She's gonna miss the fun."

Lips curving in a surely wicked smile, Jake reached into his pocket and grabbed his phone. But, after making the call, he handed the phone to Esme. "Here, you ask." No one had ever said Jacob Esera was stupid.

"It's me, Esme!" Esme cried cheerfully into the phone. "Did you finish your work?" A pause as she listened. Then, "I got my picture with a wizard!" Another pause. "Uh-huh. Are you gonna come out? *Please.*"

Yeah, that please was going to do it, Jake thought smugly. Esme wasn't yet aware of how sweet and adorable she sounded when she said it just that way, but Jake was already girding himself for when she got older.

"Daddy, can I borrow the car? *Please?*"

"Daddy, can my friend"—insert some idiot boy's name —"come study with me in my room? *Please?*"

"Daddy, can I go to this party? *Please?*"

He was going to have to grow fucking titanium armor to have any hope of resisting her.

"Yeah!" Esme bounced against his arm. "Um, we're by the..." She looked around. "There's a statue. He's all gold. He's actually a person—I saw him move," she whispered into the phone. "But don't tell. It'll hurt his feelings."

Jake bit the inside of his lip and waited.

"Uh-huh. Okay, see you!" Esme handed over the phone.

"Juliet's coming?" he asked as he slipped his phone back into his pocket.

"Yup."

He held out his hand, palm up. Grinning, his daughter gave him a high five.

And not long afterward, there was Jules, her hair damp

and her luscious body clad in jeans and a navy T-shirt with a black design down one side, gold hoops in her ears. Except for the hoops and her watch, she wore no jewelry and hadn't bothered with makeup. But she'd tucked the T-shirt in, and on her feet was a pair of black heels.

Jake's entire body pulsed; he wanted to see her in nothing but those skyscraper heels. Or better yet, have her long, long legs wrapped around him, heels on her feet as he pounded into her deep and hard.

"Love the outfit," she said, talking to Esme in that way she had of doing—as if Esme was a grown-up—and his sexual interest softened into something gentler, more tender.

"See my buttons," Esme said, pointing out the flower-shaped buttons. "Grandma lemme choose."

"Nice."

"I like your shoes." Esme eyed the heels. "I wanna be tall."

Juliet winked. "Get a little older and I'll teach you how to wear them."

Smile brilliant, Esme dropped Jake's hand to take Juliet's. "Come see the wizard, Jules."

The three of them spent the next hour wandering around Times Square, just taking in the frenetic vibe. Jake couldn't handle a constant barrage of this, but for a lazy afternoon, it was fun—especially with Juliet and Esme. His daughter was all wide-eyed innocence while Juliet's sharp commentary had him biting back laughter more than once.

When Esme yawned for the third time in the same minute, he picked her up in his arms and they began to head toward the hotel. "I'll put her down for a nap," he told Juliet. "We can talk about tomorrow's schedule then." And he could begin his not-so-stealth assault of a courtship.

Step one: Lure Juliet into his lair. Success!

Step two: Show her the two of them were friends already.

Step three: Dependent on outcome of step two, but he had hopes of a kiss. He missed her touch.

"No nap, Daddy," Esme protested while her eyes fluttered shut.

"Just a little one," he promised. "I want you to be able to sleep tonight. So don't be grumpy when I wake you after half an hour."

She stuck out her tongue at him.

Grinning, he pressed a kiss to her forehead. "Nap, and no backchat from the cheeky corner."

Snuggling against his shoulder, she yawned again. "Only short," she said, and her eyes closed.

Juliet was looking at Esme with the softest expression on her face when he glanced at her. Yep, his baby girl was going to walk all over Juliet. It made him want to grin that the prickly beater-up-of-boys-twice-her-size was putty in the hands of a pint-size girl. Jake would have to protect her from his daughter's adorable ways.

The two of them didn't speak until they were in the hotel corridor and Esme was fast asleep against his shoulder. She was making those little snuffling sounds that she'd made from babyhood when she was in a deep sleep. It was freaking adorable, and when she grew up one day and fell in love, some damn lucky man would probably grin while watching her sleep beside him.

"We can talk in the living area of our suite," he told Juliet. "If that works for you?"

"Yes. Let me pick up my laptop and notebook. Join you in a second."

Leaving the door open behind him, Jake walked into the

bedroom that Esme had claimed for herself. He fully expected her to run across the living area at bedtime and crawl into bed with him instead. His daughter was intrepid, but this was a new place and a whole new environment. She'd probably need her daddy the first night at least.

After tugging down the blanket, he put her to sleep under it. She looked so tiny in the middle of the king-sized bed, her head on a giant pillow, and his heart, it filled all over again with the love he felt for her. And also with fear. Jesus Christ, it was terrifying having a kid and knowing there was so much in the world that could hurt her.

He ensured she was covered up since the air-conditioning was crisp, then walked out into the living area. He was using the provided coffee pods to make a couple of drinks when Juliet walked in. She closed the door, then put her laptop and satchel on the coffee table.

"Here, Jules." He held out one of the drinks. "Mocha, right?"

The corners of her eyes flared slightly as she took it.

"What?" he said. "Is my hair sticking up or something?" It probably was, thanks to a habit of Esme's left over from babyhood. The times she fell asleep against his shoulder, she usually ended up with a hunk of his hair in her fist. Not pulling. Just kind of kneading.

He'd had to work her fingers gently loose before he put her down to nap.

"No." Juliet shrugged. "I guess I'm not used to a guy making coffee for me." A slight hint of suspicion around her eyes. "Why are you doing it?"

"Because I intend to talk you into swinging-from-the-hotel-chandelier sex."

She froze with the cup partway to her mouth, her lips parted. "Funny, Jacob."

Unable to resist, he tugged on a strand of her hair. "My dad always makes my mum her morning cup." A ritual he'd observed from childhood, an act so normal it just was. "Though yeah, I can't see Reid doing it. Asshole."

Juliet snorted, then had to cough to clear her throat. "Don't hold back." But the suspicion was gone, her deep sigh at her first sip of the coffee making him want to groan.

"When a word fits…" Picking up his own drink, he walked over to take the sofa facing her. "You don't have to answer, and I'm not being an ass here—I really want to know. What drew you to him?"

Smile fading, she didn't answer for so long that he thought that was it. He watched as she opened up her laptop, pulled out a notebook.

"You know how I went back to Samoa?" she said at last. "It was because my aunt caught me in bed with a boy from school. Making out. My top was off, but that was about it."

Jake hadn't realized she'd had a boyfriend at school. "Who was it?"

"No one important. Just the start of my tendency to pick the wrong men." She took another sip of her coffee. "He bolted and left me to deal with the fallout."

One thing Jake could say—he'd never done that. He'd faced up and been by Calypso's side for everything. "Your aunt was strict, traditional?"

A nod. "My grandparents were even stricter." The look on her face was difficult to read, difficult to divine. A kind of smudged sadness. "They had photos of my father from when he was a young boy, but none of him with my mother —or with me. My father was a student on a scholarship in Auckland when he met my mother.

"They weren't married when I was born, and even though they were both adults at the time, it was considered a shameful thing by my grandparents. But he was their only son and they might've come around, only apparently my mother wasn't religious and wouldn't pretend and they took it as a personal insult."

"Yeah, I've known people like that."

"They cut my father out of the family," she added.

"I've never understood how a parent could do that." Jake was so angry for those two long-ago lovers. "I'd cut out my own heart and throw it in the garbage before I'd ever cut off Esme."

Juliet glared at him. "Stop it."

"What?" He spread his hands, honestly not knowing what he'd done.

"Being so..." A wave of her hand that explained nothing. "Anyway, my grandparents didn't love like you love. They stopped talking to my dad, told him not to come back to their village, the whole feudal drama.

"Then my parents died in an accident and I was three years old, and it would've been more shameful to let their grandchild go into care, so they strong-armed my aunt into raising me. But they never forgave my parents. Out of wedlock, they said. I'd been born out of wedlock."

Jake had never heard anyone use that old-fashioned phrase. His family had shielded him and Esme from all that —they'd literally stopped seeing friends who'd tried to make judgments about Jake, Calypso, and their baby girl. The only reason the Eseras had remained with their long-time church was because the pastor was a man who understood that family and raising children with love was what mattered—he'd preached that when the news first circulated.

"Your grandmother and grandfather were unkind to you?" He had to fight to keep his voice even. She'd grown up with a resentful aunt, only to be sent to grandparents who considered her a mistake.

Juliet cupped her mug with both hands. "It wasn't so simple. They were... disappointed. In my father and in me. Not just for being caught with that boy, but for the detentions, the terrible grades, all that stuff. They blamed my mother—the bad blood coming out."

"Jesus, Jules. Tell me you didn't internalize that?" Jake had no sympathy for people who'd say such things to a child.

Juliet's smile was faded. "No. I was old enough to pity all they'd lost because of their prejudice. In the end, when I finished my final year of high school with good grades and no demerits, they softened toward me."

"Whoa, wait." Rising, he went around to her side and sat on the coffee table, so close to her that their knees touched, then reached out to lift up a lock of hair near her forehead.

Eyebrows drawing together, she said, "Jacob, what are you doing?"

"Checking for the lobotomy scars."

A laughing snort exited her lips in a burst that told him she'd lost control. The sound was so damn cute that he leaned in and kissed her. Not a sexy, come-to-bed kind of kiss, but a soft, playful, hey-you kind of kiss.

She was smiling when they went into it, was still smiling when they parted. And his heart, it went boom all over again. To have Juliet smile at him that way...

"No lobotomy," she said, the sadness no longer heavy on her features. "I was just tired, I guess—I mean, it didn't take a psych degree to realize I'd been acting out all that time to get my aunt to pay attention to me."

It might not have taken a degree, Jake thought, but it *had* taken a kind of painful emotional clarity no teenage girl should have to possess. Juliet had basically accepted that no one in her family would ever love her, and fuck but he wanted to destroy them all for the harm they'd done her.

"In Samoa," she added, "I realized the futility of trying for any kind of connection with my relatives and decided the only way out was with academics, so I put my head down. Then I heard what happened to Calypso, and..." A hard swallow. "She was the best friend I ever had. The only one who never judged me, who liked me for me."

"Sorry for being a dick to you back then," Jake said with a grimace; he was devastated that he might've added to her hurt. "But I've learned and grown."

A sudden, delighted smile. "Oh, Jake, that's different— we were dicks to each other. I called you a gearhead jock more than once, remember? The insults canceled out—and the only time I asked you for something, you came through. We're good."

That smile, it hit him in the gut, left him breathless.

Made him want to pull her into his lap and kiss her and kiss her and kiss her.

25

FIVE CHILDREN, THREE DOGS, FOUR CATS... AND AN HONEST-TO-GOODNESS GOAT IN THE BACKYARD

Instead of giving in to his compulsion to kiss that smile into his mouth, Jake leaned forward to play with strands of her hair instead. No way would he interrupt her when she was trusting him with such private memories, such closely held wounds.

An arch look at his fingers in her hair, but her smile didn't fade. "Anyway," she said, "after I completed high school, I did a vocational course that taught office skills—typing, advanced computer literacy, things like that. I was just finishing when my granddad died of a heart attack. My grandma followed six months later." A touch of sorrow in her voice—because behind her hard shell, Jules was as soft as they came, and she felt even for people who'd deprived her of love.

"After her death," Juliet said, "the village chief came to me and said my grandparents had made a will and put it in his keeping. They owned their house, and they had a small amount in savings, and it was all left to me. Let's say my aunt wasn't pleased."

Jake wondered how much Juliet had done for her elderly

grandparents while she was living with them and whether, in their twilight years, they'd realized what they'd given up by raising a child without love. "You took the money and came home?" She'd been born in Auckland, Samoa a foreign land to her.

She nodded. "I took out their savings and sold their house—it wasn't worth a huge amount compared to Auckland prices, but the chief was a nice man and he helped me get a good price for that area. After buying my plane ticket home, I transferred the balance to a new account here since I couldn't be sure if my aunt still had access to the old one. Arrived in the city knowing no one but her and well, you know I wasn't going to go to her."

"You knew me," Jake found himself saying, furious that she'd had no one on whom to lean. Not even at his worst had he ever been that alone. His family was his first and most important team.

"I knew Calypso," Juliet pointed out. "You were just the strutting gearhead jock with whom she'd had the bad taste to fall in love."

He scowled at her.

Cheeks creasing, she said, "Honestly, I shouldn't have put it that way—I wasn't quite Orphan Annie. The chief knew a pastor here, and he and his family put me up while I hunted for a place to stay."

She laughed. "They had five children, three dogs, four cats, one other houseguest, and an honest-to-goodness goat in the backyard. I'm not sure they even noticed an extra person in the mix—they fed everyone who came to their table."

"You still see them?" Jake asked, thankful for that unknown family that had opened its arms to her when she'd needed a friend.

A nod. "I drop money in the donation box at the church too. Can't make myself go to church after how my grandparents used religion to put me down, but I know they use that money to help out others—maybe even another lost girl like I was."

Soft, soft Juliet.

Esme was definitely going to make a meal of her if Jake didn't step in.

The idea of it made him want to cuddle them both close.

"I ended up only staying with them for four days," Juliet said. "Got myself into a flat with three other girls, then started applying for jobs. It took five months, and my money was just draining away, and I'd begun to panic when I applied at E. E. Designs.

"Iris, that's my immediate boss, took me on even though I had no experience. She said she liked my drive, but—and I'm definitely *not* complaining about this—I was on three months' probation. She couldn't risk offering me full-time work before I proved I could do it.

"Then our landlord told us we had to move out in two weeks because he was moving relatives into the rental, and all four of us had to scramble for new housing. We were all young, didn't know he was meant to give us a much longer period of notice."

Jake saw the answer to the question that had begun this entire conversation. "You met Reid when you were vulnerable."

Screwing up her nose, Juliet said, "I hate putting it that way, but yes. I met him one month into my probationary period and two days after the notice from the landlord. The thing with Reid is, he can be charming—in a way that I can see is superficial now, but I had no real experience with guys back then—"

"Why not?" Jake couldn't help but interrupt. "I have a ton of cousins in Samoa and the guys aren't monks, and the girls haven't taken the veil either."

Her shoulders shook. "Say that in front of your pastor. I dare you."

"My mother would clip me upside the head even if she does have to stand on a stepladder to reach."

Juliet's laughter wrapped around him, and he sat there and took the delicious punishment.

"My grandparents were elderly," she said when she'd caught her breath. "I used to come home right after school and from the office management course—I was terrified they'd fall or something."

No wonder they'd left her all they had; if he had to guess, she'd have cooked for them too, done the housework, pretty much been their lifeline. He still couldn't find it in his heart to forgive them for how they'd hurt her.

"So I was virgin territory for Reid." Juliet made gagging sounds. "I think it was how green I was that hooked him. He was a big man in sports at the time, but we met in an open-late supermarket of all places. He'd come hunting ice cream and I was doing my grocery shopping and he made a cheeky comment about all the vegetables in my cart, and..."

A shrug. "He's *really* good at paying attention to a person when he wants to; no one had ever before paid that much attention to me. And he was a big star. I mean, that day his face was actually on a woman's magazine at checkout. He picked it up and made a crack about how he'd cut his face shaving when the picture was taken and could I see where they'd covered it with makeup?"

Jake told himself to keep his lips zipped.

"Yeah, I know, *Jacob*," Juliet said pointedly. "You don't have to give yourself a hernia holding in the commentary."

"Okay, *Juliet*. I'll keep that in mind."

Her laugh was utterly impenitent. But then she leaned forward and kissed him, and the taste of her went to his head. "It's weird," she whispered against his lips, "but I'm starting to find your grump-face kinda cute."

No one in his life had called Jake cute. He sat there and took it from Jules.

"So yeah," she said, ending the kiss even as his heart kicked, "it was all probably a line, and he picked up that magazine to make sure I knew who he was, but it worked. I was awed and flattered to have his attention—I was probably like a puppy dog to him. I came when called, was always happy to see him, was delighted when he called me his girlfriend. I showered him with adoration, and Reid is all about adoration."

"Seems like a perfect match."

"Sarcasm much?"

Placing his empty coffee mug to the side, he held up his hands. "No, seriously. I know more than one guy married to his most devoted groupie. It works for them—she worships him and he basks in it." Jake found the lack of give and take weird, but he'd grown up with parents who were partners.

"Well, this groupie grew up," Juliet said. "Iris and Everett began to give me more and more responsibility, and I began to understand that I was being treated with respect, my opinions valued—and I saw that Reid didn't respect me. He put me down a lot, and at first, I let it get to me. But after a while, I began to question what he said, question him, and it was never going to work after that."

"Because he's a limp-dicked washout who needs his ego massaged on a regular basis."

"Yep and yep." She put her coffee down on a side table.

"There you have it—the short and sordid history of Juliet Nelisi."

"I see tough and inspiring."

"Sure." Despite the casual agreement, shutters were falling over her eyes in front of him, the moment of intimate connection drifting out of reach.

No fucking way was he going to let that happen. He jumped into deep water to recapture it... and invited her into a place no one else had ever seen. "Sometimes I can't remember what Calypso looked like when she laughed."

The words fell between them, raw and rough. Words he'd never spoken aloud to anyone, not even his brothers.

Juliet had been about to open her laptop. Taking her hand off it, she shifted her gaze to him. *"Jake."*

Suddenly his eyes were hot, as hot as the day when the small beating sound had stopped in Calypso's hospital room. Her parents had never liked him, but while conscious, Calypso had made them promise they wouldn't kick him out—then or ever, and so he'd been there when she went silent.

That promise was also why they'd allowed him to be a pallbearer.

Swallowing hard, he looked down. His hair fell across his forehead. "I keep wondering if she'd have survived if she hadn't given birth not that long before. Would she have been stronger? Could she have fought longer?"

"Jake, no." A rustle of movement, then Juliet was kneeling in front of him, her hand stroking over his hair. "Meningitis is a pitiless disease. And the strain that took Calypso was a vicious one—you know that. It was all over the papers, how the authorities were afraid it was turning into an epidemic."

It felt like he was turning himself inside out, and he

never did that. *Never*. But Juliet had known Calypso, the *only* other person who'd really known her. She'd loved her too.

"It doesn't matter," he admitted, the words stones grinding in his throat. "I know the logic of it, but Jules, if you'd seen her in that hospital bed..." It was too hard to speak now, his eyes so hot it hurt. He squeezed them shut, his hands fists.

Juliet continued to stroke his hair, continued to murmur comforting things that he didn't hear, but that mattered. She mattered. This strong woman who'd survived so much and yet who'd found the capacity in her to forgive, to grow.

Raising his head, he opened his eyes, saw that hers were wet. "Jules." A shaky word.

Cupping the back of her head, he pressed his forehead to hers and stopped fighting the wet heat in his eyes. Her own tears fell silent and hot down her cheeks. "I missed her every single day," she whispered. "Then I couldn't even come to her funeral."

"I read out your message," he told her through the agony wrenching them both. "I knew she'd want that."

No more words, both of them too torn. They cried, and then they just sat there in that awkward position that neither of them made any move to alter. When she shifted her head slightly, he moved with her, and suddenly their lips were touching and he was tasting the salt and wet of her, and her hands were on his thighs as she arched up to taste him back.

Wet and hot and full of need.

It was a distant siren that brought him back to his senses. Breaking the kiss, he looked over toward the room where his daughter slept. He could just see the edge of her body; she hadn't moved from when he'd last looked over.

Breath harsh, he pressed his forehead to Juliet's again.

When she went to pull away, he held her to him with the hand cupping the back of her head. "This isn't anything shallow, Jules, and we *are* friends." He'd fucking cried in front of her.

Jacob Esera never cried.

Not even in Calypso's room.

Not even at her funeral.

All those tears knotted up inside him, and it was only Juliet who'd broken the dam.

Her eyes were wide, wet, and yes, scared. *"Jake."* It was a plea. "I have the tabloids following me—your family is so private. They'll drive you insane. And... I'm messed up inside."

"So am I."

"I know." A hand cupping his cheek. "You know how to let loose, play, I've seen it, but most of the time... Jake, you like things a certain way, don't enjoy change. The steadiness in you, it draws me so much"—huge, dark eyes unshielded and open to him—"but that's not who *I* am."

She pressed her fingers to his lips when he would've spoken. "I change hair colors as often as I change my nails. I'm the air and the wind to your earth and rock. I don't know who I'll become as the years pass, but I know I'm never going to be static. And I know I can't and won't live according to someone else's rules. Not ever again."

Things hurt inside him as they shifted and repositioned. "But you don't change *people*, Jules," he said in a rough whisper. "You stick by your people even when they kick that soft heart of yours. I can't think of anything better than being your number one person."

Her lower lip quivered.

Jake wasn't done fighting for her. "What if you take my hand and lead me into a life less rigid and defined by rules?"

The idea of returning to the gray calm of a life without Juliet wasn't one he was willing to contemplate. "What if I can be the steady heart of your life and you be my wings, teach me to fly past the walls I like to build? What if, Jules?"

"Don't call me Jules." It was a shaky rebuff with no strength behind it. "What if we screw up?"

"Then we live with it." He brushed back her hair. "This is the biggest leap I've ever taken. Leap with me. Be my wings."

Scared eyes, her pupils dilated. But then she kissed him and his heart beat again. Tugging her into his lap, he held her close as he kissed her with every ounce of skill he had. He'd fight with every tool at his disposal—including the combustible chemistry between them.

But she was the one who slayed him when she began to gently, tenderly kiss the fading remnants of tears off his cheeks. Arms locking tight around her, he sat there and took that too. Because this was Jules.

26

JULIET NELISI: EXPLORER OF AN ALIEN WORLD

J uliet stared at herself in the bathroom mirror in her hotel room. She'd returned there to put herself to rights while Jake did the same in his room. He'd be waking Esme soon, and they still needed to finish their work.

"I must've lost my mind," she said, and her voice was rough from the tears she'd shed for her lost friend—and for Jake, who carried so much guilt for something he could've never stopped.

Sometimes I can't remember what Calypso looked like when she laughed.

Her heart broke all over again. To see big, tough Jacob Esera cry... Her own eyes burned once more. Not only had he cried, he'd done so for a girl he'd loved as a boy. The man could *feel* and feel deep. What would it be like to have his loyalty?

I can't think of anything better than being your number one person.

Things tore open inside her. She wanted what he was offering so much. Which was also why it was so terrifying. If they tried and it all crashed and burned, she'd have to give up Jake. At least now they could be friends—because he was right. They *were* already friends. She trusted him to keep her secrets and not use them against her. He trusted her to do the same.

With Jake, she never had to tiptoe around anything. Their every interaction was based on honesty.

But if she thought she could have him, only to have to give him up again...

It was lead in her veins, scalding ice in her gut.

Because the truth was, she was half in love with him already.

Legs shaky, she sat down on the wide tiled ledge that surrounded the bath. "Oh, Juliet." Talk about self-destructive. To fall for Jacob Esera? A man so far out of her reach that she might as well be clawing for the moon?

It wasn't only his fame or his wealth. It was his family. The Bishop-Esera name was respected in every corner of the country. Among the Samoan community, they were all but revered. While she was a screwed-up girl from the wrong side of the tracks. One who'd made good but who'd never shake her history.

Juliet hated the idea of her notoriety dragging Jake's family into the tabloids. The thought that Esme might have to go from a little girl who had a fairly normal life to a child who had to be wary of a camera flash, it made her want to throw up.

It won't be the same when you're part of Jake's family.

The words came from the few neurons that hadn't drowned in the emotional storm inside her. She remembered the call from Thea Arsana. A call that had come because Jake had contacted Molly with a request for help for Juliet. Suddenly, instead of being caught in a nightmare, she'd taken control of the entire situation.

The media against the entire Bishop-Esera clan?

No fucking contest.

Rolling her lips inward, she smiled and it was shaky. But it was there. Because in the memory of how they'd dealt with the scandal was hope. Having Jake at her back massively changed the equation.

And... he'd said he needed her. To be his wings. To drag him outside the safe gray walls of his life. He'd cried in her arms. Told her things she was sure he'd told no one else. Jake, so contained and reserved that the public called him the Saint, had opened himself up and invited her in.

Her. Bad-girl Jules. He knew her, had seen the good and the bad... and the soft. Her vulnerability hadn't turned him off—the way he'd said it, it was as if he'd always seen past her prickly outer shell. He wasn't inviting in a fantasy idea of her or the person he wanted her to be. No, Jake was inviting *her*.

Juliet just had to be brave enough to accept the invitation.

JAKE WASN'T sure Juliet would come back, but about fifteen minutes after she'd left, she used the keycard he'd given her to reenter his suite. He'd woken his sleepy baby girl in the interim and he currently held her *very* grumpy form in his lap while she rubbed her eyes and scowled. Without her glasses, her eyes were huge—she looked like a bad-tempered owl.

"I was *sleeping*," she said very precisely to him.

"I know, Boo, but we had a deal, remember?"

"He's right, Esme," Juliet said. "Also, your dad's scared

you'll turn into a vampire if you sleep all day and are up all night, and that you'll come attack him while he sleeps." She made claws with her hands, bared her teeth.

A giggle from his grumpy girl before she held out her arms toward Juliet. A minute pause... then Juliet picked her up and settled down on the other sofa. His warm, sleep-mussed daughter stayed in Juliet's lap while Juliet opened up her laptop and began to go through their schedule for tomorrow.

It was to be one of the busiest days of their trip, including a couple of meet and greets with the head honchos of the new retailer, as well as shooting for both still and moving ads. Turned out he'd be strutting his stuff above Times Square, not just staring down at it.

Juliet grinned at him when he groaned at that little bombshell.

"The other side wanted dinner too," she said, "but I made it clear that they were already pushing the hours they're asking of you. Also, where you go, Esme goes." She tugged on Esme's messed-up ponytail.

"Yeah," his daughter said firmly. "Daddy go, I go!"

"So we're going to do the meal at lunch instead." Juliet placed a kiss on Esme's tousled head. "Esme can come, but sweetie, you'll have to bring your bag with books and games so you don't get bored. That okay with you?"

Esme gave Juliet a solemn look, then patted her on the cheek. "I like you, Jules." A dazzling smile. "I'm gonna put on my glasses and pack my bag now." Tumbling off Juliet's lap, she ran into her room to organize.

Jake raised an eyebrow at Juliet. *We still doing this?* he asked silently, his entire body tense.

"Don't blame me when it goes down in flames." A bad-tempered mutter.

Good thing he knew his Jules, knew she hid fear and worry behind an armor of prickles. But even as he took his first real breath since she'd left the room, she glanced quickly over her shoulder toward Esme's room. "Not in front of Esme though, right?"

Jake had never introduced any of the women he'd dated to his daughter. He'd always meant to do it once the relationship got serious enough, but nothing had ever reached that point. This, with Juliet, was definitely at that point, the idea of a life without her in it no longer acceptable to Jake, but first, they had to figure this out between adults.

"Yes," he said. "Not in front of Esme. You understand why?" After learning how she'd been treated by her family, he never wanted Juliet to feel rejected.

"Of course I do." No tension in her, nothing but an active and protective acceptance. "It'll hurt her if she gets attached that way and we can't make it work."

"Keeping things from her is going to make things interesting." Esme was a smart cookie, and she was going to be attached at the hip to them this entire trip.

"I hear parents have trouble finding privacy for sexy times," Juliet said with a straight face. "I'll consider this a glimpse into an alien world."

"Hah." But he was smiling. She did that to him. Juliet. *Jules.*

His daughter reappeared, backpack on. "See?" She spun around to display the princess's sparkly face. "I'm ready!"

THE NEXT MORNING WENT WELL. Esme was a touch quiet, but they got through the meet and greets without problem. Having been forewarned, the relevant parties had set up the meetings in rooms with glass walls so Esme could play directly outside, beside the admin staff, and Jake could keep an eye on her the entire time.

It might not be how business was usually done, but Jake was who he was, *and* he was giving these people more time than they were contractually entitled to in return, so it wasn't as if they weren't coming out better off in the deal.

Esme chatted away to the staff for the first half of the day, but post-lunch, she sat quietly reading her book.

In the car on the way to the photo shoot, he said, "Boo, you feeling okay?"

Shaking her head, she leaned into him.

He tested her temperature with the back of his hand. She didn't feel hot. On her other side, Juliet ran her hand down Esme's back and shot him a worried look.

Turning from Jake, Esme snuggled into Juliet... and promptly threw up all over her lap.

"Sorry," she said afterward, her eyes welling up as her lower lip quivered.

Sensing real distress, Jake went to snuggle her in his lap but Juliet was already cupping her face in her hands and smiling. "Baby, don't be sad. You didn't mean to do that. You're sick."

"I feel better now," Esme said with a smile.

Jake exhaled quietly and told the driver to detour to their hotel. Then he grabbed a wad of tissues from the courtesy packet wedged in the back of the driver's seat and handed it to Juliet along with a small bottle of water provided by the driver. He also used the opportunity to clean up Esme. She hadn't gotten a spot on her dress, so all he had to do was wipe her mouth.

Meanwhile, Juliet cleaned herself up as best she could while keeping up a light patter to distract Esme, who—

despite Juliet's words—was despondent about messing up Juliet's dress.

"It'll wash out," Juliet told her. "And now I get to wear another outfit. Want to help me choose?"

Esme nodded, her spark starting to come back. He'd keep an eye on her, but from past experience, he had a feeling she'd eaten something at lunch that didn't agree with her and was feeling better now that she'd thrown it up. He made a note to more closely monitor her food intake tomorrow—he'd let her choose what she wanted from the lunch spread today because this trip was a treat with relaxed rules.

For now, he made her drink some water to replace her fluids, then caught Juliet's eye. *Thank you,* he mouthed, because her response had led to his daughter's smile.

A scowl was his reward.

Because Juliet was insulted that he'd think she'd have any other response. His Jules had grown up without love and affection. Instead of allowing that to harden her, she understood the value of being shown such softness. Esme would never want for a pair of loving arms or an affectionate word while with her.

Heart expanding on a rush of nameless emotion, Jake found a plastic bag he'd put in the side pocket of Esme's backpack—because there was always need for one with a six-year-old—and got Juliet to put the dirty tissues in there. Her dress remained a mess, but at least she could walk now without dripping.

"Let me call the studio and tell them we'll be delayed." She made the call a couple of seconds later, her voice friendly but professional.

They arrived at the hotel soon afterward.

"Esme," she whispered, "walk in front of me so no one can see the stain."

Giggling, his daughter took up position, and Juliet put one hand on her shoulder. Jake also used his body to block others from seeing Juliet, and they were soon in the elevator. While Esme skipped into Juliet's room with her, he waited in the corridor. And tortured himself with memories of Juliet's naked curves.

The two of them stepped out only eight minutes later. Juliet now wore a hot red dress tailored to fit her body. It was very much a professional dress—but va-va-voom was an understatement.

"Look, Daddy! I picked Juliet's dress!"

"Baby girl, you have excellent taste." He wanted to wolf whistle, and Jacob Esera did not wolf whistle. "You look gorgeous, Jules."

Juliet ducked her head slightly, a flustered kind of expression on her face, and oh fuck, it was adorable.

But then she smiled, and it dazzled him even more. "Let's go, team. We have work to do."

JAKE GRUMBLED the whole way to the photoshoot, but Juliet and Esme had a grand time once there.

Esme didn't blink an eye when Jake walked out in the boxer briefs he had to wear for the shoot, just said, "Daddy, those are colorful. You only wear black or white."

"Think I should switch to this type?"

A twist of Esme's lips and a thoughtful pause, followed by a decisive, "No, you're not colorful."

Juliet winced, but Jake chuckled—and the camera crew just about fell over. Mostly naked Jacob Esera was a serious punch to the senses, whichever way you swung sexually. But a half-naked Jake who was laughing with his pint-sized daughter? *Boom.*

Then he turned that special private smile Juliet's way, and her knees threatened to melt.

"Shoo." She waved him toward the camera crew. "The faster you finish this, the faster we can get—" She stopped herself from saying "home" just in the nick of time, but Jake's gaze told her he'd heard the word anyway.

As he walked away, Juliet took a deep breath and picked up Esme to put her in a high director's chair that Juliet had organized in advance. She took a seat next to Esme, ready to put a stop to the shoot if anyone stepped out of line.

Which happened way faster than she'd expected.

27

JULIET BREAKS OUT THE SCARY, AND
P.S. ESME SEES AND KNOWS ALL

A scantily clad female model walked out of the dressing area. Jake's eyes went from laughing to flat and angry.

Juliet said, "Esme, stay here."

"Okay." Esme kicked her feet. "This chair makes me tall."

Striding over to the model, Juliet said, "Go back in the dressing room. *Now*." The stunning platinum blonde skedaddled.

Juliet turned her attention to the camera crew. "Go get a coffee."

They didn't hesitate, leaving their equipment where it was and walking away.

At which point she looked at the advertising exec she'd dealt with all through this project. "The contract was very clear. No images of Jake with female models." Jake was conservative in that way, and *everyone* had agreed to his terms in advance.

"Our surveys tell us we'll have much more impact if we pair him with a female model," the other woman said.

"Especially when the model is Kseniya. She's incredibly well known."

"No," Juliet said flatly.

"We can and will pull the plug," the other woman said. "Your boss wouldn't be too happy about that."

"Everett's built his reputation on ethical manufacture and equally ethical treatment of his employees and contractors. He has zero interest in working with people who break their word." She raised an eyebrow. "You do realize you weren't the only party interested in this deal? And that your current stance is a serious breach that gives *Everett* the opportunity to walk away?"

The ad exec paled. "No female model," she said quickly. "I apologize—I didn't understand how serious you were about this."

Yeah, right. Juliet had made Jake's stance clear. "Glad we sorted that out. Let's get this shoot going so we don't fall further behind schedule."

When she turned to look at Jake again, he had his hands on his hips and was staring right at her, a huge grin on his face. "Glad I have you on my side, Jules."

"Be quiet and get modeling."

His grin grew deeper until his cheeks creased. The camera crew all but sprinted into the room to capture the shots of Jake with such a rare expression on his face. Stomach hot, Juliet walked over to see that Esme had her hands pressed together and was grinning too. Her smile was pure Calypso and oh, it hurt Juliet's heart—but in a good way. She was so glad part of her friend lived in this sweet, smart, rugby-loving girl.

"You made the mean lady be nice," Esme whispered.

"Yes." Juliet bent down to press a kiss to the top of Esme's hair without thought. "Now, let's watch your daddy strut his stuff."

"How come he has to wear only his shorts?" Esme kicked her feet again. "Uncle Danny does that sometimes at Grandpa and Grandma's. When I wake up early, I go see him."

"Yeah?" Juliet had to bite back a grin at what a twenty-two-year-old might get up to in his private flat that he'd have to scramble to hide from sharp little eyes. "What does he say?"

"Boo, I'm sleeping." Esme did an excellent approximation of a growly voice. "Then he puts his pillow over his head, like this." Esme pretended to drop a pillow on her face. "I jump into bed and tickle him and he makes me pancakes."

That hadn't gone at all how Juliet had expected. "Does he have friends to stay sometimes?" she asked, curious about how it worked with Danny living at home.

Esme nodded. "Yup. He had a big party one time and his friends were sleeping all over. On the floor and the couch and one fell asleep in Grandma's garden and squished her flowers." A shake of her head. "Grandma was *maaad*."

Okay, that was more what she'd expected. Could be Danny went somewhere else with women—on his salary, he could afford the most exclusive hotel rooms.

"I'd be mad too," she said. "Flowers take ages to grow."

"Yup, Grandma made Uncle Danny and his friends plant new ones."

Smile wide, Esme waved at her father when he glanced their way.

He still had laughter in his eyes.

Juliet clenched her stomach against the urge to run over there and kiss him silly. When the female photographer dared step closer to give Jake instructions, she was buffeted by a sudden wave of raw possessiveness.

Gritting her teeth, she made herself look away.

It had been difficult with Reid, how the groupies would swarm. It'd be a nightmare with Jake. He didn't court attention, but he was undeniably hot—and he was at the top of his career. Bees to honey was putting it mildly when it came to female interest in him. The design firm's PR team had done a workup on his profile when Everett was first considering the campaign, and Jacob Esera had a *significant* following of admirers who'd drop their panties at a moment's notice.

It was more than a little troubling to know that the man with whom she was falling in love had so many choices available to him.

But he asked you, Juliet. He showed his heart to you. He doesn't play with the rest of the world. He plays with you.

Juliet settled again. If Jake wanted a groupie, he'd had endless opportunities. Yet he'd picked a girl who'd once had elbows of doom. As she'd picked him. She had to remember that too. This wasn't a one-sided deal. The two of them had chosen each other, and it was up to the two of them to make it work.

"Uncle Danny's friends are fun." Esme's voice broke into her thoughts. "But he's the nicest."

Juliet wrenched her thoughts back to the moment. "Yeah?"

"Yeah." A gap-toothed smile. "But he fights with Catie lots."

"Yes, I saw that at the barbeque." During the wedding photos, however, she'd seen Danny instinctively stretch out an arm for Catie to grab when she nearly slipped on a step.

Catie's hand had landed on his powerful forearm as if she'd known it'd be there.

The next minute, Danny had teased her for being like a hippo in a china shop, and she'd shot back that she wasn't the Neanderthal who ran around "aimlessly" with a ball. They'd walked down the steps together.

Juliet still hadn't figured out that particular relationship.

Esme put her hand on Juliet's where she had it on the arm of her chair.

Juliet glanced over. "You feeling okay, Boo? Your tummy all right?"

"Yep." Esme rubbed her stomach. "All systems normal."

Juliet bit back a laugh, figuring one of her uncles had to have taught her that phrase. "You want to sit with me?" Sometimes, as a child, all she'd wanted was a pair of loving arms around her.

When Esme nodded, she scooped the girl's small weight over into her lap. Nuzzling her chin on Jake's baby's hair, she was *not* prepared for Esme to say, "Jules, do you like my dad?"

Juliet felt like a deer caught in the headlights. "Sure," she managed to croak out. "He's my friend."

A thoughtful pause before Esme said, "You can kiss him if you like." It was a solemn statement. "Like Aunt Charlie kisses Uncle Gabe, and Aunt Issie kisses Uncle Sailor, and Grandma kisses Grandpa."

Juliet was drowning. She thought about sending out smoke signals for help, but Jake was busy completing his work with the attention to detail that made him so spectacular on the field; she was on her own. "Uncle Danny doesn't get kissed?" she said, clutching at any available straw.

"No, but he's a kid. Like me and Emmaline. It's different."

Danny was no kid, but she could see how he'd occupy a different place in the girls' minds. The youngest Esera boy, he likely got treated like a kid by his brothers as well as his parents. Never mind that he was six feet, three inches tall and probably around a hundred kilos of pure muscle that exploded into impossible speed on the field.

That made him a couple of inches taller than Jake, but their builds were similar. In fact, the only member of the family taller than Danny was Gabriel. Obviously, given Esme's declaration, his size made zero difference to how he was treated. Juliet had seen the same immovable pecking order in other large families; Danny would always be the kid brother, even when he was ninety.

"And he's not a daddy," Esme added firmly. "Daddies need mummy kisses." A soft kind of sadness to her. "My mummy is in heaven."

Eyes hot, Juliet found herself hugging Esme tighter. "I knew your mummy," she whispered. "We went to school together."

Esme sat up straight, her eyes bright when she looked back at Juliet's face. "Really?"

"Yes. She had a smile just like yours, and she wore glasses, and her hair was silky like yours." It had been blond instead of Esme's black, but it'd had the same softness and texture. "We used to sit together at lunch and share our food." The trade had been heavily one-sided, mostly because Calypso always had way more than even she—the infamous devourer of an entire pizza—could eat.

Juliet had accepted the imbalance because their friendship was deep enough that they'd long ago stopped keeping track of favors given and received. "She was really nice, your mum."

Esme had so many questions, and Juliet answered

them all. It wasn't until Jake had dressed and was walking toward them that she wondered if she'd overstepped her bounds.

Esme piped up with "Daddy, did you know Jules knew Mummy?"

A curve of his lips. "Yep. We all went to school together," he told his daughter as Juliet shook hands with the ad executive, who still looked a little scared of her.

She was back with Jake and Esme when he said, "Want to know a secret?"

"What?"

"Juliet and I didn't like each other then."

"Really?" Eyes rounded, Esme looked from one to the other. "Like Uncle Danny and Catie?"

Jake snorted. "Those two are a whole other story." He shook his head. "But yeah, a little bit like that."

"But you like each other now?" A serious question.

"Yes," Jake said, his eyes meeting Juliet's. "I really like her now."

The knots in Juliet's stomach grew hotter, tighter.

Especially when Esme took one of their hands each and beamed. "Good! I told her she can kiss you!"

As a result of an extra meeting that had to be shoehorned in, it ended up being a long day. Jake was worried about Esme, but she caught a nap during a car ride and was so excited by all the new experiences that she was otherwise up and active, with no indication she was feeling unwell again. She'd crash tonight, sleep like a log, but that'd be good for her.

Still, all three of them were feeling the long day by the time they finally arrived back at their hotel. Running into their suite, Esme collapsed dramatically onto her back on the chaise by the window.

"I'm ex-aus-tid," she declared, each syllable sounded out.

Juliet, who'd stopped in the doorway to talk to him, sighed. "Tell me about it, Boo. At least you don't have to deal with mean ladies."

Esme giggled and popped up into a sitting position. "Can we eat in our room?"

"Room service picnic?" Jake raised an eyebrow at Juliet.

"Sounds like heaven. Give me a few minutes to change into my pajamas. I am *not* wearing proper clothes again until tomorrow morning."

Jake appreciated the sweet curves of her ass in that red dress as she walked down the hallway. His wolf whistle was quiet, but she sent him a look over her shoulder that told him she'd heard. The smile flirting with her lips said he wasn't in too much trouble.

Miming taking a blow to the heart, he staggered back against the doorjamb.

Her laughter lingered in the air after she disappeared into her suite.

Returning to his own, he first helped Esme get into her pj's too. They'd bought two pairs for this trip, and she wanted the yellow ones with brown dogs on them.

"Look at the doggies, Daddy," she said slyly as she finished buttoning her top.

Jake was onto her. "We are not getting a dog," he said for the thousandth time. "I travel too much and your grandparents can't dog-sit all the time. A dog would be lonely."

"Grandma and Grandpa stay home more. It could be *their* dog," his too-smart kid said. "We could take it for walks and pet it."

Jake knew full well that she was wearing his parents

down on the topic, but he wasn't about to be a sucker too. "You know dogs poop," he said, bringing out the big guns. "You wanna clean that up?"

A screwing up of her nose.

He popped into his room to change while she thought that over, leaving his door partially ajar. He was just pulling on a pair of sweatpants when she called out, "I saw Mrs. Dennis use a thing!"

"What thing?" He found a loose tee, was about to pull it on when he remembered the way Juliet had shaped his arms while they'd been in bed together. Throwing the tee aside, he found his white one that was snug on the arms and showed off his biceps. It had been a gift from Catie. Ísa's sister had become part of the family and, according to her, he needed to flaunt what he had.

"The poopy thing!" Esme said loudly as Jake came out of his room. She was making motions as if she had a shovel, a tiny and determined creature digging at the hotel carpet.

Growling, he ran over and picked her up, pretending to be a monster who wanted to take bites out of her.

Shrieking with laughter as he "attacked" her stomach, she said, "Daddy!" but it wasn't a request to stop. They were still playing when the door opened and Juliet walked in.

She paused on the doorstep, dressed in a pair of gray sweatpants and a dark blue hoodie under which he could see a hint of lace. Maybe a camisole?

"Jules! Save me!" Esme reached out her arms.

Juliet joined the game, and all three of them were huffed and warm and happy when they collapsed on the sofa not long afterward.

Jake picked up the room service menu. "What do you want?" he asked his ladies.

Because they were both his ladies now, even if Juliet

hadn't yet committed to it. Yeah, there were obstacles—he'd checked his phone during one of the car rides and seen that her bastard of an ex was still shooting off his mouth. Since Juliet had made it so clear that she had no use for Reid, the buttwipe had switched tactics and was now trying to paint her as a bitch who'd broken his heart by cheating on him.

28

AN INVITATION TO MISBEHAVE

J ake didn't know if Juliet had seen the latest volley, but he'd sent Thea a text to see if they should do anything. Her reply had been succinct: *Let him dig that hole. He's looking like more of a whining ass with every word he utters.*

True enough, but the problem was that he was keeping Juliet's name in the media without her consent or desire. It was something that needed to stop, but Jake put it out of his mind for tonight—this was special and Reid had no place here.

Right then Juliet was pretending to tickle Esme, and Esme was attempting to shield herself while not going far from Juliet, and they both looked so happy and at home. Jake trusted Juliet absolutely with Esme's heart, and he'd never trusted anyone outside the family with his baby.

"Ahem," he said. "Shall I order salad?"

"Ew!" Esme declared. "No salad!"

"Yeah, no salad," Juliet echoed. "I want a burger. Esme, burger? Nuggets?"

Esme put a finger to her lips and thought about it. "Spaghetti," she announced at last.

He scanned the menu. "They do burgers." Fancy burgers with ingredients he'd never heard of, but hey, it was a burger and at that price, it better be prime. "No spaghetti, but they have mac and cheese." He'd have nixed the cheesy dish if Esme's stomach had still been iffy, but she was back to her usual self, and probably quite hungry after the light snacks they'd given her through the rest of the day. "You want that, Boo?"

"Yummy in my tummy." She rubbed her stomach and licked her lips, just like Danny had taught her. "Plus ice cream."

"No ice cream today, but I'll reconsider tomorrow," Jake said. "I don't want to give your stomach too much to handle tonight."

"Tomorrow!" Esme collapsed on the floor on a giant sigh, making Jake shake his head and wonder if he was nurturing a future star of the stage.

"I'll get a burger too." He glanced at a laughing Juliet, so content in this moment that he felt... right. Exactly where he was meant to be. "You want to try this appetizer platter thing?"

"Is it weird?"

"Can't tell," Jake said, reconsidering the platter thing. "Don't think the ingredients are in English." He was already going out on a limb with that burger.

But Juliet being Juliet, said, "What the hey. Let's order it —we can play a game to see if we can figure out what we're eating."

Fully on board with the idea of playing with Juliet, he placed the order, and Esme declared that they had to have a proper picnic. Which entailed moving the dining table out of the way and spreading one of the spare blankets on the carpet. Jake and Juliet chose a spot by the windows that looked out on the colorful chaos of Times Square.

"You've always been ballsy," he said to Juliet when Esme went to the toilet. "But today, how you dealt with that ad exec, was something else." He'd been so fucking proud of her—and he'd had a Neanderthal thought: *She's kicking your ass and she's mine.*

Juliet gave him an odd look. "How come you weren't mad I took over like that?"

Reid. Fucker had left her with more than one scar. "Because it's your job," he said simply. "You knew exactly what to say to get her to back down. I'd have come across as being irrational."

"There's nothing irrational about wanting a certain brand image."

"Jules, you know I don't do it for that reason. It's because I don't want Esme confused by seeing images of her dad cozying up to a random woman while in his fricking underwear."

A twitch of her lips. "She was unfazed by seeing you in your briefs."

"Try having a kid and not letting them catch you in your skivvies." Jake remembered many a night when, bleary-eyed, he'd rocked his little girl to sleep after a nightmare or soothed her when she was feeling sick. "But it's different if there's a woman involved. Especially since Esme doesn't have a mum."

"I get it." Juliet took a cross-legged position on the blanket. "She knows something's up."

"Yeah, she's a smart cookie." He couldn't help feeling smug about that, even though most of Esme's brains had no doubt come from Calypso. "The thing is, Jules, you're part of her life now, whatever happens."

A hard swallow. "I won't let her down. I promise."

"I know you won't."

Esme ran out right then, holding out her hands. "I washed! With soap! Promise."

"Good girl." He patted a spot on the blanket just as someone knocked on the door. Esme came with him to get the room service cart. He handed the waiter a generous tip and wheeled the cart over to the blanket.

They set out their meals on the blanket, along with the bottles of water the turndown service had left behind. The service had also left behind small boxes of chocolate that he'd had to hide from his daughter.

As they ate, he was struck by the comfort of it: Juliet wasn't trying too hard with Esme. She was being herself, and the person she was happened to be kind and gentle with people who needed that gentleness. She'd snapped at him in school, but he'd never once seen her snap at Calypso.

When Esme decided she'd rather have some burger instead of finishing her mac and cheese, Juliet cut off a piece of hers before Jake could do the same. God, she was digging deeper into his heart with every second that passed. He was screwed if she decided against him. Which was why he had to make very sure she decided for him. For them.

Even when Esme began to fall asleep midway through the meal and grew bad-tempered with her inability to stay awake, Juliet took it in stride. While Jake carried his daughter through to the bathroom to clean her teeth before he put her to bed, Juliet got her laptop and returned a couple of emails.

He came back to find she'd waited for him rather than finishing her meal.

Seeing him, she closed the laptop and put it aside.

"She hates missing out," he said after sitting down on the blanket next to Juliet rather than across from her. He put his hand deliberately behind her, his arm acting as a brace for her back.

"Jake."

"She's conked out," he assured her. "Trust me, when she gets like this, I could set off a siren next to her and she'd sleep on." It amazed him, where both Esme and Emmaline could fall asleep. "My mum says she gets that from me. Apparently, one time I fell asleep while Mum was riding in an ambulance with the siren going full blast."

"Why was she in an ambulance?"

"Danny—he came early and the birth was a bit compli-cated. She was alone with me at home, so I got to ride with her to the hospital. Family legend is I crawled onto the stretcher beside her and snoozed away. Dad arrived at the ER right as she was being wheeled in—I was still fast asleep."

Juliet's eyes were on his mouth, her teeth sinking into her lower lip. "You're even sexier when you smile."

Smile turning into a grin, Jake said, "I'll use my powers for good."

Instead of making a face at him or laughing again, she turned back to her food. Three bites later: "Did you see what Reid's saying?"

"I come from a good family, but I'm pretty sure one of my cousins knows a hit man or three." Aleki had gone over to the dark side for a while in his teens, though he now ran a very legitimate security firm. "Want me to put the word out?"

"If only." She picked up a fry, stared at it before defiantly crunching it between her teeth. "Thea says I should maintain radio silence right now. That he's trying to goad me into turning this into a melodrama."

"That's what she told me too."

Juliet's brows gathered over her eyes. "Why are you talking to Thea about me?"

"Because you matter to me."

JAKE'S WORDS knocked the breath out of Juliet. To say it so bluntly, so without hesitation: *You matter to me.*

No one since Calypso had claimed her so without conditions—and that had been a childhood friendship. This... She didn't know how to react. Fear tangled with need inside her, alongside a bone-deep terror. The need won and Juliet found herself leaning into him, the hunger inside her painful. Cupping her jaw in that way he had of doing, as if she was precious, he kissed her.

Jake's kiss...

Toes curling, her slippers long ago kicked off, she leaned deeper into him, drunk on him and on how he made her feel. Cherished. Wanted. Beautiful. "You smell too good."

Her complaint made his lips curve against her own, his kiss even more potent for it.

When he went to nudge her down to the blanket, she found the breath to say, "Food."

A second, two, and he'd pushed that food out of the way. Then he was coming down over her, a strongly built man sleek with muscle. She loved feeling the weight and power of him. Nudging her legs apart, he settled himself in between. She groaned. He was already hard. Harder than the biceps she gripped as he moved his head down to the curve of her neck.

She shivered under each kiss, but she didn't attempt to

control the sensations... because this was Jake. Strong, annoying, protective, too serious Jake who devastated her when he smiled. Curling her legs around his hips, she held on for kiss after kiss. His hair was slightly rough under her touch, the strands sliding through her fingers before she managed to get a grip.

In contrast, his skin was silky and hot and when she gave in to temptation and tugged up the back of his T-shirt so she could slide her hands underneath, he made a rumbling sound in his chest that went straight through her nipples and to her core.

Clenching her thighs around him, she kissed the curve of his shoulder. He pushed up against her, once, twice, his erection hard and frankly a bit intimidating despite the fact they'd already been together twice.

He kissed her throat again, sucking for a second.

Shivers cascaded over her. "Jake." She pushed at his shoulders. "Bedroom." *He* might be certain Esme would sleep through an earthquake, but Juliet needed the security of a door and at least a second's warning.

The last thing she wanted to do was traumatize Jake's baby girl.

He rose up off her, his arm muscles flexing and his ridged abdomen taut as he went into an effortless push-up. She swooned like a romance-novel heroine. The man was *hot*. But that wasn't what caught her, held her.

With his hair falling across his forehead and a wicked smile on his face, he looked so young. And the thing was, they *were* both so young, only twenty-four. It was just that life had aged them.

"Do you think we can be young together?" she found herself whispering.

Though she'd spoken utterly out of context, Jake said,

"We already are, Jules." He rose to his feet with enviable fluidity, then held out his hand with that smile that enslaved her. "Let's misbehave."

Her own cheeks creasing, she took his hand and he hauled her to her feet—and into him. She rose onto her tiptoes, unable to resist the temptation of his mouth, of him. He moved backward as he kissed her and she followed, her breasts crushed against the heat of his bare chest and one of his hands on the back of her neck, the other on her ass.

Her skin heated at his open appreciation of her curves.

Once inside the bedroom she said, "Do we close the door?" She didn't know about children Esme's age, what they would and wouldn't find scary.

Jake nudged it shut. "She'll come in if she needs me." At her horrified look, he chuckled, and she saw a glimpse of the Jake who'd souped up his car and burned rubber. "Seriously, Jules, if you're going to be with me, you'll have to get used to the idea of occasionally being caught with your pants down."

She shoved at his outrageously gorgeous chest, though the idea of being part of such a tight little family group made her go all warm inside. "It's not that. It's because we're not together yet." It'd be different if Esme walked in on Mummy and Daddy or even Daddy and Daddy's long-term lover. You could explain that away.

A quietness to Jake's face. "Aren't we?" He cupped her jaw and cheek, rubbed the pad of his thumb over her cheekbone. "Are you going to see other people?"

"No." She fisted her hand in his T-shirt. "But you know what I mean."

He brushed his thumb over her cheekbone again. "Thank you for watching out for my baby girl, Jules." The tenderness in his voice shattered walls inside her she hadn't known she'd put up. "But trust me, she's not going to wake up."

She did, she realized. Trust him. Jacob Esera, the annoying boy from school, had grown into a man she trusted in a way she'd never trusted anyone else.

Tugging at his clothes, she said, "I thought we were going to misbehave."

He laughed, wild and young again, and tore off his T-shirt. It ended up hanging on top of a standing lamp. "Three-point throw," he quipped.

Juliet giggled, adoring this Jake as much as she did serious Jake. He caught her laughter with his mouth, her hands landing on the hard, ridged muscle of his chest. Every part of her clenched. The man was flat-out-beautiful.

It wouldn't have mattered if he hadn't also been Jake.

But because he was, she let herself indulge and she let herself fall. He unzipped her hoodie and she shrugged it off. Her camisole was a dark burgundy with matching lace at the top. She'd worn it because it was comfortable, with no intent to entice, but bared to Jake's gaze she was glad to be wearing something pretty.

Breaking the kiss, he bent his head to press his lips to the vee between her breasts.

His hand slid up the satin to cup one unfettered breast. "No bra," he said in a *very* happy tone of voice. "Naughty Jules."

Brain cells misfiring, she had to fight to get out the words. "I wanted to be comfortable." She never wore a bra while at home.

"Be comfortable around me all you like, I insist." He closed one big, hot hand around her breast, the other on the back of her neck as he took another voracious kiss.

Juliet broke it to kiss her way down his jaw and along his

throat, to the hollow at the base of his neck that had tempted her from the start. He shivered when she licked him there, and though Reid had done a number on her self-confidence in bed—she knew he was full of shit, but she wasn't superhuman, couldn't forget all his barbs—she kept going, kissing and licking and sampling the addictive taste of him as she shaped her hands over his body.

"God, Jake. Your body is ludicrous." It was the stuff of a woman's wet dreams.

He chuckled, one hand fisting in her hair. "Comes with the job."

She tongued his abs, began to slide lower, but he tugged her up with a grip in her hair. His eyes were hot.

"That can wait," he said. "First I want to see your back arch, feel you go all wet and quivering around me as I make you come."

29

JAKE IMPROVES HIS GRADE

Throat dry, Juliet braced herself against the back of the door as he hooked his fingers in the sides of her sweatpants and tugged down.

He looked up with a grin. "I like the little rabbits."

She flushed, remembering the cotton bikini panties she'd pulled on this morning. Black, with happy white bunnies bouncing all over them, they didn't match her camisole, weren't in any way seductive. But she found herself smiling back because he looked so damn delighted with her. "Wait till you see what's under them."

Leaving her pants pooled around her legs, he leaned in to press a kiss to the top part of her panties, the spot right below her navel. A tremor ran through her. For a moment, she was afraid, confused. Sex had never been like this for her. Not even the first time with Jake.

But when he looked up at her as if she was his every fantasy come to life, nothing but Esme running in could've stopped her from going forward. She lifted a foot and he tugged one leg of her sweatpants off, then waited for her to lift the other foot.

Two seconds later, her pants were gone.

Instead of getting to his feet and taking her to the bed afterward, he stayed where he was and ran his hands up her calves and to the backs of her knees, her lower thighs.

A look up out of dark eyes that ate her up. "Take off the camisole."

Her hesitation was instinctive but minute. This was Jake, and Jake had already seen her naked—and come back. Not only that, he'd just told her he loved her body. Raising her arms, she tugged the whisper of satin and lace off over her head and threw it aside. His eyes heated as he took in the bare mounds of her breasts, her nipples chocolate brown and large against the generous weight.

She'd have been fine if he'd stayed there—her breasts were sexy even if they were never going to be perky. That ship had sailed three cup sizes ago. But he moved his gaze down over her abdomen; Juliet colored, battling the instinct to suck in her stomach. She jogged and she did yoga, but she was never going to have washboard abs like him.

Her abdomen held a soft outward curve, and it was the one part of her body that she always tried to downplay or obscure with the cut of her clothes.

But the heat in Jake's eyes didn't dim.

"I love how soft you are, and I love all these dangerous curves," he said, his voice like gravel as he laved kisses over her abdomen and down to her navel. "I want to take you from behind one day so I can stroke your ass while I thrust inside you."

Juliet soaked her panties.

Never had she thought Jake could talk so dirty.

Shoving her critical inner voice to the side in favor of Jake's much sexier one, she wove her fingers in his hair and, when he rose to his knees to press another kiss to her navel, she didn't make a self-deprecating comment about the soft-ness there. Instead, she closed her eyes and drank in the sensation of his gorgeous body so close to her, his hands on her skin, his breath whispering over her.

"I just remembered I have to prove my expertise with my tongue."

Juliet looked down, her heart thudding double time. "Practice makes perfect."

A wicked grin as he hooked his fingers in the sides of her panties.

Throat dry but a smile on her lips, she didn't protest, just silently raised one foot, then the other. His next kiss was to the curls at the apex of her thighs. One big hand spread against her left inner thigh, a gentle push.

Taking the hint, she spread her legs, and he hooked one up over his shoulder. Juliet dug her heel into his bare back. She couldn't look down, was certain she'd explode. But it was almost worse, not being able to see what he'd do next.

He didn't tease.

He just spread her open with the fingers of one hand and ate her up. Stifling her cry against her forearm, she gripped his hair tighter. In response, he pushed her other leg out wider and settled in for a deeper taste. A suck of her clitoris had everything in her clenching and tiny white lights bursting in front of her eyes—she wanted him so much and he was doing the most delicious, decadent thing to her.

The first time she'd been shocked into pleasure. It was even better now that she and Jake weren't just lovers for a single night. He stroked and kissed her through the first orgasm, then set his mind to tenderly, determinedly, pushing her up over a second peak. Her knees buckled during it, but Jake caught her. A very smug Jake. She'd never before seen that particular look on his face. It suited him.

"What's my grade?" he asked, his lips slick with her.

Cradled naked in his arms, her body trembling with aftershocks, she pressed a kiss to his neck. "B plus." She patted his rumbling chest. "Gotta keep you keen to improve." Though she'd be deceased if he improved any further.

A masculine chuckle. "I think you like my tongue, Jules."

Boneless, she just kissed his throat.

Rising as if she weighed nothing—and no, that was never not going to make her swoon—he walked over to the bed and dropped her on the mattress. She might've felt self-conscious lying naked on the crisp white sheets, all skin and curves, except that he'd already done something excruciatingly intimate to her—and she'd loved it.

Holding her gaze with the glittering dark of his, he dropped his hands to the top of his jeans and undid the button. She found herself biting down on her bottom lip as she watched his hands move.

He undid the zipper, waited.

She made a sound in the back of her throat and looked up... to see a slow smile light up his face.

Instead of flushing, she felt her lips curve too. "Tease."

He leaned over to kiss her, arms braced on the bed beside her. She could taste herself on him, and it was the most intimate thing she'd ever done with another person. Raising one hand, she petted his chest as they kissed and there was an innocent, bright happiness inside her that terrified.

Nothing had ever felt this good. This right.

When he pushed back off the bed this time, he took off his jeans. His boxer briefs were a simple white. The head of his erection pushed out from the top, the tip rounded and slick. Stripping off his briefs, he dropped them on the carpet and put one knee on the bed.

Feeling wild, Juliet spread her legs.

A deep sound in his throat before he wrenched open a bedside drawer and pulled out a box he must've put in there at some stage. He swore as he fought to tear off the plastic. Removing one flat packet soon afterward, he sheathed himself with quick, efficient hands. Hands that shook slightly.

If she'd had any defenses left, they would've collapsed into dust at that moment.

She wrapped her arms around him as he came over her, and lifted her head to kiss his jaw. He looked down, cupped one hip with his hand, and began to work himself into her. He clearly knew he was of a size to make things difficult if he wasn't careful, but she was so wet from what he'd done to her that her body stretched with languorous ease.

Ripples of pleasure washing over her, she buried her face in his neck. He thrust home. It shocked a small cry out of her.

"Jules?" Taut, rigid muscle above and around her.

"Good," she gasped out. "So good, Jake." She felt full to the limit but in a way that made every nerve ending quiver. As she pressed kisses to whatever part of his body she could reach, he began to move, slow and easy at first, then into a rolling motion that had her back arching under him and her body spasming uncontrollably in an orgasm that seemed to stretch into eternity.

"Fuck!" Shoving one hand under her ass, he gripped the curve of her cheek and held her as he thrust in and out in a hard and fast rhythm that made her pleasure-drunk bones shudder on another erotic wave.

Quivering in the aftermath, she held his sweat-filmed body as he found his own pleasure. The affection she felt for him right then wasn't affection at all. It was deeper, far more dangerous.

He came with a deep groan before collapsing on her. She gave a small "oof" because he was heavy, but she wrapped herself around him too. Because it was Jake.

JAKE'S MIND WAS ADDLED. He'd lost all control there at the end, and now he was crushing Juliet, but he couldn't seem to gather together the strength to move. His muscles trembled, his entire body in a kind of shock.

The first time with Juliet had been good, really good, but this was...

He had no words.

Nuzzling at her throat, he managed to make himself functional enough to roll them both over so he was lying on his back with her sprawled on top of him. He kept his arm around her, his hand possessive on the curve of her hip. His chest heaved, his heart pounding so hard that, had he been on the field, his coach would've ripped into him for being out of condition—but there was no training for this.

For Juliet.

"Whoa."

She snorted out a giggle at his statement, a funny and adorable sound. It made him want to laugh, and he'd never laughed in bed.

"Was that normal?" he asked in a deliberate echo of their first time together.

"No," Juliet confirmed with a kiss to his pectoral. "Can I ask a question? You don't have to answer."

He stroked her hip. "I have no secrets from you, Jules. Ask."

"How did you and Calypso manage? I mean, you were both virgins at the time and you're not exactly small—but Callie told me it was good, and she was blushing and smiling at the time, so I believed her."

"Jeez, do girls really talk about everything?"

"Pretty much. Also, I was a virgin and wanted intel from my best friend."

Jake grinned at the idea of shy Calypso whispering said intel to Juliet. "I have two older brothers," he told her. "They sat me down when I began to notice girls that way and gave me "the talk"—and they gave me the best advice anyone can give a teenage boy."

Raising herself up on her elbow, Juliet pushed the tangled mass of her hair off her face. "What?" She put her hand back down on his chest, spread her fingers.

"That if I could make it feel good for my girl, chances were *much* higher she'd let me see her naked again." Jake shrugged. "I mean, most teenage boys are all about doing anything to increase chances of female nakedness, so I took serious note."

Juliet's shoulders shook. "Did they give you pointers too?"

"A few," Jake admitted, thinking back to that day when Sailor and Gabe had taken him out for a drive. He hadn't been of drinking age, but when they'd brought the vehicle to a stop by a black sand beach, the waves crashing to shore in the distance, the three of them had sat on the tailgate and Gabe had let him have half a beer while they talked.

It had made him feel like an adult, and the resulting conversation hadn't been embarrassing, rather a rite of passage he remembered warmly. He knew they'd done the same for Danny, too, when their youngest brother got to that age.

"I still messed up with Calypso," he said, then looked at Juliet. "Is *this* weird? Me and you talking about that?"

"No, Jake." A soft smile. "She was part of your life. Part of my life. It's okay to remember her—if you don't, you're shutting off a whole important chunk of your life."

Reid, he thought, was a fucking moron. He'd given up Juliet. But better for Jake. "I was so excited that I busted my nut in a matter of seconds." He'd been painfully embarrassed in the aftermath. "She was really sweet about it though. Later, she said she liked all the other stuff, and could we do more of that, so we did, and we somehow figured things out."

He smiled at the memory of that long-ago experience.

Her lips curving, Juliet put her head down on his shoulder. "Did she ever tell you that I stole the pregnancy test for her?"

Jake's hand tightened on her hip. "No. Why did you have to steal it?" Calypso's parents had given her a good allowance.

"We were both so paranoid that it'd spread all over the school if we got caught. My aunt would've assumed it was for me, and the shit would've hit the fan."

Yet she'd done it anyway because Juliet was loyal, stood by her people. "What happened?" They'd obviously gotten away with it.

"We took the bus to another suburb, then went into a supermarket and bought a whole bunch of stuff—cookies and things—while I pocketed the test. I checked to see if it had a strip to set off the detectors but couldn't find one. But the detectors went off when we went through—I swear, I almost sweated through my cardigan. Calypso went sheet-white."

A gentle laugh. "We froze while the security guard came over, and he said, 'Girls, let's see what you have there,' and we showed him the bag of stuff we'd bought and he checked the receipt and said, 'Looks all good. Off you go then.'"

More laughter. "We didn't say a word until we were around the corner from the supermarket, then we collapsed onto the curb and had a hyperventilating session. God, we were so young." She blew out a breath. "The next week, we went back and put the money for the test in a charity box at the supermarket because we felt so guilty about stealing."

Jake listened, learning of a part of Calypso's pregnancy experience that he'd never before known. The nerves she must've suffered, the worry. Made a little better because of a friend who'd kept all her secrets, no matter how big or small. "When did she do the test?"

"That day. We found a public toilet in a nice mall—all clean and shiny. Calypso wouldn't go into any of the public toilets in the parks or anywhere else."

"Yeah, she never would."

"I had to stand outside and guard the door just in case someone barged in while she did it. She came out with the finished test hidden in the box and stashed in her backpack, but I could tell the answer from the look on her face." Juliet's voice grew thick. "I gave her this big hug and told her that you wouldn't abandon her."

Jake went motionless at the echo of confidence in her voice. "Yeah?"

"You might've been a gearhead jock, but you took your responsibilities seriously."

They lay in silence for several moments, the past weaving with the present. He thought if Calypso was up there, she'd be pleased to see them this way—she'd always wanted them to be friends. And if she wasn't here to raise her daughter, then who better than the best friend who'd never let her down?

Such a leap from nemesis to lover to *his* woman, the one he'd trust to help him raise his child. It seemed too fast. But he and Juliet, they already knew each other in ways many couples never did. As Times Square blazed outside, he tightened his hold on her.

30

A KISS IN TIMES SQUARE

The next day followed much the same pattern as the first, though he had fewer work commitments. After those were complete, they returned to the hotel for a rest. While Esme napped, he and Juliet turned on the music and danced together as they hadn't at the wedding.

All slow and sexy and pasted together.

He left her only long enough to put on the sailor cap he'd bought from a novelty shop back home. "Couldn't find the full suit," he said, walking out of the bedroom. "How's this?"

Laughing in open delight, she held up a hand as she backed to the door of the suite. "Five minutes."

She returned in under that time wearing a knockout dress in dark pink, her feet in those skyscraper black heels he adored.

Bending her over his arm to re-create the famous kiss, Jake said, "You are the sexiest, most beautiful woman I've ever seen."

Her lips parted.

He kissed her, tender at first, then all tongue and sex.

Since she was wearing a dress, he also got his hand on the bare skin of her thigh. She retaliated by cupping his growing erection. Drawing her back into a standing position, he glanced at the room where Esme slept before tugging her into his bedroom.

"Quickie?"

She shimmied out of her panties in response.

That was how Jake got to live out his fantasy of taking her pinned against a wall, her long legs wrapped around him. She came quick and hard around him, setting him off. They were still entangled when he heard Esme call out his name.

Groaning, he disengaged and went to get rid of the condom.

Juliet was in the living room cuddling Esme by the time he came out.

His heart didn't stand a chance.

Then, a day later, his angelic little girl threw two uncharacteristic tantrums out of nowhere. Except he knew those tantrums weren't out of nowhere. She was picking up on the growing emotional connection between him and Juliet.

Jake wondered if Juliet would react with dismay, but she took it in stride. Jake was so fascinated by her reaction that he mentioned it while Esme was stomping around in her room, refusing to talk to them.

She burst out laughing. "Jake, honey, have you forgotten who you're talking to? I was the resident bad girl in high school. Esme can't do anything I haven't done a hundred times worse."

As a result of Juliet's calm and unfazed response—all of it backed up by hugs and affection when Esme came out of her room at last—his baby girl began to settle around Juliet in a way she'd never before done around someone who wasn't a member of the family. She was starting to learn that whether she threw a tantrum or threw up over Juliet or refused to eat the food that she'd especially asked for, Juliet wouldn't respond by rejecting her.

That night and the next, their final one in New York, Esme asked for good-night hugs from both of them. The three of them had spent that night out in the lights of the city—and though he had no sailor hat, Jake got to kiss Juliet in Times Square. He did it while Esme was momentarily distracted by watching fireworks high above. It felt as if they were inside him, tiny bursts of light and happiness.

"Be mine?" he whispered, then glanced down at the little hand she held in hers. "Be ours?"

Wide eyes, fear in them yet, but she nodded, her eyes colored in all the hues of Times Square. This time Jake kissed her while Esme was looking. His daughter cried out in glee, and they both had to go down and kiss her on the cheek, one on either side of her.

His girls. His heart.

THINGS WENT to shit the instant they landed in New Zealand. Jake took his phone off airplane mode as they walked along the air bridge, then tucked it into his back pocket. It began to vibrate over and over within seconds.

Frowning at the deluge of messages, he retrieved the phone while Juliet and Esme walked on ahead hand in hand, the two of them chatting animatedly. Esme had entrusted Juliet with Mr. Mouse but pulled her princess carry-on. Jake was pulling Juliet's so she had an arm free for the stuffed toy, his own carry-on a team duffel he had over one shoulder.

The messages were from his family and from Thea Arsana. He opened one at random. It was from Sailor: *Jake, that asshole Reid's released an intimate shot of Juliet. He's claiming it's recent and was taken with her consent. Fucker.*

Rage burned through Jake's blood like fire. He clicked the link his brother had included, felt his hand bunch into a fist when he saw it was a relatively tame photo of Juliet in bed, the sheet pulled up over her breasts. She was leaning her head on her hand and smiling at the person taking the photo. All you could see were her bare shoulders and arms, and the slope of her hip under the sheet.

Her face, however, was as it was today, not the sharper and more angular version of her past with her ex. He skimmed the "article," saw that Reid was claiming Juliet had been with him the week before the impromptu press conference where she'd blasted him to pieces. The bastard had pointed to the date stamp as proof. That date was the night Jake and Juliet had first kissed.

They'd reached passport control.

He waited until they were through and waiting for their luggage before murmuring to Juliet. Esme was busy looking out for their bags, so they had relative privacy.

"Jules, we need to deal with something."

"Oh God, what's he done now?" She went to get her phone, which he'd noticed she hadn't glanced at while chatting to Esme.

He put out a hand to stop her, then laid it out for her, including showing her the image so she wouldn't imagine anything worse. The look on her face was pure devastation. Such pain that he wanted to kill Reid then and there.

"Jake, I promise I didn't—"

"I know that," he said because he did. Juliet didn't lie. "I *know*."

"He did take that photo—it was after we were first married, when I trusted him." Her expression was fragile as she admitted that. "But I didn't look like that then, was more angles than curves. He's gotten someone to edit it."

"Yeah, I figured." Squeezing the back of her neck, he said, "We'll deal."

"No." She stepped away. "Jake, I won't drag you into this ugliness. Let me think. I can—"

"No." He was done letting Reid run the show and done having Juliet think she had to walk alone into the fire. "You've dealt with things long enough on your own. Now you have me."

"Jake, no." Her gaze went to Esme, fierce protectiveness in her next words. "Esme, your family—we need to protect them."

"Esme will be fine." Anyone who dared come after a Bishop-Esera child would be pulverized. Jake had the social and professional reach to do it on his own, but throw in Danny's power and add in Sailor and Gabe and no one would survive it.

As for any rumors or gossip that might reach Esme, they'd talk with her beforehand, give her the weapons to handle it. Tempting as it was to surround his baby in cotton wool, he couldn't protect her by keeping her in the dark. "As for my family, see for yourself." He showed her the messages on his phone.

Her lower lip began to tremble as she went through the messages. All of them furious on her behalf and in her corner.

"Your parents are out there," she said, her voice a little wobbly.

"Of course they are." Jake put his hand on her lower back. "This is what we're going to do. I'll exit and take Esme over to them, then I'm going to come wait by the doors for you to exit."

Swallowing hard, she shook her head. "See?" She pointed to his mother's message.

"I know, Jules." He pressed a kiss to her cheek, uncaring of who might see. "I know the gossip mags are out there. That's why you are *not* going to go out alone."

Another hard shake of her head. "Jake, you can't be dragged—"

"No." Jake rarely put down his foot in this way, but when he did, he didn't budge. "This isn't negotiable, Jules. You're mine, and I stand by my people."

"But Esme," Juliet argued back in a whisper, her priorities clear.

"They won't dare." Jake knew that for a fact. "Our family has cut certain magazines from interviews because they published pictures of our children. They won't risk it, especially as they're hoping to get some kind of an exclusive from Gabriel and Charlotte." Not that his brother would give them anything but crumbs—just enough to ensure they didn't start making up shit.

Another glance at Esme. "I—"

"We aren't discussing this, Jules." He kissed her hard on the lips. "You wait for me to exit, and then you give me a minute to get Esme to my parents." He held her gaze. "Promise me that."

A stubborn pause before she finally nodded, but there was a haunted wariness in her eyes. He didn't attempt to address that wariness—sometimes the only thing that worked was showing someone that their trust was valued and wouldn't be betrayed. Juliet was going to learn that Jacob Esera didn't let down his people.

He stuck.

"Daddy! Jules!" Esme pointed excitedly as Jake's bag came around. He'd tied a big blue bow on the handle especially so Esme could find it among the sea of other black bags.

"Good spotting, Boo," he said and stepped forward to get it off the conveyer belt. His daughter knew not to cross the yellow line, but she was happily pointing out her own bag, a pale blue thing emblazoned with—shockingly—the face of her favorite princess.

He took that off the belt as well and was ready when Esme said, "Jules, look!"

Jules, too, had tied a bow around her handle after Esme gave her a hair ribbon and said, "Then we can see it easy." Her bow was a bright pink. He saw Juliet step forward to grab her bag, but he was already there. Come hell or high water, he was going to teach her that it was okay if she permitted herself to rely on him.

"Do we have them all?" he asked Esme after grabbing a luggage cart and putting the bags on it.

Brow furrowed, she carefully counted. "Yup. Here, Mr. Mouse can sit on top. He likes to ride the cart."

Juliet held out a hand after another shaky glance at Jake. Esme slipped her hand into her new favorite person's, and they headed off to the Customs line, both Esme and Juliet dragging their roll-ons behind them. Thankfully, the line was moving fast today, and they got to a Customs officer in a matter of minutes. That the gray-haired man recognized both Jake and Juliet was obvious from the way his eyes flicked between them.

"Look, guys," he said, after quizzing them on their declaration cards and stamping them with the all clear, "just a heads-up. There's a media scrum outside. I think it might be for you." He glanced at Juliet. "We can get you out another way if you want."

Juliet was openly taken aback by the unexpected kindness, but she caught her breath and said, "No, it'll be worse if I try to avoid them. But thank you for the warning."

The officer nodded. "Good luck. Follow the green line to the exit."

Once past him and on their way to the doors, however, they found themselves inspected by one of the airport's drug-sniffing beagles.

"No petting," he warned Esme. "He's at work."

Esme waved at the "doggie" instead and said, "Daddy, see? He's so nice and he works hard."

"Baby girl, we are not getting a dog."

"But I gonna get the poopy thing," Esme protested as the beagle moved on, giving them final clearance to exit.

Juliet looked between the two of them. "The poopy thing?"

"Tell you later," Jake promised and stopped the luggage cart before the sliding doors to the waiting area. "Wait here." He caught the eye of a nearby security officer who seemed to be watching them. "I need to get my daughter out, then I'm going to come back to the doors so Juliet doesn't have to walk out alone."

The woman nodded. "Figured the cameras were for you."

Sometimes it was good to live in a small and rugby-obsessed nation where his face was immediately recognizable. "Thank you." He took Esme's hand. "Come on, Boo."

"Jules, come."

"Jules is going to take a couple more minutes. But she won't be far." A glance at Juliet to remind her of her promise.

She nodded though her face was torn.

He headed out, Esme's hand held firmly in his. He controlled the cart with his other hand. Despite his parents' warning, the media contingent was far bigger than he'd expected. It was, in fact, certifiably insane. It was either a slow news week or Reid's stories had somehow caused a rise in ratings.

Ignoring the camera flashes as he was recognized, he went left out of the doors—his parents always waited on that side, and that way the cart hid Esme's small form from intrusive shutters.

"Daddy, why are they taking pictures of us?"

"Because I play rugby." He kept his voice calm so she wouldn't be scared. "They're excited."

She beamed. "You're fast! Uncle Danny is faster though."

Jake would've laughed if he hadn't been so tense. Danny *was* faster; he could run like the fucking wind, the ball tucked securely in one hand. "Can you see Grandma or Grandpa?" he asked, having already spotted them.

"Um." She looked around for a few seconds before giving a happy cry and streaking forward toward his parents.

She was already in Joseph's arms by the time he reached them. His father gave him a disappointed look, his bushy eyebrows heavy over dark eyes.

Jake parked the cart. "Wait here. I have to get Juliet." He texted her to tell her he was on his way back to the exit doors.

The disappointment faded, to be replaced by firm approval.

His mother nodded too. "I don't know what the world is coming to, that the media thinks this is acceptable."

Jake was already moving and was at the doors when Juliet walked out. He took her hand before she could stop him. Her glance was shocked, startled. He just squeezed and said, "Let me do the talking this time, Jules."

A tiny frown, but she was shaken enough that she didn't protest, and then they were heading straight for the pack of media salivating out front. Camera flashes went off in a tornado of noise and light, questions shouted their way from ten different mouths.

31

SHIELD

J ake paused and waited until they'd all calmed the fuck down.

"Jake! Jake! Did Juliet cheat on you with Reid? Or did you get together in New York?"

Beside him, Juliet stiffened. "Why the hell would I go to Reid when I have Jake?" She sounded so flabbergasted that Jake found himself bursting into laughter.

"The photo!" another reporter shouted. "Are you saying you weren't with Reid that night?"

"I'm not into threesomes," Jake said with a straight face.

It took a moment for his comment to penetrate. The questions began again, harder, faster.

He let them roll over him until they quieted again. "Look, that pathetic piece of crap who can't even crack twenty-five on the wicket these days is taking you all for a ride. I was there the night Reid tried to hook up with Juliet again. Jules kicked him to the curb—her taste in men has improved drastically since—"

Juliet elbowed him, sharply and visibly enough that the cameras flashed again. Grinning, he hauled her into a kiss, one hand cupping the side of her face and his fingers in her hair.

And that was the photo that hit the online sites even as Jake's parents drove Juliet, Esme, and Jake from the airport in their big people-mover van. Juliet, stunned at what had just gone down, stared at her phone as the pings began. Jake's family, Charlie, Aroha, Iris, Everett, Kalia, Mei, Nayna, Molly, casual friends, even the eldest daughter from the family that had put her up back when she'd returned from Samoa, they were all sending her thumbs-up emojis or laughing faces or messages that broadcast pure delight.

The cameras had caught Jake laughing as he kissed her. Jake *never* laughed. Not for the cameras, not this way. And the way he was laughing, the way his hand cupped her face, it was... Things got all tight inside her. No one had ever looked at her that way before. No one had ever put himself in the line of fire to shield her.

He'd linked himself to her with a finality that was going to make his life much harder.

The articles that had begun to pop up also mentioned that she and Jake had been greeted at the airport by his parents and that Jake's daughter appeared very comfortable with Juliet. Esme, back on her feet by then, had grabbed her hand as soon as Juliet and Jake joined Alison and Joseph.

She'd been frowning. "Are you famous too, Jules? But you don't play rugby."

Needing the sweetness of Esme, Juliet had gone down to squeeze her into a hug. "I'm a little famous," she'd said after. "I don't want to be though."

Esme had patted her cheek, and the five of them had walked out of the airport unmolested by any more media interest. The reporters were all racing off to file their stories, and the photographers apparently realized there was no point taking family shots that included Esme. Not here, not in this situation.

Maybe that line in the sand would be crossed in a larger country, but in a country this small, with the Bishop-Eseras a beloved family that quietly gave a lot of financial and emotional support to disadvantaged kids who wanted to play the game, the public tended to look askance at such an invasion of privacy.

It helped that Jake was a young god on the rugby field. His devotion to his daughter was well known, as was his protectiveness. The media was well aware the public could turn against them in defense of Esme.

All the articles held a vein of shock at the unexpected turn of events. Jake had sold it with his obvious contempt for Reid's false statements. Juliet's lips still tingled from the kiss. She'd never have expected that. *Never*. Jake was so private.

She looked forward to where he sat in the front passenger seat beside his dad. Alison had chosen to get in back with Juliet, with Esme in a child seat between them. When Juliet glanced at Jake's mother, her heart trembling because surely Alison had reservations about her son hooking up with a woman like Juliet, Alison gave her a warm smile.

"You just let us handle this, dear heart." She reached over to touch Juliet's hair in a maternal caress. "You shouldn't be dealing with it alone."

"That picture," Juliet said, because she couldn't bear for Alison to be shocked by the truth should it come out. "I let him take one when we were first married, and I trusted him. I know I shouldn't have, but—"

"You trusted your husband. There's no shame in that," Alison said gently. "But no matter what the circumstances,

Juliet, it wouldn't ever mean that you or *any* woman deserved that kind of media haranguing. Reid also released an intimate image without your permission and has been lying about you non-stop—you say the word, honey, and we'll get the lawyers on it."

Juliet was going to start crying. Looking down, she squeezed her eyes shut.

A tiny hand patted her on the shoulder. "Don't be sad, Jules."

Esme sounded so worried that Juliet swallowed the knot in her throat and met the little girl's eyes with a smile. "How can I be sad when I have all of you?"

Smiling, Esme leaned her head against Juliet and went back to her conversation with Mr. Mouse about how New York had been so much fun but she was glad to be home.

"Thank you," Juliet said to Alison, one of her hands in Esme's hair.

Alison glanced to the front, where Jake and his father were involved in an animated discussion about a recent international match between two big rugby countries. Then she reached over and pulled out a pair of sparkly pink head-phones from the back pocket of a front seat.

"Want to listen to your princess music?" she asked Esme.

When Esme nodded, her grandmother set her up. Only once Esme was singing along with her tunes did Alison turn to Juliet and say, "No. Thank you." Soft eyes, full of a mother's love. "Jake stopped laughing that way a long time ago. We've always tried to be there for him, but he took all the weight of Calypso's death on his shoulders. He stopped being a boy and became a man far too young."

Juliet thought of how he'd laughed with her in bed, how he'd looked so young when they'd kissed just now at the airport, and felt a strange stretching inside her. A reminder that this wasn't a one-sided relationship where she was the recipient of all the gifts—Jake had asked her to be his wings, to take him flying.

She hugged that truth to her heart when Joseph brought the van to a stop at Jake's place. Jake invited his parents in for a coffee, and she found herself with Alison again at one point while the men and Esme went outside to check out a clothesline that had fallen over during the high winds Auckland had experienced a couple of days earlier.

As Juliet made the coffee after scoping out the machine and realizing she could work it and Alison rummaged in the cupboard for a packet of cookies, Juliet found herself settling into a space where family wasn't a cause of pain but of support and joy. She told Alison about their trip, and Alison told her about a family dinner they'd had after Charlotte and Gabriel's return from their honeymoon.

"We can be overwhelming en masse," Jake's mother said. "So if you ever want to miss a family dinner or get-together, no one will hold it against you."

Shaken inside at the simple acceptance that she'd be part of future family events, Juliet said, "I'd love to be part of a family. I don't really have any family." It was hard for her to be so vulnerable and put herself out there like that, but Alison smiled and gave her a one-armed hug.

"Trust me, you've got one now. We'll probably drive you bonkers."

Joseph Esera was less demonstrative, but he gave Juliet a pat on the back when he came inside and she almost cried again. But she didn't, because Esme was running in, excited to tell them all about how the "big wind" had made things fall down.

They stood around the kitchen counter talking and catching up, and it was just... normal. A kind of normal

Juliet had never experienced. She was starting to fall as madly in love with Jake's family as she was with Jake.

She sucked in a breath even though the realization of how deep he lived in her heart wasn't that much of a shock. How could she do anything but fall for a man who stood by her side with pride? Who was ready to be her shield against pain and hurt? Yet, aware how vulnerable it made her, she'd been fighting herself. It was too late.

Juliet Nelisi was in love with Jacob Esera.

She wasn't yet strong enough to lower her shields first, be the one who spoke the words. But as she caught him looking at her with a grin that creased his cheeks, she thought maybe she could find the courage in the future to come.

32

THREATS OF STILETTO THIEVERY

J ake pulled Juliet in for a kiss after his parents left. The three of them were still in the kitchen and Esme smiled wide at seeing them kiss again.

Bouncing up and down beside Juliet, she said, "Jules! Are you gonna stay with us now and hug me and kiss Daddy?"

"Yeah, Jules? Are you?" He knew he was being a demon, putting her on the spot in front of his daughter, but he wasn't about to let her go. Especially not today when she might have more media camped out on her doorstep.

An expanding of her pupils, a tug of her lips. "You two..." She put her hands on her hips. "I'll stay tonight and then we'll see."

"Yay!" Esme caught Juliet's hands, and the two of them spun into a dance in the sunlight that fell through the open kitchen doors.

Jake staggered, leaning back against the counter. A realization stirred at the corner of his mind, but he shoved it aside, not ready for that depth of vulnerability and the fear that came with it. Instead, he took out his phone and snapped a photo of his Jules and his daughter laughing together.

Later that day, after they'd prepped a quick dinner and Esme was in bed—with plenty of hugs and kisses from both Jake and Juliet—he and Juliet sat out on his deck with its view of the ocean while soft music played from speakers in the kitchen.

This house was the biggest purchase he'd ever made, but he was glad of it every time he sat out here or when Esme swung in the wooden swing he and his dad had made, then attached to a large tree in the yard. Her hair would stream behind her as she pumped herself up and down, the ocean her backdrop.

"Your house is beautiful," Juliet murmured. "But it feels like a home. Not perfect and styled."

"I wanted Esme to have what I did growing up." Four rambunctious boys meant Alison and Joseph's home had never been a showpiece. "If you want to change stuff, go for it. The only thing out-of-bounds is my favorite game-watching chair. Touch that and I'll steal the left shoe from your favorite pair of stilettos."

A searching look from Juliet. "You're serious? About me moving in?"

Rising, he pulled her up into his arms and began to sway to the rhythm of the music. "I don't want us to date, Jules," he said. "We're past that. I want us to be together." Being with her in New York had felt so right. "I hate the idea of not waking with you in my arms." It'd be bad enough when he was at training camp or at out-of-town games.

Juliet swallowed hard, but she'd always been tough. "Okay," she said, "let's try."

Jake's heart boomed. "You won't regret it."

Dropping his head, he kissed her slow and deep. When

she gasped in air during a break in the kiss, he smiled. She laughed and pulled away to go into the kitchen. A moment later, the music changed from slow and muted to fast—though still quiet enough to not wake Esme.

She danced her way back outside, her moves sensual and playful at the same time. It was Juliet who pulled Jake into the dance this time, and they danced as if they were in a club. Jake hadn't been in a club for years. Despite his actual age, he always felt too old in those places.

But dancing with Juliet at home, it had him grinning and breaking out moves he hadn't realized he remembered. At one point she ended up with her back to his chest, his hand splayed on her stomach as they moved with a sensual grace that could've been choreographed it was so seamless.

Feeling the lush curves of her bottom move against him had a predictable effect, and he dipped his head to kiss her neck. Raising her hand, she wove it in his hair and they kept on dancing. By the time they made it to bed at last, they were so hot for each other that she kicked off her jeans and panties as they entered, and he opened the fly of his own jeans, released his erection, and then he was thrusting into her as he pinned her to the bedroom door he'd pushed shut.

Afterward, she laughed softly against him. "I feel like a hormone-ridden teenager."

He went to grin back when his gut iced. "I forgot protection." He'd *never*, not once, forgotten protection. Not after making Calypso pregnant because he'd been too eager.

Juliet didn't get angry at him for breaking the mood. "I'm on long-term birth control," she said with a kiss. "I won't get pregnant unless I get the IUD removed." Her fingers weaving through his hair. "I promise." A pause. "Unless you have super sperm. In which case, I might have to rethink this entire relationship."

Dropping his head to the curve of her neck, Jake found himself chuckling, then laughing so hard that he almost dropped her. She grabbed hold of his shoulders, and he pressed her against the door once more before lifting his head to kiss her again and again. "My pants are stuck halfway down my thighs."

"Sexy." A big smile. "Let's get in bed before we injure ourselves. I do *not* want to end up in the ER with a sex injury."

He released her and got naked, dove under the covers. They lay facing each other, and he realized he'd laughed more with Juliet than he had for years. It wasn't over either, because she was still smiling and he felt his own lips curve in response.

"I'm clean," he told her, because after Reid, she had to worry. "We get physicals all the time, and I'm not exactly a man about town."

"Me too." Juliet sank her teeth into her lower lip. "After I caught Reid cheating, I got myself tested for everything. It was so horrible, not knowing who he'd been with while he was supposed to only be with me."

Jake cuddled her closer. "So, we can be naked with each other?"

Stroking her hands up the sides of his body even as a flush heated her skin, she nodded. "Yeah, I'd like that." A ducking of her head, her slight shyness in bed another part of his Juliet that he was discovering. "Feeling you inside me, the heat, the wet... I like it."

Groaning, he shifted so that he was fully over her, his cock nudging her entrance. "Talk dirty to me some more."

She looked utterly mortified, so he started the dirty talk.

Rocking against her, the head of his cock rubbing over her clit, he told her how beautiful he found her breasts, how he loved the sensitivity of her nipples and the way her pussy clamped around him in spasms when she came.

Perspiration on her skin, she ran her nails down either side of his spine. "You are so hot, it's not fair." She arched her body against him. "You could get me to do anything you want in bed."

"What I want is to see you come apart for me." Pushing into her again, her muscles tight and wet around him, he took it slow, his eyes looking into hers.

They held the eye contact until the very end, until he'd spent himself inside her body. It never occurred to him to question her promise that she was on birth control. Because this was Juliet.

Loyal and honest and his.

JAKE DIDN'T KNOW what had woken him, but he jerked awake to see a sleepy Esme climbing into the bed from the end, Mr. Mouse held close to her chest. He'd gotten up to open the door last night after he and Juliet began to fall asleep.

Almost back asleep already, he lifted the blanket so Esme could get in—and realized he was buck-ass naked. He usually wore boxers to bed for this very reason. Since his daughter was mostly asleep, her eyes closed, he managed to use a foot to drag his boxer briefs over from where they lay on the floor and pulled them on under the sheet. Yawning, Esme curled herself to Juliet's bare back.

And fell back asleep.

Jake looked at his two girls fast asleep and rose to kiss them both on the cheek. Then he located his T-shirt and left it on Juliet's side of the bed. She'd never woken up with a little person snuggled up to her, would likely get a shock.

Glancing at his bedside clock, he saw it was six. He'd managed to get in some training in New York, popping into a local gym for an early-morning hour each day while Juliet kept an eye on a sleeping Esme, so he wasn't out of condition. But he'd take it easy on his jet-lagged body today, do only an hour or two later in the day.

As Esme also had the day off school to recover from the trip, he decided to lie back and just relax. It felt good, his happiness a deep and warm thing. Oh yeah, except for the blinding terror. He'd spent most of his life fighting not to be an overprotective and suffocating parent. Now he'd have to fight the same urges regarding Juliet.

The idea of her being hurt in any way...

A stirring on her side of the bed. He saw her go motionless a moment later. "Jake? Are you awake?" It was a panicked whisper.

"Yeah." He leaned over Esme to kiss a sleepy-warm Juliet on the temple. "I put my T-shirt by you."

She reached down to grab it. "How do I...?"

He moved Esme away from Juliet's back with gentle hands. His daughter grumbled in her sleep but settled when he put her against his chest. Meanwhile, Juliet shimmied into the tee, then turned around to face him. "I'm going to have to remember not to sleep naked."

Esme yawned against his chest at the same moment. Her eyes fluttered open a second later. She just lay there for a while; his daughter wasn't a morning person. But today she was excited enough about something that her eyes were suddenly bright.

Flipping over to face Juliet, she said, "You slept in Daddy's bed."

Juliet sent him a "help" look, but Jake winked and left her to it.

"Yes," she said. "Is that okay?"

"Yup. Can we have waffles for breakfast?"

Juliet still appeared shell-shocked half an hour later when they sat down to breakfast. He'd pulled on his sweatpants but nothing else while she'd found her pajama bottoms in her suitcase and pulled them on. But she was here and she seemed happy under her shock, and the day passed in a hazy, happy way that left him rejuvenated for the next one.

JULIET EXPECTED chaos the next morning, but Jake and Esme had a well-oiled routine.

For a moment she felt awkward and out of place, then Jake said, "Jules, can you make Esme's lunch while I make sure she has her flute and Phys. Ed. gear?" He told her what his daughter normally took to school. "Her lunchbox is sitting in the cupboard above the sink," he said as he entered Esme's room to grab her backpack.

Juliet had never made a little girl's lunch before—except for her own—so she took care with how she put everything together. Spotting a cookie cutter in one of the drawers she'd opened while looking for a knife, she cut Esme's sandwich into the shapes of stars, then arranged grapes and blueberries together in another section.

Lastly she added two cookies, and on a whim cut a piece of carrot into the shape of a flower and put it with the fruit. "Where are you two?" she called out when the kitchen remained otherwise empty.

"Daddy's braiding my hair!" Esme shouted back. "And he couldn't find my fwoot."

"That's because you put your 'fwoot' in the drawer with your socks," Jake grumbled. "Be there soon, Jules."

"Issa safe place," Esme argued in a stubborn voice. "I just forgots it was there."

Smiling, Juliet started the coffee, then located the stuff Jake put in his smoothies and whipped him up one. She'd seen him order smoothies more than once in New York, and it was an easy thing to replicate since he had his nutritionist-suggested food list pinned to his fridge. It also made her feel part of the morning routine.

Esme ran into the room not long afterward, dressed in sparkly black leggings and a fluffy green jumper, her hair in two small braids. "Hi Juliet!" She threw her arms around Juliet.

Juliet hugged her back. "Cereal, right?"

"Yup. Plus milk to drink."

"Got it."

The coffee had just finished perking and Esme was already eating her cereal when Jake walked into the kitchen with Esme's backpack. He paused at seeing his smoothie waiting for him, then—after placing the bag by the door—came around the counter to give Juliet a big kiss. "Thanks, Jules." He poured a coffee and handed it to her. "Toast?"

"I've got it going." She ate a piece of crust left over from cutting Esme's sandwich. "Can you check?" She passed over the lunchbox. "I don't want to have missed anything."

Jake opened the lid and smiled. "She'll get a kick out of that," he said about the sandwiches. "You just missed her juice box. It goes here." He pointed out the spot she'd thought must be for an extra snack.

"B plus?" she suggested.

Rubbing his shaved-clean jaw, he said, "Nah, I'm not a tough grader like you. A minus."

Dear Lord but he was gorgeous when he was being playful. Leaning in, she kissed that jaw that had been bristly last night, scraping over her in delicious ways. "Talking of grading, I haven't showed you my oral skills yet." She flicked her tongue against his skin.

He groaned. "You're a devil woman."

She went to say that was why he loved her... but Jake had never said those words.

"Jules!" Esme was waving her milk cup. "I finished!"

"Wow, that was fast!" Juliet swiveled. "Your dad and I better hurry up."

But it turned out they didn't have to hurry—having Juliet taking charge of meal prep while Jake got Esme ready had bought them time, and they sat together at the table for a few minutes, talking and finishing up breakfast before Jake rose to walk Esme to school. "You can take my car," he said, passing Juliet his keys. "Price is a kiss."

Juliet paid it gladly.

Afterward, she bent down to hug and kiss Esme. "Have a great day at school. Make sure you show your teacher your special travel book with all your notes, and don't forget to hand in your homework. I'll see you tonight."

It was as Jake was walking out the door with Esme that he turned around and, dark eyes intent, said, "Hey, Jules— you make sure you call me if anything happens."

The world shimmered in front of her before settling into its new form where she had someone who belonged to her, someone for whom she was a priority. "I will," she promised, her voice husky.

Reid had said "I love you" weeks after meeting her.

Jake had never said it.

But words were easy. Having a man who stood by her, a steady, loyal presence who'd face the world with her, come what may? That was real, that was what mattered.

Juliet's eyes burned, her heart full.

33

GAME ON

Juliet didn't look up the news and gossip sites until she was at her desk at work. As expected, Reid was firing off a few cheap shots, but his attempts were no longer gaining much traction—not with everyone fascinated by Jake and Juliet's emergence as a couple. One reporter had managed to dig up an old school photo that featured all three of them—Jake, Calypso, and Juliet.

Her heart ached. "Miss you, Cals," she murmured under her breath. "Hope you're good with me and Jake."

An unseasonably warm wind blew through the open window, brushing the scent of freesias across her face. Throat thick, she said, "Thanks. I promise I'll love him and your baby." Could be the landscaper who looked after these premises had planted them downstairs, but freesias had been Callie's favorite flower, and on the day of her death—before Juliet had ever learned that her friend was gone—she'd been standing on a rocky beach in Samoa when she was enfolded in the scent of freesias.

Callie, saying goodbye.

Believing her friend was in a better place, from which she occasionally dropped by to watch over them, Juliet took a deep breath in readiness to start work. That was when she recalled what Alison had said about Jake's lost laughter and found herself clicking to another site, one she'd learned about during a previous promotional campaign. She was buying the tickets before she could second-guess herself.

The tickets weren't for till after his training camp and the big game to follow, so she'd keep them to give him after. No point distracting him in the lead-up. If he decided not to use them, she knew people in the office who'd love them.

Then she got to work, ignoring any and all calls from the media. Of course they were waiting outside when she walked to Jake's car after work, but she kept her comments short, not giving them anything new. As she drove to Jake's, she thought about her house, all her things.

The idea of letting it go at some point in the future was a tough one. It had taken her so much hard work to afford her own place. Part of her also remained scared that Jake would change his mind, decide she was too much trouble. It'd probably take her years to get over that. Maybe she could rent her place out so it wouldn't be such a big deal if she and Jake didn't make it.

Who're you kidding, Jules? It'll be a big freaking deal regardless. You'll be devastated.

"Shut up," she muttered to that bluntly honest voice.

A big, black SUV she didn't recognize was sitting in the drive when she arrived home. Parking behind it, she got out.

"Juliet!" Charlie, dressed for work in a slimline gray dress that did spectacular things for her petite body, ran over.

Joy welling up at the sight of her friend, a friend with the same gentle heart as Calypso, Juliet hugged her close. "What're you doing here?"

"We wanted to catch up. We brought dinner."

Again, Juliet found herself in a kitchen full of conversation and laughter. Esme was playing on the swing outside but ran in every so often to check on things before running back. Gabriel, big in every way, gave Juliet a hug when she walked in, and though she was startled, she hugged him back. He was part of the family, she realized, a family by which she'd been embraced.

"Tell me about your honeymoon," she said to Charlotte afterward.

As Charlotte regaled Juliet about the pleasures of sun and snorkeling and laziness, followed by what appeared to have been a lovely visit with the Samoa-based Esera grandparents, Jake spoke to Gabriel about the New York shoot. At one point, she heard him relaying the story about the female model and how Juliet had "spanked" the ad exec, and there was so much pride in his voice that she felt ten feet tall.

The dinner that followed was as full of laughter and conversation, with Jake ragging his brother on his workaholic ways. "If you tell me you didn't work the whole honeymoon, I'll eat my manky old running shoe."

"We negotiated a contract beforehand," Gabriel said, his arm braced on the back of Charlotte's chair. "I got two hours a day to clear major issues. I picked up the phone again at my peril—my wife would not have been amused." His smile was sinful as he looked at Charlotte.

"Don't you forget it," Charlotte said, the softest blush on her cheeks. "He was very good about sticking to our contract," she added afterward. "One day he actually forgot about his phone—to be honest, I worried he was getting sick."

Gabriel rumbled a response to Charlie's tongue-in-cheek comment, and laughter filled the air.

Juliet realized it would always be like this, whether she was with Jake and Esme alone or if they were joined by other members of the family or their friends. Family for the Bishop-Eseras meant support, laughter, ties that bound with affection and love.

Buzzing after the lovely night, she felt lazy and sexy when they got into bed. Jake was feeling the same, kissing her all over, his hand stroking her curves with unhurried patience as he murmured naughty, dirty things that made her toes curl. But it was his breath that hitched when she took over the kissing and began to make her way down his body.

In the mood to tease, she kissed him everywhere except where he wanted her mouth. His thighs were rock hard and gorgeous with muscle, his abdomen ridged, the hairs on his legs rubbing against her in delicious friction.

Though she was torturing him, he didn't tell her to hurry up.

They were both having too much fun.

His hand did fist in her hair, but he was careful to be gentle.

When she finally closed her mouth over the taut, reddened head of his cock, his back lifted off the bed, his hand shifting to cradle her nape.

"*Jules.*" It was a groan.

Moaning, she stroked his thigh and drew him deeper into her mouth, enjoying giving him pleasure. Her core grew hotter, wetter, small pulses clenching her muscles. Until by the time he tugged her up his body and asked her to ride him, she was desperate to have him inside her.

A gasp escaped both of them as she settled on him.

Sitting up with her astride him, Jake wrapped his arms around her, his mouth coming to her own. She moved on him as they kissed and the way he held her, with such possessive tenderness, it thickened her throat and made her weave her hands into his hair. As close as two people could be, they touched and made love and Juliet began to believe in happy ever after.

A MONTH later and Jake was having the best game of his career.

The lights of Eden Park blazed down on him, the field a rich green except where it was marked by the sponsors' logos.

That wasn't to say it had been an easy game—in point of fact, it had been a bruiser. The clock had eight minutes to go, Jake's team was behind by six points... and the ball had just hit Jake's hands.

Seeing a gap in their opponent's defenses, he ran, always aware of all the players around him. Right before his body smashed into that of an aggressive flanker who had his head down to tackle him, he threw the ball in a sweet, sweet pass that landed in Danny's hands.

Even as Jake's momentum crashed him into the defending flanker, he saw his brother's winged feet fly. He came up from the tackle relatively fast, just in time to see that Danny was about to be tackled. Leo was to his back and right, but Danny did sometimes have a problem with his spatial awareness on the field.

Already running, Jake yelled, "Danny! Five!" It was a simple clock reference—no need or time for complicated calls when play was moving this fast; their opposition would have no time to take advantage, not if Danny passed quick enough.

The ball left his brother's hands just before Danny went down in the tackle, the defender's hit taking him out-of-bounds. But the ball was still in play and Leo, fast and powerful, was in the clear... all the way to the try line. Jake yelled with the rest of his team, fist pumping the air as Leo slid across the line, thumping the ball down in the area behind the goal posts.

The whistle awarding the try and the resulting five points split the air.

But the celebrations had to wait. With the clock rapidly counting down, Jake quickly set up the kick awarded to his team for having successfully achieved a try. If he managed to clear the goalposts, they'd get the two points they needed to win this match. The conversion kick, however, was always lined up with where the ball had been placed during the try, and Leo had slid across at a spot that meant the kick would be from an acute left angle.

Wiping the sweat off his face using his playing jersey, Jake set the oval-shaped ball upright on the kicking tee, tilting it a fraction toward the right as was his preference. Then he breathed deep and shut out the screaming crowds, stopped seeing his teammates, and focused on the passion inside that drove him.

Juliet and Esme. Twin flames deep in his heart.

He moved back several steps, looked at the goalposts one last time in the silence inside his mind, pictured the ball flying through the posts in a perfect curve, then flowed into the kick. The ball flew in what seemed an impossible arc, one that meant it'd bounce off the posts, losing them the game.

The entire stadium was hushed.

The ball sailed through, the referee's flags went up to signify a successful conversion, and the stands erupted.

The final whistle went off at the same time and Jake was overwhelmed by his jubilant teammates, including an ecstatic Leo—who wrapped one arm around Danny's neck and hauled him down for a kiss on the cheek. "Fucking insane pass, Danny boy!"

Words were lost in the overlapping conversations, sheer joy ascendant.

Jake looked up toward the area in the stands where he knew his family and the two pieces of his heart were watching, and though he couldn't see them from this far away, he blew a kiss in that direction.

JULIET CAUGHT THAT KISS, curling her fingers against her thundering heart. It was pandemonium in the private box behind the family's seats. Gabriel had opened a bottle of champagne, the girls were yelling and dancing, and Sailor had found streamers that he'd let off before pulling his wife close for an ecstatic kiss.

"You okay?" Alison touched her lower back.

"I just... It's so dangerous, the game." She'd never truly understood the amount of force that came from two such powerful men hitting each other at speed. When Jake had gone down just before the try, she'd jerked out of her seat, her skin ice-cold.

"It took me time," Alison murmured. "But it's their passion. If I stopped them, I'd kill a part of them." She stroked her hand down Juliet's spine. "Jake's a brilliant player, rarely goes for brute force. He plays with intelligence and strategy."

Juliet nodded; she'd seen that on the field. Jake had scored tries in his career, but more often, he set up the try. It was as if his mind could see multiple steps ahead—even when all the pieces on the board were moving. "He's *really* good," she said, then flushed. "Sorry, I never properly watched rugby before being with Jake."

Laughing, Alison passed over a glass of champagne while behind them, Sailor started popping open beers for those who wanted them. Ísa and the girls already had glasses of bubbly pink grape juice in hand.

"I still get a shock sometimes," Alison said, "when I see Danny and Jake do impossible things on the field—how are these my boys? The same ones I picked up a hundred times when they were learning to walk."

Juliet could commiserate; she still hadn't internalized the fact that Jake was her man. That the world continued to question their relationship didn't exactly help. She had a firsthand demonstration of the public's lack of belief in their relationship later that night, when Jake gave in to his family's urgings to head out on the town with his team to celebrate.

"Esme can sleep over with Emmaline," Ísa said, sending the girls into paroxysms of delight.

With this being a home game, which would be followed by a break, the men's wives and girlfriends and partners were welcome to join in the celebration, and Jake laughingly told Juliet to put on her glad rags. His eyes were shining from the rush of the win, his hair wet from the postgame shower, his body all heat and skin—and more than one bruise, which he'd shrugged off.

Juliet wasn't so sanguine, but knew she had to get a

handle on her worry if she was to be with Jake—and she definitely couldn't use that worry as an excuse not to go out, no matter the urgings of her subconscious. Because the magazines were once again calling her a WAG, as if the rest of her life and her achievements held no value now that she was on Jake's arm. *Ugh.*

"Hey, Jules, how about this?" Jake, who'd been inside the walk-in wardrobe, returned with a sparkly silver dress in hand.

It was ridiculously short and she'd only ever worn it once—on a girls' night out with Aroha soon after her divorce. The slimy male attention she'd attracted had left her vowing to donate the dress to charity, but she'd liked the sparkly, pretty thing too much to let it go. "You realize I'm all boobs and ass in that dress?"

A slow, sinful grin that melted her at the knees. "How about you put it on so I can decide for myself?"

Lips twitching because the man was irresistible when he played with her, she shimmied out of her jeans and threw them on the bed, then tugged off her team sweatshirt. Jake watched with an appreciative glint in his eye, especially when she went to unhook her bra.

His groan at her bared breasts made her thighs want to clench.

34

IN WHICH JAKE HAS ONE THING ON HIS MIND (LUCKY JULIET)

Padding toward him, she leaned into his chest, her naked breasts pressed to his equally naked chest. He bent his head to meet her halfway, their kiss carnal.

She shivered when she pulled back and tugged the dress from his hand. It fell over her head in a shimmer of sparkles and long strings of silver. The actual dress barely cleared her butt, but the falling silver strings made it an inch or two more modest.

Turning so her back was to him, she swept her hair over her shoulder and to the front. "Zip me up."

He kissed a line up her spine instead, his hands stroking the backs of her thighs. "How about we stay in?" It was a rumble against her.

Juliet wanted to jump on the offer, but this was Jake's night to celebrate—and hiding wouldn't rid her of the WAG label. It would follow her around like a bad smell regardless. "We promised Leo a ride, remember?" The other man had planned to catch a ride-share car so he could have a drink or two, but Juliet had volunteered to be a sober driver.

Jake groaned but finished zipping her up.

When she turned, he wolf whistled. "Damn, you're hot, Jules."

Delight bubbled in her—where the lecherous glances she'd experienced the first time she'd worn this dress had creeped her out, Jake's honest pleasure in how she looked had her sauntering over to the makeup table, her hips swaying.

In no mood to behave, he came and stroked her butt and kissed her shoulder and whispered naughty things in her ear and generally distracted her into a breathless, panting mess who didn't protest in the least when he slid his hands under her dress to tug down her panties.

Pushing up her dress afterward, he slid into her honey-slick body, his eyes holding hers in the mirror before he bent his head to kiss that spot in the curve of her neck. She moved with him, adoring him for remembering her little pleasure spots and for giving them attention.

"Jake." A whisper that held so much love.

"Mmm." He began to speed up his thrusts even as his eyes locked with hers once more, his smile wicked. "You are so fucking beautiful."

Her heart, it melted right into his hands. Even more so when, after they'd both orgasmed, he cradled her against his body while he nuzzled her throat. Reaching back with her hand, she ran her fingernails lightly across the back of his scalp and thought, screw the magazines.

Tonight she'd forget the world was watching and party with the man she loved.

HAPPY AND SATED, the two of them were in a good mood when they walked into the chosen club with Leo. The lights were dim, the music bright, and more than one player had brought his wife or girlfriend. Juliet took it on the chin when most of those women gave her the stink eye—she couldn't blame them, not when, according to a number of Reid-fueled articles, Juliet was a voracious raptor out to snatch every man possible.

Thankfully the disapprobation wasn't total. A tall brunette with slick straight hair came over to chat while Jake was distracted talking to a teammate—though he kept his arm around Juliet's waist.

"We've never met," the other woman said, "but I worked on Everett's deal in London. I'm with Jin, Beckstead, and Partners."

Juliet began to lose the knot in her stomach. "Lawyer or accountant?" The firm was a merged one, with two arms.

"Lawyer, for my sins." A diamond flashed on her left ring finger as she took a drink of what looked to be a rum and Coke. "Name's Zuli. I'm Oliver's fiancée."

Oliver, Juliet knew, was the team captain. A solid man whom Jake deeply respected. "Thanks for not giving me the death rays from your eyes."

"Hah!" Zuli's laugh was high-pitched and infectious. "I don't listen to that gossip bullshit. Most of the ones who do are the new girlfriends—fighting to cling to their man, all that rubbish." She rolled her eyes. "My man better fight for *me*. I'm not going to scurry around behind him."

Zuli's opinion on the death-ray-givers proved to be spot-on. The long-term girlfriends and wives were fine with Juliet, and with Jake and his teammates in such an ebullient mood, she ended up having a great time, most of it spent dancing with Jake or chatting with the women who didn't see her as a threat. One of them even asked Juliet's opinion on a small business she was in the process of creating.

It was as she was coming out of the bathroom two hours into the night that reality bit. She was in the shadows, invisible from the dance floor, but she could see it clearly. Jake had been hanging around a high table to the back right of the dance area when she left, and he was still there—but surrounded by women.

Juliet's stomach jolted, cold burning her cheeks.

A second later, she caught the way he shifted subtly back from a woman who was inching closer, his eyes flicking in the direction Juliet had gone. The woman persisted. Jake sidestepped her, only to be brought up short by another woman who was determined to bag Jacob Esera.

Who was too polite to push her out of the way.

Juliet strode out. Unlike Jake, she had no compunction in using her height and her elbows to get through the horde. The look of relief in his eyes when he saw her had her giving him one hell of a kiss before she turned to pin the groupies with her "the Vice-President-is-Not-Amused" look. "Shoo."

Nearly all left.

Juliet smiled at the two that hovered.

Paling, they skedaddled.

Jake, meanwhile, had buried his face in her hair. "Why did you leave me alone? I need protection."

Her shoulders began to shake at the forlorn tone of his voice. "My big, strong man, scared of a few women?"

"They had the hunt-and-bag look in their eyes."

Shifting on her heel, she brushed his hair back from his face. "Hunt and bag?"

"Like I'm a trophy for their wall." Snagging one arm around her waist, he pressed her close. "No more bathroom breaks for you."

That was when she realized Jake was slightly drunk. Not

much, but enough that his decision-making skills had to be a bit impaired—and still he'd *looked for Juliet* even when surrounded by all that willing female attention. He hadn't lapped up the attention or basked in it; no, he'd been discomforted by it.

Jake was no Reid and never would be, and she'd never ever forget that again.

"I promise," she said, with a nuzzling kiss to her adorably drunk lover. "I'll protect you." Just as she'd love him with everything she had inside her.

THE GOSSIP BLOGS were filled with photos from the team's night out, and with so many targets, Juliet got off pretty easy. A snap of her walking into the club with Jake's arm around her, both of them laughing, and a couple of hazy ones taken inside the club. Labeled with Jake's name and hers, with "ex-wife of Reid Mescall" next to it.

It made her see red, especially as the gorgeous man she loved was lying asleep next to her, one arm around her waist as she sat up to check the news on her phone. Deciding not to let it color her mood, she flicked through a few other sites and was brought up short by what was purported to be a direct quote from Jake the night before, in response to the question: "Anything to share about your new relationship?"

"I'll tell you what—I've learned that being a vice president in a multimillion-dollar company means a hell of a lot of work. Jules does more in one day than most people do in a week. I'm amazed by her."

Wet heat burned her eyes.

Putting away her phone, she bent down to kiss Jake's cheek.

He grumbled at her. "Coffee."

"Talk first. Did you tell some reporter you were amazed by me?"

"Yes. Now give me coffee." He pretended to bite the curve of her breast.

Laughing at her morning grump of a lover, she peppered his beard-stubbled face with kisses before pulling on a robe and walking out to put on the coffee. She didn't remember the tickets she'd been carrying around in her purse until she and Jake were in bed later that night.

Not sure how he'd react but encouraged by his willingness to let down his hair the previous night, she got out of bed to rummage in her purse.

He wolf whistled.

Naked, she bent even deeper, giving him quite the view.

Saying a naughty, naughty word, he threatened to come over there, but she was already turning around with the tickets in hand. "I got you a present."

Curiosity lit up his face. "Yeah?"

Getting into bed again, she gave him the tickets. He was silent for a long time after looking at them.

"It's safe," she said, well able to read his thought patterns. "You just drive the supercar around the track at whatever speed you want."

The look he gave her was unreadable. "I'm not that boy anymore."

"I know. You're an amazing man." She squeezed his biceps. "But you still like flash cars, and this looked fun." *Let me be your wings, Jake.*

Putting the tickets on his bedside table, he turned and slid his hand across her stomach. His kiss was intense, dark, the thigh he threw over hers possessive. She didn't push the issue, just took him in her arms and loved him, her Jake who'd shut a piece of himself away a long time ago.

It wasn't obvious, not these days. He laughed often, played with her and Esme both, but despite his love of fast cars, he only drove a "responsible dad" car, had no hobbies that he did purely for fun, and their time at the club the previous night had been a deviation on his part. For the most, his world remained a small and controlled one.

Stable. Structured. *Safe*.

Juliet had no argument with any of those things, not when Jake never put any strictures or rules on her. She loved their little family and the bigger one of which it was a part. She loved each and every minute she spent with Jake and with Esme. Added to that, she was no party girl and would rather hang out at home than go out.

This wasn't about that.

It was about the fact that Jake had always had a second passion aside from rugby. Had he left it behind out of choice, that would be something else. But she'd seen how he admired Leo's Porsche, watched his eyes light up when he worked on the family's cars, heard the interest in his voice when he caught a snippet of Formula One racing news.

It was as if he'd decided his love of cars was a childish thing, a waste of time for a man who was a father.

Juliet hurt for the boy he'd once been, the boy who'd made that call.

As it was, he said nothing about the tickets the next day. Neither did he mention them in the days that followed. She decided to let it go. She'd try again later, maybe with something less intense. A car show possibly. Juliet wasn't a woman who gave up easily when it came to the happiness of those she loved.

Taking the tickets from his bedside table one night after dinner, she put them back in her handbag, figuring to pass them on to a couple of girls who worked in Administration.

Jake popped into the bedroom an hour later to grab his phone. When he came out, he said, "Jules, what happened to the supercar tickets?"

Startled, she looked up from her laptop. She was working at the kitchen table while Esme did her homework beside her. "I thought I'd pass them on to people at work."

Slipping into the chair across from her, he gave her an intent look. "You're not mad?"

Esme's head lifted, but reassured by the smiles both of them shot her way, she continued on with her painstaking lettering practice.

"Of course not." Juliet closed her hand over his. "I don't want to change you, Jake." Not when he was so damn wonderful. "I'm just trying to lure you outside the castle walls and out into the wild."

Turning his hand so the back of it lay against the table, he wove his fingers through hers. "Don't give the tickets away."

Breath tight in her chest, Juliet nodded, but she didn't really believe he'd do it until they were at the track three days later. They'd brought Esme and Danny with them. Jake wanted Juliet to make use of the second ticket and ride with him, so Danny had been roped in to babysit.

"Zoom!" Esme pressed her face to the fence around the track, eyes bright as she watched the supercars racing by.

Only one car was on the track at a time, which reduced the chances of a collision, and each person had a half-hour slot—after accounting for prep time, that meant about ten minutes on the track. Jake had chosen his car online, but Juliet didn't know what it was until they arrived.

A gleaming red McLaren P1 waited for them, a sexy curve of fire just waiting to take off.

The terms of the ticket meant they had to wear safety

gear, including helmets, and they both geared up without argument while Esme and Danny watched, Danny taking photographs on his phone.

Esme was so excited that she bounced. "Go fast, Daddy!"

Jake's grin was sharp and it hurt Juliet's heart; it reminded her so much of the teenage boy who'd done illegal burnouts on the lonely back roads where they'd gone to hang out.

"Make sure you cheer me on," he said to his daughter.

Danny took Esme's hand as a light flashed behind Jake. "Time to take our seats, Boo."

Slipping into the car after the two were clear, Jake and Juliet strapped themselves in. The McLaren started with a purr that turned into a growl as Jake moved it out to the start line.

The checkered flag went down.

Jake hit the accelerator.

Juliet screamed in pure, wild exhilaration as the world turned into a blur around them, the car powering forward like the beautiful beast of a machine that it was. Beside her, Jake handled the steering with an ease that seemed natural. Though they were going faster than she ever had in a car, she felt zero fear.

At one point he slowed down right as they passed Danny and Esme, and Juliet waved at them. Danny and Esme waved back, big grins on their faces, before Jake hit the accelerator again.

Juliet was laughing, her heart pumping when they came to a final stop, Jake doing a precision turn to park the car in its assigned spot.

Pulling off his helmet as she took off hers, he gave her a wicked look before leaning over to haul her down into a hard, hot kiss. "Let's go again."

She laughed, but he was serious.

He leaned out the car window and asked the people on duty at the track if he could buy more tickets.

Clearly starstruck, the man in charge said, "Next slot's open" in an awed tone of voice.

Jake put his helmet back on.

35

THE RESURRECTION OF THE GEARHEAD

Danny took another shot of Jake and Juliet after they exited the car, helmets held by their sides and their bodies clad in the protective jumpsuits. Juliet's hair was a mess, Jake's as tumbled, but their faces glowed.

Jake had his arm around her, his face turned to look at her.

"I love this photo," she said when Danny showed it to her. "Can you send it to me?"

"Shoot it to me too, bro," Jake said while Esme wandered around the car, touching it with reverent little hands.

Apparently the car love was hereditary.

Juliet grinned and walked over to drop a kiss on Esme's head.

Taking out his phone in the interim, Jake did something on it. She didn't know what until early that evening when Aroha sent her a message exclaiming over how cute she and Jake looked and asking about the experience.

Jake had posted the photo on his social media.

The text read: *Supercars with Jules.* ♥

That was it. No hashtag, nothing else. But Jake never posted emojis. N.E.V.E.R. NEVER. Now he was using a heart one?

Suddenly it didn't feel so scary to take the final step, throw her heart wide open.

Taking a deep breath after getting into her yoga leggings and slouchy sweater because they were just going to be hanging out at home now, she made sure Esme was happily ensconced in her favorite armchair with a book.

"I wanna car that goes zoom, Jules," the little girl said decisively. "A red one!"

"How about you get your license first?" Lips twitching, Juliet bopped Esme on the nose with a gentle touch, making her giggle. "You good here?"

"Yup." Esme snuggled down into the armchair, under the fluffy throw Juliet had tucked around her.

An ache inside her that was a kind of love she'd never experienced before Esme—maternal, fiercely protective— Juliet went out to the patio with a beer for Jake and a glass of wine for herself. He was still wearing his jeans and the T-shirt he'd worn to the track, his gaze pensive as he took in the sunset.

"Thanks, babe," he said absently, taking the beer.

Leaning against the house next to him, their hips touching, Juliet sipped at her wine. She didn't know how to go about declaring her love, was starting to lose her nerve when he put his arm around her, his hand hanging loosely over her shoulder and the scent of him seducing her all over again.

"Thank you."

"For what?" She looked up.

A glance down out of those intense dark eyes that melted her. "For beating your head against my stubborn one." No smile, but his tone was warm. "I fucking loved being on that track. Really loved it."

"After the exposure you just gave them, they'll probably roll out the red carpet if you want to go back." Jake was followed by millions of people on social media, not just in New Zealand but worldwide.

Danny might be the rising star of the team, but Jake was the rock. All his teammates—his brother included—looked to him on the field, and that calm steadiness made him a favorite with fans. The fact he had only a few well-chosen and vetted endorsement deals and rarely promoted anything he didn't love just made his power all the stronger. When Jake backed a product or service, it grew wings and flew.

"Funny you should say that," he murmured and passed over his phone.

The email he'd pulled up was from his agent. The president of a supercar manufacturer was a rugby fan who followed Jake; he'd seen not only the shot Jake had shared but the video and photos someone else in the track audience had posted. They were offering him a deal to—

Her jaw dropped open. "They want to lend you a freaking four *million*-dollar car?"

"Keep reading."

She did and felt her eyes widen. "Wow, Jake." It was a serious endorsement offer. The car manufacturer wanted him to sign on to not only endorse the supercar in the Asia/Pacific region but worldwide.

"This type of thing is usually reserved for winning race-car drivers," Jake said.

Juliet nodded. At the same time... "I can see why they want you." The sheer exhilaration on Jake's face was dazzling—you could tell he loved speed, loved cars. It was real in a way that'd speak to the public. That he was at the top of his sport and supremely hot didn't hurt.

"It feels over the top." He drank some of his beer. "I went to a normal public high school for a reason. My family's not into living the crazy high life. I mean, even Gabe with all his gazillions still throws a ball around with us in the park."

"This doesn't have to change that," Juliet said, able to feel his desire to take the offer. "I mean, most of these ads will run in places where the superrich shop. Meanwhile, you'll have a kick-ass car, and they're saying they want you to come do things at other car events, so you'd get to hang out with fellow gearheads."

"You're going to put Gearhead Jock on my tombstone aren't you?"

Grinning at his tone, she rose on tiptoe to kiss his jaw. "Do it, sweetheart. Just for fun. For you."

Another glance, his lips curving into that heartbreaker smile he kept giving her. "I'd like to do you. For fun. For me."

It was a sexy and playful comment, but the intensity in his eyes made everything inside her soften. "I love you, Jacob Esera," she said, pressing her fingers to his lips when his eyes flared. "Just take it. I'm gonna be stubborn about that."

"Jules." Turning, he crushed her to the wall, her wine splashing everywhere as he kissed her stupid while the sun set in a glorious blaze at his back.

THREE WEEKS LATER, when Coach Graves announced the team for the next major international series, Jake wasn't too concerned. He was in peak condition, and he was playing the best he'd ever done. The selectors would be idiots to drop him.

Still, his stomach was tense on the day. Juliet woke to tell him she'd taken the day off. After they walked Esme to school, Juliet took him home, cooked him a great breakfast, then sexed his brains out.

Grinning in the aftermath as he lay there, spent, his body slick with sweat, he said, "I like your remedy for nerves."

"No talking. I can't breathe yet."

He laughed, and that was when his phone rang. Sitting up, he saw it was from Coach. The news the other man had for him had his smile fading.

Juliet was sitting up, sheet clutched to her chest and her eyes worried when he turned to her. "Jake, what's happened?"

He stared at her. "Our vice-captain is out for the first game of the series as a precaution after suffering a possible concussion in an accident at home, and now Coach is having Oliver sit out the game too. He'll be coming back for the rest, but he's got a niggling injury that needs more downtime. No point losing our captain because of what will effectively be a warm-up match."

"That sounds like a good idea." Juliet frowned. "Why are you so shocked?"

"Coach wants me to be acting captain for that game."

Shrieking, she jumped on him. It was her excitement that finally had the news sinking in.

"Holy shit." Squeezing her close, he tried to calm himself down. "As long as we don't fuck up royally, it should be an easy game—the other team's at the far end of global rugby rankings. It's no risk on anyone's part."

"But Jake"—she took his face in her hands—"it's obvious

they're taking the chance to try you out in the position, see how you do." A triumphant kiss. "I know you'll be amazing!"

She twisted to get his phone. "Call your parents! And your brothers!"

"No, I have to wait until the team is announced."

"Why?"

"Because Danny's waiting too. Coach only gave me a heads-up because he knows the media barrage will start the instant the appointment is announced."

Juliet's face softened. "Oh, of course." Brushing his hair back from his forehead, she said, "Is it hard? Being part of a sports family with three of you in the same game?"

"Gabe was way ahead of us, so it's just been me and Danny waiting at the same time." He ran his hand down her back. "It's not hard, but we hurt for each other. When Gabe got injured... He was devastated. I've never seen my big brother that broken." Jake shook his head. "But then I saw him build himself back up, and now he owns half the city."

His phone buzzed. "It's Danny. Team news must be out."

"ACTING CAPTAIN! FUCKING LEGEND!" Danny's yell blew out his eardrums.

And Juliet's kiss was everything. But he still couldn't look full on at the realization in the back of his mind, a stab of terror closing his mouth when he tried to speak. If he didn't look at it, if he didn't acknowledge his love for Juliet, maybe he could keep her safe.

It was an irrational thought, but he couldn't stop it.

At least Juliet didn't seem to hold his lack of a response to her declaration against him. She just loved him, his Juliet who had never been told that she was loved.

Fuck. He had to get over this. He was not *going to be another person in her life who shortchanged her.*

· · ·

JULIET HAD to work after hours two days later. She'd called Jake to let him know, and he decided to take Esme with him to training. It wasn't one of the hard-core closed sessions but a warm-up where no one was going to worry too much about a rugby-mad little girl in the audience.

"She knows all the team people," Jake told her over the phone. "She'll sit with the nutritionist and the physio and discuss plays like she's sixty, not six. They love her."

Later, after reaching the field, he messaged to say that the assistant coach had brought along his son, who was of a similar age, so Esme had a friend to play with. *I think they're plotting Esme's rise to rugby domination.*

Juliet laughed. Messaging back that she'd be home by eight thirty, she began to clear her backlog. It was dark outside by the time she shut off her computer. Iris'd had to leave at three to catch a flight to an important work meeting, but Everett was just finishing up too, and she poked her head into his office. "Want to walk down together?"

"No, you go ahead. I'll be ten more minutes." A warm smile. "Thanks, Jules."

"Hey, I own part of the company remember?" Everett and Iris had given her company shares two weeks earlier, following her annual pay review. They'd also given her a significant pay raise after the three of them went over her duties and realized exactly how much more she'd taken on over the past year.

Jake had whooped and spun her around in his arms at the news, then insisted on taking her out to a champagne dinner to celebrate. At which point he'd put his strategic mind to creating a ten-year plan that'd leave her CEO of her own major corporation. He'd only been half joking. Because this time around, Juliet had found herself a lover who was jubilant at her success and ready to back her all the way to the top.

Smiling within at the thought, she waved goodbye to Everett and headed downstairs. She didn't bother to put on her coat since she'd soon be in the car. Hers and Everett's vehicles were the only ones in the lot, but it was plenty bright enough with the external lights Iris had insisted be installed before they moved to these premises, and there were cars passing by on the street just beyond.

She'd opened up the passenger door and put down her satchel and coat when she heard a scrape behind her. Spinning around, her heart in her throat, she groaned. "Reid, what are you doing here?" She'd thought this was all behind her—he'd gone quiet soon after her and Jake's return from New York.

He lifted a bottle in the air. "You made me... laughing... laughingstock." Alcohol fumes wafted off him, his feet not exactly steady.

Juliet wasn't afraid. Reid might be psychologically toxic to her, but he'd never been physically violent—toward her or anyone else. "You're drunk and you'll be embarrassed by this in the morning. Go home."

"I loved you," he wailed. "Why? Why?"

She had no idea what he was on about, but she took out her phone, intending to call him a taxi.

He lurched forward, staggering toward her. "Juliet, why did you leave me?" A wobble as he tripped on his own feet and into her.

Her phone dropped to the asphalt as she slammed her hands into his chest, trying to keep him from falling onto her. She heard something smash with a corner of her mind and winced because her phone wasn't that old... Then she felt a numb kind of pain in her side. Her foot was wet too. Strange.

Looking down with a spinning in her head, she stared at the bottle sticking out of her side. Reid had accidentally smashed his bottle against the car, sending vodka spilling onto her foot and driving part of the broken bottle through her thin work dress and into her body.

"Fuck! Oh fuck! Juliet, fuck!" Reid staggered backward, his eyes huge. "Juliet, what do I do?"

"Call an ambulance." She couldn't see her phone and her head didn't feel right.

Sliding down to sit on the ground, she said, "Reid. Ambulance."

He scrabbled in his pockets for his phone just as a door opened nearby.

Reid looked up, relief harsh on his features. "Call an ambulance!"

The last thing Juliet saw before she lost consciousness was Everett's horrified face coming around the car.

"Jake," she whispered and was gone.

36

LOVE

Jake and Esme had just sat down in front of the TV to watch a bit of her princess movie for the seven billionth and thirty-seventh time when he got a call from Everett. Wondering why Juliet's boss was calling him, he answered—and felt everything inside him turn to ice.

"You'll stay with her?" he said. "I have to drop my daughter off at my parents'." It was hard to form words, hard to think.

"I'll stay right here," Everett promised. "The doctors are with her."

"Daddy?" Esme was looking at him, her face scared. "What's wrong?"

"Nothing, baby," he said and hoped he was telling the truth. "But Juliet needs my help with something. I'm going to drop you off at Grandma and Grandpa's."

But Esme was too smart to fall for that. "No, I wanna come with you." She clung to him as he rose.

Gathering her up in his arms, he found his keys and took her out to the car. He didn't argue with her, just drove to his parents, and though she cried, he dropped her off into her grandmother's arms.

"Hush, Boo." A big hug, a kiss on the cheek. "I'll call you soon." A hospital waiting room was no place for a little girl who'd lost a mother and adored the new woman who'd come into her life.

Jake's heart was a rock in his chest as he drove through the night to the hospital. It wasn't far from his parents' home, and all he could think the entire way there was that he hadn't told her he loved her. Juliet might go into surgery never knowing how much she meant to him.

He squeezed the steering wheel so hard that he was afraid he'd break it.

The hospital building appeared in the distance, big and white. After finding a parking spot, he ran to the emergency ward to which Everett had told him she'd been taken. The slender man jerked to his feet as Jake arrived. A nurse appeared at the same time.

"You're Juliet Nelisi's family?" she said, looking from one to the other.

"Yes," Jake said, even though legally he had no right— and that pissed him the hell off. He was hers and she was his. He *wanted* the right. "Is she all right?"

"Yes." The nurse smiled. "She's fine. In recovery. The glass didn't penetrate as deeply as it initially appeared."

Relief shook his knees. "Can I see her?"

"Yes, follow me. We used local anesthetic to stitch her up, so she's lucid."

Jake was aware of Everett following, didn't ask him to stay back. The man'd had a hell of a shock—and he might've saved Juliet's life. "Everett, how did Juliet get cut?" He hadn't bothered to ask that question during the initial call.

"I'll let her tell you that. I'm not sure myself."

"Here you go." The nurse pushed aside the curtain around Juliet's cubicle.

She was sitting up in bed in a hospital gown, a scowl on her face. "I fainted," she muttered the instant Jake appeared. "I *fainted* like a great big drama queen."

"It was shock, dear," the nurse said soothingly before leaving.

Jake, meanwhile, was having trouble maintaining any kind of composure. Which was why he stood by the curtain while Everett rushed over to gently embrace Juliet. Their conversation was a buzz in Jake's head. He barely even saw the other man say his goodbyes and leave.

The antiseptic smell of the hospital, the noises of the machines, even the bed, it all had nausea churning his gut. Again and again, he saw Calypso's lifeless face, except his brain kept trying to superimpose Juliet's on the memory.

"Jake." Juliet held out a hand.

Jake jerked forward because he'd made a promise to himself to never let Juliet down. Sinking into the chair beside her bed, he took her hand, and then he dropped his head and his shoulders and just shuddered. He didn't cry, not this time. The waves of emotion were too huge and too merciless. He squeezed her hand until it had to hurt, and he tried to find a way through the chaos.

"Hey." Her voice cut through the mess, made him look up.

She gave him a tight smile. "Every time you run onto that field, I worry. Rugby isn't a gentle game. But I can't protect you from the world. So I live with it. Just like I live with knowing that I can't wrap Esme in cotton wool."

His entire soul twisted and torn, he looked at her and he knew he'd be savaged if she died. He'd be destroyed. Broken to pieces. "Do you know how much I love you?" he rasped out and saw an expression on her face he'd never before seen. "Until it hurts me to breathe sometimes. Until seeing you in this bed is my worst fucking nightmare come to life."

He pressed his lips to the hand he'd gripped. "Fuck, Juliet." Shaking, he rose and got up onto the bed, then—with care—wrapped her up in his arms. *"Fuck."*

Silence... and a bloom of wet heat on his T-shirt where Juliet had pressed her face.

"Jules," he said, kissing the top of her head. "God, I'm sorry to be such an ass. I should be—"

"Tell me again." A teary but firm request. "Tell me again."

"I love you, Juliet. I love you." He repeated the words again and again as she cried. "I'm sorry I was too chickenshit to say that before. If I'd lost you and you'd never heard it from me..." The idea tore him apart. "Forgive me."

She shook her head against him, mumbled, "Nothing to forgive." It came out bleary. "Words are nice," she said on a hiccup of breath. "So nice that I'm stupid-crying like a baby, but I've felt you loving me all this time. You love hard, Jake. Impossible to be yours and not know." A salt-laced kiss pressed to his lips. "It's okay, baby." She stroked her hands over his trembling shoulders. "I'm right here. Loving you back just as hard."

Unable to speak, Jake held on, just held on.

THE DOCTORS RELEASED Juliet a couple of hours later with strict instructions for her to not physically exert herself for a week.

Esme was mad at both of them when they picked her up that night and refused to say a word. She stomped to her room and shut her door. Jake, well aware his daughter had a full measure of the Esera stubborn streak, let her be.

"Did Everett call the cops?" he asked Juliet as they got ready for bed.

"I think so." Juliet sighed. "Reid didn't mean it—he was an idiot."

Muscles tight, Jake gripped her chin. "Don't you dare let him get away with this."

Smiling, Juliet pressed a hand to his chest. "No, he has to be held responsible, but I hope the judge gives him mandatory alcohol-addiction counseling along with any punishment."

Jake didn't give a shit about Reid, but he was clearly *much* more of a hard-ass than Juliet. Since he couldn't stop touching her, he gave in and took a long, deep kiss. "Behave," he said when she made a kittenish purr in her throat. "No exertion for a week." And they definitely exerted themselves when they got together in bed.

Juliet pouted.

Chuckling, he dropped a kiss on her nose before wandering into the master suite bathroom. When he came back out, it was to find the bedroom empty. Figuring she must be making a hot drink in the kitchen, he padded that way, but she wasn't there either. Then he heard a soft murmur coming from the direction of Esme's room.

Walking over, he peeked in the half-open door. Juliet was sitting on the side of the bed while Esme stubbornly faced the wall, her back to Juliet and her arms tightly folded across her chest. But Juliet had her hand on Esme's shoulder and she was telling Esme a bedtime story.

Jake's heart was already so full, but it expanded all over again right then. He stayed outside and just listened as Juliet completed the story.

Closing the book, she said, "I love you, Boo" and made sure the blanket was tucked up nicely around Esme's drowsy body.

When Esme mumbled something, Juliet said, "I know you're mad at me, but I still love you." Another kiss pressed to Esme's temple before she came to the door.

Seeing Jake, she walked into his arms.

"Will you love me too, even when I'm grumpy?"

She looked up, eyes dark. "I'll love you always."

Scared, so scared at the love that filled him up and could destroy him, Jake said, "Let's grow old and wrinkly together, Jules." He knew she couldn't promise that, that life wasn't predictable, but he needed to hear the words. A statement of intent against fate.

"We *will* grow old together," Juliet said firmly. "We have a daughter to raise, and some day we'll have grandchildren to spoil."

"Yeah?"

"Yeah. Let's do this."

EPILOGUE

HAPPY EVER AFTER

J ake glanced at the gleaming supercar in the lot of the local park where he and the family came often to hang out and play a game of rugby. A bunch of teenagers were gathered around it, snapping pics, pure awe on their faces.

He got it. It was a beautiful machine. He'd hooked up with the engineers and mechanics who'd worked on the engine and knew that the car was as beautiful inside as it was on the outside. Thanks to Juliet's encouragement, he was thinking seriously about continuing his education and getting into something to do with high-performance cars when he eventually retired from rugby.

Her laughter broke the air.

He looked to where she stood chatting with Charlotte and Ísa under the spreading branches of a flowering cherry tree, unable to believe how his life had changed so much in the space of a year and a bit. All because of her. A woman who loved openly and without fear, and who challenged him to do the same.

"Spot! Wait!"

He laughed as he saw Esme's mutt of a rescue puppy race away from her with a Frisbee in his mouth. Danny took off after the dog, his long, powerful legs eating up the ground. Emmaline ran over from the other side at the same time to try to cut Spot off from absconding with the Frisbee.

Given how much Sailor's daughter adored the puppy, Jake had a feeling another dog would soon be joining the family. Lawyers had nothing on the pint-sized negotiating team of Esme and Emmaline.

Gabriel and Sailor were at the portable grill they'd brought out for today's picnic, and their parents—plus Ísa's mum—were on loungers, watching the shenanigans. They were also taking turns cuddling Ísa and Sailor's happy, healthy baby boy—who seriously looked like a miniature copy of Sailor.

The newest human member of the family was named Joseph Connor, in honor of his grandfather. Said grandfather was already predicting another generation of rugby greatness. To avoid mix-ups between Joseph senior and junior, everyone referred to the baby by his second name. Connor took it all in his baby stride.

Alison called out right then, and Ísa and Charlotte headed her way while Juliet stayed behind to flip out a picnic blanket on which he knew she planned to put snacks for the kids. The dark pink petals of the cherry tree fell around her where she stood, and she looked up, a soft smile on her face, her hair as vibrant a pink as the petals.

Juliet was wild color, and she'd drenched his life with it.

Jake was walking toward her before he knew it. Digging into his pocket, he pulled out what he'd hidden there. She smiled at him as he neared, said something, but he didn't hear. His heart was pounding too hard.

He'd meant to do this at another time and place, but this moment felt right.

Going down on one knee in front of her, he opened his hand to expose the ring within. A burst of color. Not only diamonds but all the hues of Juliet.

Her hands flew to her mouth, her nails shimmering gold and her eyes shining.

"Marry me?" he said, his mouth dry.

Nodding jerkily, she held out her hand and he slipped on the ring. She jumped on him the instant it was on, tumbling him to the picnic blanket. Laughing, he rolled on it with her as the cherry blossoms fell on them, and he felt young and alive and invincible.

"Daddy! Is Jules gonna marry us?"

Opening his arm as Juliet opened hers, they enclosed Esme in the hug, her delight added to theirs. Spot, not to be left out, jumped into the pile, and it dissolved into a thing of wild joy with the wiggling puppy butt in Esme's face causing her to laugh hysterically.

Across the blanket, he kept one hand linked with Juliet's, and when she turned her head, he said, "I love you, Jules."

She said, "I know," and it was the most wonderful thing she could've said.

I LOVE WRITING about the Bishop-Esera clan, and I hope you love reading their stories just as much. There's only one more brother to go now—Danny's turn in the spotlight is coming up next. If you'd like to be notified when his book is available, please join my monthly newsletter at: www.nalinisingh.com Along with release information, I send our free short stories and/or exclusive deleted scenes several times a year.

I'd also like this opportunity to acknowledge my friend and fellow author, Wendy Vella, and her son, professional rugby player Nathan Vella. They were incredibly generous with their time and knowledge of professional rugby. Any mistakes are mine (and I confess I did take some small artistic liberties).

If you've missed the stories of the other brothers, they are: CHERISH HARD (Sailor) and ROCK HARD (Gabriel). —Nalini

ABOUT THE AUTHOR

New York Times and *USA Today* bestselling author of the Psy-Changeling, Guild Hunter, and Rock Kiss series, Nalini Singh usually writes about hot shapeshifters, dangerous angels, and sexy rock stars. With the Hard Play series, she decided to write about a sinfully gorgeous set of brothers and their friends, all of whom will make your blood pump and your heart melt.

Nalini lives and works in beautiful New Zealand, and is passionate about writing. If you'd like to learn more about the Hard Play series or her other books, you can find excerpts, behind-the-scenes materials, and more information on her website: www.nalinisingh.com.

Made in the USA
Middletown, DE
05 October 2023

40298716R10203